THE ORPHAN SONGBIRD

CHRISSIE WALSH

Boldwood

First published in Great Britain in 2024 by Boldwood Books Ltd.

Copyright © Chrissie Walsh, 2024

Cover Design by Colin Thomas

Cover Photography: Colin Thomas

The moral right of Chrissie Walsh to be identified as the author of this work has been asserted in accordance with the Copyright, Designs and Patents Act 1988.

Every effort has been made to obtain the necessary permissions with reference to copyright material, both illustrative and quoted. We apologise for any omissions in this respect and will be pleased to make the appropriate acknowledgements in any future edition.

A CIP catalogue record for this book is available from the British Library.

Paperback ISBN 978-1-78513-489-0

Large Print ISBN 978-1-78513-490-6

Hardback ISBN 978-1-78513-488-3

Ebook ISBN 978-1-78513-491-3

Kindle ISBN 978-1-78513-492-0

Audio CD ISBN 978-1-78513-483-8

MP3 CD ISBN 978-1-78513-484-5

Digital audio download ISBN 978-1-78513-486-9

Boldwood Books Ltd
23 Bowerdean Street
London SW6 3TN
www.boldwoodbooks.com

For Charles, Martina and Harry.

Music is very spiritual, it has the power to bring people together.

— EDGAR WINTER

PROLOGUE
BRADLEY BRIGG, NOVEMBER 1909

Thomas Earnshaw lay propped on his pillows in his bedroom at Ashcroft House, his pallid cheeks sheened with sweat and his lungs wheezing with every breath. The dimly lit room smelled of sickness and despair.

'You're my only close relative, Abe, and I look to you to love and care for Darcy until she's of an age to lead an independent life,' Thomas gasped, his feverish eyes searching his older brother's face.

Abe Earnshaw met Thomas's gaze, his cold, grey eyes devoid of compassion and his expression inscrutable.

'This damned tuberculosis has me beaten and I must be sure that Darcy will be taken care of before I go,' Thomas continued, his every word laboured. 'What I would like is for you to give up Northcrop House and move into Ashworth with Darcy and her nanny.' He struggled to raise a smile. ''Twill be no hardship to you. My house is far grander than your own.'

Abe nodded his head, his lips verging on a sneer. 'And then what...?'

'Then you will be there to offer her guidance... attend to her schooling... and deal with her financial needs. She is but thirteen... too young to manage her own affairs and...' Exhausted for the moment, Thomas closed his eyes. Mucus gurgled in his chest. He coughed then spat into a bloodstained rag, and with his airways clearer, he appeared to rally. His pale blue eyes sharpened.

'I have deposited money in the Yorkshire Bank which will pay for her education, her keep and her clothing. You'll not be out of pocket, Abe. And whilst I don't expect you to give up your position as clerk with Hepworth's, I would like you to keep an eye on my sawmill and its finances. Harry Chadwick will continue to manage it until Darcy is eighteen. I've spoken with him and...' Thomas waved a weary hand, incapable of further explanation. He gazed beseechingly at his brother, his breathing ragged as he implored, 'All I ask... is that you have Darcy's best interests... at heart and that... you protect her as I would do if...'

Utterly spent, he closed his eyes.

'Have no fear, Tom, I'm more than willing to do all you ask.' Abe Earnshaw placed his hand on Thomas's, his smile insincere and his steely grey eyes glinting with avarice. 'I'll love Darcy as if she were my own.'

1

NORTHCROP HOUSE, APRIL 1911

'Shall ye be wantin' me to put a light to the coals for ye, Master Earnshaw?'

Polly Oldroyd bobbed a deferential curtsey in order to lessen the audacity of her question. Her wrinkled face wore the blandest of expressions but her grey eyes glinted wickedly. A chill wind rattled the windows of the bitterly cold, sparsely furnished parlour in Northcrop House as she spoke, and a vicious draught caused the gaslights to throw ugly dancing shadows on the walls.

'Indeed, I would not,' Abe Earnshaw barked, his whiskery jowls wobbling with irritation under his ferocious glare. 'You know the rules as well as I do, or you should by now. No fires after the first day of spring, Polly, and seeing as we're now into April you shouldn't need to ask.'

Undeterred, the aged housekeeper tried again.

'It'll take but a minute, sir. I think perhaps Miss Darcy's feeling a mite cold,' she persisted, her eyes pitying as she glanced at the shivering girl.

Darcy sat with her head bowed, her cornflower blue eyes fixed on her plate and her pale, finely sculptured features hidden by the curtains of her shimmering blonde hair, straight as a die.

'That's because she's nesh,' Earnshaw sneered. 'Now, clear the table then be off with you to your own home, you interfering old baggage.' Pushing back his chair, he stamped over to the couch by the fireplace.

Darcy jumped to her feet. 'I'll lend Polly a hand,' she said, the desperation in her voice letting the housekeeper know that she was not so much offering to help as to escape being left alone with her uncle.

'Thank ye, miss, that be very kind of ye.' Polly's reply sounded overly grateful as she began clattering dishes and plates into piles on a large, wooden tray. Darcy eagerly followed suit.

'Stop that this instant, girl,' Earnshaw bawled. 'Leave the chores to the hired help. That's what she's paid for.' Then, his harsh tones softening, he patted the couch and said, 'Come, sit here by me.'

Darcy visibly quailed, and the dishes in her hand rattled perilously. She turned wild eyes on Polly, begging for her to intervene. The housekeeper shook her head hopelessly and pursed her lips in a remorseful grimace. 'Sorry, lass,' she mouthed, 'I did try.' Lifting the tray, she backed out of the room saying as she went, 'G'night, Master Earnshaw, Miss Darcy.'

Darcy lingered by the table, gazing round the cheerless room, its dark panelled walls and bare, cold flagstones offering neither warmth nor comfort. The ham and pickles she had just eaten turned sour in her belly. The clock on the mantelpiece chimed nine.

'Don't keep me waiting, Darcy,' her uncle called over his shoulder. Darcy took a deep breath but it did little to calm the thudding in her chest.

'I have a headache, Uncle Abe. I think I'll go straight to my room,' she said, sounding far braver than she felt.

He sprang to his feet. 'I ordered you to come sit by me and that is what you will do,' he roared, taking two quick strides and dragging her across the room. She winced as his fingers bit into the tender flesh of her upper arm. 'Sit,' he growled, tossing her onto the shabby velour couch. He flopped down beside her, his thigh pressed close to hers and his sour breath wafting in her face.

'Please, uncle, I feel unwell,' Darcy whimpered as he placed a wet kiss on her cheek. Ignoring her plea, he began kneading her budding breasts through the thick flannel of her dress. She sat rigidly, praying that he would soon be satisfied. Her stomach began to churn and a burning sensation flooded her chest. Then, bile rising in her throat, she started to retch.

Abe Earnshaw reared his balding head and shoved her aside. 'Go to your bed this instant, madam.'

Darcy needed no second bidding. Feet flying, she ran from the room and up the stairs to her bedroom. Shivering in the icy chill, she undressed and put on her nightgown then plumped down on the end of the ancient feather bed. It creaked ominously. Like the rest of the house, her bedroom was shabby and spartan even though Abe Earnshaw wasn't a poor man. Yet, he seemed to take some sort of twisted pleasure from eschewing creature comforts. But as Darcy tucked her freezing feet up under the hem of her nightdress, such comforts were the last thing on her mind. Tonight she had been subjected to another mauling, and the fear of what her uncle would do next jangled inside her head.

It had all started some three months ago, shortly after her fifteenth birthday.

At first it had been no more than lewd appraising looks as he had eyed her burgeoning body, his gaze resting too long on her pert breasts and shapely hips. If that had made her squirm it was nothing compared to what he had taken to doing in the past few weeks.

Now he insisted on touching her, his large, rough hands groping her backside when he came up behind her, or, like this evening, forcing her to sit whilst he kissed her cheeks and groped at her breasts. She detested the feel of his hands and mouth. Tonight, had her retching not deterred him, he would have started to pant, sweat springing to his blubbery upper lip and the bulge in his trousers swelling then subsiding as he grunted and groaned.

Darcy knew very little about the facts of life, but she knew that what her uncle was doing to her was very wrong. Feeling sick to her stomach, she curled up into a ball on the bed and wished with all her might that she still had a mother to guide her and a father to protect her. But her mother had been dead seven long years and her father almost two.

Her heart and head aching and her tears dampening the quilt, she asked herself yet again how it had come to this? How was it that her father had left her in the care of his widowed childless brother when surely he must have known what an evil man Abe Earnshaw was?

Rolling onto her back and staring up at the cracks in the ceiling, Darcy recalled the last time she had spoken at length with her father. She pictured his pallid face and imagined she could hear his ragged breathing as he had said, 'Uncle Abe will take care of you. He is coming to live here at Ashworth.' Thomas had forced a wan smile. 'A man about the place to do as I would if only that were possible. It breaks my heart to leave you, my darling, but I am leaving you in good hands.'

Darcy shuddered at the memory. She had been left in the filthiest hands imaginable.

Her father's death had left her numb. Lost in her grief, she had been incapable of taking control over what had happened next and now she was suffering the consequences. Uncle Abe had immediately sold Thomas's fine house in Bradley Brigg, the busy mill town that had been Darcy's home for the first thirteen years of her life and taken her to live with him in Northcrop House. Then he had readily given up his job as a clerk and had taken over the running of the sawmill. He was now a wealthy businessman.

Darcy was unaware that by rights she was the owner of her late father's enterprising business that supplied timber to all manner of developments in the prosperous West Riding. New, gigantic cloth mills were being built along the banks of the River Colne, and engineering works were springing up in the towns in the valley, the merchants and industrialists building fine mansions in the countryside. The sawmill was a lucrative source of income, but at thirteen years of age, Darcy had understood none of this. She presumed that the sawmill now belonged to her uncle, and Abe Earnshaw encouraged that belief.

To the outside world, Abe styled himself as a gentleman and the benevolent guardian of his dead brother's daughter. In his own home, Darcy and Polly knew him to be a parsimonious, miserable taskmaster and, just lately, a disgusting pervert. With no one to turn to, Darcy was at his mercy.

Downstairs, slumped on the couch in the parlour, Abe Earnshaw ground his teeth. The girl was driving him out of his wits. Initially, he had only taken her in as a means of getting his hands on the sawmill's finances and making himself a fortune into the bargain. But now the child had blossomed into a pretty young woman tempting him with her every movement. He'd be damned before he let her inherit the sawmill, and he'd deal with that when the time came, but for now he had other things on his mind and his frustration turned to seething desire. Shifting uneasily on the couch he recalled his most recent fumble with the landlord's daughter in the yard behind the Cock and Bull. She was but twelve, yet she had known just how to satisfy him. His loins grew hot at the memory of her eager little hands and mouth and he reared to his feet. His brother's namby-pamby daughter needed to be taught a lesson.

* * *

The stairs creaked and Darcy jumped to her feet, her heart leaping up into her throat and her breath pent as she listened to her uncle's heavy tread on the landing. The footsteps stopped outside her door. Unable to move a muscle, she willed them to go on, taking Abe to his own room. Then, mesmerised, she watched the doorknob turning. Her uncle stepped into the room.

He had removed his jacket and waistcoat and the collar of his shirt. His trousers, suspended by a pair of striped braces, were unbuttoned. Too late Darcy realised that she was trapped between the confines of the bed and the dressing table. She backed up to the wall, her eyes darting left and right as she looked for a means of escape. Abe watched her impassively; she had nowhere to run. Locked in the narrow space, Darcy cowered against the wall, her heart jolting against her ribs. Slowly, like a wolf teasing its prey, her uncle closed in on her.

Darcy broke into a cold sweat. 'Please uncle,' she begged brokenly, 'what you are doing is not right.' She pressed her back harder against the wall, rage and desperation bringing tears to her eyes.

'I'll tell you what's not right,' he snorted, two strides bringing him close enough for her to smell his breath. 'It's not right that I should have to pay for the services of the filthy whores in town when I have a peach in my own home that's ripe and ready for plucking.' He grabbed her arms in a vice-like grip. Then, laughing loudly at her feeble attempt to break free, he pulled her with him as he backed onto the bed.

She filled her mouth with saliva and spat in his face. He flinched. His grip loosened and Darcy struggled all the more, but her twisting and wriggling seemed only to excite him. She butted her head into his face and he clamped his teeth round a lock of her hair and yanked it. Darcy screeched, her scalp on fire as the roots of her long blonde tresses protested. Abe let go of her left arm but, still holding the other in an iron grip, he tugged back her head, forcing her to look up at him, and as he held her captive in this way, his free hand fiddled with his underwear.

The fetid smell of stale sweat and the lavatory seeped into Darcy's nose, and her cries were smothered as he pressed her face down into his lap. Frantically, she twisted her head to one side. As she did so, she felt something hot and hard brushing against her skin. She swivelled her eyes. A monstrous worm throbbed against her cheek, bloated and smelly.

Darcy jerked her head left and right, attempting to put distance between her face and the thing in his crotch, but Abe held fast to her hair. When the stinking, brown skin touched her mouth, it only encouraged the vile thing to swell and throb all the more. She gasped for breath. Bile seeped into her throat and she began to choke. Her uncle yanked on her hair, raising her face a few inches.

'Kiss it,' he ordered, his voice thick with lust. 'Take it in your mouth and make like it's a sugar treat.'

'I... I can't... I...' Darcy mumbled. 'Please, uncle, please!'

Snorting with frustration, he raised her head until she was looking up at him. Sick with loathing, she blanched at the carnal desire burning on his face. Then he grabbed her hand, forcibly placing it round the stiff brown thing. 'Hold it. Move your hand up and down like this,' he growled, his large mitt encasing hers and moving faster and faster.

Darcy's wrist ached and her body was so tense she felt that her spine might snap at any moment. The sight of the wrinkled skin and glistening head on the thing in her hand was so obscene that she shut her eyes, but she could not blank out the feel and the smell of him.

Strangled growling noises and moans escaped Abe's lips and his body jerked and shuddered. Was he having a heart attack? Darcy prayed that he was. She opened her eyes. A stream of sticky white mess shot out of the thing in her hand, catching her full in the face. It clung to her skin, festooning her lips and chin. Vomit filled her mouth and she swallowed it noisily, afraid of what he might do if she spewed on him. Abe made a strange snarling noise that gurgled up his throat. Giving a final shudder, he let go of her and fell back on the bed, gasping.

The thing in Darcy's hand shrivelled so that it looked like a squashed sausage in a bed of matted, sticky grey hair. She drew away her hand as though she had been stung and wiped her wet fingers on her nightdress. Then, on legs that barely held her weight, she got to her feet and stood, trembling, fear and intense hatred surging through her. Too overwhelmed to think of making her escape, she tottered over to the window, watching distastefully as her uncle pulled himself upright, his hair awry and his jowls flecked with spit.

'Now you know what you have to do next time to please me,' he said coldly. 'Let that be a lesson to you.' Clutching at his trousers, he strutted from the room.

Darcy stood rooted to the spot until the sound of his footsteps faded. She had never before detested someone as much as she did Abe Earnshaw.

Feeling utterly violated, she leaned against the window, struggling to gather her wits. The icy coldness of the glass penetrating her nightdress made her skin tingle, and her dazed mind suddenly cleared, a fiery anger replacing her fear. She dashed over to the nightstand, pulled off her nightdress and washed her hands and face and then her entire body to expunge the vileness of him. As she did so, she told herself that there would not be a next time. Never again would she allow him to subject her to such depravity.

Ignoring the sickening feeling, partly of disgust but mostly anger, that still churned in her insides, she put on fresh underwear then her grey flannel dress and the one pair of boots that still fitted her. Then she emptied the drawers and cupboards of her meagre possessions. She had outgrown the fine clothing she had brought with her to Northcrop House and her wardrobe was scanty to say the least, her uncle begrudging every penny he spent on her. She had but the one dress she was now wearing, bought so that she might look presentable at church on Sundays. The only other garments she owned were a shabby tweed skirt and blouse that she wore every day, a few pairs of bloomers, and a petticoat that she had made for herself out of a fine lawn sheet that she had bought from the market on one of her rare shopping trips with Polly.

The drawers and cupboards empty, she stuffed her possessions into a canvas valise that had belonged to her father. Then she lifted the corner of the feather tick and took from underneath it the small purse containing the few coins Polly had slipped her whenever there were any left over after she had paid the tradesmen. It had been their secret, something Abe had been unaware of, otherwise he would have punished both of them severely.

'Ye never know when ye might need a few coppers, so put them by for a rainy day,' Polly had said each time she handed them over. Well, today certainly was a rainy day. It had been an absolute deluge even though not a drop had fallen from the sky, Darcy thought, as she counted the pitiful amount of money. She wouldn't get far on that, she told herself bitterly. Not for the first time, she wondered how it was that her father had left her so ill provided for.

They had lived an extremely comfortable life in their lovely home on the far side of Bradley Brigg and she'd wanted for nothing. But her father had never confided his financial affairs to her, and her uncle had told her that the sawmill made barely any profit and that he only kept it running out of the goodness of his heart to give employment to the workers. Her father had made her aware that he had left money for her education, but on the day of her fourteenth birthday, her uncle had told her the money had run out and she had left Miss Compton's Academy without any prospects.

Counting the coins again, and calculating that they would provide her with food and shelter for no more than a day or two, she dropped the purse on the bed and crossed the room to her secret hiding place. Down on her knees, she prised up a short, loose board in the wooden floor and lifted out her father's gold timepiece. This was her greatest treasure, the only thing she had of any value, and although she would hate to be parted from it, she might find herself faced with no choice.

When she had been forced to leave her own home, her uncle had told her that he would have her parents' possessions packed and brought to Northcrop House. Even then, something deep inside had told Darcy he wasn't to be trusted and she had slipped the heavy, gold timepiece into her pocket, desperate to have something that would hold the memory of her beloved papa.

Her instinct had proved true. Abe had sold every scrap of the house's contents along with the house, leaving her with nothing but her school books, her own clothing, and a fine woollen cape and a felt bonnet that had been her mother's.

The watch had been her mother's gift to her father on their wedding day, and Darcy knew he treasured it above all else. Sadly, whenever Darcy thought about her mother, she couldn't recall what Alicia Earnshaw had looked like. The only memories that had stayed with her were the scent of a musky perfume and a gentle voice. However, she remembered everything about her father with startling clarity.

Sitting on the bed with the timepiece nestled in the palm of her hand, she saw the gold Albert chain draped across her father's slender abdomen, its little T-bar snug in the third buttonhole up from the point of his pin-striped waistcoat, and his long, lean fingers flipping the watch from his waistcoat pocket as he checked the time. Tears sprang to her eyes. She wished with all her might that he was here to put his arms around her and press her to his chest as he had so often done in happier times. The feeling was so strong that she imagined she could smell his spicy cologne mingled with the fuggy aroma of his tobacco. Her tears spilled over. Pressing the watch to her lips she rocked back and forth, sobbing her heart out.

One day, when she had been about ten years old, he had shown her how to keep it ticking. On the day she had claimed it, the hands had stopped moving. She had twisted the small gold knob on top that wound the spring and set the hands to the right time. And every night since then, before climbing into bed, she had taken the watch from its hiding place and turned the winder. It was her way of keeping her father's heart beating even though he was dead.

She cried until she was empty, then wiping her eyes on her sleeve, she flipped open the watchcase. The hands on the pearly white dial told her that it was five minutes after ten. She got off the bed and crossed to the window, staring out into the pitch-black night, not a star in the sky, and she trembled at the thought of walking the dark roads into Bradley Brigg and beyond to God alone knew where. Silently cursing her lack of knowledge of the wider world, she tucked the timepiece into the deep pocket of her dress and went back to sit on the bed and think.

Her thoughts were dismal as she contemplated the narrowness of her experience. Her parents had cosseted her; her expeditions to the town and into the surrounding district had been taken in a carriage that knew exactly where it was going, and her weekday journey to and from school had been in a pony and trap. Since leaving school, the furthest she had ventured was to the grocery less than a mile away. She had never wandered the streets freely and the cold realisation that she had led a far too sheltered life filled her with a sense of hopelessness. Who could she turn to for help?

She thought of Polly. The old housekeeper had shown her nothing but kindness since she had come to live in Northcrop House and it occurred to her that it might be wise to seek her advice before setting off to... where and what, she didn't know. Furthermore, she wouldn't want her sudden disappearance to distress the old woman. So, with that in mind, she decided to call on her before leaving the hateful Abe Earnshaw and the town of Bradley Brigg behind. There was nothing to keep her here.

Her thoughts tumbling, her mouth dry and her hands trembling, Darcy placed the valise by the bedroom door, and taking the dark blue woollen cape from where it hung on the back of the door, she laid it on the bed. Should she leave the house now whilst her uncle slept and find somewhere to shelter until she called upon Polly, or should she wait? Polly had told her that she rose at four every morning, but that was almost six hours away.

Confused and afraid, she sat on the edge of the bed again wringing one hand with the other. Her scalp still tingled from her uncle's cruel, clawing hand and she rubbed the sore patch. As she gently moved her fingers in circles under her hair, she realised that even raising her arm hurt and that her entire body ached with tension. She didn't feel fit enough to walk anywhere.

The silence was oppressive. When an owl hooted outside in the yard, Darcy almost jumped out of her skin. The bird's cry lured her to the window. A mere sliver of a pale, watery moon moved slowly across the heavens but its pale, sickly light did not reach the yard below. Darcy imagined walking between the dark hedges that lined the road to Polly's cottage and Bradley Brigg. Filled with terror, she decided to bide her time. Her uncle was a heavy sleeper and rarely got out of bed before seven. All this worry made her feel dreadfully weary so she went back to bed. Propped up on the pillows with the timepiece in her hand, she settled down to wait.

2

Darcy woke with a start, her heart pounding and blood singing in her ears. Had she slept too long and left it too late to make her escape? Frantically, she glanced at the timepiece, breathing a sigh of relief when she saw that it was but ten minutes past four. Time to make a move.

She rolled to the edge of the bed, panic making her throat tight at the thought of what she was about to do. The bed creaked as it always did whenever she removed her weight from it, and as she planted her feet on the floor she waited, and listened. The house was still. All she could hear was the moaning wind against the windowpanes. She put on the cape and bonnet.

Stealthily, she crossed to the door. It rasped on its hinges and she silently cursed her uncle's neglect – he never maintained anything in Northcrop House. Trembling on feet that didn't seem to belong to her, she lifted the valise and stepped out onto the landing. Again, she waited and listened. All she heard was the thudding of her own heart and the faint rumble of Abe's snoring, so picking up her feet, she descended the stairs nimbly, avoiding the loose treads that rattled. At the bottom she listened again then crept into the kitchen. Desperate to ease her parched throat, she filled a glass with water from the jug on the table.

The refreshing drink calmed her jangling nerves. Steeling her resolve, she lifted the valise then opened the back door and, closing it softly behind her, she walked out into the black night and gusting wind.

The darkness thickened and gathered round her. Her cape flapped like the wings of a frightened crow. Clutching at its edges with one hand, she hoisted the strap of the valise over her shoulder with the other. Then, head down against the driving wind, she hurried across the yard and into the lane leading to Polly's cottage. She dared not look back.

High above, the branches of the trees swayed, their witch-like arms creaking. Shivers ran down Darcy's spine. She had never before been out at this hour and now the familiar lane seemed like a strange and fearsome place. Mustering her courage, she set out at a brisk pace, the wind buffeting her back and the valise dragging at her shoulder.

A faint light glimmered in Polly's window. Darcy breathed a sigh of relief. The housekeeper was up and about. She tapped softly on the cottage door. A few minutes passed before it cautiously opened. Polly peered round the jamb.

'Miss Darcy!' she exclaimed, her wrinkled face masked with confusion. 'What be ye doing here at this hour?'

'I'm running away,' Darcy replied, thinking that she sounded foolish and childish. 'I can't stay with my uncle a moment longer.' The memory of what he had made her do caused her cheeks to redden with shame, and she had to fight back the sobs choking her throat.

'Come in, child, come in.' Polly opened the door wider then placed a finger to her lips. 'Keep your voice down, they still be abed,' she hissed and pointed to the ceiling above, where her husband and two grown-up sons were sleeping. She eyed the valise curiously. 'What be this all about?'

Tears welled in Darcy's eyes. She dropped the valise. 'He... he forced me to... to do terrible things to him,' she sobbed, her hands flying to her face and wiping it as if to remove the smelly sticky mess that felt as though it were still there.

Polly curled her lip and nodded. She wasn't surprised. She too had seen the lascivious look in Abe Earnshaw's eyes when they lingered too long on his niece's nubile body and she had pondered more than once on how long it would take him to make a move. 'Filthy beast,' she muttered. 'He didn't break ye, did he?'

Darcy gave her a blank look. 'Break me?'

'Aye? Did he put his thing in ye?' She patted her own groin.

Then Darcy understood. Her stomach churned. Bile crept into her throat and she swallowed forcibly before shaking her head. 'No, he made me kiss it and hold it,' she cried, her voice rising to a scream. 'It was horrible! Horrible!'

Polly clamped a finger to Darcy's lips. 'Shush, ye don't want them upstairs to hear ye. Best not to mention it to anyone.'

'But what am I to do? I can't go back. Where will I go?'

The old woman's heart was torn, but she had little help to offer. She patted Darcy's arm.

The comforting touch gave Darcy an idea. 'Do you think I could stay with you for a while until I gather enough money to take me somewhere? I can find work,' she gabbled, clutching at what she knew were fragile straws.

'That ye could not,' Polly said harshly, stepping back to put a distance between them. 'He'd only find ye and drag ye back. What's more, I have my job to think of and those of my husband and sons. Earnshaw's wicked. He'll sack the lot of us if I help ye.' She softened her tone. 'I'm sorry for ye lass, but I cannot risk us losing our livelihoods. Ye must make your own way, or go home and suffer the consequences.' She walked over to the range and, with her back to Darcy, she began riddling the embers as if that was the end of the matter.

Shocked by the housekeeper's lack of compassion, Darcy felt as though she had been dowsed in icy water. 'I'll be going then,' she croaked, willing herself not to fall to her knees and beg.

'Aye, off ye go afore the streets get busy,' Polly said without looking at her. 'Get on your way lest he finds out ye've gone and comes looking for ye.' Hardening her heart, she made a busy show of clattering coals on the fire.

Darcy's heart shrank at the coldness in Polly's tone. In a daze, she hoisted the valise up onto her shoulder and stepped out into the howling wind. She hadn't felt so bereft since the loss of her father. With her plans in tatters and the fear of the unknown making her nerves jangle, she trudged along the road that would take her into Bradley Brigg. The wind whipped at her cape and skirts making her feet unsteady. Her eyes watered and the valise grew heavier with every step.

By now, the first streaks of dawn were lighting the sky, a pale-yellow glow appearing from behind the foothills of the Pennines. The wind dropped, making Darcy's passage somewhat easier, but it did not make her feel any happier. The horrors of the night before kept creeping unbidden into her thoughts making her stomach churn, and Polly's callousness made her chest feel bruised, as though she had been kicked. The sickening feeling turned to outrage at the unfairness of it all. She had done nothing to deserve this.

The burning anger spurred her steps and fired her determination to carry on. However, within a mile or so she came to the sawmill and the sweet scent of freshly hewn timber made tears spring to her eyes as she thought of all she had lost. Slowing her pace, she let her mind dwell on happier days.

Darcy had loved visiting the sawmill with her father. He would lead her in, her hand clasped inside his, warm and safe, as she watched the huge saws cutting through the wood as easily as cutting through cheese. Fine clouds of yellow dust misted the air, and as curling shavings spiralled to the floor, she would scoop up handfuls and play a game with them. As she had grown older, she had shown an interest in the workings of the mill and her father had encouraged her, for it provided them with their living.

She recalled how he had taught her to recognise the different woods. She could still hear his gentle voice saying, 'This is oak, Darcy, a good, strong timber for spars and floorboards, and this is beech for the crafting of fine cabinets. And this beautiful stuff is mahogany that's come across the seas all the way from the Americas.'

Since her father's death, her uncle had strictly forbidden her to visit the sawmill. Paying him no heed, she had disobeyed him on three occasions. Harry Chadwick, her father's manager, had greeted her warmly and she had spent a few happy hours watching the men work. However, she had paid the price for her pleasure. On each occasion when her uncle found out, he had taken off his leather belt and, lifting her skirts and pulling down her drawers, had beaten her bare rump. The whip and crack of the leather had been agonisingly painful, and almost as bad had been the sight of him clutching at the front of his trousers after delivering the last swipe, spittle glistening on his lips as he grunted and moaned with pleasure. Darcy had learned her lesson, and it had been almost a year since she had last visited the place.

Her memories were so painful that she came to a standstill, and standing outside the long, low buildings that were still silent at this hour of the morning, she put down her bag and leaned against the gatepost at the entrance to the mill. Lost in thought and heedless of the time ticking by, she wondered if the workers were as happy and cheerful as they had been in her father's day. It had always pleased her to see them laughing and joking with him as the saws buzzed and the planks were loaded onto the wagons. She could tell they held him in high regard and he them, and she couldn't imagine that her miserable, penny-pinching uncle was appreciated in that way. Polly had told her that since Abe had taken over, he had twice reduced the men's wages and increased the working day by an hour, much to the workers' dismay.

'Damn him to hell,' she muttered, grimly conjuring up all manner of cruel punishments that Abe Earnshaw so rightly deserved. A pleasing image of his smelly, wrinkled thing roasting over hot coals formed in her mind and fired her determination to get as far away from him as was possible. Vengeance spurring her steps, Darcy reached the centre of the town in no time at all.

The streets were just coming to life, the factory smells mingling with that of fresh baked bread, the creak of cartwheels on the cobbles and the stink of horse dung. Men in cloth caps and stout clogs, and women in aprons and turbans were making their way to the mills that were the main workplaces in Bradley Brigg. Even at this early hour, a pall of grey, soot-stained clouds hung over the manufactories and the streets of terraced dwellings that the mill owners had built in the last century to house their employees.

Nobody paid Darcy any heed, but bearing in mind that her uncle might have already found her missing, she avoided the main streets and went down a ginnel between the towering, soot-blackened mills. It led to the towpath that ran alongside the river and the canal beside it. If he were to come in search of her, he would do so in the pony and trap and that meant he'd have to keep to the main thoroughfares. It was highly unlikely he'd come looking for her on foot, Abe being an overweight, lazy sort of chap. Besides, Darcy felt safer in the shadow of the mills.

Although it was barely six o'clock, the mighty heart of the

cloth-weaving industry was belching out thick, black smoke from its soaring chimneys and the air quivered with the rumble of the gigantic boilers that powered the machinery. Clouds of steam and noxious smells spouted from huge pipes protruding from the mill walls, the warm air gusting in Darcy's face as she trotted along. As the clock in Bradley Brigg's church tower struck the hour, the mills' hooters blared, their mournful wail signalling it was time for work to begin. Within minutes, the steady clack of the weavers' looms accompanied Darcy's steps.

She began humming a song about weavers that her nanny had taught her. She loved singing, and from an early age she'd had a sweet, clear voice and was quick to pick up a tune. Sometimes in the evenings she'd sing for her father, and as she softly sang about weavers and doffers and clacking looms, sad memories surged back. Abe Earnshaw had even taken the pleasure out of singing.

At the end of the towpath, she came to a wharf where goods were being unloaded from a brightly painted canal barge. On its deck a swarthy young girl of about her own age was heaving sacks of cabbages up to an older man standing on the wharf. He loaded them onto the back of a wagon. The girl was chattering and laughing as she worked. Darcy envied her. Not because she wanted to heave sacks of vegetables, but because the girl had a purpose and was enjoying fulfilling it.

She doesn't have to think about running away, Darcy thought peevishly. *She most likely lives on the pretty barge with her parents and the man loading the wagon is her father.* Overcome with jealousy, and her shoulder aching, she dumped her bag on a low wall, wishing she could board a barge and glide down the still, deep waters of the canal with her father. As she sulked, the loading was finished. 'That's it, Sam,' the bargee shouted to the wagon driver. 'Tha's getten a full load. See ye next week.'

'Thank ye kindly, Joey,' Sam yelled back, and clucking his tongue and flicking the reins, he set the wagon in motion.

Joey jumped aboard his barge, the girl waving and shouting a cheery farewell as they prepared to sail away.

Darcy hitched her bag back onto her shoulder and began walking on. The loaded wagon drawn by two fine shire horses trundled behind her, and as she stepped to the side of the path, the elderly wagon driver gave her a friendly smile and slowed the wagon to a halt.

'That's a heavy load to be carrying at this hour of the morning,' he quipped.

Darcy blushed as she returned his friendly smile. It suddenly struck her that riding on a wagon would be a much quicker way of putting distance between her uncle and herself. She set down the valise and, looking up at the driver, fixed a rueful smile on her face.

'I've been called away to nurse my sick grandmother,' she said, hopeful that such a sad event might encourage him to offer her a lift. 'Where are you travelling to?'

'I'm bahn for Brighouse wi' this load.'

Darcy's eyes twinkled. 'That's fortunate because that's where I'm going,' she cried. 'Maybe I could take a ride with you.' Ignoring an inner voice warning her that she knew nothing about the man – or Brighouse for that matter – she gave him a pleading smile.

'Aye, put your bag in the back an' hop up alongside me. I'm glad to help you out. The sooner you get to your grandmother's the better,' he said, noting the fine quality of her cape and dress and thinking it strange that a girl of her means should be begging a lift on a wagon and not travelling by carriage or one of the horse buses that travelled from town to town.

Swallowing her deceit, Darcy tossed the valise on top of the sacks and climbed up to sit by the driver.

Her spirits lifted. For the first time in what had been the most horrendous hours of her young life, she felt the tension in her neck and shoulders ease. Pushing her terrible ordeal into the darkest corner of her mind, she sat back to enjoy the ride. Sam proved to be a pleasant man with a lively turn of conversation as he chatted about his own daughters, one a seamstress and the other training to be a nurse.

'You could do wi' taking a page from our Mary's book if you're going to nurse your granny,' he said. 'I hope for your sake she's not too badly.'

'She's not really sick. She's had a fall and broken her arm,' Darcy lied, feeling uncomfortable in the face of Sam's sympathy. 'She just needs me to do the chores till it mends.' She began to wish she really had a grandmother with a broken limb, and as she embroidered her story she found herself almost believing it.

'Your mam must be right proud of you, an' your granny's a lucky woman to have a willing girl like you to help her,' Sam remarked, his praise bringing tears to Darcy's eyes. He was so kind and thoughtful, Darcy had to struggle to prevent herself from spilling out the whole sorry story. Sweating at the thought of it, she diverted his attention from the reason for her journey.

'Where are we now?' she asked as they drove through a quaint little village, its streets lined with terraced houses and shops and a magnificent mansion set far back on a rise of land off the main thoroughfare.

Sam gave her a puzzled glance. 'We're in Holywell Green, lass. Have you not come this way afore when you were visiting your granny?'

Darcy realised her mistake and mumbled, 'I just forgot what it was called,' but her curiosity got the better of her when she spied the mansion through the trees. 'Is that a castle?' she cried craning her neck to get a better view.

Again, Sam was bewildered. 'Nay, that's Brooklands, the home of Samuel Shaw, the textile merchant. I'm surprised your mam or your dad hasn't pointed it out to you afore. It's one o' t'grandest houses in these parts.'

Darcy thought she had better take more care with what she was saying in case Sam became suspicious, so she asked him what his horses were called. It turned out that Sam loved his shires, Vulcan and Thor, and for the rest of the journey he talked of nothing else. The wagon trundled down a steep slope and over a bridge, Sam announcing, 'Well, here we are lass. Brighouse. I'm going to deliver this veg to t'market down by t'canal. Where do you want me to let you off?'

Darcy glanced wildly about her. She'd never been here before. On her right stood a huge cloth mill, the river on her left, but further down the street she could see shops and houses. 'At the end of this street,' she replied blithely. 'My grandmother lives just round the corner.'

By now Sam didn't believe a word that came out of her mouth, but he had his load to deliver so he brought the wagon to a halt at the end of Commercial Street. 'Will this do you?' He turned to face her, and pushing aside the niggling doubt that Darcy had spun him a pack of lies and that he was leaving an innocent young lass unprotected in a place he thought she knew little about, he gave her a warm smile. 'Take care now,' he said as Darcy lowered herself to the pavement.

She lifted her valise from the back of the wagon then stood smiling up at him. 'Thank you very much. You've been most kind, and I've enjoyed travelling with you.' Then, fiddling with the clasp on the valise, she tentatively asked, 'Should I pay you? I have money.'

Sam widened his eyes in astonishment at her naivety and felt even sorrier to be leaving her alone. 'Nay, lass, I don't want your money. An' you be careful who you tell that to,' he advised, his face wrinkled with concern. 'Now, like I said, you take care, wherever it is you're going.' He clucked to the shires and, giving Darcy a parting wave, he trundled out of sight.

Darcy stood uncertainly on the pavement, watching him go. The street was busy even at this early hour, the shopkeepers raising their shutters and setting out their wares, and housewives with their baskets nipping in and out of a nearby bakery to buy freshly baked bread still warm from the ovens. Brighouse, like Bradley Brigg, was a child of the Industrial Revolution, its fortunes thriving due to the Calder and Hebble Navigation, and the mills that dealt in wool, wire and cotton crowded the banks of the waterway. But all of this meant nothing to Darcy. She didn't know where to go or what to do.

'Are you lost, love?' The friendly woman about to enter Sowden Stansfield's boot and shoe shop carried a pair of heavy boots by their laces. She gave the mesmerised-looking young girl a quizzical frown.

'Er. No. Not at all.' Darcy sounded far more confident than she felt. Realising she was drawing attention to herself by standing and staring about her, she moved on down the street past Turner's painters and decorators and then Lancaster's Fish, Poultry and Game shop, the strong smell of wet fish and dead animals making her quicken her pace until she came to the Ring O' Bells public house. By now, she felt dreadfully confused. Running away with no idea of where or what you were running to wasn't at all easy. She knew exactly what she was running from, and her hatred of Abe Earnshaw bubbled up inside her chest. He was to blame for forcing her out into what now seemed like a very foolish venture indeed. But she couldn't go back to Northcrop House. Never!

Then she spied something that made her realise she hadn't run far enough. A heavy wagon loaded with planks slowly trundled past, the sweet smell of freshly hewn wood catching her attention.

She saw the painted board on the side of the wagon bearing the name 'Thomas Earnshaw, Timber Merchant'. The sight of her father's name galvanised her into action.

What if the driver had seen and recognised her? Would he report back to her uncle, tell him of her whereabouts? She needed to go further to escape his clutches. Quickening her pace, she hurried to the crossroads. There she saw a horse bus at a standstill, the horses standing patiently as the driver waited for people to alight and others to climb aboard. The sign above the driver's window read 'Halifax'. Darcy dashed to join the queue and, her fingers fumbling, hurriedly opened the valise and pulled out her purse.

'Halifax,' she said, proffering her fare, her disappointment showing when she saw how depleted her purse suddenly was. 'Thank you,' she muttered, and almost wishing she could change her mind and reclaim the coins, she climbed the stairs to the upper deck, pleasantly amazed by the view of the town: a towering building bearing the name Sugden's Flour Mill, a fine church with a square tower, and tall mill chimneys belching smoke over long glass-roofed sheds that she knew housed weaving looms and spinning mules, just as they did in Bradley Brigg. To Darcy, one place seemed very similar to another yet totally unfamiliar.

3

'What do you mean gone, Master?' Polly turned her rheumy eyes from the pan in which the rashers of bacon sizzled, and looked innocently at Abe Earnshaw.

'Gone, you blithering idiot. Gone and taken her clothing with her,' he bawled, neglecting to add that he had discovered Darcy's absence when he had gone to her room with the intention of furthering what had occurred the night before.

'Taken her clothes, you say?' Polly ruminated, flicking over the bacon in the pan. 'But where would she go?'

'That's what I'm endeavouring to find out, you old fool,' Abe snapped, dragging a chair from the table and sitting down. 'You know more about the girl's doings than I, that's why I'm asking you.'

'She said nothing to me, Master Earnshaw. I've no idea where she's taken herself off to. She has no kin but you as I knows of, an' who she'd be visitin' I couldn't rightly say.' Sounding thoroughly disinterested, Polly slapped the bacon onto a plate and set it on the table in front of him.

Abe began shovelling his breakfast between his blubbery lips.

Hands on hips, Polly stared into his florid, unshaven face, her wizened mouth quirking at the corners in what looked dangerously like a smile of satisfaction. *Wherever she is, she's better off away from you, you dirty beast,* she silently opined as she poured tea into Abe's pint pot. 'Will ye inform the police?'

Abe ignored her. He slurped his tea, deep in thought.

Informing the police was the last thing on his mind. Darcy might accuse him of forcing her to submit to his perversions – and they might believe her. He didn't want that. Neither did he particularly want Darcy back. It would be better for him if she were to disappear and never be seen again. That way there would be no awkward questions when she came of age and, by rights, inherited the sawmill. He still couldn't be certain how much his brother, Thomas, had confided in the sawmill's manager regarding that matter. Harry Chadwick and Thomas had been close friends as well as colleagues, and Abe had considered sounding Harry out as to how much he knew of Thomas's dying wishes. In the end he had decided to leave matters as they were. The less they discussed the future of the sawmill, the more likely he could claim it as his own. He had been tempted to sack Harry in case he knew too much about Thomas's affairs, but Harry knew how to run the mill and was popular with the workforce. Abe's own knowledge of sawing and selling timber was limited, and the men in the mill treated him with contempt, so he'd kept Harry on. Still, he couldn't pretend he wasn't concerned.

He pushed aside his empty plate then roared at Polly to pour him more tea.

Taking her time, she hovered over him with the large teapot in her hand, musing on whether or not to smash it over his head. When his cup was full again, Abe grabbed Polly's free wrist so hard he made her squeal.

'You keep your gob shut about the girl,' he snarled. 'If anybody asks, tell 'em she's gone to stay with a distant cousin in the Lake District. Otherwise, it'll be your job and those of your husband and sons that'll be forfeited.' He flung her away from him, her old bones quaking and the teapot smashing to the floor. 'Do you understand me?'

'Aye, master,' Polly growled, rubbing her aching wrist.

'Good! Now clear up this mess, you old witch.'

* * *

Darcy's first impression of Halifax was that it seemed much larger and grander than Brighouse or Bradley Brigg. The buildings were bigger, the architecture finer and it spoke of a wealth far greater than that of the other two towns.

She alighted from the bus in Gibbet Street and stood gazing about her with no idea of where to go or what do.

Her insides felt empty and she realised she had had nothing to eat or drink since the evening before, save for the glass of water she had snatched in the early hours of the morning. Perhaps she'd feel better if she ate something, she told herself, and she set off down the street in search of a teashop. Her nose soon located one, the warm waft of a savoury smell emanating from a door that had just swung open to let two women pass through.

A youth in a shabby jacket too large for him lolled against a wall close to the shop door. Darcy looked in the shop window at the meat pies, bread and pastries. Her stomach rumbled.

She set the valise down on the window's narrow sill, wedging it in place with her knees so that she could take out her purse. No sooner had she withdrawn it than a long, bony arm clad in a ragged sleeve shot under her nose and a dirty hand snatched the purse from her grasp. She tottered, the swiftness of the grabbing hand unbalancing her. Then she screamed, 'Stop! Thief!' The valise slid to the pavement, and by the time she had regained her balance the lad in the shabby jacket was almost out of sight.

'What happened there, love?' A passer-by, alerted by her scream, hurried to her side. The theft had left Darcy so shocked that for a few moments she couldn't speak, and when she did open her mouth all that came out was a pitiful wail.

'He... he... stole my purse,' she sobbed, pointing to where she'd last seen the fleeing boy. 'It... it had all my money in it.'

'Eeh, that's a bad job,' said the elderly man. 'There's some bad buggers about this town. They don't want an honest day's work; they'd sooner go thieving.' He patted Darcy's arm. 'There's nowt you can do about it, lass. You'll not catch him an' neither will t'police.' He shuffled off, leaving Darcy to dry her eyes and try to stem the rising panic that was threatening to choke her.

She was penniless, without money for food and lodgings, a vagrant. She was now the sort of person she had avoided or spared a halfpenny for when she had come across them on her few outings to Bradley Brigg. Her father had always been more than generous with them, handing over a shilling or maybe a florin and advising them to spend it wisely, not on strong drink but a good hot meal and a bed for the night.

Devastated, Darcy picked up the valise and trudged along Gibbet Street, seeing and hearing nothing, her mind whirling with dreadful thoughts of what was to become of her now that she had no money. Gibbet Street was long and winding, and had she known the reason for its name, she might have contemplated that it was just the place for the lad who had stolen her purse to be dealt with, for this was the street where thieves had been executed in days gone by. She passed by the stump that once held the guillotine, oblivious to its purpose and too numb to even notice the crowds swarming the pavements. By now it was well into the afternoon, shoppers hurrying to make their final purchases and workers on their way home after a hard day's graft.

At the end of Gibbet Street several roads met and Darcy wandered into Crown Street, her boots, which had seemed comfortable when she had set out that morning, now rubbing blisters on her heels and nipping at her toes. Spying a monument in the middle of the crossroads, she went and sat down on the base of it, the valise at her back. Wagons and carts trundled past, and a steady stream of men in cloth caps and overalls made their way to a nearby public house, their clogs striking a brisk tattoo on the cobbles. The dizzying clouds of dust stirred by the constant spinning of rumbling wheels and the smells of greasy wool and horse dung made Darcy feel faint. She closed her eyes and let the feeling of utter desolation engulf her mind and body.

She must have dozed, for when she next opened them dusk had fallen and the gaslights cast an eerie yellow glow over the street. She stood and stretched her stiffened limbs, amazed that no one had accosted her to enquire why was she sleeping in the middle of the busy thoroughfare. Then sadly telling herself that they had done so because they didn't care, she lifted her bag and plodded on. It seemed like a lifetime since she had left Northcrop House.

Unbidden memories of her warm bed and food on the table flooded Darcy's mind and she realised that, miserable though she had been, at least the house had provided shelter from the cold night air. She had taken that for granted, and just for a moment Northcrop House seemed a better place than this awful street she was trudging down. Then she recalled why she had run away.

Darcy began to shiver from head to toe, not just from the chill, damp air but also at the memory of what her uncle had forced her to do. In her mind's eye she saw again the wrinkled brown skin and the glistening head of the smelly thing he had wanted her to kiss.

She imagined she felt it brushing against her cheek and her free hand flew to her face, wiping it clean of an illusory sticky mess. Would her face truly feel clean ever again? The thought made her retch, a dry croaking sound that hurt her throat, but she didn't vomit. Her belly was so empty it had forgotten what food was.

Incapable at that moment of walking any further, she leaned against the wall of a public house, weary to the bone. She could hear men's raucous laughter, shouts and the clinking of pint pots, and when the door opened, a gush of warm, smoky air rushed out into the street. A man in clogs clattered unsteadily on to the pavement. Pausing to adjust his flat cap, he saw Darcy. His slack mouth turned up at the corners.

'How much do you charge, love?' He stepped closer, close enough for her to see the stumps of his blackened teeth and smell his sour breath.

Darcy had no idea what he meant by the question, but sensing danger she pushed herself from against the wall and swung the valise with as much force as she could muster. The bag caught him across his knees and he staggered then fell, his cap rolling into the gutter.

Darcy ran, his shouts and curses ringing in her ears.

Her heart thudded painfully in her chest and the soles of her feet burned but she kept on running, barely noticing where she was treading, regardless of the piles of horse dung, the dog droppings and the rotten vegetables that lay mouldering on the pavements in front of the closed-up market stalls. Fear drove her through a maze of narrow streets and she only slowed her pace when she was sure the man hadn't followed her.

The street she was now on was very dark, as though the smoke from the nearby mill chimneys had formed a thick blanket and descended to street level, but here and there lights shone from behind the curtained windows of the shabby houses. Darcy halted outside one such house, gazing at the rosy glow and envying the people inside. When the sound of laughter floated out from behind the window she began to cry. Her shoulders heaved and big, fat tears trickled down her face.

Painfully aware of how alone she was, she contemplated knocking on the door and begging to be let in. Then realising how foolish that was, she reluctantly walked on, too dog-tired to worry about what might be lurking in the shadows. She had to find somewhere to rest, a place where she wouldn't be disturbed. But where?

There were no gaslights to show the way and it was now so dark that Darcy could barely see ahead. She trod in something that slithered under her boot and her knees buckled. She knew she couldn't go much further. If she did, she'd most likely faint and fall in the filth under her feet and lie there all night. She pressed on to the end of the street. In a different mood she might have smiled had she known that the street was called Hunger Hill.

Rounding a corner, her senses were alerted by a familiar smell. She breathed in the sweet, clean smell of newly sawn timber, and just like iron filings being drawn by a magnet she followed her nose to the large building a few paces ahead. It was a cabinet maker's workshop. At the side of it was a ginnel, even darker than the street. Feeling her way between the walls of the pitch-black narrow passage, she came to a stop when her way was barred by a stout wooden door. With her heart in her mouth, and thinking it foolish to even try, she pressed the lever above the large iron handle. To her amazement, the door opened. She poked her head through the gap and looked into the enclosed yard at the rear of the workshop. Light from a gas lamp behind the far wall cast a sickly yellow glow over the yard and she peered through the gloom at a conglomeration of eerie shapes and shadows. Her ears pricked. Silence. Cautiously, she stepped inside the yard, which was sheltered from the chill night breeze.

She looked around her and spied some long planks that were stacked on their ends against the workshop's wall so that they formed a tent-shaped shelter. She looked at it speculatively then crawled inside. The sweet-smelling wooden boards gave off a certain sort of warmth all of their own and Darcy decided that this was as safe a place as any to bed down for a few hours. It was off the street, away from the drunks and anyone else who might wish to harm her. Taking the tweed skirt from her bag, she spread it on the cold flagstones then piled the blouse and her underwear together to form a pillow. Her bed made, she took off her boots and sat down. It felt good to take the weight off her feet. Gently, she massaged them through her thick lisle stockings then took off her bonnet and did the same to her scalp, still tender from Abe Earnshaw's grasping fingers. These simple actions relaxed her, and feeling the tension drain from her body, she lay down and closed her eyes.

She was so tired that she had imagined she would fall asleep instantly. Instead, she found herself making plans for the following day. She would look for work, anything that would provide her with money to pay for food and shelter. She'd ask in the shops and make enquiries at the mills. Surely she could find something to support herself; other girls did. Today she hadn't been prepared for the rigours independence so obviously demanded, but tomorrow would be different, she told herself firmly. She had seen and learned things she hadn't known existed, yet she had managed to survive them without coming to any great harm, even though the theft of all her money had left her badly shaken. Tomorrow she would be more careful.

She turned over on her side. The timepiece in her dress pocket pressed against her thigh. She had quite forgotten it was there. Her fingers stiff with cold, she wrapped them round the smooth gold case and withdrew it then held it up to a gap in the planks that let in the light from the yard. She saw that the time was seven minutes to eight. Four hours and seven minutes to a new day, she mused, a day in which she would prove she was capable of tackling whatever life might throw her way. That's what her father would expect from her.

After her mother's death he had often told her what a brave, resilient girl she was, and now, as she gazed at the opalescent dial, she determined not to let him down. Just holding the watch gave her comfort and made her feel stronger. She turned the winder. Then, with the watch nestled in her palm, she tucked her hand under her cheek against the pillow, listening to the steady tick, her mind filled with positive thoughts as she let sleep overtake her.

The nightmare that then took hold was terrifying. Darcy dodged this way and that trying to avoid a wrinkled brown snake with a glistening head that was feverishly attempting to reach for her mouth. Summoning all her courage, she grasped it tightly, intent on choking the life out of it, and in response it squirted a sticky, smelly mess up into her face. Then it shrivelled and flopped its head, but just as she thought she had killed it, it stiffened and sprang back to life, startling her into wakefulness.

Despite the chill night air, she was bathed in sweat, her heart thudding painfully. Beneath her ear the timepiece ticked steadily, its mesmerising beat doing much to calm her. Gradually her heartbeat slowed and her breathing had just resumed its normal, steady level when she felt something brushing against her leg.

Darcy squealed. She shot up into a sitting position thinking that the snake had returned to torment her. Her common sense told her it was most likely a rat. Whatever it was, it didn't scurry away. Frozen with fear, and her breath tight inside her chest, she felt the thing brushing its way up her leg. A pair of round yellow eyes gleamed in the dark space. Afraid to move, Darcy stared into them. They eyed her curiously then loomed slowly nearer until they were level with her own. Darcy's pent breath whooshed from her lungs.

'Hello, puss,' she said, her voice cracking with relief as she tentatively stroked the large ginger cat's back. The cat mewed, its long tail swishing as it coiled its body and tucked itself into her side. The cat's fur was warm under Darcy's cold fingers, and the steady rise and fall of its soft, plump body let Darcy know that she was no longer alone. It's purring lulled her into a deep, dreamless sleep.

When she wakened, she didn't know where she was, and when she did remember that she was in the wood yard, she was most surprised to think that she had slept at all. Her throat was parched and she was ravenously hungry. She stretched out her hand, feeling for her friendly ginger sleeping companion, but the cat wasn't there. Darcy wondered if she had dreamed its presence. Then, from behind the wall against which the planks were propped, she could hear the repetitive thud of a steam engine and the high-pitched whine of a circular saw. The workshop must be open.

Her father's timepiece had slipped from her hand whilst she slept and she scrabbled under the makeshift pillow to find it, gasping when she saw the hands pointing to a quarter to nine. Hardly daring to move, she got up onto her knees, and slipping the watch inside her pocket with trembling fingers she crouched there, listening and waiting.

A door creaked, and she heard men's voices in the yard. She shrank further into the corner of her hideout and listened to the sound of running water, her tongue cleaving to the roof of her dry mouth. The splash of water ceased and a deep voice said, 'Tek these in first, lad, then shift them planks over to that pile.'

Darcy cowered in her hiding place, praying that the man didn't mean her planks.

Scrapes and thuds and clatters let her know that things were being moved and she reckoned that the noise would mask any sound she herself made. Still on her knees, she stealthily stowed the clothing she had used for a bed back into the valise. Her heart pounded, and although her body ached from lying for so long on the cold flagstones, she tensed, ready to make a dash for it.

At last, the noises stilled and with the slamming of a door the yard fell silent. Inching forward, she peeped out from behind the pile of planks. There was no one in the yard so she ducked out. She knew she ought to leave at once but the lure of the water pump beckoned and her parched throat and empty belly impelled her to cross the yard and crank the pump's handle. Water gushed out and she placed her open mouth under the flow and swallowed, the water gliding deliciously over her furred tongue and gurgling in her empty stomach. Caring not that it was wetting her bonnet and cape, she drank greedily, her ears deaf to the creaking workshop door as it opened.

'Oy! What are you doing?' Someone was walking towards her.

Startled, Darcy let go of the pump handle and hastily wiped her face with her fingers and batted her eyelashes free of the droplets blurring her vision. The lad was about her age, and he didn't look particularly threatening. Thinking on her feet, she said, 'I've lost my cat. I thought he might have wandered down here.'

The lad grinned. 'An' you thought you'd gi' yoursen a bath whilst you wa' lookin' for 'im?' he quipped.

'I was thirsty,' Darcy mumbled, embarrassed by her damp appearance. A trickle of water dribbled down her nose from the edge of her bonnet and she swiped at it impatiently.

'What does your cat look like?'

'Black with a white shirt front.'

'Only cat round here is yon big ginger tom.' The lad pointed to a pile of timber on which Darcy's night-time friend was now stretched. She was glad that the cat couldn't talk, but the thought made her aware that she hadn't had a conversation with anyone since her arrival in Halifax. The boy looked friendly and she was tempted to stay and talk to him. It would make her feel less alone.

His smile was replaced by a frown as he asked, 'How did you get into t'yard?'

Darcy pointed to the door in the wall.

The lad groaned. 'I must have forgotten to put the bar on it.' Anxious to cover his mistake, he glanced nervously over his shoulder at the open workshop door. 'I'd best be getting on wi' me work, an' you need to go or else t'boss'll have me guts for garters. I hope you find your cat.' He walked over to the planks under which she had slept and lifted one.

'So do I,' Darcy replied, and picking up her bag, she hurried to the door then down the ginnel, leaving behind a bemused young boy who was thinking that, even though she looked half drowned, she was still very pretty.

4

Darcy emerged from the ginnel, and back on the street she joined a throng of people who all seemed to be heading in the same direction. Housewives carrying shopping baskets chatted and laughed as they walked along, small children skipping beside them, a sharp reminder of how alone Darcy was. Then, recalling the notions she'd had the night before about finding work, when they reached the junction and had to wait for the traffic to ease, she turned to the woman at her elbow. 'I'm new to the town. Do you know of any place I might find work?'

Taken aback, the woman looked Darcy up and down, frowning. 'Work did you say? Eeh, lass, there's not a lot going in t'mills right now an' I can't say off top o' me head where you're likely to find a job.' The passage of carts and wagons eased and they crossed the road. 'You could allus try t'Borough Market,' the woman added. 'There might be a stallholder looking to tek someb'dy on.'

'Where is the market?' A flame of hope flickered in Darcy's chest.

'Just down here, lass. I'm goin' there meself.'

Darcy kept pace with the woman until they came to a busy market overflowing with stalls and people looking for a bargain. The woman stopped at a stall selling vegetables and Darcy thanked her and kept on walking. The noise and bustle seemed somehow cheering and she asked at one stall after another if they needed any assistance. None did, and, her spirits sinking, she wandered towards a towering, foursquare edifice with an arched entrance. She walked through the gateway and found herself in an immense courtyard surrounded on all sides by galleries three storeys high. The walkways thronged with shoppers, and there were shoeblacks, knife grinders, match sellers and vendors selling all manner of goods and things to eat, but having no money to make a purchase of any kind, Darcy sauntered past them, too disillusioned to ask if they required an assistant.

A blowsy woman of middling years with a heavily rouged face was standing on a box, singing raucously. She was wearing a garish frilly dress that exposed a copious amount of bosom and Darcy was reminded of a poster she had seen outside the theatre in Bradley Brigg advertising a burlesque show. The singer wiggled her ample hips and pulled lewd faces as she sang, and the small crowd gathered round her tittered and made coarse remarks.

Darcy thought they were being rude and felt sorry for the woman, but as her ears tuned in to the shockingly vulgar ditty, she realised why they were laughing. As the song ended the singer made a sweeping curtsey, her bosom almost spilling free of its trappings. To Darcy's amazement, the crowd clapped and cheered and threw coins at the woman's feet. The singer scooped them up.

What a terrible way to have to make a living. The woman was making a spectacle of herself, Darcy thought as she walked on. What was more, she had a dreadful voice, yet her bawdy ballad had earned her something Darcy didn't have: money.

Silently damning to everlasting hell the lad who had stolen her purse, she stood for a while watching a man juggling plates, his feet treading on broken crockery as he tried in vain to keep his plates spinning. Further on, a man playing a ukulele was doing his best to make his music heard above the shouts of the vendors and the chattering shoppers.

Hunger pains gnawed at her empty stomach and she paused on the edge of a large crowd who were standing round a platform watching the antics of a tall, muscular man with swarthy skin and flowing black hair. He wore nothing but a pair of tight-fitting trousers made from shiny black satin. His bare torso glistened under a sheen of sweat. Darcy thought his handsome, finely sculpted face looked rather noble, like a prince from foreign parts. A blackboard propped against the platform read 'Tarquin the Tartar, Tumbler and Fire Eater'.

The crowd oohed and aahed as Tarquin somersaulted across the platform then gasped as he cartwheeled high into the air and suddenly dropped like a stone onto his belly, squirming snake-like across the wooden boards. Before his audience had time to catch their breaths, he flipped upwards, coiling his body in mid-air so that when he landed on his feet he was facing them, his sinewy arms raised in triumph. The crowd clapped and cheered.

Quick as a flash, he scooped up a bowler hat and leapt into the crowd, yelling, 'Show your appreciation,' as he began collecting money.

Hunger growled like an angry dog in Darcy's belly. *That's what I need. Just a few coppers to buy...* As she imagined a tasty pie or a dish of meaty stew, she noticed that most of the spectators had wandered off before Tarquin could get to them, and seeing the look of disappointment on his handsome face, Darcy suddenly had an idea that could serve them both.

Seizing her chance, she tossed the valise under the platform. Then whipping off her bonnet, she held it out to the people nearest to her. Coins clinked in, so she scurried in and out of the crowd, crying, 'Show your appreciation,' and gushing, 'Thank you kindly,' as they made their donations.

'Hey, them's my earnings!' Tarquin bawled at the top of his lungs as he dashed over to where Darcy was still collecting coppers in her bonnet. His face was red with ill-concealed outrage.

'I know that,' Darcy scorned, tipping the coins in her bonnet into the bowler hat in his strong, brown hand. 'I was just helping you out, it being a pity to let the crowd go before you got to them. I wasn't stealing, if that's what you thought.' She sounded highly offended and her clear blue eyes were devoid of any shame.

Tarquin looked abashed, and shrugging his muscular shoulders, he muttered his thanks. Then, taking a long look at the girl wearing a cape and boots of good quality, he wondered what her game was.

There being nothing to hold their attention, the crowds continued drifting away from the platform, and seeing the look of desperation in Tarquin's eyes, Darcy remembered the tawdry woman with the raucous voice. She clambered onto the platform and burst into song. At the sound of her clear, high voice the passers-by faltered then turned to look where it was coming from. Darcy continued singing, her sweet rendition of 'Scarborough Fair' floating high above their heads. The onlookers smiled and nodded along with the refrain. Tarquin saw she was holding the crowd. He dashed behind the platform and liberally dowsed himself with water. As the last sweet notes of the song faded and the spectators applauded, he leapt back on the platform carrying a flaming torch in either hand.

Darcy jumped down as he flourished the burning brands, the

sparking arcs of fire swirling magically and the crowd holding their breath as, never flinching, he swished the flames up his bare arms and across his chest. Darcy watched, wide-eyed, afraid that at any moment his long dark hair would go up in flames or his entire body combust in a fiery demise.

The crowd whooped and cheered. Tarquin darted to the edge of the platform and, placing the torches in a stand, he then lit a smaller torch and whirled back to face the crowd. Opening his mouth wide, he inserted the burning taper. The crowd gasped then roared their approval as he blew out streams of fire. Tarquin responded with a daring fiery somersault before landing on his feet and making a low, sweeping bow. The crowd screamed for more.

Grasping the moment, Darcy ran amongst them, thrusting her bonnet under their noses, delighted by the clink and rattle of the coins as the bonnet's weight increased. Flushed with success, she gave Tarquin a cheery smile as he passed by her, his bowler in his hand. He smiled back, but Darcy knew he was keeping a sharp eye on her in case she fled with the takings.

When she felt him grip her arm, she turned to face him, the bonnet heavy in her hands. Maybe he would see fit to give her a few coppers for her trouble. If he did, she could pay for a bed in a cheap rooming house and buy a hot pie for her supper. She was dreadfully hungry, and she didn't fancy sleeping rough again in the city, where there might be all kinds of dangers. Last night she had been lucky.

She handed the bonnet to Tarquin. He looked into it and then at her, his face showing nothing short of amazement. She was a pretty, little thing with her long blonde hair and elfin features. She also had none of the roughness of the other girls who hung around the markets, on the make. Her manner of speech and the way she carried herself was far more genteel, and her honesty was astounding. Weighing the bonnet in his hand then tipping the coins into the bowler, he gave her a puzzled smile. 'You did well, lass. But why?'

Darcy returned his smile. 'You couldn't perform and collect at the same time. I thought if I lent you a hand you might reward me with a few coppers that will buy me a hot pie and pay for a night's lodgings.'

Still amazed by Darcy's integrity, and more impressed by the way she had broken into song and kept his audience from wandering off, he said, 'You've a fine pair of lungs on you. Where did you learn to sing like that?'

'I've always been able to sing, and my old nanny taught me the songs,' Darcy replied modestly.

Tarquin was now even more puzzled. The girl must belong to gentry if she had a nanny. Yet why was she alone in the market collecting coppers for him and looking for a place to sleep and a pie to fill her belly? Her innocence and naivety touched his kind heart.

Loath to abandon her after she'd improved his day's takings to more than double, he contemplated handing her a few coins or taking her home with him, where she would be safe. As he was deliberating, ominous rain clouds gathered overhead. It wasn't yet midday but the light had gone out of the sky and the wind was rising. Tarquin packed his fire sticks into a hessian sack.

'What brings you here? And why have you no place to rest your head?' he asked bluntly. 'You shouldn't be out alone. The town can be a rough place for a young lass on her own.' He tipped the contents of the bowler hat into a leather pouch he had taken from the sack. Darcy choked back tears as she watched the coins disappear, and a gulping sob leapt from her throat as she watched him fasten the bulging pouch to the broad belt round his waist.

She hung her head. 'My uncle, with whom I lived, has turned

me out,' she said, hopeful that, contrary to the old adage, dishonesty would prove to be its own reward. 'We quarrelled and he barred the door on me, leaving me with nothing but what I stand up in. I have no money and nowhere to go.' She shifted from one foot to the other, her pride forbidding her from repeating her request for money.

'Then I suggest you turn around and go back the way you came. Tell him you are sorry and—'

'No! I'm never going back,' Darcy cried, her blue eyes blazing. 'I'd rather die than go back to suffer his filthy perversions.' She grabbed her bag from under the platform, her disappointment at not having persuaded Tarquin to hand over a few coins bringing tears to her eyes.

'Wait!' he cried, horrified by the word 'perversions'. Whatever had her uncle subjected her to? He took her hand firmly in his before she could make a run for it. 'If you've nowhere to go for the night you'd best come along with me,' he said.

Darcy raised her tearstained face and looked into his. He was gazing down at her, his dark eyes conveying something she could not quite fathom. She pulled her hand free, her mind working overtime as she debated whether or not to accept his offer. Supposing he turned out to be like her uncle, expecting her to do disgusting things to please him? Then where would she be? Out of the frying pan into the fire, she thought. But where else could she go without money?

He caught hold of her arm. 'Come along, the weather's turning,' he said as a spatter of raindrops carried on the rising wind fell from the darkening sky.

Darcy began to tremble. She couldn't possibly wander the streets in such foul weather. She looked up at him again, and seeing nothing but kindly concern in his darkly handsome face, she shrugged. 'If you're not prepared to pay me for helping you, then I suppose I will have to accept your offer.'

Tarquin relaxed his grip on her arm. 'It isn't that I don't want to give you the money. You've earned it. But lodgings will be hard to find, with it being Easter week and the town thronging with folks come to stay for the markets and the fairs.' He gave her a pleading smile. 'I wouldn't want you to come to any harm.'

The heavens opened. Rain lashed down and without another word he held on to her arm and began to run, Darcy having no alternative but to keep up with him. They pelted across the market place and down an alley off the main street, Darcy's heart pounding not only with the effort of moving at such speed, but with rising panic. Where was he taking her? And what was he going to do to her?

Soaked to the skin, they hurried through a warren of narrow streets until they came to a ginnel that led into a dismal little court of six two-storeyed dwellings, the houses on three sides of the yard, ash pits and two water closets on the fourth. Darcy's first thought was that it didn't look very inviting.

'Welcome to Burgos Court,' Tarquin said, letting go of her arm. 'Its name has something to do with the Duke of Wellington. He had to fight the Frenchies, but all we have to contend with is rising damp and rats.' He chuckled grimly.

Darcy was debating whether or not she should turn tail when he rapped on the door of the house nearest the end of the ginnel. It opened immediately, letting out light and a gush of warm air. The woman who had answered his knock flung the door wide crying, 'Come in, come in, you're wringing wet.' Tarquin stepped inside, pulling Darcy behind him.

Darcy blinked her eyelashes free of raindrops and glanced round in a daze, taking in the sparsely furnished living kitchen, a fire blazing merrily in the grate, and the plump, smiling face of a pretty woman. A bonny, little girl of about four years jumped up from the hearth rug, her glossy brown ringlets bouncing as she ran to Tarquin, looking to be hugged. Seeing the state of him, her arms fell to her sides and she pulled a face. 'Daddy, Daddy, you're all wet,' she cried, her voice high with concern.

'Hold on, my little angel, I'll lift you in a mo,' he said, ruffling her hair.

Then she noticed Darcy. Her big, brown eyes widened. Casting anxious glances from her father to her mother, she said, 'Who's she?'

'Aye, John, who have we got here?' The woman spoke pleasantly as she helped him out of his wet coat, smiling fondly as she accepted a kiss on her cheek.

He gave a lopsided smile. 'That I don't know, for we didn't get round to making introductions. What I do know is that she's in trouble an' needs a bit of help.' He turned to Darcy. 'I'm John Carver an' this is my wife, Betsy. An' this little princess is our daughter, Angela.' He lifted the little girl in his arms then addressed Darcy. 'What name do you go by?'

The happy faces helped Darcy to recover her wits. Her fears that Tarquin – or John – had intended to harm her rapidly diminished and she replied, 'Darcy Earnshaw.'

'Well, Darcy Earnshaw,' Betsy Carver said with a warm smile, 'let's get you out of your wet cape and boots an' then John here can tell us how he came by you.'

There was no malice or suspicion in her voice, so Darcy peeled off her cape and slipped her feet out of her boots. Betsy went over to the fireplace and took two towels from the brass rail above the range. Tossing one to John then handing the other to Darcy, she said, 'Give your head a rub. You don't want to catch a chill sitting about with wet hair.'

At Betsy's bidding, Darcy sat by the blazing fire, and John and

Betsy sat at the table with Angela on Betsy's knee. Although the room was nothing grand and its walls displayed damp patches of peeling plaster, Darcy could see that it was spotlessly clean. The brightly coloured pegged rug beneath her feet and the pink and grey lino that covered the rest of the floor showed not a speck of dust, and the white cloth on the table was pristine. Betsy Carver was clearly a proud housewife.

'Well, go on then,' Betsy urged, 'let's be hearing what you've been up to.'

John chuckled and cast a mischievous glance in Darcy's direction. 'I was working the crowd in the Piece Hall, as I usually do of a Saturday, when this one came along,' he said, flicking his thumb at Darcy. 'The next thing I sees is her collecting coppers from the crowd – coppers I'd done my damnedest to earn. I thought she was a thief.' He broke off, laughing as he related the rest of the story. However, whilst he told Betsy that Darcy had been turned out of her home, he made no mention of Darcy's uncle's 'filthy perversions'.

'An' what's more, she has a voice like a nightingale,' he continued, loosening the leather pouch hanging from his belt. 'She stopped them good an' proper in their tracks when she started to sing, I can tell you.' He upended the pouch, Betsy clapping her hands to her mouth and her eyes sparkling as the coins streamed out to form a glittering heap under the light from the oil lamp.

'My goodness me! The pair of you have certainly earned your dinner,' she cried, shunting Angela from her lap and jumping to her feet. 'We've already had ours.' Betsy crossed to the hearth, Angela at her heels.

The little girl sat down on the hearth rug, gazing up at Darcy, her eyes alight with curiosity. Betsy opened the door of the fireside range. A gust of hot air warmed Darcy's cold feet. Using a pot-holder, Betsy lifted out a large, iron dish and carried it to the table.

Darcy's empty stomach growled. Angela heard it. Giggling, she gave Darcy an impish grin. Darcy grinned back, and when Betsy removed the lid from the dish, her mouth watered as the delicious aroma of stewed meat and vegetables wafted her way.

'Darcy, come to the table,' John called out. 'As my good wife says, you've earned your dinner. An' her stew knocks a hot pie into a cocked hat.'

Darcy needed no second bidding, and fondling Angela's curly head as she stepped by her, she crossed to the table and sat down. 'Your daughter's very pretty,' she said, before spooning up a mouthful of stew. After that she had no time for talking. She ate ravenously, the hot gravy warming the cockles of her heart as she listened to John and Betsy sing their little girl's praises.

Eventually, her dish scraped clean, Darcy sat back feeling replete and rather drowsy. 'Why do you call yourself Tarquin if your name is John?' she asked, as Betsy cleared the table.

'"Tarquin" is more exotic and it goes with "tumbler", whereas "John" is meek and mild and only goes wi' "jumper",' he said, grinning as he leaned across the table. 'You see, you have to make the crowd think that you're a mysterious foreigner with special powers. It wouldn't do for them to think I was the son of a cobbler born not a stone's throw from here.'

'But how does the fire not burn you?' Darcy could barely contain her wonder.

'It's all in the way you do it. Timing is the thing. Did you not notice that I'd dowsed my body with water before I lit the torches?'

'I thought you were just cooling off.'

John shook his head. 'I was wet through when your song ended so that when I let the flames play up my arms and legs and across my chest, they had to evaporate the water before reaching my skin. And when I put the little torches in my mouth, I'd already filled it with spit and a drop of alcohol.' He grinned ruefully as he added, 'Of course, there are times when I have blisters inside and out.'

'Indeed, there are,' Betsy piped up. 'I've never done telling him to stick to the tumbling. That's enough to please any crowd.'

'Ah, but where's the danger and the thrill?' John crowed. 'The crowd want me to burst into flames and shrivel into a melting ball of blubber before their very eyes. Breaking a leg or me neck's not half as exciting.'

5

'What do you reckon we should do about her?' John asked Betsy as he climbed out of bed and began pulling on his clothes. It was Monday morning, Darcy's third day in the Carver household.

Betsy leaned up on her elbow and looked at him thoughtfully. 'She's a lovely little thing, and she's been no bother over the weekend. In fact, she's been really helpful with the chores, an' she played ever so nicely with Angela. I like having her here.'

Now it was John's turn to look thoughtful. 'I suppose we should let her stay until she sorts herself out. She doesn't have anywhere else to go, so she says. An' like you say, she does make herself useful.'

'She certainly did that the other day when she helped you out in the Piece Hall – an' you were right about her voice. I heard her singing to Angela. Mebbe you could let her work along with you until she finds her feet.'

John looked up from fastening his boots and smiled. 'Then that's what we'll do till such time as she feels ready to move on.'

Betsy pushed back the bed covers and got to her feet. 'I'm glad you agree,' she said. 'I'd like to think we were helping her out, 'cos she seems like she needs it.'

'Will you be coming along wi' me this morning, or will you stay at home with Betsy and the bairn?' John cocked his head and looked enquiringly across the table at Darcy. Her mouth full of porridge, she couldn't reply immediately and John continued. 'You can be my bottler again. That was Betsy's job before this one came along.' He patted Angela, perched next to him at the table.

Darcy swallowed and gave him a puzzled look. 'What's a bottler, John?'

'The one that collects the money from the crowd,' he said, reaching for a slice of bread smeared with jam. 'Some buskers use a bottle to gather the coins 'cos it prevents folk from filching the coppers out when they're pretending to put some in. There's them on the markets that 'ud steal the eye out of your head if you're not careful.'

'But you collected the money in your hat,' she said, feeling even more confused.

'Aye, so I do, 'cos it's quicker, an' it's all a matter of holding the hat just at the right level to make sure the dippers – that's what we call them that pinch coins – can't help themselves.'

'Ah, now I see what you mean,' Darcy said, her eyes lighting up. 'When I was running round with my bonnet there was a lad whose hand lingered too long as he put in his penny. He must have been "dipping" as you say.' She grinned, proud to be acquiring the knowledge of how John made his livelihood. 'But what's a busker?'

'That's what we street performers call ourselves. It comes from an old Spanish word,' John replied. 'My granddaddy was a Spaniard. That's why my skin's so dark. He came over here with a band of players an' married my granny here in Halifax. He taught my daddy to busk an' my daddy taught me.'

'I thought you said he was a cobbler.'

'He was. He busked at the fairs an' the markets in the summertime, an' when the weather turned bad, he mended shoes. That's what I do.'

Darcy was thrilled to be in such exotic company as someone whose ancestors had come from Spain. It made her feel wild and adventurous, and she longed to be part of John's world. It was far better than mouldering away in Northcrop House with her evil uncle.

'I'll be your bottler then,' she cried, her sweet spontaneity causing Betsy and John to laugh out loud. 'I'll collect as fast as I can, and I'll make sure nobody dips in the hat.' And, her eyes sparkling, she added, 'And when you need to get ready for your next act I'll keep the crowd by singing.'

'It sounds as though you've got yourself a lovely apprentice, John,' said Betsy, coming to the table with a pot of tea in her hand. She gave Darcy a warm smile. 'I had to give up the busking when Angela was born, for I'd not trail a baby into the crowds, but that made me feel bad about leaving John to do all the work,' she said as she filled Darcy's beaker to the brim. 'He did try using a lad or two to collect for him but they stole more than they were worth, so I'm glad you've come along. You've already proved how honest you are.'

Darcy smiled her appreciation of Betsy's kind words then drank her tea. 'I'll go and put my boots on,' she said, getting up from the table and going into the small back room where she had slept the two previous nights. It was no bigger than a broom cupboard, but Betsy had made up a narrow pallet bed with clean sheets and warm blankets, and on each of the nights, before she had fallen asleep, Darcy had thanked God for placing her in the care of John and Betsy Carver.

* * *

Yesterday being Sunday, and street performances banned by the authorities, John had stayed at home. 'The church don't take too kindly to people enjoying themselves,' he'd said, 'but I believe God wouldn't object. To my mind, God's everywhere, not just in the chapels an' churches we've built in his name. He's in the fields an' the parks, and in people's houses. I think he'd want the workers to be happy on their day off, not down on their knees listening to the preachers ranting on about fire an' brimstone an' the wages of sin.'

Darcy heartily agreed with him, and when he'd suggested they go to the People's Park in the afternoon, she hadn't felt one bit guilty about not attending a church service, as she would have had to do if she had still lived with her uncle. She'd reflected bitterly on Abe Earnshaw's false piety and the manner in which he ingratiated himself with the dignitaries at the chapel in Bradley Brigg. Then she'd thrust him out of her mind. She was no longer in his clutches. She was free to do as she pleased. And as they had walked to the People's Park it had pleased her mightily to be in the company of the lovely Carver family.

After Saturday's lashing rain the sun had shone brightly, and the pathways and the grass had been dry underfoot as they had strolled through the park. Darcy had been impressed by its beauty and amazed to find such a place slap bang in the centre of the town that she had thought of as dismal, with its busy, dirty streets and the towering mill chimneys puffing out black smoke.

'It's as though someone has planted a part of the countryside in the town,' she had marvelled, her cornflower blue eyes shining to match the cloudless sky.

'It was given to the people by a wealthy manufacturer called Francis Crossley,' John had told her as she admired the grand pavilion, 'and it was designed by the famous landscaper, Joseph Paxton.'

'Oh yes. I've read about him. He's the one who designed the

Crystal Palace for the Great Exhibition, isn't he?' she'd replied, and Betsy had commented on how knowledgeable Darcy was.

They'd sauntered along pathways, stopping every now and then to admire the statues and the verdant lawns and flowerbeds. When they had arrived at the bandstand they'd been delighted to find that a brass band was just about to start playing. They had sat down to listen to the music, but after a while Angela had become restless, so Darcy took her onto the grass to play, leaving John and Betsy to rest and enjoy the lively airs the smartly uniformed bandsmen were pumping out.

For Darcy the afternoon had been a wonderful reminder of when her father had taken her on such outings. Living with Abe Earnshaw had involved no such pleasures, her daily life narrowed to Northcrop House, and she had rejoiced in the glorious feeling of being released from what had been more like a prison than a home.

Now, as she laced her boots and donned her cape, she was ready for more of this marvellous feeling of being her own person, and as she left the little room that she already looked on as hers, she determined to repay John and Betsy for their kindness in whatever way she could. She'd start by making sure that she was the best bottler John had ever had – save for Betsy – and that his hat was full after each performance.

* * *

John took a different route to the Borough Market and the Piece Hall so that Darcy would get to know the town. 'Can't do wi' you gettin' lost,' he joked.

'What's that place over there?' Darcy asked, pointing into the distance to a massive mill that dominated the manufactories around it.

'That's Dean Clough Mill. The biggest mill in the world, so they say,' John replied. 'It's over a mile long. That's where the Crossleys weave carpets for kings and queens an' other rich folk.'

They turned left into Northgate, John pointing out the Exchange Chambers and Hemingway's Pianoforte and Harmonium Warehouse and the Northgate Hotel. When they arrived at the Piece Hall, Darcy still wanted to know more about the town she was beginning to look on as home.

'Why is it called the peace hall? Was it built to mark the end of a war?'

'Nay, it's not that "peace" spelled with an "a". It's p-i-e-c-e,' he explicated. 'It's where the handloom weavers used to bring their pieces of cloth to sell. All those little rooms on the galleries were for buying and selling the weavers' wares. Now that all the cloth is woven on machines in the mills they're shops selling all sorts.'

'The Industrial Revolution,' Darcy said.

'Aye, summat like that,' John replied.

When they arrived at the platform John preferred to work on they found it already occupied by a group of accordionists, so they moved on until they found a place to his liking. It wasn't as central as he would have liked but they did well enough, and by the end of the day, having given another performance in the Borough Market, they moved on to Gibbet Street. At the stump where the guillotine had once stood, John went into his routine. A small crowd gathered. Amongst them was a plump matron with a stern face.

'If this were still in use young man, you should be under it,' she heckled, gesturing with her rolled umbrella at where the gibbet had been. 'Cavorting about half naked in full public view is not only disgusting, it's against the laws of God and a sin of the worst kind.'

'You don't have to watch if you don't like what you see,' Darcy retorted.

The matron heaved her bosom. 'And you, young lady, should know better than to associate yourself with such indecency,' she snorted, her fat cheeks wobbling with indignation. 'You'll pay for your sins. The good Lord will see to that.'

By now there were more eyes on the fat matron than there were on John. He stopped performing, intent on defending Darcy, who was receiving the brunt of the matron's spleen.

A frowsy young woman who had been ogling John with lustful eyes turned on the matron. 'Oh, bugger off! Go home to your husband,' she yelled, sniggering as she added, 'I'll bet you a bob neither of you 'as ever seen one another wi'out your clothes on. You don't know what you're missin', you prudish old bag.'

The matron's cheeks turned purple. She raised her umbrella, bringing it down sharply on the young woman's shoulder.

'Here, you can't do that,' the young woman bawled, grabbing at the matron's bonnet and ripping it from her head.

As they began to tussle, Darcy tried to intervene but all she got for her pains was a fist in her eye. Suddenly the whole crowd erupted, John struggling to hold back a man who was supporting the matron and others joining in the free-for-all just for the fun of it.

Eventually, when two policemen arrived on the scene, the crowd rapidly dispersed, the young woman with them. The matron voiced her complaints to the officers of the law and they, in turn, cautioned John. 'Take care not to incite any further disturbances,' warned the young policeman who seemed to think it was all a bit of a joke.

'I think we'll call it a day,' John said, as the policemen escorted the matron away. 'It doesn't usually get as rough as this, but you've got to learn to take care.'

'Now you tell me.' Darcy giggled and rubbed her puffed eye. Far from being upset, she'd found the incident amusing and exciting. 'Did you hear what that woman said about the fat one never seeing her husband without his clothes?' she said, as they walked down King Cross and headed for home.

'Aye, I did, an' she wa' probably right. Some folks have a funny take on life.'

Out of the blue, Darcy thought of her Uncle Abe. He had a very strange take on life, but it wasn't funny. She shuddered at the thought of it.

Later that evening, after Angela had gone to bed and John for a pint in the Dyer and Miller, Darcy and Betsy sat by the fire, Betsy with her large pile of mending and Darcy gazing into the flames. She told Betsy about the debacle between the matron and the young, frowsy woman. Betsy laughed, and responded with a few tales of her own from the days she had worked the streets with John. Then, almost echoing John's words, she said, 'Some folks have a very different view as to what's right an' wrong in life.'

'My uncle certainly did,' Darcy replied bitterly.

'Tell me about him. What was it made him so bad you had to run away?'

'Well, for a start, I cannot imagine why on earth my father entrusted me to his keeping.' Darcy's voice wobbled and she looked close to tears.

Betsy's face creased with sympathy. She put down the sock she was darning and reached out to pat Darcy's hand. 'But was there no one else? Someone from your mother's family who might have taken you in?'

Darcy shook her head. 'I don't really remember my mother,' she said softly. 'I do know that she was an only child and that her parents disowned her when she married my father.'

'Good gracious! Why ever did they do that?'

'Dad told me that they were very conscious of their place in society, and also very religious. My grandmother died before I was

born and my grandfather when I was very young. He was a
gentleman farmer. He left all his lands and money to the Roman
Catholic Church instead of to my mother.'

'And she his only child,' cried Betsy. 'That was downright
cruel.' She resumed her darning. 'And was there no one on your
father's side other than this uncle of yours?'

Again, Darcy shook her head despondently. 'There was just the
two of them, and their parents died of the influenza within days of
each other when I was about four.'

'So your poor father had nobody to turn to other than his
brother.' Betsy shook her head despairingly, her voice thick with
sympathy.

'I don't think my dad could have known how horrible Uncle
Abe really is,' Darcy said in his defence, 'otherwise he would never
have left me with him.' She swallowed the tears that clogged her
throat and gazed hopelessly at Betsy.

'How bad was he?' Betsy sounded as though she was afraid to
find out.

Darcy gave a disconsolate shrug. 'He doesn't have a charitable
bone in his body. Other people are of no account to him whatsoever, so long as he gets what he wants.' Her voice harshening, she
cried, 'He deprived me of all of my dad's possessions and forced me
to leave school before my time, and he kept me like a prisoner. He's
one of those hypocrites who goes to church every Sunday
pretending to be an upright Christian, but on the inside he is positively evil.' Her voice began to shake. 'He is the filthiest, vilest man
I've ever known.'

'How come?' Betsy, believing that Darcy's wounded spirit might
be healed if she got all the hurt and hatred off her chest, urged her
to go on.

Then, sobbing and gulping, and at times almost choking on

her words, Darcy related the events of her last night in Northcrop House.

Betsy was stunned into silence, a silence so deep that both she and Darcy felt bathed in it. When she at last found words her voice shook with burning anger.

'Don't let that ruin the rest of your life, love,' she said forcefully. 'That man is a pervert, a dirty brute who defiles women. He should rot in hell. But don't let what happened between you an' him put you off men, Darcy. His actions were wrong, but when you truly love somebody that sort of thing can be beautiful.'

And for all Betsy was no more than ten years older than Darcy, she went on to tell her the facts of life in a most gentle, sincere manner. 'That's how me an' John got our lovely Angela,' she concluded, with a fond smile.

Darcy smiled at the woman who was turning out to be the sister she had always longed for, and as she gazed into Betsy's warm, brown eyes she felt as if a heavy burden had been lifted from her shoulders, taking with it all the hatred, the shame and the pain that she had been carrying for too long.

6

Over the course of the next few days, rain lashed from the heavens. John devoted his time to cobbling rather than performing and Darcy helped Betsy with the household chores.

'I'll do that,' she volunteered, on the morning Betsy began to fettle the range. 'I do know how. I did it for Polly to save her aches and pains,' she continued in response to Betsy's surprised look. 'She was very old, you see.'

'I'll gladly let you do it,' Betsy said, wincing as she got up off her knees. 'To be honest I'm not feeling too cracky. I sometimes have days when I don't feel like moving. The doctor says it's me heart that's weak.' She did indeed look pale and her lips had a bluish tinge.

Darcy took her place at the range. Kneeling, she cleared the ashes and soot then applied black lead, brushing and polishing until the range gleamed. After that she offered to do the laundry. 'It'll clean my hands,' she excused when Betsy was about to refuse.

Helping in this way came easily to Darcy. She was so grateful to have found shelter and friendship with the lovely Carver family she would have gone to greater lengths if it meant staying with them, but as one week ran into three, she worried that they might be expecting her to move on.

On the Wednesday morning of her third week with the Carvers, Darcy wakened to the sound of lashing rain once more. She dressed and went into the kitchen. The family were sitting at the table eating their breakfasts and greeted her with smiles.

'Help yourself to porridge,' Betsy said, indicating the pot on the range.

'Aye, get your breakfast. There'll be no performing today again in this blasted weather. It'll be another day for cobbling,' John grumbled.

Darcy filled a dish and sat down at the table. In between mouthfuls of porridge, she voiced the problem uppermost in her mind. 'I suppose it's time I started looking for a place to live and a proper job,' she said, her heart thudding painfully at the thought of it.

John and Betsy exchanged quizzical glances.

'What do you mean, a proper job? You're my bottler,' said John.

'I know, and I love doing that, but you were just being kind and helping me out. It's very good of you but I don't want to take advantage of your hospitality.'

'You're not,' said Betsy firmly, 'so let's have no more talk like that.'

Darcy breathed a massive sigh of relief.

Betsy Carver smiled inwardly. She knew what it was to have an unhappy childhood. Her bullying father had moved them from town to town, and her mother had been too wrapped up in her own misery to care about her only daughter. Betsy's brothers had all flown the coop as soon as they were old enough and she had borne the brunt of her father's drunken rages. From the moment she'd met kindly John Carver he had been her hero and her saviour. He'd stood up to her father, threatening him with a beating if he ever laid a finger on her again, and as soon as she had turned eighteen they had married, giving Betsy all she had ever wanted: a loving husband and a home of her own. She was an innocent girl not given to deep thinking, but now as she mulled over the future of their unexpected lodger, she supposed that that was all Darcy wanted: a home where she felt safe and loved. However, it was a rather unusual arrangement to take in a girl they knew so little about, and Betsy looked to the longer term.

'What are we going to do about her?' she asked, taking the opportunity to speak to John in private whilst Darcy was running errands.

'I don't really know,' said John, scratching his head in confusion. 'What I do know is she'd not last a crack out there on her own. She's far too innocent.'

'You're right about that, an' to say she's fifteen years old...' Betsy shook her head in bewilderment. 'She seems to know nowt about life. She's been too well bred to deal wi' hardship. When I think back to what I wa' like at fifteen...' She threw up her hands in despair. 'So, what do wi' do?'

'It's up to you, love,' John replied, rubbing his chin as he mulled things over. 'She costs nowt but the food in her mouth an' the few coppers I've handed her for doing the bottling – an' look at the way she's helped you out with the chores when you were havin' one of your bad days.'

'Aye, I wa' thinkin' that meself,' Betsy said. 'An' although it didn't lay me up this time, there'll be other times when it will.' She pulled a face, irritated by the incapacity that frequently afflicted her. 'An' she's awfully good with Angela. Why, only the other day the little darlin' said it wa' like havin' a big sister.'

'So, do we let her stay, or what?'

When Darcy returned with the shopping, Betsy took her to one side. 'John an' me have been talkin', an' we think it's best if you stay here for as long as you like, love. Be part of our little family.'

Darcy threw her arms round Betsy and hugged her. Then she waltzed Angela about the room, her gratitude spilling over in a tumult of laughter and tears.

* * *

Living in Burgos Court with the Carvers and working the streets, markets and fairs with John certainly opened Darcy's eyes and changed her view of the world. She soon made friends with most of the other inhabitants of the court, a disparate bunch of all ages. She ran errands to the grocery or the bakery for Nellie Helliwell, an ancient widow who lived with her five cats next door to the Carvers, played games in the yard with Angela and with Tilly Whittaker's large brood of scruffy children, sat on the steps and chatted with old Jimmy Pickles, a retired cabinet maker, and always passed the time of day with Meg and Peter Horsfall, a young couple just recently married.

The only occupant she avoided was Norris Firth. A down-at-heel, saturnine man in his forties, Norris skulked in and out of the court without acknowledging any of his neighbours. That he never spoke to her didn't perturb Darcy in the least, Betsy having told her that he was an oddity best left to his own devices. However, she didn't like the way he looked at her whenever their paths crossed. He reminded her of Abe Earnshaw. Norris aside, and having endured the remoteness of Northcrop House with only Polly for company, Darcy loved the neighbourliness of Burgos Court.

* * *

'Will you pop along to Chalice's Herbalists in King Cross and get another bottle of Sloane's Liniment? We've run out of it, and John's complaining of pain in his legs.' Betsy lifted her purse from the mantelpiece and handed Darcy two shillings. 'An' get some teacakes an' a bag of broken biscuits from the bakery whilst you're at it.' She grinned impishly at her young lodger. 'Let's have a bit of a treat, eh, to celebrate the coronation?'

Darcy grinned back, but the grin quickly disappeared as she said, 'I didn't know John was having pains in his legs. He seemed all right yesterday.' She had been living with the Carvers for nearly three months and felt like one of the family. It was a lovely feeling.

Yesterday being 22 June and the day of King George's coronation, Darcy and John and Betsy and Angela had travelled as far as Leeds to take advantage of the huge crowds celebrating in the big city. John had found a good pitch for his performances and Darcy, in between singing to the spectators, had bottled energetically.

That had been a day to remember, the grand buildings decked with bunting and people lining the streets waving Union Jacks as the marching bands paraded through the streets. They had gone to Leeds early in the morning, and after a very lucrative few hours they had arrived back in Halifax in time to catch the last of the parades as the Duke of Wellington's Regiment, based in Wellesley Barracks, marched through the town. Darcy marvelled at all these things, for she knew that had she not run away from Abe Earnshaw, she would never have had such splendid experiences.

Now, as she prepared to go shopping, her face screwed up in consternation.

'John's not hurt, is he? He never mentioned anything to me about his legs.'

'Oh, he wouldn't let on to you, big, tough man that he is, but he wa' moaning about 'em in bed last night.' Betsy pulled a comical face. 'I think he wa' looking for a bit of sympathy an' summat else, if you know what I mean.' She winked saucily.

Darcy giggled.

Still giggling, Darcy left the house. It was a glorious day, puffy white clouds high in the sky and the sun shining. Outside, by the steps, John had set up his workbench and was tacking a thick leather sole to a heavy working boot. He looked up as Darcy approached, and grinned. 'Where are you off to?'

'Chalice's, to get some liniment for your pains.'

John flushed. 'Oh, aye, me pains,' he mumbled, 'they were bad last night.'

'So I heard,' said Darcy, her flippant reply coupled with a mischievous wink.

John roared with laughter and raised his hammer, pretending to threaten her. 'Get out o' that, you cheeky besom.'

'Would you strike a defenceless maiden?' Darcy said in mock horror.

'There's nothing defenceless about you, lass, not these days,' John replied, a glint of admiration in his dark eyes.

Taking it as a compliment, Darcy dropped a curtsey. 'I'll just go and see if Nellie wants anything from the town,' she said.

She let herself into the dingy, cluttered house that stank of cats and old age.

'I'm going to Chalice's,' she said, 'do you want anything from anywhere?'

Nellie screwed up her wizened face. 'Aye, lass, get me some jallop to loosen me bowels. I'm constipated.' She broke wind noisily to prove her point.

Darcy tried not to breathe too deeply as she waited for Nellie to find her purse.

Back in the yard, she walked past the closets on her way to Jimmy Pickles's to ask the same question. Here the smell was worse than that in Nellie's house and Darcy wrinkled her nose. She, who had only ever lived in a house with an indoor lavatory, detested having to use the outdoor closet, but worse than that was having to help clean the one they shared with Nellie and Tilly. Thankfully, she or Betsy had to scour it out only every second week. It should have been only every third, but out of the kindness of her heart and in respect for Nellie's great age, Betsy had taken it upon herself to take Nellie's turn.

Jimmy greeted Darcy with a cheery smile. 'Come to keep an old chap company, have you?'

'Not just now, Jimmy, I'm going into the town. Can I get you anything?'

'I'd be most obliged if you'd fetch me a fresh loaf,' he said, plunging his hand in his pocket and extracting two pennies.

Darcy set off on her errands feeling pleased with herself, for just at that moment she believed that every part of her life was perfect.

* * *

As Christmas approached, Darcy could barely believe that she had been living and working in Halifax for almost nine months and that, with John, she had worked the fairs in Hebden Bridge, Ovenden, Hipperholme and Sowerby Bridge to name but a few. Month on month her horizons had broadened and with them a confidence in her own worth. She now knew she could survive in this busy, exciting world.

On Christmas Eve, the trade in the markets was brisker than usual. The crowds in the Piece Hall were looking forward to their holiday and spirits were high. In between shopping for bargains and haggling over the price of a tasty chicken, a plump rabbit or toys for their offspring, they flocked to the sideshows for entertainment. As John performed his stunts, Darcy dashed in and out of the throng, the bowler hat held at just the right level to deter the dippers and her face wreathed in smiles as she gushed, 'Thank you kindly,' at every clink of a coin.

She was dressed for the occasion in a bright red bonnet trimmed with white pom-poms that Betsy had knitted, and over her cape she was wearing a bright red shawl that she herself had crocheted. 'You look like a Christmas elf,' John had quipped as they had set out that morning.

Street performers were allowed to demonstrate their skills for two hours between ten and twelve in the Piece Hall, and as it was a special time of year John faced a tremendous amount of competition. There were ballad singers, a Punch and Judy show, a plate juggler and a wrinkled old man with a monkey on top of a barrel organ all within a few yards of where John was doing his act. However, he was drawing a fine crowd, the takings plenty, and every now and then, to give John a rest, Darcy sang carols, her high, sweet voice encouraging the spectators to join in as she sang old favourites such as 'God Rest Ye Merry Gentlemen' and 'Joy to the World'.

The buskers were a friendly lot and Darcy had got to know many of them by name. When, after an hour of performing, John took a short break, he and Darcy made their way over to a nearby stall selling hot toddies and cinnamon buns. It had yet to snow, but there was a definite nip in the air.

'This is just the ticket,' said John, shivering as he swigged the spicy honey and lemon drink. Clad only in his leotard, his bare torso was rapidly cooling now that he had stopped leaping and tumbling.

'Never mind,' Darcy replied, giving him a wicked grin, 'you'll soon warm up when you set yourself on fire.'

'Cheeky madam.' John laughed and gave her a playful push.

His strength being what it was, the push had more impact than he'd intended. Darcy reeled back, her drink slopping over the edge of the glass as she cannoned into someone standing behind her.

She turned round, ready to apologise, and found herself looking into a pair of amused, dark, almond-shaped eyes in a handsome, swarthy face framed with blue-black, glossy hair. A jaunty yellow neckerchief lent a brilliant splash of colour to a dark brown, knee-length frockcoat with a velvet collar, the flamboyant cut of it suiting its wearer perfectly. Then, before Darcy could utter a word, the young man's lips curved into a warm smile.

'I am admiring you from afar. I am thinking you are *bellissima*.' He touched his fingers to his lips. 'A beautiful *signorina natale* who sings like the nightingale.'

Darcy stared, open mouthed, her cheeks flushing and her heart fluttering for, whilst she had not understood some of his words, she understood enough to know that he thought she was beautiful. Thoroughly flustered, she turned to John for help. He was talking to the plate juggler, so she tugged at his sleeve.

When he turned he cried, 'Well, if it isn't Danny Capp.' He stuck out his arm and clapped Danny on the shoulder. 'I haven't seen you since we last met in Hebden Bridge. How are you doin'?'

Only then did Darcy notice that Danny had a guitar strapped to his back.

'I am well,' Danny replied. 'Working hard. I go to Newcastle then Scarborough but I come to Halifax for Christmas.' He glanced at Darcy. 'And I am admiring your assistant with the voice of an angel.'

'She has that all right. She's a proper songbird, an' a damned fine bottler,' John praised. Darcy's blushes deepened. He placed his arm about her shoulders and by way of introduction he said, 'Darcy Earnshaw meet Danny Capp, the finest tenor in the land.'

Danny held out his hand. Darcy slipped hers inside it but

instead of just shaking it, he raised it to his lips, brushing the back of her hand before saying, 'I am Danilo Cappelini and I am charmed to meet you, Darcy Earnshaw.'

The fluttering in Darcy's chest quickened to a pounding and her breath caught in her throat. 'I'm pleased to meet you.' Her voice wobbled embarrassingly.

'Better get back to work,' John interrupted. 'See you around, Danny.'

'And I will go back to my pitch.' Danny seemed reluctant to let them go.

They made their farewells, and as they walked away John gave Darcy a knowing wink. 'I think you've got yourself an admirer, lass.'

Darcy's heart fluttered afresh. 'He's foreign, isn't he? Where is he from?' Her tone casual, she tried to hide her eagerness to learn as much as she could about this exciting new acquaintance.

'He's Italian. He roams up and down the country with a band of fellow eyeties, singing for a living.'

Darcy wondered if she would see him again.

They finished their stint, and as they walked through the Piece Hall, Darcy paused to give the organ grinder's monkey the remains of her sticky bun. She had been so overcome by her meeting with Danny Capp that she hadn't been able to swallow another mouthful. As they left the Piece Hall Darcy heard a beautiful tenor voice singing 'The Rose of Tralee', and when she looked to see from where it came she saw Danny entertaining a small crowd with his lovely rendition of the song.

She tugged at John's sleeve, indicating that they should stop and listen. Danny's voice soared above the noise of the busy street as he hit the high notes. The onlookers clapped.

'Give me a couple of coppers, John.'

Rummaging in his pouch, John handed Darcy the coins, and

pushing her way to the front of the bystanders, Darcy dropped them into the open guitar case at Danny's feet. His face broke into a wide smile. 'It's not just me who sings like an angel,' Darcy said.

Danny nodded his thanks, and eager not to lose his audience but also keen to make an impression on Darcy, he hurriedly said, 'I do hope we meet again. I'd like to get to know you.' Then, flashing a smile at the spectators and addressing them in a rapid flow of Italian, he burst into song again.

Reluctant, but aware that John was impatient to get back to Betsy and Angela, Darcy went back to join him, and as they walked away the strains of 'Santa Lucia' pulled at her heartstrings.

Later that night when she was in bed, Darcy thought about the strange effect Danilo Cappelini had had on her. She had never had much to do with boys, Miss Compton's Academy being an all-girls establishment, and since her father's death her Uncle Abe had so curtailed Darcy's social life that there had been no opportunity to meet young people of either sex.

She had read stories that told of beautiful girls and handsome youths who met and fell in love but she had never imagined it for herself: she had considered herself too young for such things. Now, as she recalled the way her heart had fluttered when Danny's dark eyes had gazed into her own, and the touch of his lips on the back of her hand, she realised she was no longer a child. She was a young woman whose feelings could be stirred by the admiration in a man's eyes, a woman capable of making a man feel the same emotions that were now flooding her thoughts. *You've grown up, Darcy Earnshaw*, she told herself as she closed her eyes ready to sleep and to dream.

7

With the coming of spring 1912, Darcy had lived with her new family for almost a year. Every aspect of her life had changed in that time and she couldn't have been happier. She rarely dwelt on the awful years she had spent in Northcrop House, although she knew she would never quite forget the misery of living with Abe Earnshaw.

She was now very familiar with Halifax and knew her way about the town. She shopped in the Cash Supply Stores for groceries, breathing in the intoxicating smell of freshly ground roasted coffee beans as she waited to be served, or did the rounds of the market stalls with Betsy as they looked for bargains. She made no objection to having to go to Chaffer's rag and bone yard in Gaol Lane to buy paraffin for the lamps, even though the yard stank of something so evil she couldn't quite name it. Such errands were all part and parcel of living with the Carvers in Burgos Court.

Today, as she was making her way back from the shops, Darcy stopped to buy kindling from Tommy Cheesebits. Tommy made his living selling firewood on the street corners for tuppence a bundle. Very short in stature, he wore a large flat cap perched on his high forehead above the grumpy expression on his broad, flat face. He was prone to quoting from the Bible, and as Darcy handed over her two pennies, he intoned, 'The Lord giveth and the Lord taketh away.'

'So he does,' Darcy replied cheerily then went on her way, and when she entered Burgos Court she saw Meg Horsfall taking in a line of washing. Darcy liked the young woman, and she called out a greeting.

'Hello Darcy,' Meg mumbled through the clothes peg gripped in her teeth. She removed the peg. 'I don't know why I bother pegging out 'cos the whites allus get soot marks an' all me washing smells of smoke.' She dumped the garments in the wicker clothes basket at her feet. 'It won't be like this in Boston, so Peter says,' she continued, referring to her husband and their imminent departure to join Peter's brother and his family in America.

'It's not long before you go, is it?' Darcy's eyes sparkled with the excitement of such an adventure even though she wasn't the one about to undertake it.

'We leave for Southampton the day after tomorrow. The ship sails on the tenth of April an' it'll get to New York seven days later.' Meg looked anxious. 'I can't say I'm looking for'ard to the journey. I've never been on a ship before.'

'It'll be an amazing experience,' Darcy assured her.

'Aye, that's what Peter keeps tellin' me,' said Meg looking awfully doubtful. 'He says the ship's unsinkable an' that it's the fastest there's ever been. It's called the *Titanic*. Peter says it means big.' Looking perfectly miserable, she picked up the basket. 'I'd best get on. I've to iron this lot ready for packin' tomorrow.'

Darcy was saddened to see how miserable and worried her friend seemed. 'Just think of it,' she gushed. 'In a week's time you'll be in a whole new country. From what I've read about America it sounds a marvellous place. I know that you're not looking forward to the sea crossing but it'll be worth it in the end.'

'I hope you're right,' Meg said dolefully. 'I'll call in an' say goodbye afore we go, an' when we get there I'll send you a postcard.'

'I'll look forward to that,' Darcy said, and leaving Meg to her ironing and packing she went into her own house to enthuse some more about the Horsfalls' trip to America.

'You'd not get me on a ship for love nor money, no matter how big it is,' Betsy said, shuddering at the very thought of it. 'All that water 'ud sicken me.'

* * *

'Ship hits iceberg!' 'Unsinkable ship sinks!' 'Titanic disaster!'

The cries of the news vendors in Cheapside stopped Darcy in her tracks as she and John were making their way to the Piece Hall.

'Titanic, John!' she cried, 'Meg and Peter were going to America on that ship.'

'Are you sure?' John bought a newspaper from the nearest vendor, Darcy almost snatching it out of his hand to scour the reportage.

'Not everybody was drowned,' she said, her voice high with relief. 'Some of them got into lifeboats and were rescued by another ship. Maybe Meg and Peter were amongst them,' she continued, hopeful.

John peered over her shoulder to read. 'Still, they reckon more than a thousand have lost their lives. You'd think they'd have seen the iceberg an' sailed round it.' He shook his head in disbelief. 'They said nowt could sink that ship, but it just goes to show that nature is more powerful than owt man can make.'

They carried on to the Piece Hall, and as they made their way through the throng all they heard was people talking about the tragedy. For the rest of the day Darcy thought of little else, her usual cheery thank yous subdued, and when it was her turn to sing she sang 'Mary's Dream', a mournful ballad about a girl whose loved one is lost at sea. There was hardly a dry eye in the crowd as her sweet voice told the sad story, and although they showed their appreciation by filling the hat, it did little to comfort Darcy.

She remembered Tommy Cheesebits' quote on the day she had bought the kindling, the same day that she had chatted with Meg about her voyage to America. 'The Lord giveth and the Lord taketh away.' He'd given Meg and Peter the courage to go in search of a new life, she thought, sending up a silent prayer that he'd seen fit not to take their lives.

Over the next weeks she waited for a postcard to arrive from Boston, disappointed when one didn't, and when the *Halifax Courier* reported the story of Margaret and Peter Horsfall, a local couple who had drowned with the sinking of the Titanic, she knew her prayers had been in vain.

* * *

However, throughout the following summer, Darcy didn't have time to dwell on unhappy thoughts. She had a new interest in her life in the shape of Danny Capp. Whenever he was working the streets in Halifax they met up, taking strolls through the People's Park or down along the banks of the River Calder. As September arrived with all its mellow softness, it lent an air of romance to their outings. When the days grew shorter, the night air chill, they went to the Electric Cinema. Darcy particularly liked the atmospheric music that the manager played on the piano to accompany the scenes on the screen. At other times they went to the Cinema de Luxe where they shivered with horror at *Dr Jekyll and Mr Hyde* or laughed until they cried at the antics of the Tilly Girls. A favourite was a film about a bear tamer whose wife became famous, and Danny had whispered in Darcy's ear, 'When you become a famous singer you won't forget about me, will you?'

Darcy had laughed at the notion and told him that he would be the first to achieve fame with his magnificent voice.

During these outings they swapped stories about their lives, Darcy confiding in him that she had run away from home because her uncle had abused her. Danny had been horrified even though she had spared him the gruesome details of her last night in Abe Earnshaw's house, Darcy finding it too painful and shaming to share. Danny had folded her in his arms and sworn to protect her from such evil occurring again.

In turn, he had told Darcy that he was an orphan raised in Florence by his maternal grandmother. After her death, he had joined a band of strolling players and eventually travelled to England with them. Danny talked wistfully about his beloved, warm city with its magnificent churches and the beautiful River Arno. Then it had been her turn to take him in her arms, reassuring him that, one day, they would go there together because she had always wanted to go to Florence after reading about its splendours in a book she had borrowed from the library.

These outings were innocent and involved no more than holding hands or chaste goodnight kisses, yet they had an understanding that they were meant for one another. Just lately, having grown weary of travelling the length and breadth of the country and wanting to be near to Darcy, Danny had taken lodgings close by and was a frequent visitor to the Carver household, where he was always made welcome.

The bite of winter took hold, November arriving with a vengeance. Thick fog and flurries of snow made it unsuitable for John's performances, so he earned his living mending shoes.

Braving the elements, Darcy and Danny joined forces, singing on the streets, then returned for one of Betsy's good, hot dinners in the evening. Their coppers were hard earned but it did mean that Darcy could make a contribution to the household. She would have hated to burden John and Betsy with the expense of keeping her in food and clothing.

* * *

One evening towards the end of December, Danny ate his dinner with the Carvers and Darcy, then stayed on to play cards. They played for matchsticks, Darcy and Betsy laughingly protesting that both John and Danny were cheating when they lost game after game. The fun was high, but Betsy couldn't fail to notice the love in Danny's warm, brown eyes whenever they met Darcy's startling blue ones, or the way they sat as close as was possible to one another.

Like all good things, the evening came to an end, and Danny went back to his lodgings and John to his bed. The two women alone in the kitchen, Darcy set about clearing the table and washing the cups. Betsy got down on her knees to bank up the fire so that it would burn slowly throughout the night and keep the house warm for when they wakened the next day. As she shovelled black, dusty slack onto the burning embers, she said, 'I think young Danny Capp has set his cap at you, Darcy.'

Darcy turned bright red and the cup in her hand dropped with a splash into the sink. Warm soapy water slopped over the side, wetting the front of her dress.

'We're just very good friends. I like him and I think he likes me, but that's all. Aren't I a bit too young to be thinking about things like that?' she gabbled in a desperate attempt to hide her true feelings.

Betsy got up off her knees and came to dabble her hands in the soapy water. 'Come New Year you'll be seventeen, just the age I was when I first met John. I knew from the moment I saw him he was the man for me,' she said, drying her hands then taking the cups to the table ready for breakfast the next morning. 'When Danny looks at you I think he's thinking the same thing.'

Darcy flushed again. 'Do you really think so? I like him a lot; in fact, I think I might be in love with him, but seeing as I don't know what love is, I can't be sure. All I do know is that when he looks at me with his lovely, dark eyes or holds my hand I get these funny fluttering feelings inside.' She bit down on her bottom lip and hung her head, embarrassed.

Betsy chuckled. 'That sounds like love to me.'

'Is that how you used to feel when John looked at you?'

'Aye, an' I still do. I couldn't wait to marry him, nor he me. But me dad made us wait until I was eighteen.' She gave a fond, little laugh. 'We had to fight tooth an' nail to keep us hands off one another, me tryin' me best to be prim an' proper an' poor John near bustin' to preserve me honour.'

Darcy laughed at the comical look on Betsy's face.

'It's all right you laughing,' Betsy piped, 'it wa' damned hard work, I can tell you.' Her expression became serious. 'An' that's why I'm tellin' you all this. Danny's a lovely fellow and you're right to like him, but don't let him bamboozle you into doin' somethin' you know is wrong. Men are different from women. They get these urges they find hard to control, so it's you that has to be strong to prevent owt bad happening.'

Suddenly, Darcy burst into tears and Betsy, misinterpreting them, cried, 'Oh, don't tell me he has, an' that you've let him...'

'No! No!' Darcy sobbed. 'Danny's never tried to do anything like that. I was just reminded of my uncle.' She shuddered. 'I wasn't strong enough to stop him doing the terrible things he did to me, but I wish I had been. It makes me feel dirty.' She collapsed into the nearest chair, her shoulders heaving.

Betsy pulled her up and cradled her in her arms. 'Eeh, I'm sorry, Darcy. I spoke without thinkin'. That wa' cruel of me.' She took a step back so that she could look directly into Darcy's face, and her voice was harsh as she said, 'What your uncle did wasn't natural. He was an evil pervert. Not all men are like that. What I meant to say was just keep yourself safe no matter how much Danny might tell you he loves you.' Realising that she had handled things badly, she gave Darcy another hug, hopeful that she hadn't done too much damage.

'So you think Danny really loves me?' Darcy's voice wobbled pathetically.

'Oh, I'd say he does,' Betsy said firmly, 'but he's a bit of a charmer used to wandering wherever he pleases. All I'm saying is don't do owt afore you're wed. Now, get yourself off to bed an' have sweet dreams.'

In bed, Darcy puzzled over Betsy's warning words. She had let Danny kiss her. She liked the feel of his lips against hers and the way it made her blood sing in her ears and her heart drum inside her chest. Had Betsy been trying to tell her that Danny might expect her to do the things her Uncle Abe had demanded? The thought of it made her break out in a shivering sweat. And as for Betsy thinking that Danny was going to ask her, Darcy, to marry him, well that was just plain silly. She was far too young to marry anybody. With these thoughts tumbling through her head, she fell into a restless sleep.

* * *

Christmas was a joyous affair, the four adults and Angela celebrating the festive season by going along to the Piece Hall on

Christmas Eve to listen to the Black Dyke Mills Brass Band. Angela attracted her own audience. Dressed in a pretty red and white outfit that Betsy and Darcy had knitted and crocheted, she'd jigged up and down to the oompah, oompah of trombones, cornets and tubas, curtseying precociously when the bystanders applauded.

'You should take her with you the next time you're performing, John,' Betsy commented wryly, but she couldn't hide her pride.

On Christmas morning, Darcy looking delightful in her red crocheted shawl and jaunty beret, they attended a sing-along of carols performed by the Halifax Choral Society, Darcy's sweet soprano and Danny's resounding tenor earning them appreciative glances from the crowd. Singing being a form of expression that appealed strongly to the inhabitants of the rugged Pennine Hills, events like this brought great joy to the often downtrodden, hard-working people who toiled in the mills and the manufactories for the rest of the year.

In the afternoon, they sat down to a tasty stewed rabbit and all the trimmings then played games and opened presents. They all knew that the simple gifts had been made or purchased with love.

'This is for you, Betsy.' Darcy handed her a pale blue shawl that she had secretly crocheted. 'And for you, young lady,' she turned to Angela. 'Seeing as how you're a big girl now and starting school in January, I've knitted this.'

Angela whooped when she saw the grey beret. 'It'll go with my new school uniform,' she cried, pulling it on and doing a twirl.

Darcy gave John a pamphlet that she had found in a second-hand bookshop about Charles Blondin, the tightrope walker who had performed his high-wire stunt across the Piece Hall in 1861. In return, Betsy, John and Angela gave her a pair of thick, black stockings and gloves and a copy of L Frank Baum's *The Emerald City of Oz*.

Danny's gift was a set of guitar strings. 'These are from all of us,' Darcy told him.

Danny reciprocated with embroidered handkerchiefs for Betsy and Angela and tobacco for John. Darcy's smile slipped.

Then, looking slightly unsure of himself – a most unusual occurrence for Danilo Cappelini – he gave a little bow as he handed Darcy a small velvet box. Darcy's fingers trembled as she opened it. The tiny, blood red heart crafted from some sort of base metal was beautifully worked, and although the chain wasn't made from pure silver it was delicately fine. 'Now you have my heart,' he said.

Darcy gasped. 'It's beautiful,' she said on her breath as she lifted it from its case and dangled it from her fingers. Danny took it from her and fastened it round her neck. The feel of the little heart nestled in the hollow of her throat made her own heart flutter and a swarm of butterflies take flight inside her tummy. Betsy had been right. He really must love her.

8

The foul weather persisted into the New Year, 1913. John and Darcy worked the streets and the Piece Hall whenever they could, and on the more inclement days when John cobbled shoes, Darcy continued to sing with Danny. If the spectators had been generous, they treated themselves to a night out at the Cinema de Luxe, where they held hands, unlike some other couples who saw very little of the film as they canoodled in the back seats of the cinema. Then Danny would walk Darcy back to Burgos Court, where they exchanged kisses in the dark ginnel, kisses that he delivered with passion and that Darcy found delightful but disturbing in case Danny suddenly took one of those urges that Betsy had talked about.

Snow fell again, blanketing the streets, and as Darcy made her way across the yard one morning in early February her feet sank into the thick, white crystals which spilled into the top of her boots. Shivering in the outside closet, always on the lookout for a rat or a spider, she contemplated what she had to do for the rest of the day.

Her ablutions performed, she called in on Nellie to ask if she required anything from the shops. The gloomy, cluttered house that always held the scent of old age and cats smelled even more rank than usual. Nellie was just smoothing down her grubby skirts as Darcy entered. She gave Darcy a gummy smile.

'Come in, lass, an' welcome,' she croaked, the greeting ending in a wracking cough. Nellie thumped her chest, hawked, and then spat a globule of green spit into the fire. It sizzled on the coals. Darcy tried to ignore it. Nellie hawked and spat again.

'That's an awful cough, Nellie.' As Darcy went to pat Nellie's back, her look of concern changed to one of disgust. 'What is that awful stink?'

Hacking and spluttering, Nellie shooed two mangy cats away from the chair behind her. 'What do you think to that then, Darcy?' she cackled, pointing to the upright chair, its rush seat cut away to leave a ragged, round hole. Beneath that was a steaming bucket.

'What is it?' Curious, Darcy stepped closer, gagging when she saw the gruesome contents in the bucket.

'That's my indoor lavvy. It saves me having to go out in that bloody awful snow and like as not skid on me arse,' Nellie declared as though she were revealing the secrets of the universe.

Darcy dashed for the door, tripping over a large ginger tom in her haste to escape into the fresh air. Nellie called after her, 'Don't forget to fetch me milk and bread.'

Back in her own home, Darcy told Betsy about Nellie's invention. 'It stinks to high heaven, even worse than the cats – and she has a terrible cough.'

'I'll pop in an' rub her chest wi' goose fat when I've finished this.' Betsy set the flat iron on the hearth. 'Now, have you got your money an' your list? An' watch your footing whilst you're out. We don't want you breaking a leg.'

Darcy laughed at the idea, but she was touched by Betsy's

concern. Where would she be without her adopted family? The thought stayed with her as she trudged through the snow to the shops.

By the time she had fulfilled her errands, a watery sun had turned the snow into slush on the pavements. It seeped into her boots, and she was hurrying for home when, out of the corner of her eye, she caught sight of Danny. He was leaning against the wall of the Dog and Partridge, his guitar case at his side. Her heart somersaulting, Darcy waited on the kerb to cross over to be with him. How dashing and handsome he looked in his coat with the velvet collar, turned up against the cold.

A stream of wagons and motors trundled by, Darcy kicking her heels impatiently as she waited for a break in the traffic. When it came, she saw that Danny was no longer alone. A girl with long, red hair was standing by his side. He gave her the kind of smile that Darcy thought of as hers and hers alone. Jealousy flared, hot and searing, and at the same time a cold hand clutched at her insides. Even across the distance, Darcy could see that the girl was very attractive and expensively dressed, her camel-coloured coat with a large fur collar cut in the latest style.

Her eyes on stalks, Darcy stood rooted to the spot even though the traffic had eased. Danny and the girl exchanged a few animated words and smiles. Then Danny picked up his guitar case and they walked off up the street, not holding hands but close enough to make Darcy think they knew each other very well.

Feeling as if her heart was sinking into her boots, she watched until they were out of sight then plodded miserably through the slush back to Burgos Court.

When Darcy entered the house, John was sitting at his little workbench shaving the excess leather from the heel of the boot he was repairing. Angela was taking a nap in the chair by the hearth, her rosebud lips put-putting as she dreamed.

'Betsy's next door with Nellie,' John said.

Darcy mumbled a response. She felt too miserable to make conversation.

'Nellie's still coughing her lungs up, she's worse than she was when I called with her this afternoon.' Betsy brought a flurry of cold air with her as she came back from next door into her own cosy kitchen.

Darcy was emptying her basket: cabbage and carrots on the draining board then the tin of corned beef and packets of tea and sugar in the cupboard. She moved slowly, her eyes downcast and her mouth drooping at the corners.

'Is something the matter?' Betsy asked, giving Darcy a searching look.

'Er, yes... No...' Darcy stuttered, hiding her face behind the open cupboard door. For a moment she had been tempted to spill her misgivings about Danny, but on second thoughts she'd decided that Betsy would only tell her she was reading more into it than it deserved.

'Well, which is it? Yes, or no?'

Darcy shrugged her shoulders then walked over to the window, staring out into the yard as though she was looking for someone.

Betsy wondered if the girl was sickening for something or maybe, like John, she was weary of the freezing cold weather that prevented them from going about their daily business. Deciding on the latter, she let the matter drop. But it wasn't like Darcy to let things get her down, she thought, as Darcy mooched into her bedroom and shut the door.

She stayed there for the rest of the afternoon trying to read her new library book, but Elizabeth Bennett's romance with Mr Darcy only exacerbated her troubled thoughts. Her dismay at seeing Danny with the red-haired girl had by now turned into bitter disappointment and she could think of little else. Her imagination running wild, Darcy tormented herself by thinking that perhaps there were lots of girls who shared Danny's affections. Did he kiss them like he kissed her, and maybe more? This thought was so awful that she wept into her pillow and was almost relieved when Betsy rapped on the door and called out, 'Darcy, love, will you come and give me a hand with the dinner?'

Betsy was rolling pastry for the pie crust. Darcy chopped the cabbage with alacrity, imagining it was fiery red hair and a fur collar, and made no attempt to chatter as they usually did when they were performing the household chores. She tipped the cabbage into a pot and washed her hands.

'Cat got your tongue?' Betsy cocked her head to one side and gave Darcy an enquiring look that took in her red-rimmed eyes. 'You've not spoken two words since you got back with the shopping.'

Darcy gave a bleak little nod, her fingers toying with the tiny, red heart nestled in the hollow of her throat. Maybe Danny's heart wasn't just hers alone, after all.

* * *

Later, at the fireside, Darcy still felt miserable as she sat listlessly playing a game of cat's cradle with Angela. Over dinner, she had tried to convince herself that what she had seen was just an innocent encounter, that her fears would be groundless when Danny gave her a perfectly reasonable explanation. She had hoped that he would call at the house so that she could quiz him about the girl. But it was now half past eight and she had given up hoping.

Betsy, worried by Darcy's strange mood, had brought it to John's attention as they ate, and he had tried to cheer Darcy up, without success. Now, Betsy sought for another distraction.

'See, rather than sitting moping, nip over to the Dyer and

Miller an' ask Willie for a drop of whisky for Nellie,' said Betsy, taking a washed-out bottle from under the sink. 'My mam allus swore by hot whisky an' honey an' lemon to shift a bad cough.' She handed the bottle to Darcy. 'I'd ask John to go if he wasn't out delivering them boots to the funeral director, but it'll not take you two minutes. If you tell Willie who it's for, he'll no doubt give you a double measure for the price of one. After all, Nellie wa' one of his best customers in her younger days.'

Darcy put on her coat and shoved her feet into boots that were still damp from her earlier walk into the town. She didn't really fancy going out into the cold night and traipsing through the slush, but if Betsy thought a hot whisky would help ease poor old Nellie's cough, then she'd go.

The ginnel was pitch dark, and as Darcy stepped into the street and turned right she did not see Norris Firth slouching along the pavement in the opposite direction. But he saw her.

The taproom at the Dyer and Miller was fuggy with warm male bodies sitting in a pall of cigarette smoke and beery smells. As Darcy entered, a young wag called out, 'Are you lookin' for me, love?' The men laughed and cheered him on.

Ignoring him, Darcy pushed through the crowd of customers at the bar and made her request. 'It's for Nellie Helliwell, she's bad with her chest,' she said, embarrassment reddening her cheeks.

The landlord gave her a sly wink then bumped the bottle twice under the optic. 'No charge, love,' he said, sliding the bottle across the counter, 'an' tell Nellie I hope it touches the spot.'

Darcy thanked Willie and made for the door, the same lad calling out, 'Aw, don't tell me you're leavin' already, darlin'.'

Out on the treacherous pavement, she hurried back to Burgos Court, her feet slipping under her in her haste to get back indoors. Leaving the dim glow of the gas lamps behind her, she ducked into the ginnel and was plunged in darkness. Halfway down the passage she collided with something large and unyielding. A pair of clammy calloused hands gripped her by the neck, taking her breath away.

The bottle fell from her hand. Smash!

Her feet skidded from under her, and with the hands still clamping her throat she fell flat on her back. A heavy body landed on top of her. She tried to scream but all that came out was a pathetic croaking noise.

Instinctively, she knew who her attacker was. Norris Firth. She recognised his putrid, greasy smell. He removed one hand from her neck but pressed the thumb of his other hand so hard against her larynx that it made her head swim. A sudden chill on her legs told her that he was lifting her skirt, and she kicked her legs and tried to wriggle from under him. Then he was clawing at her knickers, the flimsy cotton tearing like tissue paper under his frantic hand. Again, she tried to shout for help but all she could manage was a few choking sounds that fizzled into whimpers.

When Norris squashed his face into Darcy's, she sank her teeth into his foul-tasting flesh. He grunted and increased the pressure on her throat. Darcy struggled to get air into her lungs. She was drifting through a thick fog, a haze clouding her brain as though someone had stuffed her head full of cotton wool. But before she lost consciousness, Norris removed his hand. Darcy gasped, raking in the cold air. As one icy draught after another filled her fevered lungs, her wits sharpened. The bottle. She'd heard it smash.

Still trapped beneath Norris's bulk, Darcy felt his cold hands fumbling between her thighs. Frantically, she stretched out her hand. A piercing pain in her index finger let her know that she was close to finding what she was looking for. As she let her fingers roam the ginnel floor, something hot and stiff was thrusting its way between her thighs. Her fingers closed round the neck of the broken bottle. She raised her arm and stabbed, again and again.

Norris's grunts suddenly became agonising bellows, and at last Darcy found her voice and screamed and screamed. John, on his way back home after delivering the funeral director's boots, heard and recognised her agonised cries for help before he entered the ginnel.

'Darcy!' he yelled. 'Oh, my God! Darcy!'

He dashed into the ginnel, his feet kicking against the thrashing bodies. Then lifting Norris like a sack of potatoes, he pinned him against the wall, driving his fist into Norris's face and stomach again and again and cursing him to hell. When John let go of him, Norris slithered downwards in a blubbering heap.

Darcy scrabbled to her feet, the broken bottle clutched in her hand. Her trembling legs barely holding her upright and tears streaming down her cheeks, she fell against John's chest. He cradled her in his arms, rocking her like a child. 'You're all right, love, you're safe.'

Darcy clung to him, choking on her sobs.

John delivered a final hefty kick to Norris's ribs. Norris rolled over groaning.

'He's not dead then?' Darcy asked in hollow tones.

John fumbled in his pocket and found his matches. Darcy loosened her fingers round the neck of the bottle. It clinked on the flagstones. John heard it fall as he struck the match. In its faint flickering light, they both peered down at Norris. The flame glinted on the bottle's jagged edges.

'Jesus! What did you do to him, Darcy?' Norris's thin raincoat was pockmarked with bloody patches.

'I stabbed the monster.'

'Go to Betsy. Go now.' John gave her a gentle push. On feet that felt as though they didn't belong to her, Darcy stumbled to the house and fell through the door, the strength that had been with her when she had fought to save her virginity suddenly dissipating as she fainted at Betsy's feet.

'Where is she now?' John enquired when, a short while later, he entered the house, his jacket stained with Norris's blood and his expression one of outraged disbelief. 'More importantly, how is she?'

'Shocked senseless, but unharmed in that way. He didn't break her, if that's what you mean. She stabbed him before he got that far,' Betsy replied, her expression mirroring John's own. 'I'd taken me bath so I dragged the bath into her room an' topped it up with warm water. I thought if she had a good soak an' washed away the filth of him it might help settle her.' She shook her head despairingly then in a low voice asked, 'What about him?'

John's lip curled. 'They're only surface wounds,' he said. 'I was all for getting the law on him, but then I thought of what it would mean for her if they got involved. He'll not show his face round here again, you can be sure of that.'

In the days following Norris Firth's brutal attack, Darcy refused to leave the house. When she wakened each morning her skin felt dry and sore to touch, as though she had been flayed. Even so, she dragged herself out of bed then spent the day listlessly carrying out the household chores, barely speaking a word. Even chatty, cheery Angela failed to cut through Darcy's misery.

'I was telling her the story Miss Chippendale told us but I know she wasn't listening,' Angela complained. It was her first term in the Misses Chippendale's Academy, and she was eager to share her everyday experiences with anyone who would listen. 'Why is Darcy so sad?' she wanted to know.

'She's had a bit of an upset,' Betsy replied, 'but she'll soon feel better.'

Darcy overheard her. *A bit of an upset*, she thought bitterly. Did Betsy think that was all it was? She, who had managed to bury the disgusting ordeal at Abe Earnshaw's cruel hands, was now reliving that along with the terror of what Norris Firth would have done to her had she not stabbed him. During daylight hours the horror of these incidents was never far from her mind, although she did her best to function, but at night her sleep was shattered by lurid dreams that suddenly wakened her. Then she'd wipe away the fine, fair strands of hair that were plastered to the sheen of sweat soaking her brow and cheeks, and she'd weep into her pillow until she was empty. She had no appetite and her pale, gaunt face grew thinner by the day. *My life is ruined and I'll never feel better again*, she told herself over and again.

Throughout those dreadful days, Danny was a constant visitor. Each day, after he had finished working the streets, he sat on the step outside the house in Burgos Court like a faithful puppy waiting for its mistress to spare it a moment. Sometimes John kept him company. Danny had wept when John had related the details of the terrible attack, explaining why Darcy steadfastly refused to speak to him. He ached to comfort her, hoping against hope that his love for her would once again make her the beautiful, happy girl to whom he had given his heart.

'You'll catch your death sitting there, lad,' Nellie remarked one evening. Despite not getting her whisky on the night Darcy had been attacked, the old bird had made a surprising recovery. 'T'poor lass doesn't know whether she's comin' or goin',' she continued, 'an' I don't blame her. That bugger Firth should be strung up, an' if he comes back here, I'll do the stringing.' Nellie hawked phlegm from her chest and spat in the gutter. 'You'll just have to be patient, lad. She'll come round given time.' Coughing and wheezing, she left Danny to keep his vigil.

On some evenings Darcy would peep through the window, gazing at Danny's mournful but still beautiful face – more beautiful than ever, for his sorrow seemed to lend it the poignancy of an old-fashioned hero or a Michelangelo painting – and she would feel herself weakening. Then the horror of what men did would come rushing back and she'd run and hide in her room. And as night fell, Danny would get up and brush himself down, as though to shake off the shrouds of misery that enfolded him, and return to his lodgings.

'No! No!' Darcy cried when Betsy or John told her he was outside begging to see her. 'I don't want him near me. Men! They're all the same. They only want to use women for their own filthy satisfaction.'

'Not all men,' Betsy insisted, trying any ploy that would break through Darcy's stubborn belief that her life was ruined. 'My John's not like that.'

Darcy couldn't disagree with that, for John was her hero, but she still held fast to her refusal to see Danny. He was just as steadfast and continued to call, bringing sweet treats to tempt her appetite and sending messages of his undying love via John or Betsy.

Come spring, Darcy still refused to see him, but she now ventured out again with John, working as his bottler and singing to the crowds. But her heart wasn't in it. That morning she had struggled out of bed after another night filled with strange dreams. Danny had been kissing a girl with long, red hair and Darcy had thrown herself at the girl and grabbed her, only for the girl to suddenly become Norris Firth. Darcy had kicked and screamed, the sickening smell of greasy sweat making her retch as, with a broken bottle in her hand, she had stabbed and stabbed. Her fury spent, she had looked down at the body. Danny lay broken and bleeding at her feet. The red-haired girl and Norris were laughing, and Darcy had wakened, her heart pounding and tears wetting her face.

It was a beautiful day in late April, the streets crowded and the spectators in a generous mood as she moved amongst them with the bowler hat. Yet the glorious sunshine did little to brighten her mood, as every now and then a throbbing pain invaded her body, bringing back shattering flashes of Norris Firth pressing down on her. When it was her turn to sing she gritted her teeth, and only for John's sake did she play her part in earning money. However, the songs she chose to sing often told the stories of girls who had been badly misused, whilst others told of lost love.

Today, her rendition of 'The Butcher Boy' was so emotional that a woman in the crowd yelled, 'Bloody hell! You're as miserable as a wet week in August. Give us summat cheerful, for Christ's sake.' But Darcy had nothing to feel cheerful about, and as she and John left the Piece Hall she was glad the day was over so that she could go home and crawl into her bed and cry.

As they turned into Cheapside they came upon a group of women carrying placards bearing the words 'Votes for Women' and other such sentiments. The crowd around them were either heckling or cheering them on. Darcy knew of the suffragettes and their struggle to gain the right to vote. She believed it to be a very worthy cause, but other than that she had not given it any deep thought.

Now, as she read 'Men don't have a right to rule women'

scrawled on one of the placards, Darcy's interest flared. 'You go on home, John. I'm going to stay and listen,' she said.

John gave her a quizzical look and shrugged. He had nothing against women being allowed the vote, but he was tired and hungry.

'If you're sure,' he said. 'You will be all right, won't you?'

Darcy patted his sleeve, touched by his concern. 'I'll be grand,' she said, giving him the kind of smile he hadn't seen on her face in a long time.

Reassured she was on the mend, he went on his way.

The tall girl carrying the placard looked extremely confident. Her dark hair parted severely and pulled into a tight bun at the nape of her neck, she gave the impression that no man would dominate her. She was handing out leaflets and Darcy took one. As she studied the leaflet, a woman of middling years wearing a stiff, black hat mounted a wooden box and began addressing the crowd.

'That's Isabella Ford,' the tall girl informed Darcy. 'Isn't she just marvellous!'

'We must make the government understand that we women have the right to vote.' Isabella Ford's impassioned voice rang out above the noise of the crowd. 'We must force them to acknowledge that we are every bit as worthy as men. Then, and only then, will we see the changes that this country of ours so desperately needs.'

Darcy listened, spellbound.

Will getting the vote and the changes she's talking about stop men like Norris Firth and Abe Earnshaw preying on women? Darcy wondered, as Isabella talked of equality, death in childbirth, sweated labour and pitiful wages.

'Bugger off home back to your husband,' a burly man at Darcy's elbow bawled as the crowd jostled round them.

Darcy whirled to face him. 'You shut your mouth,' she yelled.

'Go back to your wife and children, not that they'll be pleased to see you,' she added, looking him up and down scathingly.

'Here, I'm not havin' a skit of a girl like you tellin' me what I should do,' he bellowed, his fist rising. Before it could connect with Darcy's jaw, a placard descended on to the top of his head. He staggered under the blow.

'That'll teach you not to threaten a woman,' the tall girl sneered as she waved the placard dangerously close to his face.

Giving both her and Darcy the filthiest of glares, he strode off, but by now a general unrest was running through the crowd. As the women cheered Isabella Ford and shouted their own grievances, some men were doing their utmost to browbeat them into silence. Scuffles broke out. Placards were broken and hats ripped from heads, women thrown to the ground. The sharp blast of a whistle had most of the crowd dispersing as three stout policemen shoved their way up to Isabella Ford.

'Get down off that box. You're causing a public disturbance.'

'I'm only saying what's right and true,' Isabella replied calmly but defiantly. 'It's that rabble over there that are the troublemakers.' She pointed out a group of men who were confronting the women protestors. 'Call themselves men,' she sneered. 'They're afraid of us getting the right to vote.'

Darcy watched in awe. How calm and courageous Isabella Ford was. She turned to the tall girl and echoed her words. 'She's marvellous, isn't she?'

'You should come to our meetings to find out just how wonderful she really is.' The tall girl smiled at Darcy. 'I'm Phyllis Boothroyd. And you?'

'Darcy Earnshaw.' She stuck out her hand. 'Pleased to meet you, Phyllis.'

'Are you one of us then?' Phyllis cocked her head and grinned.

'Not really,' Darcy said. 'Well, not until today that is. But I'd very much like to be.'

9

'Are you going to another one of them meetings again?'

Betsy's face was creased with anxiety, for whilst she did not entirely disagree with the demands the suffragettes were making on the government, she was appalled by the violence that took place on many of the demonstrations and marches. More to the point, she was afraid of Darcy being hurt or, worse still, being given a prison sentence.

'Yes, we have to give our support to women's suffrage. Our meetings let the women know that they have to stand up for their right to a earn a fair wage or own property and vote for who rules us. We do it peaceably by spreading the word. I don't agree with everything the suffragettes have done but...' By now Darcy was all fired up. 'If we women don't fight for our rights we will always be oppressed by men. Without the right to vote, our voices will never be heard.'

'They'll have a job keeping you quiet. All you've done this last while back is lecture us on what you learn at them meetings.' For all John's choice of words seemed harsh, he spoke jokingly, a wry smile on his face.

'It's because it's important that everyone comes together to fight the cause,' Darcy said as she shrugged into her coat then patted the white, green and scarlet badge that was pinned to her lapel.

'You're beginning to sound like Emmeline Pankhurst,' John said with a grin. 'She came to Halifax a couple o' years back to tell the women not to complete the national census. She wanted to muck up the government's counting. You do know she spoke in the Mechanic's Institute, don't you?'

Darcy gave an imperious sniff. 'Of course I do. I know all about it. The women went into hiding so that the enumerator couldn't register them. Mary Lister read out Mrs Pankhurst's speech to us at one of our meetings.' She went and plopped a kiss on Betsy's cheek. 'Don't look so worried. I won't be late.'

'Have you owt you want me to say to Danny if he calls round?' John called after her as she headed for the door.

Darcy pretended she hadn't heard.

At the meeting Darcy sat entranced. The visiting speaker was Florence Lockwood from Huddersfield. She opened her speech by declaring, 'We are sick, we suffragists, of being told by men what we may do, ought to do, what is womanly.'

Darcy, seated next to Phyllis, reached out and squeezed her hand. Phyllis returned the squeeze as they exchanged looks of agreement and excitement.

On the stage from which Florence was delivering her speech was the exquisite banner that she herself had embroidered. Its depiction of the Pennine Hills and the monstrous mills with their towering, smoking chimneys immediately captured Darcy's attention: it summed up all that was evocative of a Yorkshire mill town. A heading on the banner read 'Votes for Women'.

'The game of cat and mouse that the government is playing with the women they have incarcerated in their filthy gaols is demeaning to all women,' Florence stated. She explained that the women who had gone on hunger strike in protest at their imprisonment were being released on licence when they neared death's door and then, when the licence expired and the women had recovered their health, they were imprisoned again.

'That's downright wicked,' Darcy whispered to Phyllis, at the same time wondering if she had the courage to starve herself for the cause.

* * *

Two days later, she travelled to Leeds to join The Great Pilgrimage, a march organised by the National Union of Women's Suffrage Societies. There she and her companions were to march through the city with the pilgrims before returning to Halifax in the evening.

Barely able to suppress her excitement, she stood on the crowded pavement with Phyllis, waving their Society banners as they waited for the pilgrims to arrive. She felt awfully important in her grey skirt and white high-necked blouse, her white, green and scarlet sash emblazoned across her chest and a cute grey cloche covering her long, fair hair. The women had been given strict orders to dress femininely and smartly in grey, black or navy with white blouses so that their attire would show them to be intelligent, decent women and not riff-raff.

'Here they come,' the cry went up as the weary marchers entered Briggate, having walked the Great North Road for days on end to reach the city. Darcy roared and cheered with her companions until her throat ached. Then, as they listened to speeches from several of the pilgrims, the anti-suffragists broke loose.

Suddenly, there was pandemonium, the speakers' words drowned by an angry mob of men wielding batons.

Someone behind her tried to rip off Darcy's sash. She reeled backwards then managed to turn on her heel. 'Let me go, you brute!'

Her assailant laughed in her face, so she swung her fist, slapping him on the side of his head. It took him by surprise and he let go of the sash. Darcy followed with a swift kick to his shins.

Phyllis was struggling with a lanky youth intent on tearing her banner to shreds as, at the same time, she continued yelling, 'Votes for Women!'

Darcy dived between them, the lad catching her cheek with the back of his hand as he tugged at the banner. The blow was so forceful that she saw stars.

'Votes for Women!' shouted Phyllis again, clutching the remains of her banner.

Darcy took up the chant. 'Votes for women.'

'Shut yer stupid gob,' the lanky youth yelled back.

'She needs a bloody good beltin', that's what she needs,' his mate roared.

He grabbed Darcy by the arm then clamped his dirty hand over her mouth. Darcy bit into it with as much force as she could muster. He howled and let her go.

'She's a bloody wildcat is that one,' he snarled before disappearing into the angry mob.

Phyllis deftly elbowed the lanky lad in his guts and he sloped off, defeated. The two girls looked at one another then burst out laughing.

'You've got a black eye, or at least you will have by tonight,' Phyllis said.

Darcy fingered her bruised cheek and felt the swelling under her eye. 'I've lost my hat as well.' She giggled. 'And so have you.'

Feeling rather battered and very dishevelled, the girls followed the pilgrims down the street, meeting up with their companions on the way. Although they all looked as though they had been dragged through a hedge backwards, they bravely made their way to the train station, chanting, 'Votes for women,' as they marched along. Darcy had never felt so invigorated and powerful.

* * *

'Just look at the state of you,' Betsy cried as Darcy put dishes of porridge on the breakfast table the next morning. She'd said much the same thing the night before when Darcy had arrived back from Leeds minus her hat. Now, she was horrified. Darcy's eye was red and swollen.

Darcy had brushed aside her concern, saying, 'It's a small price to pay if we succeed in getting votes for women.' Now, she repeated her words.

'Small price, my arse,' John growled. 'You could have been really hurt.'

'But I'm not.' Darcy's tone was assuaging for she hated to distress them. 'Look upon it as a badge of honour. I will.'

'You won't do owt daft like that lady who threw herself under the king's horse, will you?' Betsy was wringing her hands as she spoke. 'An' don't be goin' on hunger strike if they send you to gaol.'

'Oh, Betsy. Don't take on so. That won't happen.' Darcy reassured her with a hug. Then, letting her go, she said, 'I don't think I'd have the courage to do anything like that.' She shook her head emphatically. 'No! I know I wouldn't, so stop worrying. I will, however, give my support to raise funds for those women who are brave enough.'

John wagged his finger at her. 'Aye, make sure that's all you do.'

* * *

Throughout the summer months, Darcy deliberately kept very busy attending meetings, rallies and marches. By doing so it made it easier to put Danny Capp out of her mind. He still called regularly with the Carvers, and whilst Darcy did not avoid him she gave him no encouragement to renew the friendship they had once known. Most of the time when he was there she kept to her room, and if she saw him when she was out and about in the town she altered her route so that their paths wouldn't cross. If he happened to stop by when she and John were working their pitch, she acknowledged him coolly yet, in her heart of hearts, she yearned for the days when they had walked through the park or down by the canal, talking and making one another laugh. Just the sight of him turned her insides to water, the way his dark curls flopped on his forehead and curled about his ears and, if he stood close enough, the very scent of his skin set her nerves jangling. She missed the warm feel of her hand in his and his goodnight kisses. But he was a man, and men always wanted more.

Whenever their paths did cross Danny never bore her any ill will, neither did he press her to resume the close relationship they had shared: he was playing the long game, certain that, given time, she would come to realise just how much he loved her. He would smile, his soft brown eyes sad as he gently asked after her wellbeing. Darcy would respond with a wintry smile. Her heart was hardened to men and their disgusting behaviour, and no amount of warm smiles and gentle words from Danny or impatient pleading from Betsy would alter her opinion.

Danilo Cappelini had known plenty of girls in his twenty-one years. His handsome, swarthy face and lean physique coupled with his charming, gentle nature gave him plenty of choice, but from the moment he'd met Darcy Earnshaw he knew that he wanted no other. He was in love, and although for the time being his love was spurned, it was unshakeable.

Orphaned at seven years old, Danny had soon learned to take care of himself in the back streets of Florence. He had also taken care of his grandmother, with whom he had lived after his parents' death. An ailing, old woman living hand to mouth and oblivious to the needs of a young boy, she had offered him little more than food and shelter. Even the food had been scarce, Danny earning their suppers by singing on street corners to the many tourists that flocked to Florence. By the time he was sixteen, Danny's beautiful tenor voice had earned him a place with a successful group of street musicians, and when his grandmother died and the group announced that they were going to tour Europe, homeless Danny enthusiastically agreed to go with them. What had he to lose?

But now it seemed he had much to lose if Darcy persisted in shutting him out. He respected her youth and innocence, satisfied to hold hands and share a few kisses, anything just to be in her company. From the start, he'd known that she was the girl he wanted to spend his life with and, cursing the perverts who had so cruelly destroyed her faith in men, he was prepared to wait. Time was a great healer.

And so, he had taken to watching over her from afar. Whenever he knew she would be marching with the suffragettes – John kept him up to date with Darcy's activities because he pitied the young man whose love he believed was sincere – Danny would be there, in the background, to see that she came to no harm.

Darcy was sometimes aware of his presence but she pretended not to notice. She didn't require a nursemaid.

* * *

To all intents and purposes, Darcy convinced herself that she was happy and that she had put the gruesome ordeals with Uncle Abe and Norris Firth behind her, but in her heart of hearts she yearned for the friendship she had once had with Danny. In order to smother these feelings, she kept busy. If she wasn't bottling for John, she was attending a suffrage meeting or a rally, and in the evenings she had started to tutor Angela.

Angela had taken to going to school like a duck to water and came home each day eager to share what she had learned, and Darcy had willingly undertaken the task of furthering her education. Angela was a lovely child with a lively intelligence, and Darcy enjoyed imparting her own knowledge to encourage the little girl.

'Neither me nor Betsy have much book learning,' John had solemnly told Darcy, 'an' it can be a drawback if you want to make your way in the world.'

'Aye, that's why we deliberately scrimp an' scrape so we can pay to have Angela privately educated,' Betsy had explained. 'We made that decision shortly after she wa' born,' she had continued proudly, 'an' to that end we've been saving ever since.'

So, desiring nothing but the best for their daughter, Angela now attended the Misses Chippendale's Academy and rewarded her parents by gaining top marks in all the subjects that were taught in that establishment.

Evenings were the time when Darcy missed Danny the most, and tonight, as on many previous nights, she was sitting at the table with the little girl doing her best not to think of him.

Angela's tongue stuck out of the corner of her mouth as she carefully formed two letter O's then added a long-legged K on a page in the copybook she used to practice her handwriting. Laying down her pencil then raising her rosy-cheeked face, she looked for Darcy's approval.

'Very good, Angela.' Darcy's praise made the little girl smile.

'Now, if you add that pattern to each of these letters' – Darcy jotted alphabet letters into the copybook – 'what words can you make?'

As Angela completed her task, Darcy looked at the clock above the mantelpiece. It was almost seven o'clock.

'Finished,' Angela crowed, triumphantly tossing the pencil aside.

'Right, what have we got?' Darcy pointed to the copybook.

Angela rattled off the list. 'Look, book, took, cook, rook, hook.'

Betsy, who was sitting close by in the armchair with her feet up on a footstool, clapped her hands. 'Well done, love,' she rasped.

She was having one of her 'bad days', and the lips that curved into a smile were tinged with blue. Betsy's sudden lapses of energy no longer frightened Darcy, and she now knew that if she did all the chores and let Betsy rest, she'd be fine in a day or two. Darcy grinned at her, as pleased with Angela's success as her fond mother was.

'Excellent,' Darcy gushed, 'you've done really well, Angela.' She got to her feet. 'Now, I've got to go and get ready for the march.'

Betsy harrumphed. She still wasn't happy about Darcy's involvement with the suffragettes. 'Why don't you give it a miss for tonight?' she said, her anxiety making it sound like a plea.

'I'm committed. We have to make a show of strength,' Darcy piped as she headed for her room.

'Have you seen what it says there?' Betsy croaked, picking up the copy of *The Suffragette* newspaper that Darcy had left on the chair the night before. Out loud she haltingly read, 'Women's Revolution – Reign of Terror – Fire and Bombs.'

'It's just to make the government sit up and take notice,' Darcy called through the open door of her bedroom. 'Last week the Nottingham branch burned down the Boat Club just to let them know we mean business. If they're going to keep putting Mrs

Pankhurst and Sylvia and countless other suffragettes in prison, we have to fight back.'

Betsy gasped and put her hand to her mouth.

John looked up from the boot on which he was stitching a new sole. 'Nothing short of bloody vandalism, that's what it is. You make sure you don't go smashing any windows or setting fire to owt.'

'I won't,' Darcy said flippantly, looping her white, green and scarlet sash over her white blouse ready to march through Halifax in protest of yet another defeated bill in Parliament that denied women the right to vote.

* * *

A motley collection of women had gathered outside the Mechanics Institute by the time Darcy arrived. Some still wore aprons and turbans, having come straight from the mills. Weavers and spinners and doffers mingled on an equal footing with the more refined ladies and one or two aristocrats, their allegiance to the cause lending an air of camaraderie to the proceedings.

'I thought you weren't coming,' Phyllis said, shoving a placard into Darcy's hand. Phyllis, a schoolteacher, never missed a meeting and had even been to London to join the Pankhursts in a demonstration in Hyde Park.

'Well, I'm here now,' Darcy replied brightly, 'and I'm raring to go.'

The march got underway, banners flapping in the gentle evening breeze and the women in good voice as they chanted, 'Votes for women.'

* * *

Less than an hour later what had been a peaceful but exhilarating march through the town suddenly turned into chaos as an opposition of men – and women – began hurling tomatoes, eggs and stones. Banners were torn from hands and shredded, the marching women roughly handled and beaten with their own placards. Darcy fought valiantly to hang on to hers, only for it to be snatched and smashed to matchwood on the pavement.

'Courage, ladies! Keep together! Keep marching!' bawled one of the aristocratic women, her large blue hat with feathers askew as she stormed through the mob, Darcy and Phyllis at her heels.

'Votes for women!' they yelled as, ducking and dodging, they forced their way down the street.

Just when Darcy thought they were making some headway a posse of policemen on horseback charged through the rioters, but to Darcy's amazement and disgust, their targets were not the rioters but the suffragettes.

'Run for it, Phyllis,' Darcy yelled as the police bore down on them.

They fled into the opening of a ginnel and the horses thudded past.

'We mustn't give in,' Phyllis gasped, two bright red spots burning on her ashen cheeks. 'Come on,' she urged, grabbing Darcy by the arm.

Darcy needed no coaxing and the two women charged back on to the street.

The march forgotten, Darcy's blood sang in her ears and her heart thudded painfully as, grabbing at flailing arms and kicking shins, she fought to protect her sisters. And still the police did nothing to protect the suffragettes.

Darcy's anger boiled over, and in the heat of the moment she lobbed a brick through one of the Exchange Chambers' windows. It shattered to smithereens.

Darcy whooped. If she lived to be a hundred, she'd never forget this day. Frantic for retribution, she stooped to pick up another brick. But before she had chance to let it fly, a burly policeman grabbed her by the shoulders and hurled her to the ground.

She landed heavily, the breath knocked out of her and her back feeling as though it was broken. She stared up into his face. He raised his truncheon. Darcy rolled into a ball and tensed her body, waiting for the blows to fall.

The policeman gave an ugly grin that suddenly changed to a scowl as a sinewy brown arm grabbed the truncheon and flung it down the street. Then a broad shoulder heaved the policeman aside. He staggered back, roaring, and in one swift movement Danny scooped Darcy up and ran with her into the ginnel. As he ran, he smothered her face in tiny kisses. 'Oh, my love, my *bellissima*, you could have been killed,' he cried, setting her down on her feet and clutching her to his chest.

Darcy felt the strong arms holding her and smelled the scent of Danny's skin. She let her body sag against his, and sobbed. Inside his warm embrace she felt safe, as though she had come home after a long, lonely journey.

Danny dried her tears with gentle fingers, and Darcy saw the love blazing in his dark eyes.

'Tell me you no longer love me.' He spoke with immense intensity, his face close enough for her to feel his breath. 'Tell me truthfully.'

She saw the anguish with which he waited for her reply. She thought how faithful he had been during the last few months, never giving up on her, and she was mindful of how foolish she had been to drive him away when her heart had been telling her all along that she loved him. She gazed into his face, her own filled with remorse.

'You do love me,' he cried, pressing his hands to her face, his palms hot against her cheeks. 'Say it! Say that you love me.'

'I love you. I love you with all my heart. And I've missed you,' she said softly.

'I'm taking you home,' Danny said, his heart rejoicing as they made their way to the end of the ginnel and through the back streets.

When they came to a quiet corner where no one was about, Darcy pulled Danny to a halt.

'I've been very silly,' she said, almost in a whisper. 'I have allowed the hideous incident with my uncle and that of Norris Firth to rule me.' Tears spiked her lashes as she hardened her voice. 'Through no fault of my own I became their victim and I let them destroy my trust.' Positively shaking with anger, she gripped the lapels on Danny's coat and looked deep into his eyes as she cried, 'I don't want to be their victim! I won't allow them to ruin the rest of my life. I want to live it as my heart tells me I should.' Her tears spilled over, wetting her cheeks and spattering the backs of Danny's hands as he gently cupped her face in his palms.

'And you will, my love, you will.' Her blue eyes made him think of cornflowers after a shower of rain, and he had never loved her more than he did now. 'I swear you are the loveliest creature I ever set eyes on. I always thought so and I will move heaven and earth to show you that my love for you and yours for me can overcome all the bad things that have happened.' He paused, a pleading grin twitching at the corners of his mouth. 'And you will love me, won't you?'

'I will, Danny, I will,' said Darcy, blinking away her tears. 'I do so want to feel whole again, and with you by my side I know I can.' She sealed her words by kissing him full on the mouth.

Danny felt a lump of emotion rise up in his throat. He could barely speak. Instead, he let out a great whoop followed by a stream of excited Italian. Darcy looked puzzled, not understanding a word of it.

'I am saying you have made me the happiest man in the world,' he explained and returned her kiss.

Then, hand in hand, they ran the rest of the way to Burgos Court, both feeling as though their hearts might burst, so full were they of love and happiness. They had ridden the storm and found each other again.

When they reached the neck of the ginnel into the court, Darcy pulled Danny to a stop again. Her eyes narrowing and her tone cool, she asked, 'Who was the girl with the red hair?'

Danny gave her a blank look. 'Girl with red hair,' he repeated, curious.

Darcy told him about the day she had seen him with the girl. Then he remembered.

'Oh, her! She wanted me to sing at her wedding. I did, too. In the minster, no less.' He puffed up with pride. 'And what a splendid affair it was, me singing along with the mighty organ and the music soaring up to the heavens.' His eyes gleamed with the memory of it.

Then it was Darcy's heart that soared to the heavens. 'I'm even sillier than I thought I was,' she exclaimed, leaving Danny looking rather bemused as she brushed his lips with her own then ran down the ginnel and into the house.

'Oh, my good God!' Betsy screeched when she saw the state Darcy was in.

Indeed, she did look a sorry sight with her blouse sleeve ripped from the shoulder, her skirt streaked with mud and her beautiful hair in tatters. Then, as Danny appeared in the doorway and he and Darcy exchanged amused, loving glances, Betsy let out another cry, this one filled with sheer joy.

Over a welcome cup of tea, the happy pair related the events of the last two hours, Betsy gasping when she heard about the policeman and his truncheon, and John growling his disgust for the law.

'Well, there's one good thing that's come out of it,' John said, smiling broadly and fixing his eyes on Darcy, 'and it must tell you something. This daft lad here' – he flicked his thumb at Danny – 'must really love you. If he was brave enough to walk the streets with you looking like you do now, then there's no knowing what he'd do for you.'

Darcy laughed until she cried.

10

HALIFAX, JANUARY 1914

'Happy birthday, Darcy,' said Betsy as Darcy, still half asleep, shuffled into the kitchen of the house in Burgos Court.

'Happy birthday,' Angela echoed, her voice high with excitement as she ran across the room and threw her arms round Darcy's waist. 'Mam says this is a very special day an' we're gonna have a cake with candles on it at teatime.' Barely able to contain her glee, Angela jigged a circle round Darcy.

Darcy, unable to hide the look of surprise on her face or the bluntness in her voice, asked, 'Why is this one special? It's just another birthday.'

The two birthdays she'd had in the three years she had lived with the Carvers had been acknowledged with greetings from John and Betsy and the cards Angela had made out of scraps of paper that she had decorated with gaudy bunches of flowers or bunny rabbits, but there had been no great celebrations.

'It's your eighteenth, love,' Betsy replied, 'you're a woman now, that's what we're celebrating.' She ladled porridge into four dishes on the table. 'I know it's not as important as your twenty-first, 'cos that's your coming of age, but I allus remember how I felt when I turned eighteen. I wa' no longer me mam's little girl. I wa' getting ready to wed John and become a wife. Talking of which' – she turned to Angela – 'go an' waken your daddy or else he'll sleep all day.'

Angela darted into the bedroom off the kitchen, singing 'Wakey, Wakey.' A lovable child with a lust for learning, and a generous pinch of mischief, the lively seven-year-old kept the household on its toes.

She bounced back into the kitchen. 'Me dad's getting up. I sang right in his ear.' Minutes later John appeared, his hair tousled and his eyes heavy with sleep.

'Which one of you sent the town crier in to waken me?' John glanced accusingly from Betsy to Darcy but he was laughing as he spoke. He was always affable even when times were hard, as he knew they would be in the months ahead as winter and the inclement weather denied him the opportunity to perform his street shows. And when he could, his earnings were few, the spectators unwilling to linger in the cold air. He'd made money over Christmas but he knew it wouldn't last long. The landlord had raised the rent, and the price of food was always higher at this time of year. Now at the end of January, his funds were depleted and the little family had to rely on what he earned cobbling shoes.

Money was the last thing on Darcy's mind. As they sat down to eat their porridge, she thought how fortunate she was to be in such splendid company on the morning of her special birthday. And she had a cake with candles to look forward to at teatime. What more could a girl ask for?

'Go and put on your uniform, love,' Betsy ordered when Angela had finished her breakfast, 'you don't want to be late, 'cos you've got your handwriting an' spelling test today.'

Both parents were conversant with her daily school routine and enjoyed learning along with her. Darcy was their invaluable ally. Not only was she clever, she had been well schooled and she delighted in sharing her knowledge with the Carvers. She had always loved reading and losing herself in books borrowed from the library in Bradley Brigg when she had accompanied Polly on her weekly shopping trips to help carry the groceries. Books had made many of the solitary hours she'd spent in Northcrop House more bearable. Now, they were all reaping the benefits of time well spent.

In fact, when Darcy looked back on the last three years she viewed it as a learning curve not only for Angela and her parents but also herself. She was no longer the unhappy girl whose future had seemed hopeless. She was a young woman capable of making her own way in the world. She now knew that she had the confidence and ability to do whatsoever she chose, but she had no desire to put it to the test. She was happy with her lot. Working with John had also taught her to recognise and value the good in people and to be wary of the bad. She knew how to fend off unwelcome advances from men who might take advantage of her. Being an extremely beautiful young woman, she attracted plenty of attention from that quarter, but working on the streets had made her wily and she was quick to spot a rogue out to get what he could from her.

And most precious of all, she had the love of a decent, thoughtful man in whom she could trust. Danny had faithfully stuck by her through thick and thin, and as she reflected on her fears and her stubbornness, she shivered to think how close she had come to losing him. The past year had seen their love for one another deepen, and Darcy now knew that she would love him for eternity.

'If you see Danny, don't forget to tell him six o'clock sharp,' Betsy said, appraising her daughter's grey pleated pinafore dress and crisp white blouse. Then they all donned their warmest topcoats and left the house together, Betsy to walk Angela to Misses Chippendale's Academy in Temple Street, and John and Darcy to make their way to the town centre.

'The sun's shining for my birthday,' Darcy remarked, pleased that it wasn't raining and that, whilst the air was frosty, there was no sign of snow.

'Aye, I told it it had to, and long may it last,' John replied.

In Gibbet Street, they began performing close by the stump of the ancient guillotine. As John leapt and tumbled, his rippling muscles and handsome good looks clearly angered a downtrodden man standing with his drab wife. Her eyes on stalks, she oohed and aahed at John's feats then bawled, 'I'd take you into me bed anytime, bonny lad.' Her husband rewarded her with a thump. A woman standing next to her yelled, 'Oy, you can't do that,' and hit him with her umbrella. The man turned on her, only to be threatened by her husband.

'Let's get out of here,' John shouted to Darcy as he speedily brought his act to a finish. Disturbances like this often attracted the attention of the law, and seeing as how they looked unfavourably on the street performers, it was best to steer clear of any trouble.

They moved on to a pitch close by the Borough Market. The dry weather had lured the shoppers out and they soon acquired a few spectators. Towards the end of the performance, as John prepared his torches, Darcy gave a sweetly tuneful rendition of 'I Dreamt I Dwelt in Marble Halls'. It was one of the many Irish airs her Irish nanny had taught her. Standing on a crate before the small audience, she not only sounded enchanting, she looked remarkably lovely, her red shawl lending colour to her cheeks and the dark green dress she and Betsy had sewn from a piece of woollen cloth showing off her neat waist. She was wearing her pale blonde hair loose, and the silky curtains framing her face gave her the look of a mystical maiden.

At the front of the crowd, an elderly man in a finely tailored suit and top hat stood leaning on his silver-topped cane entranced as Darcy's clear soprano voice soared above the noise of the market. She brought such pathos to the refrain that his eyes filled with tears, and as the last sweet notes faded, he reached up and caught her hand.

Darcy was all for pulling it away. She'd come across his sort before and didn't like being mauled by men with dubious intentions, even those who looked as frail as this one. But when he spoke she left her fingers inside his.

'Thank you my dear. That was my late wife's favourite song and you sang it beautifully,' he said, his voice dry and quavering, and his accent letting her know he was Irish.

'I'm pleased you enjoyed it, sir,' Darcy replied, 'it's one of my favourites too.' She gave him a dazzling smile.

Still holding her hand, he fished in his trouser pocket with the other. Finding what he was looking for, he withdrew his hand then slipped some coins into Darcy's palm, closing her fingers round them and holding them in place.

'Thank you, sir, thank you kindly.' Clutching the coins in her closed hand, Darcy bobbed a little curtsey.

'The pleasure is all mine,' he said, tipping his hat and moving off. In seconds he was lost in the crowd.

Darcy stood for a moment thinking what a lovely man he seemed. Then she opened her palm. Her cornflower blue eyes boggled at what she saw. Vainly looking out for a top hat she cried, 'Oh, no sir! Come back! It's far too much.'

Phelim Convery heard her cry and smiled. What a sweet, lovely girl. She had put him in mind of his beautiful late wife with her fair hair – straight as a dye, as Bridget had been wont to say – and her startling blue eyes. He kept on walking, thinking how pleased his wife would be to know that he was bringing a little happiness into the lives of the less fortunate. She had always maintained that they should share their good fortune, and in the short time he had left on earth Phelim was doing just that.

He had come to England from the bogs of Ireland when he was a boy and over the years he had created a very lucrative business in concrete. Now, having already dispersed much of his wealth between his workers, he was doling out the remainder in a most satisfying way. Chuckling softly, he strolled on.

Stunned, Darcy stared in the direction he had gone, too amazed to carry on singing. Then she gazed at the three gold sovereigns sitting supreme in the palm of her hand. At first, she had thought, by the feel of them, that they were florins and she had been thrilled. Pennies, halfpennies, thrupenny bits and silver sixpences were what they usually collected unless, of course, on rare occasions a drunk, too free with his money, or soldiers on leave from the barracks in the town, tossed in a shilling. But never before had anyone handed her a sovereign – let alone three.

John was lighting his torches and at the same time looking rather bemusedly at Darcy. Why wasn't she singing to keep the punters entertained? He was even more confused when she rushed towards him, her face flushed and her bright blue eyes flashing.

'Look, John! Look! Three gold sovereigns!' Her squeals hurt his ears. 'A gentleman's just after giving me them for singing "I Dreamt I Dwelt in Marble Halls",' she gabbled, holding out the coins for his inspection.

Heedless of the flaming torches, John stared wide-eyed at the coins. Then he took them and bit into one and then the others with his strong, white teeth. 'Bloody hell!' he exclaimed. 'Three sovereigns! An' they're real.'

His eyes ranged the crowd. 'Who was he? Where is he now?'

'Gone,' Darcy replied, her eyes following John's gaze. 'He was wearing a tall hat and carrying a cane with a silver top. He told me it was his wife's favourite song and that I sang it beautifully.'

'You did indeed,' said John, his voice thick with emotion as he gave Darcy an affectionate smile and ruffled her hair. He tucked the sovereigns into the pouch on his belt. 'Right, let's get this show over,' he cried with alacrity, his eyes gleaming at their unexpected good fortune.

* * *

On their way back to Burgos Court, dodging in and out of the cabs and wagons as they crossed the busy thoroughfares and almost pushing people aside on the pavements in their haste to give Betsy the good news, they talked of little else but the gift of the sovereigns.

'He must be somebody important to part with that much,' John panted as they hurried down Commercial Street and into New Road.

'I'd like to think he'd stop by again. I can sing lots of Irish airs, and at a sovereign a song we'd be as rich as the king in no time,' she replied, laughing at the idea as she raced down the ginnel ahead of John.

* * *

'By rights it's Darcy's,' John said as they sat at the table and told Betsy how she had come by the coins. Betsy wiped the tears from her eyes and stared at the sovereigns. Then, with her forefinger, she slid them one by one so that they sat in front of the little sponge cake on a platter in the middle of the table. 'What a wonderful birthday gift, Darcy,' she said on her breath.

'It's not *my* gift! It's *ours*,' Darcy protested. 'I'd never have earned it if you hadn't taken me in and cared for me all these years. It's for all of us: you, John, Angela and me.' She reached across the table and laid her hand on Betsy's. 'Think of it, Betsy, no more scrimping and scraping. We could even move to a better house, one where we don't have to share a lavatory with Nellie and Tillie. Angela can have whatever she needs, we all can,' she cried, her joy at being able to repay these beautiful, kind people spilling over.

Angela listened, bouncing in her seat and already planning what she would ask for.

A rap on the door startled them all. In their excitement they had quite forgotten about the birthday party. The door opened and Danny stepped in.

* * *

'So, you are now a rich lady,' Danny said, his eyes dancing with amusement after he had heard the story from Darcy as they ate cheese sandwiches and pickles.

'Can we sing "Happy Birthday" and light the candles?' Impatient, Angela rattled the box of matches her mother had placed on the table beside the cake.

John lit the candles and they all sang 'Happy Birthday' lustily.

'Blow them out, Darcy. Take a deep breath and don't forget to make a wish.' Angela squealed, then anxiously warned, 'Don't say it out loud or it won't come true.'

Darcy blew and made her silent wish. *Let us always be as happy and as loving as we are now.* Everyone clapped and cheered. Darcy sniffed the waxy smoke from the extinguished candles and thought what a wonderful scent it was; it seemed to signify love and joy.

Then Betsy presented Darcy with a new straw boater with a

scarlet ribbon to replace the one that had suffered on the march. 'This is from me, John and Angela,' she said sternly, 'an' it comes with a strict warning from all of us. Don't let it get squashed or battered and don't lose it, or else you'll have us to answer to.'

Darcy set the boater on her head at a jaunty angle and pouted prettily.

They all laughed, reminded of the sorry state of Darcy on the day Danny had rescued her from the irate policeman: the day that Darcy had buried her demons once and for all.

'Now it is my gift,' Danny said, taking Darcy's left hand with both of his own.

Darcy gasped as he slipped a delicate band decorated with three small, white pearls on her third finger. She could tell that it was neither new nor expensive, but it was so beautiful that tears sprang to her eyes.

'Thank you, thank you,' she sobbed, her tears perturbing none of them for they knew they were tears of joy.

'Does this mean you're bahn to wed this flibbertigibbet of a lass of ours then?' John grinned at Danny, and Angela squealed her delight.

'If she will have me,' Danny replied, turning his dark eyes on Darcy and losing himself in the pools of blue that gazed back at him.

'She will,' she said firmly.

11

Two months after her eighteenth birthday, Darcy and the Carvers were still in a celebratory mood. After a lengthy search to find new accommodation, they were leaving the cramped unpleasant conditions in Burgos Court and moving to a better part of town. The excitement levels were high.

'If anyone had told me I'd be livin' in a house in Pellon Lane with its own lavatory an' three proper bedrooms, I'd never have believed 'em,' Betsy was heard to remark on several occasions, and her joy knew no bounds as she and Darcy cleaned the parlour in readiness for their new furniture.

At Betsy's suggestion, they were leaving some of their old furniture behind in Burgos Court for the next occupants. 'They might be glad of it,' she'd said, delighted to think that she was sharing her newfound affluence.

They had tremendous fun shopping at the Halifax Furnishing Company in Northgate for a walnut table and chairs, and two matching armchairs with button backs. 'It's lovely to be able to buy just what you want without having to worry where the money's coming from,' Betsy said.

Darcy agreed wholeheartedly. She was still amazed to think that her rendition of an old Irish air had given her the opportunity to repay Betsy and John for their kindness, and she delighted in helping them furnish their new home.

However, when they had passed by Hemingway's Pianoforte and Harmonium Warehouse, and Betsy had wondered if they should buy a piano for Angela, John had thrown up his hands in despair. 'Don't be ridiculous, woman. Do you know how much they cost?' he had cried, shocked by her naivety. 'We need to use this money wisely,' he had said, a thoughtful frown on his face.

* * *

Moving into Pellon Lane was to everyone's advantage. Darcy and Angela each had their own bedroom, Angela delighted not to have to share a room with her parents, and John and Betsy relieved. 'I can get me wicked way wi' you now without Miss Inquisitive wakening an' spoiling it,' John had said, giving Betsy a saucy wink then nodding at their daughter, who was in her own bedroom busily arranging a teddy bear with one eye, a floppy rabbit and a rag doll on her new bed.

But the most surprising move was the one John decided to make. He hadn't worked the streets since the day Phelim Convery had given Darcy the sovereigns. He had his reasons, one being that he had strained the muscles in his back and another being that his cobbling skills were keeping him very busy, and with those in mind whilst he'd been searching for their new home, he had also been making discreet enquiries that he hadn't divulged to Betsy and Darcy.

They were sitting comfortably in their new parlour one afternoon in the first week of May, John reading the *Halifax Courier* and

Betsy and Darcy sewing a patchwork quilt for Darcy's bedroom, when he made his announcement.

'I'm not going back to working the streets,' he said, glancing from Betsy to Darcy over the top of the paper.

Betsy gasped, and Darcy was so startled that she pricked her finger. Two pairs of eyes, one warm brown and the other corn-flower blue, stared at him. John loved performing, and neither Betsy nor Darcy could imagine him doing anything else. It was in his blood.

'An' what will you do if you don't work the streets? I know we've got money in the bank now, John, but it'll not last forever.' Betsy's voice wobbled, and she clutched her hands to her lips as if to stem a rising tide of anxiety.

'I'm nigh on thirty years old, Betsy, too old to be somersaulting in all weathers,' John replied wearily. 'An' what I intend to do is set meself up in a business that'll provide us wi' a good living for the rest of us days.' He sat back, a determined expression on his face as he waited for Betsy's and Darcy's reactions.

'I don't know what you mean.' Betsy looked and sounded thor-oughly flustered.

'It means I'm going to open a boot an' shoe shop.'

'A boot an' shoe shop,' Betsy echoed faintly.

'Aye, I'll not only mend shoes, I'll make 'em an' buy some in. Make a proper business out of it. I've found a little place down the street to rent. A shop at the front an' a workshop at the back.' He folded his arms across his chest, his eyes glinting with pride at his perspicacity.

'You've given this a lot of thought, haven't you?' Darcy said, her voice rich with admiration. 'I think it's a marvellous plan.'

'But what if it doesn't make any money and you lose what we have?' Betsy had been raised in extreme poverty and was terrified of being plunged back into that parlous state.

John gave her a look full of understanding and reassurance. 'It will, love. I'll make certain it does. The money the old fellow gave us has set us up nicely, and the cobbling I'm doing now is bringing in more money than I earned working the streets. Even when I've paid me rent on the premises an' bought the bends of leather for repairing an' making, there'll still be a bit left in the bank. Don't you be worrying about Angela's schooling, 'cos there'll allus be money for that.'

'If you're sure.' Betsy sounded doubtful.

'I am, an' I'll work me arse off to prove I'm right. Now, stop moping an' come an' give us a kiss for being such a level-headed fellow.'

Betsy got to her feet and crossed the room and John stood to take her in his arms.

'I can just picture it,' Darcy said enthusiastically. 'I can serve the customers whilst John makes and mends shoes in his workshop. I think it'll be a great success, Betsy.'

John grinned and gave her a fond wink, and Betsy's face brightened.

12

Before the end of the month John was certain that he had done the right thing. His venture was proving to be a wise move. With Darcy's help he had cleaned and refurbished the shop, building shelves to display the shoes that he had purchased from a wholesaler in Nottingham. In the workshop, where he had installed his lasts and leather and a heavy-duty sewing machine, second hand but in good condition, John cobbled boots and shoes, and Darcy charmed the prospective customers with her ready smile and helpful nature. And on a glorious sunny day at the start of July she was willingly applying both.

'Good afternoon, Mrs Spivey, your husband's boots are ready and waiting.' Darcy plonked a pair of stout brown boots, to which John had recently attached new soles and heels, on the counter. 'Lovely day isn't it?'

Maud Spivey inspected the repaired boots. 'Nice job, they're like new.' She fished in her purse to pay, but instead of taking the money Darcy stepped from behind the counter looking every bit the charming saleswoman in her smart navy skirt and crisp, white blouse.

'Have you seen our new line in ladies' summer shoes, Mrs Spivey? They're very light and comfortable.' Darcy lifted a pair of cream shoes with a T-bar and low heel. 'You can walk miles in these without your feet getting hot.'

Maud looked down at her own button boots that were pinching her toes, swollen now with the heat of the day.

'They do look comfortable,' she murmured, taking a shoe out of Darcy's hand. 'I'll try them on.'

Darcy rewarded her with a beaming smile. 'I think this is your size,' she said, kneeling down to place Maud's foot into the shoe and then fastening the strap.

'Ooh, that feels like heaven after those tight boots. Put the other one on.'

The sale completed, Maud walked out of the shop wearing her new shoes, Darcy calling after her, 'Don't forget to tell your friends about us. We've plenty of stock to suit them.'

As it was Saturday, the shop was busy with customers collecting their repaired shoes in time to wear for church the next day, and a spate of those who were just plain nosy and wanted to see what the new shop had to offer.

Towards the end of the afternoon, an old man called in to collect his boots. 'That's bad news about that archduke they assassinated in Sarajevo,' he said, his heavy jowls wobbling. 'It'll bring us nowt but trouble. Mark my words.'

'Oh, yes. I heard about that – and his poor wife too,' Darcy replied as she handed him the boots and took his money. 'It's very sad, but why would it trouble us? Sarajevo's a long way from here.'

The old man harrumphed. 'You need to learn your history, lass. Them that runs this country allus poke their kneb in to other countries' affairs just to show the world what a great country we are. They don't give a damn for the young men who go to war and pay for it with their lives.'

He stamped out of the shop, leaving Darcy of the opinion that he was a curmudgeonly old misery. Even so, his notion that the news might cause England to go to war made her uneasy. But why would an incident in a place with an unpronounceable name do that? Giving a careless shrug, she forgot about it. It was time to go home.

'I sold seven pairs of ladies' shoes and two pairs of men's boots,' she told John as he came out of the workshop. 'That's our best day yet. What with those sales and the money for the cobbling, you were right to say we'd make a go of it.'

'A go of what?' Danny asked as he came into the shop ready to walk Darcy home. When she told him of her success he quipped, 'How could they refuse to buy shoes when they are given such pretty service.'

'Aye, she wa' a damned good bottler an' now she's an even better saleswoman.' John bestowed upon Darcy a proud smile.

She flushed with pleasure. 'We're just a good team, John. You do your bit, I do mine, and it all works out well in the end.' The satisfaction she got from helping out her adopted family in whatever way she could was reward itself, and for the millionth time she blessed the day she'd met John Carver.

The first week in August promised more hot sunny days, and John decided to close the shop and take a holiday, so on the Tuesday Danny was taking Darcy out for a trip into the countryside. She was looking forward to it immensely.

'Breakfast's ready,' she carolled as John and Betsy entered the neat, shiny kitchen. Betsy was inordinately proud of her new home and was never done with the cleaning and polishing. However, she'd had a couple of her 'bad days' in the previous week. John blamed it on too much unnecessary housework.

'You need to slow down. The house is just grand,' he'd grumbled, but Darcy could tell it pained him to see his beloved wife utterly sapped of energy and her breathing shallow. As usual, Darcy had insisted Betsy rest and she had taken on all the household chores, at the same time nursing Betsy with nourishing beef broth and milk and honey.

This morning, to Darcy's delight, Betsy looked much better. The blueness that had tinged her lips had faded and she seemed quite perky. So much so that when Angela skipped into the kitchen, having heard Darcy's cry, Betsy said, 'I think I'd like to go to the People's Park. We could take a picnic and listen to the band.'

Angela whooped her agreement, the relief in her eyes evident. She hated to see her mam unwell. John, too, looked relieved and tucked into the bacon and eggs Darcy had set in front of him.

When Betsy cleared her plate of two rashers and a fried egg, Darcy knew she was definitely on the mend. However, still concerned for her health, Darcy washed the dishes and packed two picnic baskets before dashing up to her bedroom to get ready for Danny's arrival at eleven.

Darcy dressed carefully in a flimsy sprigged muslin dress and her new straw boater. She was wearing the same sort of lightweight shoes she had sold Mrs Spivey and six other ladies the day before. When she went downstairs John gave a loud wolf whistle.

'You daft ha'p'orth,' Darcy said, blushing prettily.

'You do look lovely though,' Betsy said, 'an' you've the kindest heart. I don't know what I'd do wi'out you.'

'And I don't know what I'd do without you,' Darcy replied, her eyes full of love.

'He's here,' Angela cried, jumping up to answer Danny's knock.

She, too, was a little bit in love with Danny and the three adults laughed at her eagerness.

In he came wearing a collarless white shirt that looked all the whiter against his smooth, swarthy skin. Darcy's breath caught in her throat, his handsomeness and his dark, laughing eyes making her fall in love with him all over again.

'You look *bellissima*,' he said softly as she went to greet him.

* * *

'Any word on Miss Darcy?' Harry Chadwick stopped Abe Earnshaw in his tracks as he was leaving the Clothier's Tavern in Bradley Brigg. Abe turned, his lip curling as he glared at the sawmill's manager. Blast and damn the man. This wasn't the first time Harry had enquired after Darcy's wellbeing, but this time he seemed more intent on getting a proper answer rather than being brushed aside as he had been in the past three years.

'And what business is that of yours?' Abe growled, then pasted a saccharine smile on his face as the Methodist minister passed by on his way from the chapel.

Bloody hypocrite, Harry thought. 'I was just enquiring. It seems a bit odd for her to stay away for so long. Is everything all right with the lass?'

Abe noted the determined look on Harry's face, his chin jutted out as he blocked Abe's path and his large, powerful hands clenched into fists. *I should have sacked him when I took over the sawmill*, Abe thought bitterly, even though he knew he could not have run the mill without him.

'She's well,' he said brusquely. 'Now if there's nothing else.' He made to move past Harry, but the manager wasn't going to be fobbed off this time.

'Nay, I was just thinking that she must be eighteen by now,' he said.

Abe dithered. 'What the hell does that have to do with things?' he growled.

'She must have had her fill of the Lake District by now,' Harry continued, 'and if Thomas's wishes are to be carried out, she should be ready to come back here.'

A cold sweat broke out on Abe's forehead. 'What are you blethering about, man? What wishes?'

Harry's brow wrinkled in consternation. 'That at eighteen the lass should be introduced to the workings of the mill so that when she attains her majority and takes over the business, she's not ignorant as to how it runs.' He looked and sounded surprised that Abe didn't appear to know of his brother's plans.

Harry's grey eyes, sharp as gunmetal, pierced into Abe's, his filled with consternation, and Harry's filled with suspicion and intense dislike.

Panic seized Abe's chest. It appeared that Harry knew as much about Thomas's intentions regarding Darcy's future as he himself did.

'The girl has no interest in the sawmill,' he snarled, attempting to shoulder past Harry, only to find that it was like trying to batter down a barn door with a feather.

'I find that hard to believe,' Harry sneered into Abe's sweating face, his scepticism apparent. 'She allus showed a deal of interest whenever she called in with her father. Thomas tutored her from no age and she lapped it up.'

'She was just a child trying to please her father,' Abe blustered. 'She's a young lady now and has no time or interest in the trade. Now, let me by, man, and in future keep your nose out of my family's affairs. Remember your position.'

Head down, he charged at Harry, almost knocking him off his feet.

Harry let him go. He'd certainly put the cat among the pigeons, he thought grimly, his suspicions deepening. He knew a guilty man when he saw one.

* * *

Whilst Abe Earnshaw was beating his neglected little pony into an unaccustomed gallop and cracking the whip so fiercely that the poor beast stumbled and almost tipped the trap into a ditch in Bradley Brigg, Darcy Earnshaw and Danilo Cappelini were on the top deck of the bus taking them to Shibden.

The sun was beating down on them but they cared not a jot. 'This must be one of the hottest days of the year,' Darcy said, taking off her boater and fanning her face.

'The sun is shining because he loves us. He is warming our hearts with his,' Danny said.

Darcy giggled. 'Danny Cappelini, you do say the loveliest things.'

'I say them because I am with the loveliest girl in the world. In my country the sun shines like this on many days.'

'One day we'll go there together,' Darcy said dreamily.

'We will. But for now we go to Shibden,' he said, standing and helping her out of her seat as the conductor bawled, 'Anybody for Shibden.' With the picnic basket over her arm, Darcy followed Danny down the winding staircase. On the pavement he relieved her of the basket and they set off to explore the pretty hamlet.

* * *

The door crashed on its hinges as Abe Earnshaw barged into Northcrop House.

In the parlour he poured himself a stiff brandy and downed it in one. Refilling his glass, he sat down at the hearth, glowering into the soot-blackened grate, his thoughts equally black.

Did the girl know of these arrangements? Had Thomas made his wishes known to her? Now that she was eighteen was she likely to suddenly turn up demanding to take her rightful place in the sawmill? Had she been playing him for a fool all along, letting him run the mill for her before tossing him aside when the time was ripe? Questions buzzing in his head, he drained his glass again.

By God! He'd not stand for that. He wasn't about to lose out to some skit of a girl. Seething with rage, he got to his feet and shambled over to the sideboard, this time bringing the brandy bottle back to the chair. Topping up his glass, he forced himself to sip and to think. He needed a clear head. He'd quiz Harry Chadwick about how much he knew. Were there documents lodged with a solicitor that he himself wasn't aware of? There were certainly none with the solicitor who acted for the sawmill, he'd made sure of that when he took over.

He emptied his glass again and again, the veins bulging in his forehead as he flung the empty bottle across the room. He stood, pacing back and forth then, venting his spleen, he hurled the glass into the fireplace. He knew what he had to do. He'd find her. And when he did he'd make sure she never came back to Bradley Brigg. When he'd finished with her she'd never go anywhere again.

13

The pretty hamlet of Shibden basked in glorious sunshine, its cottage gardens a riot of colourful blooms, and for all it was but a mile from Halifax with its bustling streets and smoky manufactories, the air smelled sweeter and cleaner.

Hand in hand, Darcy and Danny strolled along Old Godley Lane then, taking a turning into a narrow, winding lane, they wandered willy-nilly, not caring where the lanes might lead. The day was theirs and they were content just to be in each other's company. Every now and then they stopped to admire the view or share a kiss or two, and when at last they came to a fast-flowing brook they sat down on its mossy bank and ate their picnic.

Afterwards, lying back on the grass with Darcy in his arms, Danny lazily said, 'You remember the girl with the red hair, the one I sang for at her wedding?'

A stab of jealousy made Darcy sit up. 'Yes,' she said tersely. Was he about to ruin a perfect day?

'Her guests also heard me sing. They like what I do and they asked me to sing at their weddings. I have three to sing for before the year is over.' He gazed up at her, his dark eyes proudly gleaming.

'Oh, that's wonderful, Danny, 'cos you love to sing in churches with the organ.'

'Ah, but that is not the best of it,' he said mysteriously, sitting up to face her. 'The girl's father, he asks me to sing in a concert at The Canterbury. He organises the shows.'

'Sing! At The Canterbury?' Darcy squealed, her excitement bubbling over at the idea of Danny singing on the stage in a proper theatre. 'That's marvellous! Why didn't you tell me before now?'

'I wanted to surprise you. If I sing well and they like me, I will give up working the streets and sing only in theatres and churches.'

'Of course they'll like you. It's wonderful news, Danny. You're far too good to spend your days singing on street corners.' Her eyes dancing, Darcy threw herself on top of him and they fell back on the grass hugging and kissing.

After a while, they brushed themselves down and continued walking. They hadn't gone far when they saw a large house with a black and white timbered façade through the trees. Darcy tugged at Danny's sleeve. 'I think that's the house where Anne Lister lived,' she said excitedly as she came to a halt to get a better view. 'It's called Shibden Hall. A speaker at one of our meetings told us all about the woman who used to live there. Anne wasn't a suffragette, but she believed that women were just as good as men and could do anything that a man could do. She even ran her own coalmine.' She cocked her head on one side to judge Danny's opinion of what she had just told him.

He gave an amused shrug, his eyes twinkling wickedly. 'I know of one thing women cannot do without men to help them,' he said slyly, laughter twitching the corners of his mouth.

Darcy was still peering through the trees at the house and thinking about Anne Lister. 'What's that?' she asked innocently.

'Make bambinos. You cannot do that without us.' He chuckled at his own wit.

Darcy felt her cheeks grow hot, but an icy hand clutched at her insides. Was he about to suggest that they should do that now that they were alone in this quiet spot? Was Danny like all other men, after all? Firmly telling herself that was impossible, she quickly changed the subject.

'I'll come and listen to you when you sing at The Canterbury. Didn't I tell you that one day you'd be famous?'

Danny pulled her into his arms. 'I am not yet famous, and maybe I never will be, but I think I am on the path to being a man of means. That being so, will you marry me very soon, Darcy Earnshaw?'

Fear flared again. Did he think that if she said yes he could...?

'Marry you? You mean...?' She bit down on her lip, her eyes troubled.

Danny heard the unspoken meaning behind her words. He placed his fingers under her chin, tilting her head so that she could see his face.

'You do not have to be afraid. What I am offering is not like those other men who hurt you. I would never harm or degrade you. I come to you with love.' He spoke so sincerely that Darcy's heart turned over.

'And I don't mean one day when I'm famous,' he continued, gazing seriously into her smiling eyes, his words urgent. 'I mean now, tomorrow or next week. I don't want to wait a moment longer to make you my wife.'

Darcy was stunned into silence. She stared up at him, her blue eyes darkening. Not for a moment in the past year or so had she doubted that one day she would become his wife: she loved him with every bone in her body. But so soon! Was she ready to be a wife with all that it entailed? She gave a violent shudder.

Danny tightened his arms around her. Was she going to make him wait forever because she was still too damaged by her terrible ordeals with the men who had so cruelly abused her? He stepped back, holding her at arm's length.

'I love you with all my heart, Darcy. I would never give you cause to fear me.' His voice was gruff with emotion, the hand stroking her long, fair hair soothing. 'So why, in *nome de Dio*, do we let things that have hurt us in the past keep us apart?'

He sounded as though he might cry, and his dark eyes were so full of love and pleading that tears clogged Darcy's throat.

Danny felt his stomach tighten. One wrong move now and he could lose her forever. Her tears spilled over, wetting the long, fair lashes fanning her cheeks, clinging like drops of dew on early morning cornflowers. He was tempted to kiss them away. He resisted, his eyes never leaving hers. He saw the gamut of emotions flitting across her beautiful face, and he smiled ruefully.

Darcy felt his pain as his words tumbled inside her head. Then suddenly she saw it all quite clearly. She was being foolish again. Letting evil men ruin her chance of happiness when this man standing in front her would never dream of hurting her. Hadn't he proven it time and again? All at once she felt a loosening in her chest as though someone had pulled a string deep inside her and set free all her fears and misgivings. Her lips parted in a glorious smile.

'I would marry you tomorrow. Or next week, or whenever,' she cried, flinging herself against his chest.

Danny felt her heart pounding against his own as they embraced, two hearts beating as one.

* * *

Darcy and Danny arrived back in Pellon Road in a joyous mood. They burst in on the Carvers, huge smiles on both their faces and words tripping from their tongues.

'We're getting married,' they chorused.

'Have you not heard the news?'

Seeing John's doleful expression and hearing the despair in his voice, the smiles fell from their faces. Darcy was the first to recover. 'Why, what's happened?'

'What's happened is we're being dragged into a war we don't want,' John growled, rustling the newspaper and scowling blackly as he shifted uneasily in his chair. 'The assassination of that arch-duke has caused more trouble than you can imagine.' He flourished the *Halifax Courier*. 'T'papers are full of it.'

Angela was standing in front of the fireplace taking in every word. 'Full of what?' she asked, sounding puzzled.

Betsy never read the newspapers and took little interest in affairs that didn't immediately affect her family and, ashen-faced, she looked just as confused as her daughter.

Darcy and Danny exchanged fearful glances. They had been so wrapped up in each other that neither of them had paid particular heed to Germany's declaration of war against Russia. Now they were both agog to learn why John was so concerned.

'What are they saying?' they chorused, consternation sharpening their voices.

His expression wry with ill-concealed anger and his tone acerbic, John replied, 'In a nutshell they're saying that if the Frenchies back the Ruskies – an' believe me they will – then we'll back the French an' go to bloody war.' He slapped the paper across his knee.

'I don't know why we should.' Betsy's voice wobbled and she pulled Angela down on her knee as if she expected a German to crash through the door and snatch her daughter from under her nose. To Betsy's mind those countries were so far away and so foreign she failed to see why it should affect her family, but if John said it would then she'd have to believe it.

The joy had gone out of the day. Danny and Darcy sat down on the couch, so close they might have been glued to one another. She took comfort in the heat emanating from his body but her insides were like ice. She recalled what the old man in the shop had said and shuddered.

'Well, we can't sit here frettin',' John cried, getting to his feet. 'But I do believe congratulations are in order.' He went to the sideboard and took out the bottle of whisky they kept for medicinal purposes. 'Fetch some glasses from the kitchen, Darcy, so that we can make a toast.'

Darcy brought back four empty glasses and a jug of water and as John poured the whisky she went back into the kitchen for a glass of lemonade for Angela.

John gave small measures with plenty of water to Betsy and Darcy, and much larger ones with barely any water to himself and Danny.

'To Darcy and Danny,' he cried, raising his glass. 'May their marriage be as happy and fruitful as my own.'

Betsy echoed John's sentiments with a wan smile, and not to be outdone, Angela shouted, 'To Danny and Darcy,' lemonade slopping from her glass as she gabbled. 'Can I be your bridesmaid and wear some flowers in my hair?'

John's attempts to lighten the mood hadn't worked half as well as his daughter's, and as she jigged from foot to foot on the hearth rug they all laughed and exchanged warm, loving smiles. Life would go on.

* * *

Later that same evening, after Angela had gone to bed, they went out into the garden and talked. The night air was balmy, the heat of the day still warm on the steps they were sitting on. Betsy leaned against John's knees, looking thoroughly miserable. He placed his hand comfortingly on her shoulder.

'I know you don't want to hear this, love, but we have to be prepared for the worst,' he said gently. 'If there's going to be a war – an' I say *if*,' he qualified, seeing the look of horror on his wife's face, 'I might be called up to fight, and so might Danny.' He glanced at Darcy.

Darcy paled and looked at Danny. Would he have to go and fight? She didn't know much about the impending war, but she did understand that the German kaiser was intent on seeking retribution for the killing of Archduke Ferdinand and his wife. Did Danny think of himself as an Englishman now that he had lived here for five years? Or did his loyalties lie with his own country? Italy had refused to ally itself with the kaiser and declared their neutrality, but wars were terrible and no one could foresee what the future might hold.

'I don't even want to think about there being a war,' Betsy cried, leaping to her feet. 'I'm going to bed.' She hurried indoors, and John followed her.

'What will you do, Danny?' Even to her own ears her voice sounded full of dread, and as much for his sake as her own, she wished that she hadn't let him hear how afraid she felt.

'If England goes to war – and I do not think it will – I may have to go and fight. And if I do, I will be doing it to keep you safe,' Danny said confidently.

'But you are an Italian, so it isn't really your war,' Darcy argued.

'Anything that threatens your safety is my war, *mia bella signorina*,' he replied, taking her hand to drop a kiss in her palm.

Darcy loved to hear the odd Italian phrases he often used, and his words brought a smile to her face and calmed her. Danny didn't appear to be concerned, so why should she? *Maybe I'm just being a worrywart...*

Danny stood and held out his hand for her to do the same.

'But what if the kaiser—'

He stooped and pressed his finger to her lips. 'Let us not talk of things that might never happen. Let us live for today and let tomorrow take care of itself.'

* * *

In the days that followed, Britain declared they would defend Belgium against the German invasion, and the words on everyone's lips were to do with the war. The weather continued to be hot and sunny, and in the sweltering heat of an afternoon in the second week of August Darcy and Betsy were shopping in Waddington's Drapers in Northgate. No sooner had they told the woman behind the counter what they wanted than she started 'the war talk' as Darcy now called it. Irritated, she sighed, but when she saw how unhappy the woman looked, she regretted doing so.

'My son went off this morning to join the Dukes.' The woman was referring to the local regiment based in Wellesley Barracks. 'He's only seventeen,' she moaned, her tears falling on the length of white muslin she was measuring out.

My wedding dress is already marked with sorrow, thought Darcy, as she watched a damp spot spreading on the pristine fabric.

The dress material purchased, they walked down Northgate to Marshall's Bakery for a fresh loaf then turned into Prescott Street. Outside the Drill Hall a long line had formed of eager young men waiting to enter, the soldier on the door letting them in a few at a time. The lads were laughing and joking.

'You'd think they were going on a picnic,' Darcy said, shaking her head and pulling an incredulous face. 'Instead, they'll end up being turned into killers when most of them have never seen a gun, let alone fired one.'

'John says they'll get plenty of training before they go to fight so they know what to do.' To Betsy, her husband's opinions were sacrosanct. 'He says he'll wait and see how things turn out before he enlists.' She bit her lip with the worry of it. 'It could all be over in a week or two,' she said, her voice high with hope.

'Danny says he'll do whatever John decides,' Darcy replied. 'And maybe you're right, Betsy. They might never have to make a decision.'

Darcy had rarely thought about getting married, and when she had she'd imagined it would be a flurry of excitement – choosing a dress and flowers, who to invite and which hymns to sing in church – and she was doing all of these, but somehow it didn't seem so exciting now the shadow of war was hanging over them.

* * *

Darcy Earnshaw and Danilo Cappelini were united in marriage in St John's Church on Saturday, 12 September 1914. John proudly accompanied Darcy down the aisle, Angela walking solemnly behind looking a picture in her blue cotton dress and new white shoes that her dad had made.

The bride was radiant in her white muslin dress with its close-fitting bodice and long, slender skirt that showed off her trim figure. A circlet of white rosebuds crowned her sleek fair hair, one of the onlookers outside the church commenting that she looked like a fairy-tale princess. The dashing groom wore a green velvet jacket, his crisp white shirt flattering his Mediterranean features and his glossy black hair that curled round his ears and in the nape of his neck. He turned to watch his bride approach, his dark eyes gleaming with love and admiration.

Darcy had never felt more beautiful, and as they exchanged their vows clearly and firmly she had never felt more precious. They had bought inexpensive gold rings from Davies's, the jeweller in Old Market, and as Danny slipped her ring on the third finger of her left hand and uttered the time-honoured words, she felt a wealth of emotions she hadn't known she possessed. When it was her turn to place his ring on his finger she held his strong, brown hand in hers and knew that his promise to love and protect her was the greatest gift she had ever received.

The organ thundered the 'Wedding March' and out they came, arm in arm, into the sunshine, everyone declaring that they made a very handsome couple.

'Did I do it right?' Angela jigged from foot to foot awaiting her mother's approval.

Betsy, in a smart new grey two-piece, gave her daughter a hug and told her she had carried out her duties perfectly. She handed her a bag of rice.

'Wheeeh,' Angela squealed, showering Danny and Darcy with a hail of tiny pellets.

Darcy and Danny exchanged a kiss as it sprinkled down on them, which encouraged the other guests to follow suit, the happy couple laughing and turning up their faces to a shower of rice. When Darcy tossed her bouquet of white and red roses high into the air, Phyllis Boothroyd caught it. She waved it triumphantly and shouted, 'Votes for women.'

Danny and Darcy posed for a photograph before leading their neighbours, street performers and suffragettes to the Dyer and Miller for a wedding breakfast. There they ate a tasty spread of roast beef or egg and onion sandwiches and sweet pastries.

'I don't think I'll be following in your footsteps any time soon even if I did catch your flowers,' Phyllis said as she came to sit with Darcy. 'I'm giving up teaching and going to train as a nurse. I think it's more worthwhile. The hospitals will need all the nurses they can get now we're at war.'

Darcy didn't hide her admiration. 'You'll make a good one too. But won't you mind if they send you to one of those field stations at the front?'

'I jolly well hope they do,' Phyllis said stoutly.

'If they do you'll soon see off the Germans.' Darcy chuckled. 'You were never afraid of bashing a policeman over the head with your placard or kicking some rotten fellow in the shins. The Hun had better watch out.'

Phyllis laughed. 'I always knew being a suffragette would come in handy.'

Danny was standing with John and the men, a pint of beer in his hand, but every now and then his eyes strayed to his bride. Just at that moment he believed he was the luckiest man in the world.

'You'd best be quick an' get that lass o' yours in t'family way,' Jimmy the plate juggler said, giving Danny a crafty nudge. 'You'll be expected to join up. We all are. I'm off to Clipstone next week to start me training.'

The beer in Danny's stomach soured. He wasn't a coward and would fight if he had to, but the thought of leaving Darcy did not hang well with him. He left the men and claimed his bride, not wanting to waste one precious moment.

14

It was John's idea that Darcy and Danny should start married life living with him and Betsy, so they delayed finding a place of their own.

'If we enlist – an' we might have to afore long – I'd be happier if Darcy wa' here with Betsy an' Angela,' he'd explained. 'Then if Betsy has one of her bad turns there'll be somebody to look after her an' see to Angela. An' you'd not want to leave Darcy on her own in lodgings.'

Darcy and Danny had agreed it was for the best, so as their wedding day celebrations drew to a close they bid their guests farewell and returned to Pellon Lane. Two weeks before, they had shopped for a double bed to replace Darcy's single. Laughing and joking, they had bought a bed with high brass ends from the second-hand dealer in King Cross, Danny remarking that he hoped the springs didn't squeak.

It was only late afternoon and far too early to go to bed when they arrived at the house, so Danny had to be content to sit and talk over the wonderful day and drink cups of tea. Darcy didn't mind the delay one bit. She'd shooed Danny out of their bedroom when she went to change out of her wedding dress and he had followed her. He'd shaken his head and given her an amused smile. Then, like the perfect gentleman, he'd left.

Later, after eating a light meal of scrambled eggs and toast, Betsy packed a tired and over-excited Angela off to bed, and not long after, John announced, 'I'm fair whacked. I think I'll have an early night.'

Startled, Betsy glanced at the clock on the mantel. 'But it's only...'

John's meaningful look and the nod of his head in Darcy and Danny's direction brought her up sharp. She giggled. 'Oh, me an' all. I'm tired out.' She gave a wide yawn to prove it.

'You go on in.' John flicked his thumb at the young couple sitting on the couch. 'Me an' Betsy'll see to t'lamps an' lockin' up.'

Danny took Darcy's hand and pulled her to her feet. Feeling like a lamb to the slaughter, she let him lead her up to the bedroom.

It was a large, pleasant room that Darcy had furnished to her liking, but now all she saw was the big double bed with its high brass ends dominating the room. In a few minutes' time she would be expected to share it with Danny. She had, of course, slept in it on her own, but now they would have to decide which side of it would be his and which side of it would be hers.

Danny appeared not to be thinking of any such thing. He was stripping off his white shirt and then his vest and unbuckling the belt on his trousers. Darcy's breath caught in her throat as she gazed at his muscular chest, a light covering of black hair snaking down to disappear below the top of his trousers. Slowly, she began to unbutton her blouse, her fingers fumbling with the small, pearl buttons.

Danny gave her a tender smile, and suddenly her fingers became thumbs and she stopped what she was doing. He could see and smell her fear, and being the gentleman that he was he mumbled something about going to the lavatory and left her on her own. Outside, on the landing, he lit a cigarette and when it had burned down he opened the window, flicked out the stub and went back into the bedroom.

Darcy was standing in front of the dressing table brushing her hair, her slender body encased in a white, high-necked nightgown. Danny shucked off his pants and climbed into bed. On legs that felt like jelly, Darcy dithered then climbed in beside him. A swarm of butterflies had invaded her belly and she laid there willing them to stop flapping their tiny wings.

Gently, Danny pulled her into his embrace and kissed her. It wasn't a passionate kiss, more one of reassurance. Darcy liked the feel of his lips on hers, but she couldn't stem the feeling of abject fear about where his kisses might lead. When the kiss ended she gave a wobbly, little smile, and whispering, 'I love you,' she turned her back to him. He kept his arms around her and buried his face in her hair. She felt the hardness of his lean body against hers and liked the feeling. Before she knew it she had fallen into a thoroughly exhausted sleep.

She woke next morning to find him still lying beside her, snoring gently, his broad chest rising and falling and his lips curved in a smile. She loved him dearly, but before he could demand anything of her she slipped out of bed and dressed hurriedly and stealthily in case he wakened.

The next three nights followed the same pattern as the first, but on the fourth night Danny didn't leave the room whilst she undressed. He climbed into bed and lay back against the pillows, a mischievous glint in his eye. Darcy had no alternative but to start taking off her clothes. She fiddled with the buttons on her blouse and skirt and when they were loosened, she slipped her nightgown over her head then began removing her garments from underneath it.

Danny laughed out loud. 'You look like a mouse trying to fight its way out of a paper bag,' he chortled. Darcy was embarrassed.

The next night, reluctant to appear foolish, under Danny's watchful eyes she swiftly divested her garments and just as swiftly enveloped herself in her nightgown. Climbing into bed, she told him she loved him, kissed him and turned over, her body rigid against his. Her heart bumped painfully against her ribs. She knew they couldn't go on like this but she didn't know what else she should do.

Danny placed his arm round her, his fingers flicking open the buttons down the front of her nightgown. Darcy held her breath and clenched her muscles.

Danny slipped his hand inside the opening, his fingers gently teasing her nipples. She felt them spring to life. As his lips nuzzled the nape of her neck and his hand continued to knead her soft flesh, Darcy felt her insides starting to melt. Strange, fluttery feelings ran from her toes to the top of her head and she rolled over on her back, the better to experience them. Danny kissed her passionately and she felt the heat of her own body rising to meet his as he raised her nightdress and placed his fingers between her legs.

After that, Darcy couldn't tell quite what happened. She was no longer wearing her nightdress although she couldn't recall taking it off, and as one beautiful sensation after another rippled through her entire being, she found that she didn't care. Her skin tingled under his caresses and she responded, trailing her fingers across his chest, toying with the hairs, and down to his stomach. When he covered her body with his own she felt his stiff, hard manhood press against her and she stroked his broad back as she began to move with him. Then he was inside her and they clung to each other, their passion rising to a glorious frenzy.

She lay back panting, her skin sleek with sweat, and gazed up at her husband. The ecstatic smile on his face touched every fibre of her being, leaving Darcy wondering what it was that she had been so afraid of. Danny ran a gentle finger down her wet cheek. 'No more fears, *mia bellissima*,' he whispered against her lips. 'No more fears.'

15

Darcy was immensely happy now that she was a married woman. Each morning when she awoke to find Danny lying beside her, she revelled in their love for one another. But when she went about her daily business selling shoes, the glow encompassing her faded and was replaced by worrisome fears.

The war was uppermost in everyone's minds, and Darcy dreaded the moments when her customers wanted to engage her in conversation about it. They talked as though it was some great game being played out like a football match, their insensitive remarks making her blood boil. Had they not read the newspapers? At the Battle of the Marne more than twelve thousand British soldiers were wounded or had lost their lives.

The shop door opened and a stout man in his fifties walked up to the counter.

'That wa' a victory for t'British t'other day at Wipers,' the wire worker who had come to collect his mended boots spouted as though he'd personally seen off the Germans. 'We're stopping 'em rightly. Honour an' justice, that's what it's all about.' The spit in Darcy's mouth turned sour.

'It's pronounced Yeeps,' she snapped, 'and I doubt the wives and mothers of those lads who were killed there would see it that way.' She slammed his boots on the counter. 'And for your information, it wasn't a victory.'

'Aye, well, you win some you lose some,' he said, without an ounce of compassion as he handed over his money and strutted out of the shop.

It seemed as though every day was a waiting game. How long would it be before Danny had to go and fight for a country that wasn't his?

The shoe shop was doing a brisk trade, John's handmade boots and shoes in demand by his more discerning customers and those who could afford to pay for such a luxury. He was still vacillating about volunteering, although there was great pressure to do so from his pals in the pub who had enlisted and were keen for others to join them.

Darcy had stared into Field Marshal Kitchener's piercing eyes on the posters that were plastered on walls and billboards throughout the town, her own eyes anxious as she read the slogan 'Your Country Needs You'. Was his pointing finger aimed at men like her Danny? She dreaded the thought of him enlisting and tried not to think about it, but the worry never really left her. Married life was wonderful, each day and night bringing them closer, and the thought of living without him was beyond bearing.

As well as making sweet music in bed, they sang together, Danny teaching Darcy songs from his country, and in return she taught him to sing the old English and Irish folk songs that she had learned from her nanny. They also sang the popular songs that were on everybody's lips. Life was sweet, but far too often affairs that were happening in the wider world managed to spoil it.

'I'm sick of hearing the words "honour" and "justice" and reading about "national pride",' she cried as she stormed into the workshop for a pair of shoes a customer was waiting for in the shop.

John raised his eyebrows at her outburst. 'You'll hear an' read a lot more before it's all over.' Pragmatic as usual, John didn't encourage high drama. 'Mrs Walton's shoes are over there.' He pointed to a shelf. 'Charge her a bob.'

When they closed the shop, John told Darcy he was going to the pub for a pint.

He might have sounded disinterested when Darcy had let off steam, but in truth he was giving serious thought to what he was going to do. Not a day went by without one of his mates going missing from the taproom in the Dyer and Miller. Only last night he'd remarked on not seeing Smoky Brown for a day or two.

'Joined up,' Willie, the landlord, had replied as he pulled John's pint of stout. 'Him an' Billy Rothery an' Sam Sykes all went off to Catterick.'

John entered the smoke-filled bar wondering who would be missing this time.

Deep in thought, he sipped his stout, and although he hated the thought of leaving his beloved Betsy and darling Angela, he arrived at a decision. He'd wait until Christmas, and if the war wasn't over by then, he'd volunteer. He shared his thoughts with Danny when he joined him in the pub after attending a rehearsal for the concert in The Canterbury. Danny agreed to do the same.

'It will break my heart to leave my Darcy but I will not let you go alone, John.'

'I'd appreciate your company,' John replied gruffly. He called for two more pints.

On their way back to Pellon Lane, they were walking down Northgate when a young woman came hurrying towards them. As she drew abreast of them, she plucked a white feather from the bunch in her hand then thrust it at Danny. 'Shame on you,' she snarled. She was in the act of extracting another feather, to give it to John, when he stayed her hand.

'Hold on, lass. Not so quick. We might not be in uniform but we will be any day now, so stick your feathers in your hat, love, an' leave us in peace.' His tone of voice brooked no contradiction and the girl dodged by him in search of another man she would accuse of not doing his duty to king and country.

John and Danny exchanged concerned glances.

'She thinks I am a coward,' said Danny, his voice high with disappointment.

'Me an' all, lad. An' I think that says it all. It leaves us wi' no option but to do what we agreed to in the pub. Come Christmas I'm enlisting, like it or not.'

They walked on in silence, each man lost in his own thoughts.

Outside the house in Pellon Lane, John caught Danny by the arm and gave him a stern look. 'No point in mentioning owt to t'lasses just yet,' he said, 'it might never happen.'

* * *

'When it's Danny's turn to sing I'm going to clap louder than anybody,' Angela announced to Darcy, Betsy and John as they took their seats in the long, narrow room that was The Canterbury. They sat facing the small stage on one of the plain wooden benches with ledges fixed to the backs of the seats to hold pint pots and spirit glasses.

John took a swig of his beer and, placing it back on the ledge, he grinned at his excited daughter, but Betsy frowned. 'You'll behave like a proper young lady. Remember where you are.' Betsy wasn't used to going to the theatre and she felt slightly in awe of some of the rather grand people in the audience.

Darcy's eyes roamed the crowded room, pleased to see that a

large number of the audience seemed to belong to the better off. She hoped that Danny would make a good enough impression for them to ask him to sing at weddings or the concerts they often held in their own homes. He had already performed at three weddings since his own, Darcy delighted, for the money he earned meant that he didn't have to sing in the streets as often in the bitter, wet weather coming up to Christmas.

The lights went down, the noisy audience falling silent as the show began. A small choir of lusty singers opened with a rendition of 'O, Come All Ye Faithful', then an elderly gentleman recited Rudyard Kipling's 'Gunga Din'. He was followed by a fat soprano with a rather wobbly vibrato. Angela had to smother her giggles, and Betsy gave her a warning nudge. As one act was followed by another, Darcy's mouth got drier and drier, even though she had a glass of lemonade to sip. She sat with her hands clenched in fists, pressing them against her chin in silent prayer.

Danny strolled onto the stage, looking extremely dashing in the green velvet jacket he had worn at their wedding. He seemed supremely confident as he gave the audience a warm smile. When he addressed them, Darcy noticed that he deliberately stressed his Italian accent, and she gave a little smile. Crafty Danny. She had been charmed by it, and now he was charming the men and women waiting for him to sing.

The pianist rattled the keys and Danny's voice soared. 'O Sole Mio' received rapturous applause and 'La Donna è Mobile' almost brought the house down. As the audience clapped and cheered, Danny's eyes searched the benches. When he spotted Darcy, he beckoned for her to join him on the stage. She looked aghast. They hadn't planned this. Her heart pounded against her ribs and a shiver ran down her spine. As she dithered, half in and half out of her seat, Danny spoke softly to the crowd.

'Your country is not my country, but you have made me so

welcome with your generosity of spirit that I feel I belong here. We are at war with Germany, but no matter what our enemies do they will not stop us making our beautiful music.'

Someone in the audience shouted, 'Well said,' and others clapped.

'Me and my beautiful wife make beautiful music,' Danny continued, 'and so I ask her to join me to sing for you a song that is dear to all our hearts.'

Her knees trembling, Darcy mounted the stage to stand beside him. He grasped her hand and whispered in her ear. She nodded. Now she knew what to do. She sang 'Till the Boys Come Home', her sweet soprano blending with Danny's magnificent tenor as they raised their voices to the rafters. As the final strains rose to a victorious crescendo, there wasn't a dry eye in the house, and the clapping and cheering and stamping of feet could be heard streets away. Danny raised Darcy's hand to his lips, then together they took their final bows.

* * *

'Bloody hell! The pair of you certainly know how to capture your audience,' John remarked as they walked back to Pellon Lane. 'You were magnificent.'

'I've never been so proud in all my life,' Betsy gushed, and Angela shouted over her, 'You were the best in the concert.'

Darcy, her arm linked in Danny's, was walking on air, the exhilarating feeling making her dizzy with joy. 'But why did you do that?' she squealed.

'So that they know you, too, make beautiful music and they will ask you back to sing again for them. You will sing for them and for me when I'm not here.'

Darcy stopped walking. Her euphoria of a moment ago fizzled and died.

'What do you mean "not here"?'

They had all come to a standstill.

'What he means, lass, is this. The war isn't going to be over by Christmas, as they said it would be. Danny an' me will have to go an' fight.' John's voice was flat and he'd lowered it so that Angela, skipping ahead of them, wouldn't hear.

'He is right.' Danny looked grimly at Darcy. 'We cannot stand by and let others fight for us.'

'You can't mean that, John.' Betsy began to weep. He put his arm round her and she sagged against his shoulder, mumbling, 'It's less than two weeks to Christmas.'

'I know, love, but I can't see it ending afore then, an' it's only right that we go.'

The wonderful evening had been ruined and they walked on in silence.

* * *

'I don't want you to go,' Darcy whispered against Danny's bare chest as they lay in bed. 'We've only just really and truly found each other and I don't think I can live without you.'

'You might have to, even if I don't join up. If the Germans invade Britain, who can tell what will happen to any of us? It will break my heart to leave you, but I must do whatever I can to keep you safe,' he said, cupping her face in his hands. 'Don't cry. Let us live for the time we have left together. Let us be happy.'

Danny made love to her so sweetly and tenderly that Darcy thought her heart would break into a million pieces.

16

Abe Earnshaw slammed the door of the solicitor's office and lumbered across the busy street in Brighouse to the Black Bull public house. Another wasted journey had put him in a filthy temper. Over the past few months he'd trekked from one town to another in the vicinity of Bradley Brigg, calling on one solicitor after another, each one informing him that they held no documents appertaining to the late Thomas Earnshaw or his daughter, Darcy. This last call had been to the offices of Farrar and Son in Briggate.

From the window of his office looking out into Briggate, young Albert Farrar watched Abe enter the pub. Abe Earnshaw was an unpleasant piece of work if ever he'd met one, Albert thought, a little smile quirking his lips. No wonder the late Thomas Earnshaw had insisted that his brother should not be privy to the will he had left with Farrar and Son before his death. Albert had followed Thomas's instructions to the letter.

The only problem was that he had been unable to trace Darcy Earnshaw and make her aware of the will's contents. He had called at the sawmill in Bradley Brigg shortly after the girl had turned eighteen only to be told by the manager, a Mr Harry Chadwick, that Darcy Earnshaw had suddenly left Bradley Brigg three years before and that he didn't know where she had gone. 'There's summat not right about it,' the manager had said, 'and if you want to find her, the only one that can tell you where she is is Abe Earnshaw.' His lip had curled malevolently as he had added 'You'd best ask him what he's done with her.' The manager had stamped off, and Albert's suspicions had been aroused.

He supposed that he could have asked Abe if he knew where his niece had gone, but bearing in mind his late client's instructions regarding his brother, Albert had a nasty feeling about Abe Earnshaw. Better to wait and see if the girl turned up of her own accord. She most likely would now that she had attained her majority. Albert went and sat back down at his desk to deal with more pressing matters. Christmas Eve was less than two weeks away and he wanted to clear his desk before taking a holiday.

Abe stamped into the Black Bull's taproom. 'Give me a brandy,' he snapped, his surly attitude so apparent that the landlord, normally a chatty fellow, served the drink without saying a word. Abe took a seat by the window, scowling through it whilst he plotted his next move. It was imperative that he found the documents stating his brother's wishes, and when he did he'd destroy them. But a more pressing issue was to find the blasted girl and put an end to her making a claim on the sawmill.

He drained his glass and stamped back out onto the street. At the rear of the pub, he collected his pony and trap. It had snowed earlier in the week and slush and patches of ice meant the roads were treacherous, the poor nag slipping and stumbling and suffering Abe's ire all the way back to Bradley Brigg.

He decided to break up the journey by stopping at the Olde Ship Inn.

'I thought I'd find you here,' he snarled at the big, burly fellow lounging against the counter, a pint of ale in his hand. 'I'm paying you good money to look for her, and you'll not find her here, you lazy lout.'

Seth Senior looked at Abe over the rim of his glass. He downed a mouthful of beer then set his glass on the bar, his lips twisting into a sneer. 'I'm doin' all I can,' he growled. 'I've asked after 'er in every bloody town an' village for twenty miles round here an' nubbdy's seen or heard of her.' He pointed to his empty glass. 'An' you can get me another pint an' pay me a bit extra if you want me to keep lookin'.'

Abe slammed the flat of his hand on the counter. 'You've not looked bloody hard enough an' you're getting no more money from me,' he roared, quickly turning tail as Seth raised his meaty fist. 'I'm done with you!'

Abe got back in the trap and lashed the poor pony all the way back to Northcrop House. He regretted having lost his temper with Seth. It had been difficult enough finding someone who was willing to snatch a girl off the street and bring her back against her will. Now, he'd have to go in search of another petty criminal to do his dirty work. He regularly frequented the slums in and around Bradley Brigg in search of young girls or boys who, for a few pence, would satisfy his needs, but it went against the grain to have to deal with grown men. If word got out that he was dallying with such low-life characters as Seth Senior, his reputation would be ruined.

'Damn and blast,' he cursed out loud, entering the empty house and going straight for the brandy bottle. Slumped on the couch in the dismal parlour, he sat drinking and fuming. As the drink took hold, Abe's anger turned to self-pity. If the girl had played her cards right, they could have been living here quite happily, he told himself, his maudlin thoughts conjuring up a picture of Darcy attending to his every need and he treating her kindly. He opened his trousers, his hand massaging his manhood as he imagined her pretty face and her pert breasts.

'I'd have given her a share in the bloody sawmill if only she'd seen sense,' he grunted as he reached a climax. Then, as his euphoria dissipated, he began calling Darcy every foul name he could think of. 'You bloody stuck-up, ungrateful little whore,' he roared to the empty room. By God, when he found her he'd make her pay for all the trouble she was causing him.

He staggered to his feet, his face livid and his thoughts black. She couldn't hide forever. He'd hunt her down if it were the last thing he did. He stumbled up the stairs to his bed and crawled into it fully clothed, his brain in turmoil as he tried to make sense of where he had gone wrong. He, who had believed that cheating Darcy out of her inheritance was a simple matter of applying guile and authority, had been outwitted by his brother, who had obviously gone to great lengths to hide his will from him. And did Darcy know where it was deposited? The disappearance of that chit of a girl meant that he couldn't force her to divulge its whereabouts – and he would have done if he could. And all the while, he'd had to suffer that nosy bastard Harry Chadwick's suspicious looks and interfering questions. It was beyond bearing.

* * *

Darcy and Betsy entered the house in Pellon Lane, their cheeks rosy from the chill wind and their baskets heavy with all sorts of goodies. They were in a merry mood, having just spent the afternoon doing the first of their Christmas shopping. They'd had great fun choosing a Pollock's toy theatre for Angela and some colouring books and crayons. They had also purchased baubles for the real spruce tree that John was going to get from one of his customers, and Darcy had bought Danny a broad-brimmed black felt hat.

'We'd best hide these before Angela gets back,' Betsy said, lifting the gifts from her basket and handing them to Darcy. 'Put them in your room. She'll not think to go hunting there.'

'I wouldn't put it past her.' Darcy chuckled. 'Do you remember last year when you hid the doll in the airing cupboard. She found it the day after.'

Betsy giggled. 'She's a right little madam, make no mistake.'

'Put the kettle on whilst I take these upstairs. I'm as dry as a bone.'

They were sitting down by the fire with their tea when Danny arrived back.

His face was pinched with cold despite the warm red scarf wound several times round his neck and a thick overcoat he had bought from the Cohen and Morris's pawnbroker's shop in King Street. Danny liked the good old-fashioned clothes such establishments sold. A newspaper stuck out of his pocket.

'Brrr!' He shivered. 'I love your country but I hate your winters.'

'Come and sit by the fire. I'll get you a cup of tea to warm you up.' Darcy got to her feet, pecked his cold cheek and went to fetch another cup.

'Where is little Angela?'

Betsy seemed not to notice the seriousness in Danny's tone. 'Gone to a tea party at Suzie Crossley's. Suzie's dad's bringing her home about six.'

Danny shrugged out of his coat and unwound his scarf, relieved that the little girl wasn't present, and his usually smiling face was solemn as he hung up his coat. He took the newspaper out of his pocket then went and sat in front of the fire. Darcy handed him his tea and sat back down. Danny cupped his hands round the mug to warm them, then looking first at Darcy then at Betsy and back to Darcy he said, 'Have you not heard the news?'

Darcy flashed him a smile. 'What news?'

'Here, in the *Evening Courier*,' he said, rustling the newspaper. 'The Germans have bombed Scarborough, Hartlepool and Whitby.'

'Scarborough!' Darcy gasped. Betsy let out a loud wail. Scarborough was a seaside town they had both visited, and although it was more than seventy miles away, it made the war seem very close. They stared at Danny, aghast.

'And Whitby and Hartlepool.' His face crumpled. 'I sing in both those towns.'

Darcy snatched the newspaper from his hand. She scanned the front page, her eyes widening in horror. 'They bombed the Grand Hotel in Scarborough. I stayed there once with my father.' Tears sprang to her eyes. 'It says 119 innocent men, women and children were killed.' Her voice cracking, she carried on reading. 'The bombs on Hartlepool killed over one hundred and left nearly five hundred injured, and in Whitby a bomb landed on the Abbey.' Sheer disbelief masked her face as she looked at her husband. 'The Germans are getting nearer, Danny.'

Betsy was weeping, but when she heard the door handle rattle she quickly dried her eyes on the hem of her dress and hissed, 'That'll be Angela. Don't say owt to her. I don't want her frightening.'

Angela burst through the door bringing a draught of cold air with her. The bitter chill had nipped her little nose bright red but she was all smiles. 'Suzie's party was smashing, and I won pass the parcel,' she piped, 'and guess what?' Her big, brown eyes were dancing. 'Miss Chippendale says I'm to be Mary in the Christmas pageant and give birth to the baby Jesus.' She tossed her coat onto the nearest chair then went and sat by her mother, awfully pleased with herself.

Somehow, her mother, Darcy and Danny all managed to smile and make congratulatory comments but their thoughts still dwelt on the newspaper report. A war that they had thought of as taking place in towns and cities they had never before heard of had come home.

* * *

Christmas Day dawned bright and sunny but bitterly cold. After a hearty breakfast of bacon and eggs, the Carvers and Darcy and Danny attended the service in the church where the young couple had married. A light covering of snow had fallen during the night making the drab, soot-stained streets look pretty under their white mantle. No smoke belched from the mill chimneys, the air fresh and the sky blue.

'You'd never believe there was a war going on,' Darcy said as they crunched along the pavements. 'On a morning like this the world seems perfect.'

'No talk of war today, *mia bellissima*.' Danny squeezed her hand. 'Today is for happy celebration.'

'Aye, no matter what comes after, we'll make this a Christmas to remember,' John said, his warm breath clouding in front of him. 'An' can we walk a bit faster? It's proper brass monkeys out here.'

The others laughed and quickened their pace.

The church service was uplifting. They sang their hearts out. Then, after trooping back to Pellon Lane, stopping for a snowball fight on the way, they kicked the snow off their boots and pulled off coats, gloves and scarves, ready to put the finishing touches to the Christmas dinner. Darcy and Betsy had peeled potatoes, chopped carrots and parsnips and pared sprouts the night before. They'd made sage and onion stuffing and, before leaving for church, the stuffed goose had been put in the fireside oven to roast.

'Can I open another present before we have us dinner?' Angela gazed longingly at the wrapped presents under the tree that she and Darcy had trimmed with red and golden baubles and glittering tinsel. Betsy had allowed her to open one gift before breakfast and she'd been thrilled with her colouring book and crayons.

'Go on then,' her mother said as she mashed potatoes into a fluffy heap.

Angela squealed her delight when she saw the toy theatre. Whilst Darcy and Betsy set the table then loaded the plates with vegetables, Danny and John helped Angela build the cardboard theatre and arrange the little paper people on the stage. Darcy kept one eye on filling the plates and the other on the three people knelt by the fire acting out a little play, her heart swelling with love. There might be a war on, and Danny and John might have to go and fight, but for now they were here together and that was all that mattered. And when they all sat down at the table and John carved the goose, she vowed to make this a Christmas filled with joy and laughter and love.

17

John Carver and Danilo Cappelini enlisted on the 26 January 1915, two days after the naval battle of Dogger Bank and the day after the muted celebration of Darcy's nineteenth birthday. Once again it seemed that the Germans were very close at hand, the site of the battle being in the sea that lapped England's north-east coast, the same sea that holidaymakers from Halifax and the surrounding towns let their children paddle in when they made their annual Wakes Week visit. It seemed that the enemy was one step nearer to marching through the streets of Halifax.

Late into the night, John and Danny had mulled over the decision to enlist. The depressing news of British soldiers fighting in the trenches, up to their knees in mud, and the black-edged death lists in the papers lengthening by the day left them with little doubt that they had to do their duty.

'We can't just stand by an' watch the kaiser's mob take over our country,' John said. 'If we don't join up now, we might be too late to do owt about it.' He gazed forlornly about his comfortable home, the thought of leaving Betsy and Angela tearing at his heart.

'I will do anything for our loved ones. I will give my life for them.' Tears sprang to Danny's dark eyes as he spoke. He was already missing his beloved Darcy.

The next morning Danny and John joined the queue of men outside the Drill Hall. They were fewer and quieter than those who had enlisted in the first flush of enthusiasm between September and Christmas, when spirits had been high and the rush to fight for king and country had brought them flocking to sign up. They now knew the gory details of fighting in the trenches, and many of them had already lost a brother, a cousin or a good friend.

'I can do this,' Danny muttered as he watched a young lad emerge from the hall waving his papers with one hand and raising the pocket Bible issued to all new recruits. A smattering of cheers from the queue made the lad smile as he marched off down the street.

'Here we go,' said John, as the soldier on the door beckoned them in. Another soldier directed John to a desk on the right of the long room. The elderly sergeant behind the desk looked up.

'A big, strong lad like you is just what the British Army needs,' he said, his eyes admiring John's strapping physique.

The recruiting officer at a desk to the left of the room raised his eyebrows and gave Danny a quizzical look. 'Italian, eh? Your country's declared neutrality.'

'I know,' Danny replied, 'but England is now my country.'

In a room off the main hall, John and Danny were ordered to strip down, their fine physiques causing the army doctors to exchange glances. 'These two look as fit as butcher's dogs,' one murmured to another as they set about weighing and measuring them. It made a change from seeing puny, underfed men who were prematurely aged by the long hours they worked in unhealthy conditions in the mills and manufactories.

When an army doctor cupped Danny's balls in his hand then

asked him to cough, John gave Danny a saucy wink. Then it was John's turn. Behind the doctor's back, Danny cupped his hands and pretended to stagger under the weight. John laughed out loud and the doctor looked up at him, surprised.

A bony little lad of about seventeen who was watching burst into a song of his own making. 'Balls to the kaiser, balls to the Hun—'

'Cut that out,' yelled the sergeant overseeing the proceedings.

The lad grinned cheekily. 'Wi' fellows wi' balls like them two have got, I reckon we'll give the Hun a run for his money.'

Amidst laughter, John and Danny dressed and went back into the main hall. They stood alongside the other recruits as the padre solemnly inducted them. Then they were back out on the street, no longer a cobbler and a singer but soldiers in the Duke of Wellington's West Riding Regiment.

'I can't really believe this is happening,' Darcy said as she undressed that night. She had done her best to be brave when Danny and John had returned making jokes about what they would look like in uniform. She tried to convince herself that they might never be sent to where the war was being fought. Betsy had spent much of the past two days silently weeping, John comforting her with positive words, then begging her to pull herself together for Angela's sake. Now, as she slipped into bed, Darcy felt wearied by it all.

'Where is it you have to report to?' She already knew the answer but she wanted to fix in her mind where her beloved husband would be when he left her in two days' time.

'Clipstone,' Danny replied, shucking off his trousers. 'It's a training camp in Nottinghamshire. That's not too far away, is it?'

Darcy shook her head. It might as well be a million miles away.

Danny climbed into bed and took her in his arms. She laid her head on his chest, listening to the steady beat of his heart and thinking how much she would miss the feel of him when the bed was half empty. Danny was stroking her hair but she could tell that his thoughts were elsewhere. *He doesn't want to go any more than I want him to*, she told herself, trying to think of something to say that might ease his pain.

'You might get to stay in England,' she said, recalling a conversation she had had with a customer in the shop. 'Mrs Shaw's son is stationed in Blyth and he told her that his regiment won't ever be sent overseas. They'll stay here to protect our shores.' She propped her elbow on the pillow the better to see Danny's face, hopeful that he would see the possibility in what she had just told him.

He gazed back at her, his eyes warm with love and understanding. He knew she was trying to look on the bright side for both their sakes. 'You could be right,' he said, pulling her gently back down then straddling her, 'but for now I am here and we will make love like there is no tomorrow.'

Their lovemaking, familiar now as drawing her daily breath, took Darcy to a place where nothing else mattered and war didn't exist. But later, after Danny had fallen asleep, she let the tears that she had been holding at bay trickle silently down her cheeks and into her pillow.

* * *

They spent the next morning in a flurry of packing, John having to remind Betsy that the army would provide everything he needed. 'Just some underwear an' me shaving kit is all I'm taking,' he'd said, laughing when, with a forlorn look on her face, she came out of their bedroom carrying his good suit. 'I'm going to war, love, not a wedding.' This jocular remark brought fresh tears.

'Put these in your bags.' Darcy handed John three photographs of him and his wife and daughter that she had taken in the People's Park with her Box Brownie camera the summer before. John leafed through them, his eyes moistening. He brushed away the threatening tears with the back of his hand. To Danny she gave the photographs captured on their wedding day: one of her in her wedding dress and two of them as a married couple. He tucked them into the pocket of his jacket next to his heart.

The rest of that day was spent being as kind and thoughtful and loving as any family could be. Later, in the privacy of their bedroom, John Carver made love to his wife Betsy, and in the room across the landing Danilo Cappelini made love to Darcy, each couple stamping the touch, taste and scent of their beloved partners deep into their memories to carry with them through the long and lonely days when they were apart.

* * *

Early the next morning, it was a solemn little group that walked to Halifax train station, Angela swinging on her dad's arm and Betsy clinging to John's other arm like a drowning man clings to a rock in a windswept sea. Darcy and Danny walked behind, arms linked and their bodies pressed close, neither of them saying much in case the tears clogging their throats spilled over.

They arrived at the station just as a train was leaving, clouds of steam and the acrid smell of smoke and oil thickening the air under the roof. On the platform a gamut of emotions was playing out: smiling faces and whoops of joy greeting loved ones who had just arrived home on leave, and muffled weeping or wails of distress from those saying goodbye.

Darcy and Danny and the Carvers found a space in amongst the crowd. Darcy stood almost in a trance, drained of emotion as she watched another train chug into the station. The doors flew open and gaunt, weary, mud-caked soldiers tumbled out. Home for a week or two from the unspeakable hell they had left behind. They fell into the arms of those waiting to greet them. *This could be us in a few months' time,* she thought, and shivered.

A group of soldiers in clean uniforms stood nearby. They'd had their leave and were now returning to battle. They eyed the new recruits with expressions ranging from sceptical to pitying. One of them, a stocky fellow wearing his cap at a jaunty angle, turned and addressed Danny. 'I hope tha's not freetened of a bit o' mud an' rats as big as bloody cats,' he said, grinning.

'Aye. Or gettin' your bloody head shot off if tha looks over t'top o' t'trench,' his mate growled, his face bitter as he stamped out his cigarette butt.

Darcy felt Danny give a little shiver, but he grinned back at the soldiers. 'I'll try to remember not to do that,' he said cheerfully. 'I want to keep my head.'

'We all do, lad, but t'bloody kaiser wants 'em on a plate, so you take care.'

'Where are you returning to?' Darcy's curiosity was aroused. She wanted to hear what it was like from the horse's mouth.

'Wipers,' the stocky chap replied, his face grim. 'An' don't ask what it wa' like, lass, 'cos it doesn't bear bloody thinkin' abaht. Pardon my French, miss.'

Darcy knew he meant Ypres, and she shuddered. She'd read about the battle in the papers. 'Well, good luck, wherever you go next,' she said sincerely.

Men were now boarding the train standing at the platform, their wives, mothers or sweethearts clinging on to them to the very last minute or reaching through open windows to those who had already boarded.

'Well, this is us,' John said, taking Betsy in his arms and kissing her. 'Look after yourself, love, and you...' He swung Angela up into his arms. 'You look after your mam for me an' be a good girl.'

Up until now Angela had been too excited by the bustle and the noise to realise the seriousness of her dad's departure. She wrapped her arms round his neck. 'Don't go, Dad, don't go! Stay with us,' she sobbed.

Holding back his own tears, John set her down. 'I have to, love, but I'll be back as soon as I can.' He drew his wife and daughter into a last fond embrace. Then he hugged Darcy. 'Take care of 'em for me, Darcy. I know I can rely on you to help Betsy get through this.' He ruffled her hair. 'You're a good lass, allus have been.' He walked over to the train then stood by an open door waiting for Danny.

Danny held Darcy tightly, and she could feel his heart thudding in tandem with her own as his lips caressed her eyes and cheeks and then fastened on her mouth. In between fervent kisses they promised to love one another forever.

The train whistle blew with a piercing shriek that penetrated every fibre of Darcy's being and she let go of him. Paralysed, she watched as he and John boarded the train. Porters ran along the platform slamming doors, and with a grinding of wheels and huge puffs of steam, the train snaked away.

'Come on, Betsy, let's go home.' Darcy offered her arm to the weeping woman then turned to Angela. The little girl was still waving and crying even though the train was now a speck in the distance. 'Hold your mam's hand – we don't want to lose you – and on the way home we'll stop at D'Agostino's and get ice creams.'

18

Darcy was feeling the weight of responsibility as she got ready to go and open the shoe shop. It was only a week since Danny and John had left for Clipstone. She had lit the fire, made the breakfast, tidied the kitchen, hung the washing out to dry and walked Angela to school, and now she was feeling guilty at leaving Betsy alone in the house.

Betsy was slumped in the chair by the fire wringing one hand round the other. Darcy felt a stab of impatience. It wasn't that she didn't feel sorry for Betsy. She loved her, but she knew that it wasn't healthy to let her sit and wallow in grief, refusing to eat or take care of her appearance. And it was certainly having a bad effect on Angela. The little girl had wept on her way to school.

'Why is my mam so sad? I know she doesn't like it when my dad's not here, but he's coming back soon, isn't he?' Angela's voice had risen an octave, her big, brown eyes begging Darcy for reassurance.

'She'll be as right as rain in a day or two,' Darcy had lied. 'She's just not used to being without your dad. You wait, once she gets a letter from him she'll be grand.'

Darcy hadn't believed a word of it, but now as she pulled on her coat she decided to be cruel to be kind.

'I'm going to open the shop, Betsy, and you're going to stop moping. Sitting crying all day won't bring John back any sooner, so get up out of that chair, get yourself washed, and if it looks like it'll rain, bring that washing in.'

Aching at the harshness of her words, Darcy flounced out of the house.

In the quiet of the empty shoe shop she stood and gazed at the shelves. The manufacturer in Nottingham was too busy making boots for the army to bother with deliveries to a small business likes John's, and their stock of ready-made shoes was depleted. John had left her with instructions to try and sell as much of their stock as she could and then close the shop until he returned. Their attempts to find someone to take over the repairs had proved fruitless. Like every other town in the country, Halifax had sent its men to war.

The town was changing by the week, the streets almost devoid of younger men, and in the mills and manufactories women were doing the jobs that their husbands and sons had once done; shopping for shoes was no longer a priority.

Darcy picked up a duster and polished the counter, the silence from the workshop playing on her nerves. She so missed the hammering and tapping and the click-clack of John's sewing machine that she felt like crying. She was also regretting having spoken so harshly to Betsy. Supposing she had made things worse, perhaps causing Betsy to do something foolish. The thought sent a shiver down her spine.

The shop doorbell rang. Darcy pasted a smile on her face. 'Good morning, can I help you? What is it you're looking for?'

The stout, middle-aged woman wore a cross-over pinny under

her open coat, the turban covering her hair denoting her as a mill worker.

'A pair of strong black shoes with rubber soles,' the woman replied. 'I've just started back at the weaving in Bentley's mill an' I need summat on me feet that'll stop me slippin' on them greasy floors.'

Darcy cast a doubtful glance at the shoes on display. 'I'm sorry, we don't have anything like that,' she said, looking at the dainty shoes on the shelves.

The woman left, disappointed.

By midday she hadn't had another customer, and her nerves were playing havoc with her mind. She shouldn't have chastised Betsy like that. But she'd been desperate. It was bad enough nursing her own grief and missing Danny so much that she felt as though she had lost part of herself, but that didn't excuse her lack of compassion. She'd go home and put things right with Betsy.

Locking up the shop, she ran full pelt back up Pellon Lane, dreading what she might be faced with when she got there. She burst into the house calling out, 'Betsy, Betsy! Where are you?'

'In here, love,' Betsy called back, emerging from the kitchen with a tea towel in her hand. She'd changed the stained dress she had been wearing for the past few days and her hair was freshly washed and neatly rolled.

Darcy sagged with relief. 'I'm sorry, Betsy, so sorry for saying those cruel things this morning,' she cried, crossing the room and hugging her.

Betsy hugged her back. 'You've nowt to be sorry for, love. You were right. I wa' being selfish. You must be missing Danny just as much as I'm missing John, but I wa' only thinking of meself.' She grimaced. 'I needed a good talkin' to, an' you gave me one.' She stepped back, smiling. 'You get your coat off an' I'll put t'kettle on.'

Darcy had to choke back her tears. Things were going to be better.

When Angela arrived home from school, she could barely contain her delight at seeing her mam up and about looking clean and tidy. She opened her school bag. 'Miss said that girls whose dads had gone to fight could write letters so I wrote this one.' She flourished a sheet of creased paper.

'It's lovely,' Betsy said, perusing the neatly written words and the drawing of three figures holding hands, big red lips on their faces wearing bright smiles. 'Look at this, Darcy.' She handed her the page.

'That's us,' Angela pointed out, 'letting Dad and Danny know we're getting on all right without them, 'cos we are, aren't we?' She looked anxiously at her mother.

'We are,' said Darcy, hopeful that from now on they would continue to be. 'And you've sent enough kisses to keep your dad and Danny going till they come home on leave,' she added, laughing at the rows of crosses at the bottom of the page. 'We'll put it in an envelope and take it to the post office as soon as your dad or Danny writes to tell us where to send it to.'

The letters arrived two days later just as Darcy, Betsy and Angela were sitting down to breakfast. When the letterbox rattled, Angela scooted to the door and picked them up off the mat. 'One for you, Mam, and one for Darcy.' She handed them over then leaned against Betsy's shoulder as she peeled open the envelope.

'He says his uniform doesn't fit, an' it's rough and itchy,' Betsy read out loud, 'an' he's missing my cooking.' She read on with tears in her eyes, her voice breaking as she said, 'He sends his love to us, Angela, an' says he's missin' us.' John had clearly tried to sound as cheerful as possible, telling them about the big, hairy sergeant who shouted orders and the running they had to do to get fit.

'As if he needs it,' Betsy croaked, 'there's not a fitter man in Halifax.'

'What does Danny say?' Angela was bouncing with excitement.

'Much the same thing,' Darcy replied, wanting to keep Danny's words of love to herself. She could tell from the crossing out of words that he had taken pains to say what he wanted to say, for whilst his spoken English was good – beautiful in fact, with his Italian accent – his command of the written language was sadly lacking. However, Darcy loved every funny turn of phrase and every spelling mistake. She tucked the letter in her pocket. She'd read it again in the privacy of her bedroom where she could savour his thoughts and feelings and store them in her heart.

* * *

'I'm closing the shop for good today,' Darcy announced, setting the teapot on the breakfast table and sitting down to eat her porridge. 'We've hardly any stock left, and what we have is never the right size,' she added glumly. 'It's pointless me standing there all day and not earning a penny.'

Betsy looked dismayed and plopped her spoon back into her dish. 'But what will you do? That bit of money you took eked out the army pay – an' I don't want to dip into our savings. Angela's school fees are due next month.'

'Don't worry about that, Betsy. There's still a small amount of money left over from the sovereigns and I'm going to get a job working for Bentley's at Dunkirk Mill. A woman who came into the shop told me they need more weavers to work the looms. They've got a huge army contract to weave khaki for uniforms.'

'But will you know how to do it?' Betsy had only ever worked for a short while in service before marrying John and couldn't imagine learning something as complex as weaving.

'I'll learn,' Darcy replied stoutly. 'I'm going to the mill first thing tomorrow to see if I can get set on.'

* * *

'You will keep an eye out to see that nobody breaks in and steals the machinery, won't you?' Darcy gave the young constable a dazzling smile. He had happened to be passing the shop as she turned the key in the lock.

'You can put your trust in me, miss,' he replied enthusiastically, at the same time thinking how pretty she was and wondering if he should ask her out.

'It's Mrs, actually. Mrs Cappelini.' Darcy loved her married name and she said it proudly, dashing the young chap's hopes in one fell swoop. 'I'm so glad I can rely on you, constable. You have my heartfelt thanks.'

The young chap looked disappointed. He'd rather have had something more. Saluting her smartly, he strolled on his way.

Darcy hurried up Pellon Lane, feeling immensely pleased with herself. As soon as she was through the door, she carolled, 'I start learning to weave first thing tomorrow morning.'

* * *

Darcy stood outside the gates at Dunkirk Mill feeling rather conspicuous in her neat white blouse and grey skirt. She was surrounded by a horde of chattering girls and women all wearing cross-over pinnies and turbans as they waited for the gates to open. Behind the gates loomed the formidable, grey, three-storeyed building with its towering chimney. No one took any notice of her, and when the hooter blasted out its mournful wail it made her jump. A crabby old man opened the gates. The girls and women surged forward carrying Darcy along with them.

Inside the mill yard the girls and women scurried over the cobbles, their heavy shoes and clogs clattering as one by one they disappeared into different parts of the huge mill. Feeling stranded and rather overwhelmed, Darcy looked around her as she tried to locate the door to the office that she had visited the day before. The gatekeeper slammed the gates shut.

'Atta lost, lass?' he said, turning his rheumy eyes on Darcy. 'Where dust tha want to be?'

'I'm one of the new trainee weavers,' she replied, her voice wobbling.

'Over there. That blue door.' He pointed a gnarled finger at a door in the end of the building. 'There's two already there afore you.'

Darcy thanked him and ran towards the blue door. *Am I late?* she thought, worried that it might make a bad impression on her first day. Catching her breath, she tapped the door. A girl of a similar age opened it. Darcy gave a wan smile and stepped inside the small, dusty office that smelled of raw, greasy wool.

Behind a long counter were shelves holding files and boxes. Samples of fine worsted and hanks of yarn hung from brackets on the walls. In front of the counter stood a plump girl with mousy hair. The tall, red-haired girl who had opened the door went and stood beside her. Darcy noted that they were already wearing aprons and had tied scarves over their hair. Her pinny and scarf were in her bag and she felt rather foolish and unprepared.

Over by the small, grimy window stood a round, motherly woman with fat, rosy cheeks, her meaty arms folded across her ample bosom. Greying wisps of hair peeped from under her brightly coloured turban. Her capacious cross-over pinny covered her plump body from neck to ankle.

'Right! Now we're all here, I'm the "Mrs Weaver" in charge of learning you how to work a loom,' she said, looking the new recruits up and down with a practised eye. 'I'm Lizzie Brocklebank, but you'll address me as missis or Mrs Brocklebank, never just Lizzie. Got that?'

The three girls nodded obediently. Darcy liked the twinkle in her eye and thought she'd enjoy letting this pleasant woman teach her how to weave.

'Now then, lasses, gi' me your names so I know what to call you.'

'Molly Pickersgill,' the plump girl answered.

'Nora Hanlon,' said the red-haired girl.

'Darcy Cappelini.'

'You'll not want to be weavin' in them togs, Darcy. They'll get covered in fluff. Have you got a pinny an' summat to cover your crowning glory? It 'ud be a shame to get that lovely hair of yours tangled up in t'piece your weavin', lass. Looms can be dangerous if you don't take care. Remember that.'

Darcy suddenly recalled the pain she had felt when her Uncle Abe's clawing hand had ripped the hair from her scalp. She shivered and hurriedly pulled on her pinny then knotted her scarf at the back of her head.

'Right, Molly, Nora an' Darcy, let's go an' learn how to weave.'

* * *

Darcy had never been inside a cloth mill before and nothing could have prepared her for the grinding roar and clack of machinery as they entered the weaving shed. The cacophonous din reverberated off the walls and up through the greasy floor like a monstrous beast charging into battle. Shimmering dust motes danced in shafts of sunlight piercing the glass roof, the hazy air catching in the back of her throat.

'This is "Weaver's Alley",' Lizzie Brocklebank bawled as she led the girls down the wide space that separated the rows of looms. 'Mind your heads on them.' She pointed up to the low hanging leather belts attached to the drums and pulleys that powered the looms.

Darcy was struggling to hear what Lizzie was saying, and when she glanced at Nora she could tell that she was having the same trouble. Nora pulled a comical face and tapped her ears. Darcy responded by raising her hands palms upwards and giving a shrug.

On either side of the alley, row upon row of looms were working full tilt, shuttles flying back and forth trailing yarns through warp and weft, weaving heavy khaki cloth. The women at the looms darted their eyes this way and that, keeping a sharp look out for broken threads and empty bobbins as the beaters thrashed faster than the eye could see. Darcy began to have second thoughts. Weaving looked much harder than she had anticipated.

At last they came to the end of the shed. In a space that was separated from the main body of the building, the noise was less and there was no need for Lizzie to shout at the top of her lungs. 'Now, lasses, I'll not be bawlin' me head off like that in future, so you'll all have to learn to read my lips. All t'lasses do it, so when I'm tellin' you summat watch me mouth.'

Six eyes, one pair cornflower blue, one anxious brown, and the other pair flecked with hazel, fixed intently on the 'Mrs Weaver's' lips.

'How to thread a shuttle,' Lizzie mouthed. Then she nodded at each of the girls. 'What did I say?'

'Cow do bread and butter,' Molly stuttered. She looked thoroughly bemused.

Lizzie raised her eyes to the roof.

'Go to bed and shuttle?' Nora asked.

'How to thread a shuttle,' Darcy piped.

'Good lass, Darcy, I can see you'll be a quick learner.' She turned to one of the two looms standing behind her. 'Right, let's make a start.'

'I'm absolutely frazzled.' Darcy flopped into a chair at the table and gave Betsy a weary but triumphant grin. 'Today I've learned what warps and wefts are. I know how to start and stop my loom, and I can load a shuttle and send it whizzing from one side to the other – although I got into an awful mess when the yarn broke and I didn't catch it in time.' She pulled off her scarf and shook her hair free, then stretched her aching neck and shoulders.

'I'm right proud of you, Darcy.' Betsy's eyes glowed with admiration. 'Have a cup of tea, I've just mashed it ready for you coming home.' She lifted the teapot and filled two cups.

'Is it very hard learning to weave?' Angela gave Darcy a sympathetic look.

'It is, but don't you worry. I'll master it, if it kills me.'

19

Learning to weave didn't kill Darcy, and two weeks later she had her own loom in the main part of the weaving shed. She had also made good friends with Nora, the lively redhead. Molly, the plump, quiet new recruit, shunned their company, seeming to prefer to sit with the older women at breakfast and dinner breaks. However, Darcy and Nora got on like a house on fire, and as they chatted they told one another snippets about their lives – but not everything. Darcy didn't divulge Abe Earnshaw's terrible abuse or that she had run away from home.

Nora had the same ready wit as Darcy, making her laugh as she related the capers of her own large family. They discovered that they both enjoyed reading and had something in common with their love lives, Nora's intended already serving in France, and Danny no doubt soon to be sent there.

The war was never far from the minds of the inhabitants of Halifax. The first patriotic frenzy of young men enlisting to take the king's shilling and fight for the honour of their country had faded, and suddenly the streets were almost empty of horse-drawn vehicles, the army commandeering those animals to serve in the front line. Pictures of the king and queen went up in shop windows, but the shopkeepers were finding it increasingly difficult to stock their shelves as supplies ran low, the army's needs taking priority over everything else. The German kaiser had announced in February that he would sink all sailing ships flying the British flag, and submarines were torpedoing the ships carrying goods from across the world. Darcy thanked God that neither Danny nor John had enlisted in the British Navy.

In April 1915, the war turned particularly nasty when the Germans used poison gas for the first time. Nora's Bob wrote to say that the chlorine had made his eyes run and his lungs burn. Tales like these only helped to heighten Darcy's fears.

At the beginning of May, a German U-boat torpedoed the RMS Lusitania, a British ocean liner on her way from New York to Liverpool. She sank off the coast of Southern Ireland with the loss of over a thousand lives. Once again the war seemed to be closing in on the British Isles. The more Darcy read about it in the papers and heard about it at the mill from those who had already lost a family member, the more she feared for Danny's and John's safety.

Each day brought with it something else to worry about.

'Prices are shooting up,' Betsy moaned as Darcy returned from work one day, tired and not in the mood for more misery. 'The price of sugar's doubled and they've put another tuppence on a loaf of bread.'

'Try not to worry, Betsy,' she said wearily. 'I'm earning good money. We'll not go short.'

Another day Darcy arrived home to find Betsy in tears, her face ashen.

'What's the matter?' Darcy's spirits drooped at the thought of yet another problem. Much as she loved Betsy, she sometimes wished she wasn't so fragile.

'It's the Goldsteins,' Betsy wailed, 'you know, the nice old couple that did the tailoring at the top of the road. Somebody burned them out last night. They daubed "Huns get out" on the door, then smashed the windows and threw burning torches inside.'

Darcy quailed. It wasn't that long ago she'd served lovely Mrs Goldstein with a pair of shoes. 'But they've lived here for years,' she cried, 'they're not Huns like the kaiser, even if they are German.' She paused to let the horror sink in, her voice wobbling as she asked, 'Were they killed?'

Betsy shook her head. 'Both of them were badly burned trying to fight the blaze. They're saying he's unlikely to make it.' She bit her lip to stem more tears.

'That was downright wicked,' Angela piped. 'He made my dad's best suit.'

Darcy sat down to eat her tea but she had lost her appetite. When would there be an end to the evil that the world was facing? she wondered. What did the future hold for any of them? Her beloved Danny and lovely John Carver had yet to see action, and every day things just got worse.

* * *

'I had a letter from Bob yesterday,' Nora said as they ate their eight o'clock breakfast sitting out in the mill yard. 'He's been stuck in the trenches somewhere in France for ages – I don't know where exactly 'cos the army put thick black lines through anything that might give the game away if the letters fell into enemy hands – and he says every time they make a bit of progress the Germans drive them back.'

'The government led us to believe this 'ud all blow over by Christmas. Seems like a big, fat lie now,' Darcy replied dismally.

'Aye, and we don't know the half of it. Bob says he's up to his knees in mud all the time 'cos it never stops raining, and he says the food's rotten. I sent him some sweets and a tin of pilchards in my last parcel but I'd have loved to be able to pack a nice bit of ham and some pickles. My Bob loves his food.'

Darcy bit into her cheese sandwich and wondered how Danny would cope in the trenches. He rarely complained about the food or his accommodation at Clipstone, and he had made plenty of new friends. The only thing that seemed to irk him was being told what to do every minute of the day. Danny was a free spirit and had lived that life for so long that obeying someone else's orders day in and day out made him feel trapped.

'I just hope they let Danny and John come home on leave before they send them somewhere else,' she said. 'I miss him so much it hurts.'

'I know how you feel,' Nora groaned, 'but they will give him leave before he goes off to the front. They'll send him back to Wellesley Barracks for a march out. That's what they did with Bob's lot. You'd think with all the flags flying and the band playing they were going off to something smashing. Then they end up in a bloody trench with shells and bullets flying over their heads.'

The hooter wailed, signalling them back to their looms, Darcy quite relieved. The conversation had made her feel depressed.

Back at her loom, watching for loose ends and seeing her piece grow by the inch, she began to sing to cheer herself up.

Nora, at the next loom, caught Darcy's eye. She raised two fingers to her lips. 'What are you saying?' she mouthed, her raised fingers having let Darcy know she was about to speak. Both girls were now adept at lip reading.

'Singing,' Darcy mouthed back. '"Till the Boys Come Home". It's the song me and Danny sang at The Canterbury.' Her corn-flower blue eyes sparkled as she fondly recalled the evening.

Nora looked bemused. Darcy hadn't mentioned that she and

Danny had sung in a proper theatre. Nora grinned then joined in, although not a sound could be heard above the rattle of the looms. Darcy grinned back and raised her thumb.

At dinnertime, out in the yard again, sitting with the women from the weaving shed, Nora quizzed Darcy. 'Go on then, tell us,' she said, her hazel eyes alight with curiosity. 'What was that about you and Danny singing at The Canterbury?'

Nora already knew that Darcy had worked with John on the streets, collecting the money as he performed his feats. 'I've seen him. He's fantastic,' she'd said at the time, admitting that she would have loved to do something like that instead of standing behind a counter in Wadsworth's dress shop serving snooty ladies. However, in her typically modest manner, Darcy hadn't mentioned anything about singing in between John's acts. Now, she went on to tell Nora about how she'd sung to keep the crowds entertained. Then she told her about the weddings Danny had been asked to sing at, and finally about the concert at The Canterbury.

Nora was suitably impressed. 'Oy, did you hear that, lasses?' she called to the other women. 'We've got a singing star among us.' She flicked her thumb at Darcy.

The women stopped their chatter and all eyes turned on Darcy. She blushed, embarrassed to be the centre of attention.

'Go on then, give us a song. Sing summat to cheer us up,' a voice cried.

'Aye, go on, lass! Don't be shy. Let's hear you,' the women chorused.

Darcy went hot and cold. It seemed rude to refuse. But what should she sing? They wouldn't want a ballad telling of lost love and dreams. These were rough, tough women who called a spade a spade. They'd want something rollicking, something they all knew.

Suddenly she had an idea. She often listened to the popular music on the wireless, and now she recalled a song that she'd heard many times before. Fortunately for her, she had only to hear a song a couple of times for her to commit the tune and the words to memory, but the song she now had in mind wasn't the sort she had ever sung in public.

She jumped to her feet. If she had to sing she'd give it all she'd got.

Swinging her feet and stretching out her arms then twisting round and round she gave them her version of 'Ballin' the Jack'.

Her sweet, strong voice accompanied by the actions to the words soared above the rumble and rattle in the mill yard. The women exchanged glances of admiration, one shouting, 'By! She's better than Marie Lloyd,' and another calling out, 'Good on you, lass, you're a fair treat.'

Darcy carried on singing. By the time she got to the second chorus the women roared their approval and, as one, they were up on their feet copying her actions and singing and dancing along with her. Darcy allowed herself a grin of triumph and gave Nora a saucy wink. Nora winked back, bursting with pride at her friend's success.

'Hey up! What's all this?' The chief overlooker barged out of the weaving shed, looking askance at the cavorting women. When they saw him, some of the women raised two fingers in a V shape and sneered at him. God hadn't blessed George Thwaite when he made him, his scrawny body and slack mouth below a beaked nose and eyes like slits a most unpleasant sight as he leered back at the women.

'Bugger off back to your cave,' Darcy heard Florrie Moorhouse yell. She had noticed that Florrie was always having run-ins with the overlooker; rumour was that she bore him a grudge from way back when she had been much younger.

George glowered at Florrie, his glare turning to one of utter fury as Dolly Murgatroyd shouted, 'We're ballin' the Jack, Mister Thwaite, an' afore long we'll be jackin' your balls.'

George's eyes stood out on stalks as the women, roaring with laughter, cheered Dolly on. The hooter blared.

'Get inside an' get to bloody work the lot of you,' George roared, his back pressed against the shed door as the sniggering women trooped past him back to their looms. As Darcy drew level with him he caught her arm. 'It wa' you that started that. You want to be careful, or else you'll have me to deal with,' he snarled.

'Yes, Mr Thwaite,' Darcy sounded contrite. She knew fine well that he could make her life a misery if he so chose. He had the power to determine whether or not her pieces were up to standard, and should he choose to find fault, he could dock her wages or give her shoddy yarn that would keep breaking, thereby making her job twice as difficult. It paid to keep on the right side of George Thwaite.

But Darcy was damned if she was going to let him intimidate her, and whenever the women asked her to sing during their dinner breaks, she did so.

One day, as she was giving them her rendition of 'If I Had My Way', Joseph Bentley, the mill's owner, happened to be crossing the yard. He paused to listen. The women let Darcy sing the song through, then they all joined in to sing it again. George Thwaite was lolling against the weaving shed door looking sour.

'You are in good voice, ladies,' Joseph Bentley called out. 'It pleases me that I have such a happy workforce.' He went on his way.

After that, George kept his mouth shut but it didn't prevent him from glaring at Darcy whenever their paths crossed.

* * *

Molly Pickersgill fumbled with the empty shuttle on her loom, her eyes darting this way and that as she looked out for a tuner to rethread the shuttle. She hated having to suck the thread through the shuttle's eye, the fluff going down into her throat and making her cough. She was also keeping an eye out for George Thwaite, dreading that at any moment he might appear and give her the nod.

He had been nice to her at first, helping her fix her mistakes and keeping Lizzie Brocklebank off her back. The 'Mrs Weaver' had already warned her that if she didn't improve she'd have to give her notice. But Molly desperately needed the job to support her and her mother, her father having died a short while ago. When George had offered his assistance, she'd readily accepted even though she hadn't liked the way his grimy hands kept coming into contact with her plump backside and ample bosom. She'd tried to brush his unwanted advances aside, pretending it didn't matter, but just lately he had begun expecting more than a casual fumble. He'd told her in no uncertain terms that if she wanted to keep her job then she had to do something for him in return. Twice in the last week he'd ordered her to go out to the women's closets, where he had taken advantage of her.

Now, with no tuner in sight and the added threat of Lizzie Brocklebank appearing and finding Molly's loom idle, she shuddered at the memory of the disgusting things the overlooker had forced her to do. For two pins she'd leave this horrible job, but then what would she do for money? Her hands slippery with sweat, she lifted the shuttle to her lips.

'Nay, you don't want to be doin' that, love,' George said, coming up behind her and squeezing her buttocks.

Molly jumped as though she'd been stung.

'Gi' us it here.' George took the shuttle out of her hand. 'You go off to t'lavvy an' get ready for me whilst I do this,' he hissed in her ear.

Molly felt nauseated as his wet lips brushed her earlobe, but fearing his ire she traipsed out of the weaving shed to the women's closets.

George grinned lewdly. By, but he knew how to pick 'em. It was always the unattractive, quiet little things that were no good at their job that succumbed to his filthy perversions, and he could spot 'em a mile off. He'd had his eye on Molly Pickersgill from the start, and it didn't matter that she wasn't pretty like Darcy Earnshaw or Nora Hanlon. In George's opinion you didn't look at the mantelpiece when you were poking the fire.

20

'They're coming home,' Angela screeched as soon as Darcy entered the house one sunny late afternoon on a Wednesday in June. 'Me dad and Danny! They'll be here on Saturday.' Angela bounced up to Darcy waving John's letter, her round brown eyes alight with tears and laughter.

'There's a letter for you an' all, Darcy.' Betsy's face was wreathed in smiles but Darcy could tell that she'd been crying, no doubt tears of joy that her beloved John was coming back to her. 'Just think, three more days an' they'll be here,' she said wondrously as she set the teapot on the table.

Darcy untied her scarf and ruffled her fingers through her hair. Then she took off her pinny before sitting down at the table to read her letter. She blushed when she read what Danny had written about what he would do once they were together again. She squirmed with embarrassment, wondering what the soldier who vetted the letters thought about Danny kissing her all over. But Danny wouldn't care what anyone thought, so why should she? She couldn't wait for Danny's sentiments to become reality.

* * *

'By, but it's good to be back in Halifax,' John said as he and Danny
alighted from the train that had brought them from Nottinghamshire. The sergeant bawled out his orders and they fell in line.
Smart in their uniforms and looking extremely fit, they began
marching with their battalion from the station to Wellesley
Barracks.

Outside the station where they had been told to assemble,
Darcy, Betsy and Angela stood with the crowd waiting for the men
they had been longing to see for the past four months or so. They
had jostled their way to the front, Angela bubbling with excitement and Darcy and Betsy straining their eyes to catch sight of
Danny and John as the troops marched past.

Darcy had dressed especially for the occasion in a new blue
dress with a little hat to match, her long blonde hair gleaming as it
caught the sunlight. Danny saw her, and his breath caught in his
throat. Although the troops were under strict orders to keep eyes
front as they marched, he risked swivelling his head so that, when
she saw him, their eyes met. Darcy waved, her face pink with
excitement and love. When Betsy caught sight of John she almost
swooned, grabbing hold of Darcy's arm to keep upright. Angela
jumped up and down shouting, 'Dad, Dad, we're here.' John
smiled and nodded to let them know he saw them.

Halifax was a garrison town, so the cheering crowd were used
to seeing soldiers marching through the streets, the tarmac
echoing with the rhythmic tramp of booted feet and the roar of
heavy lorries, but these men now on their way to the barracks were
their men: husbands, sons, brothers, uncles and cousins. The
crowd went wild. Names were called out along with loving sentiments, Angela's and Darcy's voices louder than the rest. Poor Betsy
dithered in a dreamlike state. Her John had come back.

The soldiers marched on, boots ringing out a strident tattoo on the road and their families running alongside waving and blowing kisses until they arrived at the castellated fortress that was Wellesley Barracks. The troops marched in, leaving their loved ones standing forlornly and then gradually trailing homeward to wait for their men to be released the next day.

'Didn't they look marvellous in their uniforms?' Darcy crowed, linking her arm in Betsy's as they walked back to Pellon Lane. 'I never wanted Danny to be a soldier but I thought I was going to burst with pride as he marched past.'

'I can't believe they're home,' Betsy said faintly, silent tears wetting her cheeks.

'I know. We'll have them for ten whole days,' cried Darcy, her enthusiasm waning when she thought what effect it might have on Betsy when John went away again. She knew how she would feel when Danny returned to duty, but she also knew that life had to go on. It served no purpose to sit wallowing in despair. She squeezed Betsy's arm. 'We'll make these ten days the best days of their lives,' she chirped, then immediately regretted her choice of words. What if Danny and John lost their lives when they were sent to the front? That didn't bear thinking about. Angrily, she shoved the thought into the deepest chamber of her mind.

Danny and John arrived home to Pellon Lane late that afternoon to be greeted with a flurry of hugs and kisses, tears and laughter. Betsy clung to John like a limpet, her body jerking with sobs, and Angela, vying with her mother for the feel of her dad, thrust in between them. Angela was dainty for all her eight years and John easily swung her up in his arms. She wrapped her legs round his waist and whooped joyfully.

Darcy fell into Danny's arms, breathing in the fresh, clean smell that was his alone, her arms feeling the roughness of his khaki uniform and her lips feeling the burning passion of his kisses. She could hardly wait to be alone with him, and she knew that Danny felt the same but, out of common decency, they stayed in the parlour with the Carvers.

Darcy had to almost peel Betsy off her husband so that she could fling her arms round John and hug him. In the meantime, Angela went and threw herself at Danny, squealing with delight as he picked her up. After her dad, Danny was her hero. Giggling mischievously, she tossed Danny's cap across the room and Darcy let out a scream.

'Your hair, your lovely hair.' His glossy black locks had been shorn to within an inch of his scalp.

Danny ran his hand over his close-cropped head. 'It will grow,' he said.

Angela wriggled out of his arms, and running over to her dad she flipped his cap off too. 'It's not that bloody bad,' John cried as they all burst out laughing.

Darcy scurried around serving up a splendid meal of meat and potato pie baked by Betsy, and her own apple pie and custard, tears welling up as she said, 'I suppose you're both hungry.'

'When aren't we?' John crowed.

'We could do with some decent grub,' Danny said, as the two of them sat down. They tucked in, munching like a couple of ravenous dogs. Betsy sat as if in a dream, her eyes never leaving John's face.

After cups of tea and a bit more of catching up with the latest news, the Cappelinis excused themselves and hared upstairs to their bedroom. What followed was far more wonderful than anything Danny had described in the letter that had made Darcy blush.

'Absence really does make the heart grow fonder,' Darcy giggled, as she lay sated in Danny's strong arms, her head on his chest.

'And it makes all the other bits more beautiful,' he replied, fondling her breast, 'and they work so much better for not being used for what has been too long,' he added, thrusting his stiffening manhood against her stomach.

They must have dozed, and when Darcy woke she put out her hand and instinctively reached for him. Miraculously, he was still there. She rolled over, and straddling his long, lean body she leaned forward, her breasts brushing his chest as she nibbled his earlobe.

Danny woke with a start. It hadn't been a dream. He was here with his wife. The magic had been reality. He kissed her lips, sucked on her nipples then trailed his tongue between her breasts and down. Darcy threw back her head in sheer ecstasy as he pulled her under him and made love to her all over again.

In the bedroom across the landing, John and Betsy were indulging in similar fashion whilst, in the room next door, Angela lay curled up in a ball planning the things they would do now her dad was home.

The next day was a Sunday, so they walked in the People's Park, Danny and John proudly dressed in uniform with their wives on their arms, equally proud. Angela skipped round them, her joy knowing no bounds. On some of the evenings, after Darcy had finished work, they visited the Piece Hall and the Borough Market, catching up with old friends such as the hurdy-gurdy player and the Punch and Judy man. Neither of them had enlisted, one being too old and the other having flat feet. One night they went to the

Electric Cinema and sat in the sixpenny seats to watch Charlie Chaplin in *The Tramp*, and on Saturday Danny and Darcy revisited Shibden, reliving the day he had proposed. And at night they made love.

On their walks around the town, Darcy tried to avoid looking at the tributes decked with flags and flowers in gardens or outside a favourite pub and on street corners, little offerings in memory of a dead son, father or brother. She prayed she would never have to erect one in Danny's memory.

'Is there any word on where they might be sending you?' Darcy asked over tea one evening, anxiety colouring her tone.

'They haven't told us for sure, but there's rumours that it could be Turkey,' John replied grimly.

'That's a long way away, isn't it?' Betsy sounded fearful.

'Is that where turkeys come from, Dad? Can you bring one back for Christmas? My friend Susan says they have a turkey at Christmas, and she said it was better than a chicken.' Angela's innocent take on things made them laugh.

Darcy went and got the atlas she had bought for Angela and found Turkey on the map. If her Danny was going there, she wanted to know where it was in the world. She found the page and they all peered at it.

'There has been talk of a place called Gallipoli,' Danny said. 'The allies aren't making any progress and our regiment could be sent there as reinforcements.' Darcy couldn't find Gallipoli on the map but the distance between Turkey and England looked so great that it seemed as far away as the moon.

The ten days seemed to fly by and the anxieties of being parted again started to show through. Betsy burst into tears over nothing, and Angela became sulky and fractious. On the evening before his departure, John took Darcy to one side.

'Thanks for looking after Betsy an' Angela for me,' he said

solemnly, 'You're a good lass, Darcy. I don't know how you coped wi' Betsy after I'd gone, but I reckon it wasn't easy, an' I don't know how she'll be after we leave tomorrow.'

He looked so despondent that Darcy's heart went out to him.

'Don't worry, John. She looked after me when I needed somebody and I'll always do the same for her.'

'I just wish she wasn't so fragile.' John shook his head despairingly. 'She's never been able to take hard knocks. Her father knocked the stuffin' out of her when she wa' young an' she's never really got over it.'

'Look, John, we'll be fine,' Darcy said with a lot more confidence than she felt. 'Me and Angela will make sure of that.'

Later that night, Danny made love to Darcy with a passion. Although he tried not to think of it, he couldn't help worrying that it might be for the last time. Darcy also had the same thought in mind, but she tried not to show it, fearing that admitting to such an idea might make it come true.

The next morning, amid tears and desperate hugs, Danny and John reported to Wellesley Barracks. They were off on the next phase of their journey, but to where? Only God knew.

* * *

Just as Darcy had feared, Betsy sank into a state of deep depression.

'Come on, Betsy. Please eat something,' she begged as she got ready to go to the mill. Angela was in her bedroom getting ready for school. Taking advantage of her absence, Darcy added, 'You're frightening Angela and making her unable to concentrate on her schoolwork.'

Sadly, this ploy had little effect and she left the house on leaden feet.

Danny and John had been gone for almost two weeks, brief letters from both of them informing her and Betsy that they were going to a camp somewhere in the south of England. 'They get further and further away,' Betsy had moaned, slumped in the chair, her hair unwashed and her lips bitten raw.

Darcy struggled to keep her patience, but she was finding the responsibility of a moping woman, a fractious child and all the work she had to do more onerous by the day. Sometimes she felt like screaming, 'I'm missing my husband as well,' but she let the words lie like ashes on her tongue and soldiered on.

* * *

At the mill gates she caught up with Nora, and as they waited for the gates to open she saw Molly standing a little way off. She looked wretched.

'Have you noticed how awful Molly looks just lately?' Darcy gave Nora a nudge and nodded her head in Molly's direction.

'Now you come to mention it, I have. She seems afraid of her own shadow.'

'She looks as if she hasn't slept for a month,' Darcy said pityingly. 'I'll have a word with her at breakfast time, see if there's anything we can do to help.'

At work in the weaving shed, Darcy sang to the rhythm of her loom as the length of khaki lapped round the thickening cloth beam. She enjoyed her work far more than she had anticipated and loved the camaraderie of the women, laughing at their crude jokes or sympathising with them in their sorrows.

Every now and then she caught Nora's eye, and placing her fingers to her lips, she mouthed across to her, gossip and chitchat flowing as easily as if they were in the quiet of a churchyard rather than the cacophony of a weaving shed. At breakfast time Darcy went to sit by Molly on the steps outside the shed. Molly was list-lessly picking at a sandwich, her eyes dark and troubled.

'Is everything all right, Molly?' Darcy opened her snap box and took out an apple. 'You don't look very happy these days.'

'I'm grand,' Molly mumbled, crumbling bits of bread between her fingers and looking as though she wanted to cry.

'I don't think you're being honest,' Darcy said gently. 'Is it the job? Are you finding it too hard?'

Molly shook her head. 'It is hard but Mrs Brocklebank says I'm getting better.'

'Then what is it?' Darcy pressed. 'You've looked sad this last while back and you seem all dithery and on edge whenever you're at your loom.'

Tears welled and trembled on Molly's lashes then spilled over her plump cheeks. 'It's him,' she hissed. 'Him an' his horrible, mucky ways.'

'Who?' Darcy's stomach churned. She thought she already knew the answer but mill gossip had it that George Thwaite was being kept satisfied by a pert little blonde who was more than willing as long as she got to work on one of the new looms and got the best yarns. Molly had yet to answer, and Darcy reached for her hand. Her gorge rising, she urged, 'You can tell me, Molly.'

Molly sniffed back tears. Her cheeks were scarlet. 'The overlooker.'

Nausea crept up Darcy's throat. The disgusting abuse she had suffered at the filthy hands of Abe Earnshaw and Norris Firth surged back. Her veins flooded with a fiery rage. 'When, Molly? Where? What does he do?' She was having difficulty holding back her own tears and trying not to draw attention to herself and Molly.

'He makes me do mucky things to him in the closet. He's been doing it for ages. He says I'll get sacked if I don't.' Molly's words tumbled out in between gulps and sobs. She gave Darcy a wild-eyed look. 'But I need my job, Darcy,' she squealed. 'I have to work to keep Mother and me.'

Darcy wrapped her arms round her. 'Yes, you do, but you don't have to put up with George Thwaite's rotten abuse, Molly.'

'But I do,' Molly wailed.

'No, you don't!' Darcy said forcefully. 'I won't let that happen.'

By now, some of the women were glancing in their direction, their curiosity getting the better of them. 'What's up?' Dolly Murgatroyd called out.

'Nothing,' Darcy called back, at the same time thinking of an excuse. 'Molly's just upset because her cat got run over, isn't that right, Molly.'

Molly nodded and turned grateful eyes on Darcy. 'Thanks for not saying owt,' she mumbled.

The hooter signalled them back to work, and although she had told a lie to protect Molly she had no intention of protecting George Thwaite. She'd make him pay for what he was doing to Molly.

Abe Earnshaw had got away with his crimes and Darcy knew she would never completely forget what he had forced her to do, but she wasn't going to stand by and let it happen to another innocent girl too afraid to do anything about it. Her blood boiling, Darcy went back to her loom, and when George sidled up to stand beside her she gave him a filthy glare.

He leered at her. Seething, she felt the urge to knock his broken stubs of blackened teeth down his throat. She picked up an empty bobbin, gripping it so tight her fingers ached. She stepped back, George's sweaty, greasy smell making bile spiral up her gullet. He was utterly loathsome.

'Tha doesn't seem pleased to see me, Arsy Darcy,' he scorned.

Darcy ignored the crude remark but her cornflower blue eyes

flashed dangerously as she gave him a challenging glance. She knew exactly what she was going to do to give the overlooker his come-uppance. She'd do it for herself and for Molly and all the other girls whose lives had been spoiled by filthy perverts like Norris Firth, Abe Earnshaw and George Thwaite.

* * *

Her thoughts black, Darcy trudged home at the end of her shift. She dreaded going into the house to find Betsy moping by the fire, the dishes unwashed, the laundry to do, and an unhappy little girl crippled with worry because her mother wasn't coping in her father's absence.

Darcy pushed open the door then paused, listening to the whirr of Betsy's sewing machine. She wondered if Angela was playing with it, even though she had been strictly instructed not to touch it. She pushed the door wider and stepped inside, her eyes popping when she saw Betsy industriously running the pulsing needle along a seam of a curtain that Darcy had never before seen.

Betsy looked up and took her foot off the treadle. She gave Darcy a wan smile.

'Mrs Lister asked me to alter these curtains for her so I said I would.' She pressed the treadle and the machine whirred back into action.

Darcy's breath left her lungs with such force that she felt quite dizzy.

'Mrs Lister says that when me mam's finished the curtains she has some skirts she wants letting out 'cos she's got fat,' Angela informed her importantly.

'That's marvellous,' Darcy gushed, 'what with there being little to be had in the shops and people still wanting to look fashionable, I'm sure there's lots of folks want stuff altering.'

Betsy stilled the machine. She still looked untidy with her greasy hair and crumpled frock but there was a positive gleam in her eye. 'That's what I was thinking,' she said. 'I can't do owt to help the war effort but I can sew. Maybe this can be my way of doing my bit.'

Darcy skipped across the room and hugged her. 'I think it's a brilliant idea. I'll tell the lasses at the mill. You could make a nice little business out of it, Betsy.'

* * *

Later that night when Angela was in bed, Darcy told Betsy about Molly and the overlooker. 'I'm not letting him away with it,' Darcy snapped, her eyes flashing and her jaw set grimly.

Betsy gasped, clasping her hands to her face as she heard the sordid details.

'Somebody has to put a stop to vile men like George Thwaite and Norris Firth,' Darcy continued. 'It happened to me and nearly ruined my life.'

'You're right. Summat has to be done,' Betsy said fervently, realising that her own problems weren't half as bad as poor Molly's. 'But what will you do?'

'I've got an idea,' Darcy said mysteriously, 'but first I'll have to speak to Florrie Moorhouse and one or two of the other lasses.'

'You be careful, Darcy.' Betsy looked fearful. 'You don't want to be getting yourself into trouble.'

'I won't. The only one that'll be in trouble is the stinking rotten overlooker.'

21

Danny put down his pencil and pages and sank into the biscuit-thin, hard mattress on the bed in the hut he shared with John and other members of his battalion. A little smile curved his lips as he pictured Darcy's sweet face, her startling blue eyes and her pale blonde hair spread out on the pillow. That was the way he liked to think of her, lying beside him in their bed, her silky skin warm under his wandering hand.

He looked John's way and gave a rueful smile. John smiled back, his expression apprehensive. Tomorrow they would board the ship taking them not to Gallipoli, as rumour had it, but to France and into the thick of war. They had stuck together throughout their training and now they were being put to the test.

'I don't know about you but I don't fancy this boat trip we're going on,' John said wryly. 'I've never been on the sea afore.'

'It is not so bad once you get used to the rolling ups and downs,' Danny replied, placing his hands on his belly and rolling his eyes. 'When I came to England I was seasick for two days.' He grimaced at the memory.

'When we get over there, you watch my back an' I'll watch

yours.' John's voice was thick with emotion. 'No bloody heroics, do you hear me?' he grunted. Danny's impetuosity often led him into trouble.

Danny grimaced. 'We stick together like – what is it you say – shit to a blanket.'

Chuckling, they each rolled over, ready to catch a last night's sleep on dry land, and as they closed their eyes they hoped to dream of the girls they loved and the home they had left behind.

* * *

'Can I have a word with you, Florrie?' Darcy approached Florrie Moorhouse with trepidation. She was well known for her argumentative manner and rough way of dealing with things, and Darcy was about to ask her some very personal questions. It was dinnertime, and Darcy had made a point of speaking to Florrie as they came out of the weaving shed before she had time to sit with her mates.

Florrie gave her a look that was halfway between a sneer and bemusement.

'What do you want?' she growled.

'Let's go and sit on the steps outside the spinning shed.'

Not wanting to be overheard, Darcy started to walk towards the steps, hopeful that Florrie would follow. Florrie hesitated, shrugged, then fell into step.

'What's all this about?' Florrie sounded annoyed.

'Please don't be angry with me,' Darcy said, 'and if you don't want to talk about what I'm going to tell you, I will understand.'

'You're talkin' in bloody riddles now,' Florrie snapped, flopping down on the steps and opening her snap tin.

Darcy sat beside her and opened her own tin. Sandwich in

hand, she took a deep breath. 'Did George Thwaite ever pester you to do stuff that you didn't want to do?'

Florrie's eyes narrowed. 'Who told you that?'

'Nobody,' Darcy insisted, 'but I've seen how much you dislike him and I wondered if that was the reason. He does it with other girls.'

'Is he doin' it to you?' Florrie's annoyance seemed to dissipate and her irritated expression was replaced by one of concern and pity mixed with a look of revulsion.

Darcy shook her head. 'Not me, but he is intimidating someone, threatening he'll sack her if she doesn't do what he demands. This poor girl is quiet and shy and not able to stand up to him, and she's terrified of losing her job.' As she spoke, Darcy imagined that she could feel Florrie's anger burning through her skin. She was afraid it might be directed at her for speaking out.

'The dirty, rotten, filthy pig,' Florrie exploded, cursing the overlooker with such venom that it made Darcy flinch. Then suddenly, Florrie went down like a burst balloon. 'He did it to me when I first started. He knew I wa' from t'workhouse an' had nobody who cared about me,' she said in a low, wobbly voice. 'I wa' terrified of him. But after a bit I toughened up. I started cheekin' him an' sayin' I'd report him to Master Bentley an' to hell wi' me job.' She smirked. 'He di'n't like that, an' he left me alone, but I've not forgotten, by God I haven't.'

The girls sat in silence, nibbling their sandwiches, neither of them sure what to say next. Darcy spoke first. 'Are there any other girls in the shed he's interfered with?'

Florrie sniggered. 'Umpteen, but you'll not get them to admit it.'

'I suppose they feel ashamed,' she said, recalling that, at one time, she had somehow felt she was to blame for Abe's abuse of her. 'But that's just it,' Darcy pressed on. 'I was thinking that if we all got together and let him know we're not putting up with his dirty games, we'd be doing something about it.'

Florrie's jaw dropped. 'Are you mad? He'd just deny it.'

'He could if only one girl complained,' Darcy said, her eyes alight with the fervour of her plan, 'but not if we all stand up against him.' She clasped Florrie's arm. 'It'll be like the suffragettes, you know, all demanding rights for women and not letting men put us down.' Her cheeks had turned pink as she imagined all the women accusing the overlooker of his wrongdoings.

Florrie screwed up her face. 'Do you think it 'ud work?' The possibility lingered in the air like a tantalising mirage.

'It will if we work at it,' Darcy stressed. 'We'll go round all the lasses asking them if they'll join with us, then if we get enough support we'll arrange a time for us all to stop our looms. When he asks what we're doing we'll tell him why.' She grimaced at the idea. 'What do you think, Florrie?'

'Bloody hell! I can't wait to see his face when we do. He'll most likely shit himself. I'll start askin' round as soon as we get back in t'shed.' She scrambled to her feet looking like Boadicea ready to go into battle.

'Thanks, Florrie, your support means the world to me.' Darcy stood and gave her a hug.

Florrie's eyes narrowed. 'It's you he's havin' a go at, in't it?'

'No, honestly it's not. But it has happened to me with somebody else and it nearly ruined my life.'

Florrie gave her an amazed grin. 'Bugger me. I never thought we'd have owt in common. I've always thought you wa' a right stuck-up little cow.'

Darcy's laughter was drowned by the blast from the hooter. 'Come on,' she said, grabbing Florrie's arm, 'let's get to work.'

* * *

Darcy lay on her bed, Danny's letter clutched to her heart and her tears soaking her pillow. She had run up to her room as soon as Angela had handed it to her, wanting to be alone when she read it. He felt much closer if she could linger over every word in privacy, and she liked to stroke the paper that his hands had held and sniff it in the hope that it still bore a trace of his fresh, clean smell.

Her heart had stumbled as she'd read:

We are in Southamton wating to bord ship tomorow morning. By the time this letter reeches you I will be in France.

She pictured him standing on deck as he crossed the English Channel, the wind blowing through his hair. Then she remembered. The army barber had shorn Danny's glossy black curls down to his scalp. Dreamily, she recalled the feel of it under her fingers, the prickly stubble sharp against her hand. How she wished she could feel it now. But wishing got you nowhere; only positive thoughts bore results and the last few days had proved that.

True to her word, Florrie had sounded out her closest friends and they, in turn, had approached others. Nora turned out to be a magnificent ally.

'Oh, I know all about things like that,' she'd said when Darcy told her about Molly and what she and Florrie planned to do to put a stop to it. 'It never happened to me – I was too gobby – but there were girls at the convent school I went to who were abused by the nuns, and the priests,' she divulged. 'We all knew what was going on but nobody dared to do owt about it. Maybe now's the time for me to put that right.'

And so Darcy's little team set about surreptitiously gathering the evidence they needed. It was a slow, painful task because they had to take great care that the overlooker didn't get wind of it.

Some of the girls felt too ashamed to co-operate, and a few of the older women refused to have anything to do with Darcy's plan, but there were plenty who believed that men like George Thwaite had had it all their own way for far too long. The number of supporters was growing by the day. Darcy, Florrie and Nora were exultant.

* * *

There was definitely a strange atmosphere in the weaving shed, had been for days, but George Thwaite couldn't fathom what was causing it. He lolled against the wall of the shed, a sour expression on his bristly face and his hooded eyes roaming from loom to loom and the women attending them.

There! They were at it again, the bitches. Turning their backs so that he couldn't read their lips if they thought he was looking their way. And when they did meet his gaze, girls and women that would have once dropped their heads in fear now stared at him long and hard, then smirked before looking away. Even that meek little sod, Molly Pickersgill, had ignored his orders to go to the closet, and when he'd threatened her she'd given him a defiant glare.

George narrowed his eyes, watching the women and the direction in which their heads kept turning. Ugh! He might have known that Darcy Poppelini, or whatever the bloody hell they called her, had something to do with what was going on. A hot sweat moistened his brow and top lip. Growling deep in his throat, he marched between the rows of looms. He was going to get to the bottom of this carry on, by hell he was. He glanced down the shed to the huge clock on the far wall. Its hand pointed to three minutes to eleven.

The women studiously kept their eyes on their looms as he passed by, not one of them glancing at him as they usually would.

It was as though he was invisible. His heart began to thump against his ribs.

Suddenly, the looms stopped thrashing, as though a mighty hand had swept through the weaving shed, stilling it into silence. George looked round wildly. The last loom ground to a halt, and the deathly hush that followed was as thick as treacle. He opened his mouth to roar then closed it again, flabbergasted, as the women began filing out of the shed into the yard.

'Oi, come back! Where the bloody hell do you think you're going?'

The women carried on walking and he was left floundering in the empty shed. Gathering his wits, he charged out into the yard. The women were standing in a tight huddle, nobody saying a word, but the expressions on their faces seemed to be saying a thousand.

'What's all this about?' Panic made George's voice sound squeaky.

Darcy stepped forward and mounted the steps in front of the women's closets.

The women fixed their eyes on her and held their breaths. George dithered.

'When I was a child I was abused by a wicked, evil man.' Darcy's voice rang out loud and clear, overriding the thump and rattle emanating from other parts of the mill. 'At the time I thought it had ruined my life and later, when I was attacked by another vile creature, I was sure it had. That's when I knew that I had to fight back.' She let her gaze roam the faces of the women. 'And that's what we are doing today. We're fighting back against the wickedness that men like George Thwaite perpetrate.' She swung her arm, pointing an accusing finger at him.

George's guts turned to water as all the women in the yard trained their eyes on him. He heard the rumbling and muttering growing to a roar and was about to turn and run when Joseph Bentley's big, black car swung into the mill yard. His knees buckled. How was he going to explain this to the mill owner?

Darcy gave a triumphant smile. They'd timed it just right to coincide with the millowner's daily arrival and he hadn't failed them.

Joseph Bentley's chauffeur leapt from the car, and the moment he opened the rear door Joseph jumped out, his face masked in puzzlement and annoyance. His eyes ranged over the crowd of women then settled on George. 'What's to do, Thwaite? What in the name of God is going on here?'

Darcy struck whilst the iron was hot. Blue eyes flashing and her heart pounding, she shouted at the top of her lungs, 'Raise your hands all those women who have been sexually abused by George Thwaite and threatened with the sack if you didn't comply.'

A flurry of hands shot up, accompanied by angry words.

Joseph Bentley stared aghast at his workforce.

George hurtled back into the weaving shed, hastened on by the cheering, jeering women.

* * *

Of course, there had been some explaining to do. Darcy, Florrie, Nora and Dolly had stood fearlessly in Joseph's office and he had listened like the decent Christian man he was. He had daughters of his own and his face had turned purple with outrage as the women gave their reasons for outing the overlooker.

'Will we get us wages docked for stoppin' our looms when we should o' been workin'?' Florrie, quick to take advantage of the mill owner's sympathy towards their cause, wasn't going to lose a penny if she could help it.

Darcy flushed with embarrassment at her audacity, the flush

deepening to one of pleasure and triumph as Joseph assured them otherwise, then thanked them for bringing such a serious misappropriation of authority to his attention.

When Darcy and the others went back into the weaving shed they were met with such a resounding cheer that it echoed throughout Dunkirk Mill.

George Thwaite was nowhere to be seen.

22

'By God, but it's good to feel solid ground under me feet,' John groaned as he and Danny stood on the quay at Le Havre. He hitched his pack up to his shoulder then gazed into the distance to get a good look at a town that wasn't in England. The bit that he could see didn't look much different to the view of any town, with its church spires and a conglomeration of rooftops of all shapes and sizes on large and small buildings. He wondered why he had had to travel so far to see something so ordinary.

Danny drooped beside him. The nausea that he'd experienced on his journey from Italy to England had attacked him again as they'd crossed the Channel. 'I am not meant to travel on water,' he moaned.

'Aye, well, I don't think you'll be sailing anywhere again soon, lad. Your feet'll be on dry land for t'foreseeable future, or in mud if you can believe what we've been told,' John replied pragmatically.

The port was a hive of activity, vessels being unloaded, orders shouted, and before long Danny and John found themselves tramping up and down gangways, descending and ascending ladders as they unloaded crates and cartons of military equipment.

The air was muggy and damp, the strong smell of salt, oil and human sweat hanging round them like a shroud.

'I'll not have any strength left to fight a bloody war by the time we've got this lot shifted.' John wiped the back of his hand across his forehead. It came away wet.

Danny stacked an ammunition box on a mountain of other boxes. He seemed to have forgotten his seasickness. 'So – this is France. We get to see some beautiful cities and meet some beautiful French ladies, ooh la-la,' he jested with a twinkle in his eye.

John grinned wryly. 'I don't bloody think so,' he grunted as he heaved a Lewis gun alongside several others. 'I don't know where you've been hiding for this past while back but did nobody ever mention there's a war on, an' that's why we're here?'

Danny laughed. 'I know, I know. I just try to keep up my spirits.' The smile left his face. 'Do not worry. I will not be looking at French ladies. I have the most beautiful girl in the world waiting for me in England.'

Orders came to fall in and they marched from the quay into the town, then kept on marching for a further five miles until they came to the rest camp at Graville. As they were deployed to their billets they smelled something tasty wafting on the air. John's belly rumbled. 'I don't know about you but I could eat a row of mucky kids,' he said.

Danny nodded agreement, his mouth watering.

A short while later they sat down and stuffed their empty bellies with fat pork sausages, fried potatoes and plenty of bread and butter.

'By God, I wa' ready for that,' said John patting his stomach. 'I'm as full as a butcher's dog.'

'You want I should eat your treacle pudding then?' Danny said, grinning wickedly as he reached for John's mess tin.

'Nay, I've still got room for that,' John said, and slapped Danny's hand away.

Fed and watered, the soldiers stayed in the canteen, clustered round the long tables. 'We might as well make a night of it, lads,' someone shouted.

'Aye, make hay whilst the sun shines and bugger tomorrow.' This rallying cry was answered by the banging of tin mugs on the tables.

Out came the decks of cards, and the 'Crown and Anchor' lads unfurled their little squares of linen ready to make a bob or two. They gambled for matchsticks or pennies and Danny won three games in a row. Clouds of blue smoke formed above their heads as they puffed on Woodbines and Park Drive, laughing and chattering as though there was no tomorrow.

* * *

Darcy and Betsy both cried when they received their first letters from France. To know that the men they loved so dearly had to spend days and nights in a trench dug out of clay and topped with sandbags, where the stench of the latrines was never far from their noses, was beyond bearing. Both John and Danny spared their wives the horrors of bombardment from shot and shell and the nerve-wracking moments when the orders came to advance their position. Had Darcy and Betsy known this they might not have been able to sleep at night.

Of course, Darcy had some idea of what it was like from the newspaper reports she scoured daily, but the place names meant nothing to her because she had no idea where in France Danny was. So, as letters flew back and forth regularly enough, she contented herself with the words of love and affection that accompanied his news. He always tried to cheer her by telling her about the pretty villages they had passed through and the wild flowers that grew in the fields, or the silly mistakes he made.

I am not thinking wat I am doing and when I try to burn the lice from seems in my tunic it catch fire and now I have holles in the sleeve.

Darcy had shuddered at the lice and laughed at his tattered sleeve – and his spelling.

John also kept his letters light-hearted. He knew that to do otherwise would only send Betsy into the depths of despair. His last letter had had his wife and daughter and Darcy howling with laughter.

There's a big meaty lad with a big appetite in our battalion. He's always scrounging food and has been known to pinch other men's rations. The other night we were crouched in the trench when one of the lads asked did anybody want a sandwich. Straight away the big lad said he did. They passed the sandwich on to him. It was pitch black that night, no stars, and you couldn't tell what was in the bread. He soon found out when he started frothing at the mouth. They'd filled it with a slice of soap. He's been on the lavvy ever since.

Darcy told Danny about the incident in the mill with George Thwaite, and about her visits to the cinema with Nora. Betsy wrote about Angela's achievements at school, and her own little sewing business, and as summer faded into autumn and then winter, their letters were the lifeline that kept them feeling as though they still played a very important part in each other's lives.

Darcy had worried that Betsy might sink back into depression now John was at the front, so she kept her busy by bringing garments for alteration from the girls in the mill. Betsy seemed to find treadling cathartic, and her machine was rarely silent during the day, or sometimes in the evening, the needle dancing up and down as she deftly turned a seam.

At Christmas, not at all the same without Danny and John, Darcy bought Betsy a copy of *Knitted Comforts for Men on Land and Sea* that contained patterns for balaclavas, socks, gloves and scarves.

One afternoon at the end of January, Darcy arrived home earlier than usual, the freezing weather having iced-up the pipes that carried water to the engine that powered the looms.

Kicking the snow off her boots, she entered the house, bringing with her a flurry of flakes and cold air. She stared, wide-eyed with surprise, at the group of women gathered round Betsy's hearth. They were all busily knitting, crocheting and gossiping, cups of tea at their elbows or rested on the hearth.

Betsy jumped up. 'You're early, Darcy. Get your coat off, love. There's fresh tea in the pot. I've just brewed it.' She hurried to the table and filled a cup. Then, with a wide, proud smile she said, 'Meet me sewin' an' knittin' circle.'

Introductions were made, Darcy already acquainted with some of the women, and as she sat down to drink her tea, she silently chastised herself. She would never have credited Betsy with the gumption to organise a piss-up in a brewery, let alone a circle of women providing much needed comforts for the men in the trenches. Leaving out the bit about the piss-up – an amusing phrase she'd picked up from the women in the mill – she said as much after the women had gone. 'You never mentioned you'd organised a knitting circle.'

Betsy flushed. 'I didn't like to say owt in case nobody turned up. I'd have looked a bit daft.' Her face cracked into a smile. 'But they did, an' we've had a lovely afternoon. We're doin' it again next week an' every Thursday after that.'

'Me mam's really clever, isn't she?' Angela put down the lumpy, holey bit of knitting dangling from a pair of large needles and grinned. 'Me dad's gonna be made up when he gets his balaclava, an' I'm knitting this scarf for Danny.'

From that moment on Darcy stopped worrying about Betsy.

* * *

'Does anybody know why Nora's not at work today?' Darcy's gaze roamed the faces of the women huddled in the corner of the weaving shed eating their breakfasts. It was too cold to sit outside and not much warmer inside.

'Maybe's she's come down with the flu,' Dolly suggested. 'Me mam's got it summat shockin'. It's this bloody weather.'

'She was all right yesterday,' Darcy said. 'I'll call round on my way home. We're meant to be going to the pictures tonight.'

The two girls spent a lot of their free time together either going to the cinema or for walks in the People's Park. Darcy visited Nora's rumbustious family in their small, overcrowded house in Silver Street, and Nora often came round to Pellon Lane for a bit of peace and quiet.

That evening after work, Darcy called at the house in Silver Street. Maggie Hanlon, Nora's mother, answered the door. Maggie was a Dubliner with a thick Irish brogue, and like her daughter she had flaming red hair and a ready wit. She laughed a lot, and managed her large brood of unruly sons and daughters with cheerful fortitude.

Today, as she greeted Darcy, she couldn't even raise a smile. She beckoned with her head for Darcy to enter. Her sad face and her silence frightened Darcy.

'Is something wrong, Mrs Hanlon?'

'Bob's gone. Killed at Ypres. My wee Nora got a telegram. The lad brought it just after she came home from work. Bob bein' an orphan, he had her down as next o' kin.' Her chins wobbled and she pressed her hands to her face, her moist green eyes overflowing.

Darcy's gasp whistled in the doorway. She stood, trying to comprehend what she had just heard and gazing at the broken woman before her. Fleetingly she wondered if she should comfort big-bosomed Maggie with a hug. Instead, she patted her arm ineffectually and whispered, 'I'm so sorry.'

Maggie nodded her head. 'Go on up to her,' she sobbed, 'she's in her room. Hasn't left it since she got word.'

Her heart as heavy as her tread, Darcy mounted the stairs. What would she say to Nora? Words of sympathy meant nothing at a time like this. Choking back tears, she pushed open the door.

Nora was sitting on the edge of the bed staring at the window. She didn't look round as Darcy entered. The room smelled of Nora's perfume, and misery.

'Nora, it's me, love. Darcy.' She looked at the slump of her friend's shoulders and her red hair tangled in knots, and was afraid to go nearer. The air felt stifling and she was finding it hard to breathe.

Then she slipped out of her coat, and taking a few tentative steps across the room she sat on the bed. She placed her arm round Nora's shoulders, pulling her head down onto her breast, gently stroking her matted hair. Nora seemed completely lifeless. For several minutes she acquiesced to Darcy's soothing ministrations. Then, like a volcano erupting, great wracking sobs escaped her lips. Darcy felt tears seeping into her blouse.

Suddenly, Nora reared up, tearing herself from Darcy's embrace. 'What am I goin' to do without him, Darcy? What am I goin' to do?' she screamed, her desperately pleading tone making Darcy's heart ache.

Darcy said the first thing that came into her head. 'I don't know, Nora.'

Then realising how useless that sounded, she added, 'I don't know what I'd do if I lost Danny, but I do know that life has to go on. It's a rotten, cruel shame but you don't just lay down and die, even if that's all you want to do.'

'I loved him so much,' Nora sobbed. 'I thought we'd be together forever. We would've got married, and now I'll never see him again. He'll never hold me in his big, strong arms and say daft things to make me laugh.' She gave Darcy an imploring look. 'I won't even be able to visit his grave.'

'You will, love. They'll let you know where it is and we'll go together.' Darcy spoke firmly, desperate to heal Nora's broken spirits. 'Now, love. Let's get you washed and do your hair. Bob wouldn't want to see you like this.' She stood, businesslike, and pulled Nora up to her feet. 'And wherever he is, you know that Bob will have you in his heart and that you will carry him in yours.'

'Do you think so, Darcy?'

Darcy thought she heard a tiny hint of hopefulness in Nora's forlorn little voice. 'I know so,' she said, heading for the door. 'Get undressed and I'll fetch some hot water.' She ran downstairs feeling far less sure than she had sounded.

'Did she talk to you?' Maggie's anxiety made her voice sharp.

'She did,' Darcy said as she filled a bowl with hot water from the kettle.

'Thank God for that,' Maggie gasped. 'It's t'first words she's spoken since she got news, an' she hasn't eaten a thing.'

'She's going to get washed and changed.' Darcy lifted the bowl. 'Maybe you could tempt her with a slice of toast or whatever else you have.'

'I'll boil an egg. I think we've got one.' Maggie waddled to the cupboard feeling better for having something to do that might help her heartbroken daughter.

Half an hour later, Nora was washed and changed and dipping a toasted crust into her egg. 'Thanks, Darcy, I feel a bit better now,' she mumbled. Her eyes filled with tears. 'My Bob loved his food,' she said forlornly, then fervently added, 'I'll never forget him, never.'

'Course you won't.'

They sat quietly, the half-eaten egg forgotten. Every now and then, Nora recalled something Bob had said or done, the need to talk about him cathartic. Darcy listened patiently, her belly rumbling with hunger, and for all she had never met Bob, she thought that she, too, would never forget him.

After a while, as the light outside the window faded into darkness, leaving a handful of stars glinting in the night sky, Nora's eyes drooped. She yawned, flopping back on her pillow, exhausted by the misery of the past twenty-four hours.

Darcy got to her feet. 'You have a good sleep, love,' she said, dropping a kiss on Nora's cheek. 'I'll be back tomorrow.'

Her legs felt weak as she walked down the stairs and she didn't know whether it was hunger or the sheer awfulness of Nora's loss that made them feel that way. 'She's sleeping,' she told Maggie as she went into the kitchen to say goodnight.

Nora's dad, Joe, lifted his grizzled head. He'd been sitting staring into the fire. 'Thank God for that. She'll not be pacin' the floor tonight, the poor wee girl.'

Darcy stepped out into the bitterly cold night air, trudging through the slush on the pavement back to Pellon Lane. All she could think of was how she would feel if Danny was killed, and she knew that she would want to die with him. She looked up into the starlit sky and murmured, 'Please, God, send him back to me.'

* * *

Nora returned to work three days later. Her skin looked sallow against her fiery red hair, and the deep shadows under her eyes looked like purple plums. She stood woodenly as the women commiserated with her, those who had also lost loved ones relating their own experiences until she could bear it no longer.

'Let's eat us dinner down there,' she said as she and Darcy left the weaving shed. She pointed to the low wall at the bottom of the mill yard, some distance from the women sitting on the steps and round the shed doors. Darcy walked with her, shivering when they left the shelter of the mill, for although the weather was bright and dry, it was still cold.

For the next few weeks, Darcy offered comfort and willed her friend to revert to the lively, funny girl she had once been, even though common sense told her that Nora would never be the same. Then, as the slush disappeared from the pavements and the sun became a little warmer, and the promise of another spring was just around the corner, Nora seemed to find herself again.

Since George Thwaite's dismissal, the atmosphere in the weaving shed was much happier, and bearing in mind what had happened to Molly Pickersgill and many of the other girls, and the fact that hardly a week went by without someone losing a husband, a son or a brother, the women were much kinder to each other.

Gradually, the daily camaraderie and Darcy's unfailing friend-ship worked its magic on Nora. She wasn't as carefree as she had been – that was to be expected – but she was getting on with her life.

One evening, after a trip to the cinema, Darcy was sitting in the Hanlons' cosy, cluttered kitchen drinking a cup of tea before she went home. She liked being in the Hanlon family's hectic household with Nora, Maggie and Joe; it was so much livelier than her own home and gave her less time to dwell on Danny's absence. Upstairs, Nora's youngest brothers, the twins Jimmy and Billy, were rampaging around, their feet making the ceiling shake and their wild whoops ear-splitting. Joe raised his eyes as a flake of plaster landed on the hearth rug. 'They'll bring the bloody house down on us afore long,' he groused, but he grinned as he spoke.

Maggie waddled to the foot of the stairs and yelled, 'Hey, stop that an' come down now!'

Seconds later, Jimmy and Billy thundered downstairs and into the kitchen.

'What the...?' Nora's eyes boggled. 'Have you been in my room?' She started to laugh. It was good to hear, and everyone joined in.

The boys might have looked guilty, but seeing as the bottom halves of their faces were covered with sanitary towels looped from ear to ear, it was hard to tell. Billy pulled his off. 'We're playing bank robbers an' we have to hide us faces so nobody knows who we are.' He cocked his fingers in the shape of guns.

'There's never a dull moment in this house,' said Darcy, almost choking with laughter. Later, on her way home, she was still smiling. *What we all need every now and then is a good laugh,* she thought, *'cos if we didn't, we'd cry.*

* * *

At the same time as Darcy walked up Pellon Lane under a wintry sky dotted with brittle stars, Danny was cursing his aching feet as he trudged the last few yards to his destination. He scrambled into the trench, half-hypnotised by the flashes of light from exploding shells, and his ears rang with the thud and rattle of guns. John was in the ranks behind him on rear guard duty. They had marched from Carency where they had been sent to relieve the French 17th

Division and now, in the dead of night, they had reached Berthoval.

The air was rank with cordite, and the stink of the latrines mingled with the smell of unwashed men. Danny's feet slipped on the slimy duckboards as he wormed his way along the trench. He dumped his pack then sank down with his back against the ramparts. Sometime later, John slithered down beside him.

'From one hell-hole to another,' he grunted, stretching his aching legs out in front of him.

'Where have you lads come from?' The soldier sitting next to Danny asked the question in a tone that implied he didn't really care.

'Carency,' Danny replied sleepily, 'and don't ask me what it is like there because it is just like here.'

With a terrifying screech, an explosion lit up the sky casting a weird glow on the soldier's face before plunging it back into darkness.

'Where atta from? You sound like a foreigner?'

'Italy.' Danny pulled his cap down over his face, his head sinking to his chest. He pictured Darcy lying naked on the bed and fell asleep, desperate to escape into a dream.

Seeing that he wasn't going to get much conversation out of him, the soldier addressed John. 'Where are you from?'

'Halifax,' John said as he scratched inside his tunic. Picking a louse out of his armpit he cracked it between his thumb and finger then went in search of another one.

'"From Hell, Hull and Halifax, may the good Lord deliver us",' the soldier quoted, chuckling at his own wit.

'Aye, so they say,' replied John, easing into a more comfortable position.

'I'm Barnsley meself. We're just back on duty. We wa' down in that little *estaminet* in t'town. Them French madams don't half gi' you a smashin' time.' He jiggled his crotch and rolled his eyes. 'You want to get down there, mate, get some for yoursen.'

'Not my cup o' tea,' John grunted, thinking of his beloved Betsy. What did he want with French madams?

The chatty soldier began humming 'Mademoiselle from Armentières'.

'That's the only good thing to come out of this war,' the officer slumped opposite John remarked. 'There are some awfully jolly songs to raise the spirits.'

'Aye, music makes the world go round,' said John, recalling the days when Darcy and Danny had sung at The Canterbury.

Throughout all this idle chitchat in the morass of a rat-infested trench the guns kept on rattling, exploding shells hurtling showers of muck down on the resting men. But tonight it wasn't their war, at least not until dawn.

23

Joseph Bentley sat at his desk in Dunkirk Mill, his foot tapping in time to the singing in the mill yard. Rather than being a distraction the women's voices made the tedious task of totting up figures pleasurable. He nodded along to the strains of 'When You Wore a Tulip' and even joined in with 'Sister Susie's Sewing Shirts for Soldiers' as he closed the ledger and put it back on a shelf.

Time for lunch, he thought, patting his stomach as he descended the stairs into the yard. His chauffeur-driven dark green Austin was already waiting to take him home to Heath Villas, his mansion in Free Cross Lane.

'Give us one of your favourites, Darcy,' Nora called out, just as the mill owner appeared in the yard, the chauffeur saluting him then opening the car's rear door.

Joseph raised a finger. 'One moment, Benson.'

Darcy grinned and began to sing 'If I Had My Way'. The women swayed and hummed along with her then joined in, the final strains of the sad, sweet song drowned out by the hooter's mournful wail. Conscious that their employer was standing not six feet away, the women jumped to their feet and began filing back into the shed.

'One moment, Mrs Cappelini,' Joseph called out, walking towards her.

Darcy hesitated, surprised. Was he about to reprimand her? She lifted her chin and straightened her back as he approached.

'You have a delightful voice, Mrs Cappelini.' Joseph favoured her with a beaming smile. 'In such drab surroundings the singing is a joy to the ear.'

'Thank you kindly,' Darcy replied. 'Although I can't take all the credit, sir. The women's harmonising makes me sound twice as good.' She glanced anxiously at the weaving shed door, aware that she should be back at her loom if she were to finish her piece today and earn a bonus.

But Joseph seemed loath to let her go.

'It occurred to me as I listened to your merry songs that you could help me out with a little task that my dear wife, Mrs Bentley, has undertaken.'

Darcy gave him a puzzled look. What on earth could she do for the wealthy Bentleys that they couldn't do for themselves? On pins, she waited to find out.

'My wife is to arrange a charitable evening for our brave boys fighting in the trenches. You know, raise funds to send them comforts to lighten their miserable ordeal. I thought that you and your companions could provide us with some entertainment along with the violinist and the magician she has already persuaded to perform at the gathering.'

Darcy swallowed her amazement. 'I think the women would be more than willing to sing for such a worthy cause,' she said, thinking of her poor Danny up to his knees in mud as he dodged a hail of bullets. 'I certainly am.'

'Good, good! Then that's settled.' Joseph clapped his hand

together. 'I will keep you informed about the final arrangements, Mrs Cappelini. It will be an evening concert at our home and' – he cleared his throat, embarrassed – 'there will be a small remuneration for you and your choir.'

'I'm sure the lasses will do it for nothing, sir, but thanks for the offer.' She would have said more but the doors of the weaving shed flew open and Fred Shaw, the new overlooker, barged out. Whilst Fred wasn't a pervert like George Thwaite, he was an irascible taskmaster.

'Oy! Are you bahn to stand there gassin' all bloody day?' he bawled, realising too late that the man with his back to him was Joseph Bentley.

Joseph swung round. 'Mind your language in front of a lady, Shaw, and get back to your work. Mrs Cappelini and I have matters to discuss.'

Darcy almost choked on her suppressed laughter.

When she was back at her loom, Fred glared malevolently at her as he did his rounds. She mouthed Joseph's invitation to Nora. 'Pass it round. Tell the women to wait when we knock off so I can see if they're willing.'

At the end of the shift the twenty or so women who considered themselves members of the newly formed choir gathered in the mill yard. Those who had chosen not to join gave them curious, even envious looks as they made their way home.

'Where's the concert to be held, Darcy?' Vera Scroggins, like all the women, was thrilled to be invited to sing for a charity that would raise money for their husbands, sons and boyfriends risking their lives in Flanders Fields.

'At his house in Free Cross Lane,' Darcy told them, laughing when they exchanged wide-eyed, excited glances.

'That'll be Heath Villas, the grand place that was his father's when I wa' a young lass,' Gertie Micklethwaite informed them all knowledgably. 'It looks smashin' from outside. You'll have to be on your best behaviour there.'

'We'll have to decide what we're going to sing and we'll have to practise like hell,' Darcy warned them, 'so make sure you can get away for an hour or two on a couple of evenings next week.' Suddenly, she looked downcast. 'We really need a pianist to make us sound at our best.'

'I can play t'piano,' May Cockshott quavered, her pale, thin cheeks pinking. 'I play it in t'chapel of a Sunday.'

'That's marvellous, May!' cried Darcy, her enthusiasm waning as she thought of the solemn hymns they sang in Methodist chapels. Not wanting to offend the timid, elderly woman she gently added, 'But can you play the songs we sing?'

'Oh, aye,' May said confidently. 'I sit an' rattle 'em off many's a night to keep me company.' She turned and gave the women a rueful little smile. 'You get lonely when you live on your own.'

'Three cheers for May,' Florrie Moorhouse yelled, and Dolly Murgatroyd called out, 'You'll not have time to be lonely once we start practising, May.'

'It looks like we've got ourselves a pianist, ladies.' Darcy raised May's arm in a salute. May's pigeon chest swelled and her smile was all teeth.

* * *

The women held their rehearsals in the back room of the Dyer and Miller. John had been a customer and was a good friend of the landlord, Willie Dyson. Keen to do his bit for the lads in the trenches, Willie generously supplied the women with free glasses of milk stout to wet their throats after the singing.

'You've a grand pair of lungs on you, Florrie,' Ronnie Postleth-waite called out as the women trooped into the taproom for their drinks after a rehearsal. 'An' you've a lovely pair of tits, an' all.' He cupped his hands as if weighing them.

Hands on hips, Florrie proudly pushed out her bosom and chirped, 'Pity I can't say t'same about your balls, Ronnie.' She held her thumb and index finger about an inch apart to show the size of Ronnie's anatomy to the other women.

The taproom erupted in howls of laughter.

Ronnie, not in the least offended, said, 'Maybe you'll let me have a feel of 'em when you've finished your stout.' He winked and nodded at the door that led to the rear of the pub.

Florrie took a swig of stout then wiped a creamy moustache from her top lip before scornfully replying, 'Kiss my arse an' hope to die.'

Darcy cringed. She was used to the women's crude language but she dearly hoped they'd keep it in check when they went to sing in Joseph Bentley's mansion. 'We'll want to look smart when we go to Heath Villas, so what do you say to us all wearing a nice skirt with a white blouse?'

'That's a grand idea,' Dolly agreed. 'We'll look like a proper choir.'

'We are a proper choir,' Vera protested.

'Maybe we should give ourselves a name.' May's confidence had tripled now that her piano accompaniment made her a vital member of the group.

'What about Bentley's Singing Slaves, 'cos that's what we are,' Lily Broadhead suggested dourly. Lily always looked on the black side of things.

'Aw, shurrup, you old misery,' Dolly shouted. 'Bentley's one o' t'best bosses in town. He allus treats us fairly.'

Several voices were raised in anger.

Before a full-scale row could start, Darcy butted in, raising her voice above the rest. 'What about naming it for the mill. The Dunkirk Ladies' Choir?'

There were cries of approval all round.

* * *

Betsy was so busy these days that she rarely had time to mope even though she missed John dreadfully. Her knitting circle had gone from strength to strength, and the feeling that she was doing something worthwhile buoyed her up no end. It also pleased Darcy. She no longer felt guilty about going out on an evening now and then with Nora or rehearsing with the choir. Tonight the concert at Heath Villas was taking place, and as Darcy hurried up Pellon Lane she was anxiously going over the programme she had arranged.

Betsy was just clearing away the willow-patterned cups and saucers she had bought especially to serve tea to her ladies when Darcy came in through the door. 'It's your big night tonight,' she said by way of greeting, her eyes bright with admiration.

Darcy pulled off her coat. 'Yes, we've to be at Heath Villas for seven thirty, so I'll have to get a move on. It wouldn't do to be late, not after Mr Bentley's been so kind.' She might have sounded calm and collected but inside she was buzzing with the thrill of singing in front of such a prestigious audience.

'Your tea's ready, love,' said Betsy, ladling carrot soup into a bowl and putting two fried sausages and a slice of bread and butter on a plate. Food in the shops was scarcer week on week, but Betsy was quite inventive with the groceries she managed to buy. Darcy drank the soup with relish, but she was so pent up with excitement that she only picked at the sausages.

'I got a letter from John. He loved the tin of sardines I sent him. I'll try to get some more for my next parcel. He says they had pea soup with horsemeat in it an' that it wa' flavoured wi' nettles.' Betsy pulled a face. 'Shockin' in't it?'

'Was there no letter for me?' Darcy looked surprised. John and Danny's letters usually arrived on the same day.

Betsy shook her head. 'Maybe tomorrow, eh?'

Feeling rather cheated, and wishing that Danny was here to share her big moment, Darcy hurried upstairs to wash and change into her best black skirt and white blouse. High-necked and long-sleeved with guipure lace trims on the collar and cuffs and pin tucks down the bodice, the blouse suited her trim figure to perfection. She brushed her hair until it shone and fastened Danny's little red heart on its silver chain round her neck. Her hands felt slightly clammy. To say she was nervous about the impending concert was an understatement. She wanted it to go well not just for her own sake but also for the women. It was a big moment in their lives too. And she wanted it to be successful for Mr and Mrs Bentley's sake. After all, they had put their trust in her and she didn't want to let them down.

'I'm off, then,' she said, pulling on her coat. 'Wish me luck.'

Betsy and Angela chorused their support and followed her to the door, watching and waving until Darcy turned the corner to go to the Dyer and Miller. Joseph Bentley had kindly hired a chara-banc to take the choir from the pub to Heath Villas. Once the excited women were aboard, Darcy suggested they had a final rehearsal. They sang all the way to Joseph Bentley's mansion.

On their arrival the Dunkirk Ladies' Choir was shown to a hallway on one side of the house. The floor was a mosaic of terra-cotta, dark blue and white, and against the walls large urns of calla lilies sat on polished side tables. A collective 'ooooh' from the women told Darcy they were impressed. And so was she. Her childhood home had been rather grand but nowhere near as splendid as this, and she empathised with her choir members, most of whom lived in two-up, two-down terraced houses built by the mill owners almost a century ago.

A servant in a smart black dress and crisp white apron led them to what was obviously a library. Darcy would have liked to peruse the books on the shelves but more pressing matters required her attention.

'The master says to wait in here. He'll come and talk to you shortly. You can leave your coats and, er, shawls on those chairs,' the little maid said snootily. She pointed to four upright chairs against the wall by the door and gave the women a despising look.

But they didn't notice. They were gazing around them in awe. The maid backed out of the door, closing it softly behind her.

'Toffee-nosed little cow,' said Florrie.

Darcy winced. 'Now, ladies.' She clapped her hands to divert their attention from the maid and their opulent surroundings. 'Remember to stand up straight, hold your heads up and smile. Listen carefully to May for the introductions and sing your best.'

The door opened and Joseph Bentley entered the room.

'Ah, I see we're all assembled. Very good, very good.' He rubbed his palms together and Darcy wondered if he felt as nervous as she did. Was he regretting his offer to let his rough and ready weavers entertain his friends? The women faced him, their solemn expressions obedient. He beamed back. 'Well, ladies, sing sweetly, and best of luck.' He turned to Darcy. 'My wife will be along in a moment.' He hurried from the room.

'He's a bit het-up, in't he?' May looked concerned.

'I suppose he has a lot to organise.' Darcy replied.

The door opened again and a beautifully attired woman stepped in. The weavers gaped at her green velvet gown trimmed with cream lace. Smiling warmly, Mrs Bentley held out her arms.

'Thank you, ladies, for your attendance. My husband tells me you sing delightfully.' Her cultured tones were rich with sincerity.

The women smiled, shoulders visibly relaxing at the warm welcome. Darcy also relaxed.

'Now, I want a lively introduction to the proceedings, so I would like you to open my little concert,' Mrs Bentley continued with a twinkle in her eye. 'The violinist will come after, and then the magician.' She paused before saying, 'I do hope he doesn't let the rabbit escape.'

The women tittered and Mrs Bentley did too. Then, composing herself, she said, 'We'll take a short break for refreshments, after which the violinist will play again and you will do the finale.' She turned to Darcy for her approval. 'How does that sound, Mrs Cappelini?'

Darcy was surprised that Mrs Bentley knew her name; they had never met.

'That sounds grand,' she replied, presuming that Joseph must have given her description to his wife. 'We'll do our very best for you, won't we, ladies?'

There was a murmur of agreement.

'Very well, we are organised.' Mrs Bentley clapped her palms together. 'I do hope some of your songs will have a military theme; after all, the concert is in aid of our dear, brave boys at the front.' She gave Darcy an expectant look.

'We won't disappoint you, Mrs Bentley,' she replied.

A rap on the door and the appearance of the snooty maid made their hostess whirl round. 'The master wants you, madam. A problem with the magician, he says to tell you.'

'Bloomin' heck! Has his rabbit escaped already?' crowed Dolly.

Laughing merrily, Mrs Bentley hurried off.

After she had gone, Darcy took the opportunity to express her gratitude for the women's appearance. Each of them was wearing a dark skirt and a white blouse. 'You all look smashing,' she said. 'We really do look like a proper choir.'

Then they waited nervously to be called to the stage.

* * *

'God almighty, get an eyeful of this,' Florrie hissed as the women were shown into a splendid drawing room with a thick Turkey carpet and chandeliers. An audience of about thirty people sat on sofas and in wing chairs towards the front of the room, and others on upright chairs arranged against the back wall. The room smelled of expensive perfumes, colognes and cigar smoke. A clear space had been left at the very end of the room and a butler led the group of women to it.

'Ooh, my goodness,' May squeaked. 'A grand piano.'

Joseph Bentley took his place in front of the choir. 'Ladies and gentlemen, I offer you my hearty thanks for your attendance this evening. My wife...'

The women began to dither and fidget as Joseph gave his speech, Darcy sighing with relief when he made a sweeping gesture and announced, 'Ladies and gentlemen, I give you the Dunkirk Ladies' Choir.'

May thumped out three rousing chords. 'Pack Up Your Troubles in Your Old Kit-Bag and Smile, Smile, Smile' brought smiles to the faces of the men and women lounging on the chairs and sofas and an appreciative round of applause. Darcy's solo of 'If I Had My Way' captivated the audience into silence, broken by heartfelt clapping, and the choir's version of 'Sister Susie's Sewing Shirts for Soldiers' – with actions – brought the house down. Flushed with success, the women continued, singing better than they ever had before, their rendition of 'O for the Wings of a Dove' bringing their set to a delightful end. Darcy's heart swelled with gratitude. She should have known they wouldn't let her down.

With the butler leading the way, they left the room to thunderous applause.

'I wouldn't have minded hearing the violinist,' May said as the butler led the way down a long corridor.

'I wanted to see the magician,' Lily groused.

The butler showed them into another large room, their complaints soon forgotten when they saw the delightful spread of dainty sandwiches, cream cakes, iced buns and biscuits. 'Help yourselves, ladies. Tea is in the urn over there.' He gestured to a sideboard loaded with a large, silver urn and fine bone china cups and saucers before leaving them to it.

Gaping in amazement, the women tucked in. 'Eeh, we weren't expecting this,' Vera crowed.

'There's no crusts on t'sandwiches,' Maggie remarked.

Darcy helped herself to a cup of tea and a biscuit but she felt too emotional to eat anything else. She tapped her teaspoon on the table, and when she had their attention she smiled warmly, her blue eyes brimming with gratitude.

'Thanks, ladies, you've done me and yourselves proud.' She felt like crying.

'We an't finished yet,' Florrie cried. 'We'll be even better in't next half.'

And they were. As they brought the concert to a close with a rousing version of 'When Tommy Comes Marching Home Again' followed by 'When I Leave the World Behind', there wasn't a dry eye in the room.

The women were donning their coats and still high with excitement when Joseph and Eleanor Bentley and a few of their guests entered the library, their thanks and praise fulsome.

'Our daughter, Victoria, is very musical. She would have loved it,' gushed a lady wearing a large feathered hat, her smile slipping as she added, 'but sadly she is nursing at a field station on the front line in France.'

'Eeh, fancy that. She must be a very brave lass, madam. You must be proud of her,' May uttered, her amazement that the daughter of such grand people would be putting herself in such danger quite evident.

The lady gave May a gentle, sad smile. 'We are, and thank you for your kind words. They are much appreciated.'

Darcy wasn't at all surprised that the generous-hearted friends of the Bentleys had a daughter doing war work, and casting her eyes over the choir, she said, 'We all wish her well and pray for her safe return, don't we ladies?'

The women cheered. Then Darcy turned to her employer and his wife.

'Mr and Mrs Bentley, on behalf of the Dunkirk Ladies' Choir I would like to thank you for having faith in us. We've had a splendid evening and we hope that it has helped raise funds for a very worthy cause.'

'Here, here,' the women chorused.

'Ladies, your hopes to raise funds have been well and truly answered,' said Eleanor, her eyes sparkling. 'I thank you again for making my evening a success.'

Emboldened by Eleanor's pleasant manner, Florrie called out, 'What about the magician an' his rabbit?'

Eleanor giggled. 'Oh, he fumbled all his tricks. The rabbit refused to come out of the hat. I have a sneaking suspicion it's in my drawing room nibbling at my curtains as we speak.'

The women roared with laughter before leaving Heath Villas triumphant, none more so than Darcy.

* * *

Long after the concert, and well into the summer of 1916, spirits were still high in the weaving shed, the choir basking in the glory of that successful evening. It had been made all the more glorious when they found that Joseph Bentley, true to his word, had included a nice little bonus in their wage packets. Darcy bubbled over with gratitude. Joys such as this eased the yearning she felt day and night for Danny to be by her side.

However, on the home front things were not as rosy, with talk everywhere about the 'Big Push' that was happening somewhere called the Somme. Initially the newspapers had written of a resounding victory. Then, as news trickled back through letters from the front and the black-edged death notices in the papers increased column upon column, the inhabitants of Halifax learned the truth.

Darcy treasured every one of Danny's letters, which by now were few and far between, but even his cheery optimism couldn't hide his homesickness and despair. As she read of how he tramped from place to place, unwashed, hungry and desperate for a good night's sleep, her heart bled for him.

In return, she wrote of her undying love, told him about the concert and anything else she could think of that might cheer him and make him feel close to her, but like everyone else she was feeling worn down by the war.

Betsy and Angela also lived for letters from John, but even he was losing faith. 'He's given up,' Betsy sighed, 'my John, who could face up to a herd of ragin' bulls if he had to, has had enough.' To hide her misery she immersed herself in sewing and organising her knitting circle, afraid that if she didn't keep busy she would sink into the depths and never find her way out. Even Angela, once so happy and vibrant, had grown quieter. She compensated for missing her dad by working hard at school to make him proud of her.

They, like everyone else in Halifax, had become used to the sight of Zeppelins that had crossed the North Sea and overshot their targets. Then they would hide under the stairs until the danger had passed. The very sight of these monstrous air ships floating high overhead was enough to send Betsy into a panic, but as time went by and it became clear that the Germans weren't targeting Halifax, their fears lessened and they carried on with their daily lives as best they could.

Darcy still occasionally attended her suffragette meetings and helped raise funds, but she had promised Danny not to attend any more demonstrations whilst he was away. At her last meeting, Phyllis had surprised her by announcing she was to be married.

'Catching your bouquet at your wedding obviously worked, even though we didn't believe in it,' she giggled before going on to say that the schoolteacher she sometimes went to the theatre with had asked her to marry him.

Darcy congratulated Phyllis, at the same time reminded of her own joyful wedding day, and Nora's lost opportunity. Nora took up much of her free time, for she was still struggling to come to terms with the loss of her beloved Bob, and both she and Darcy took solace from singing with the choir. The Dunkirk Ladies' Choir had been invited to further fund-raising concerts in the town, Darcy losing herself in the joy of making music each time they performed. In this way, Darcy, Betsy, Angela and their friends simply got used to the idea of war and, in Darcy's opinion, whilst things weren't good they could be a whole lot worse.

24

Nightfall, and a mist had come down, the sort that seeps into your tunic, and Danny felt damp and chilled to the bone. They had the order to move forward under cover of darkness, carrying their full equipment. As well as his backpack, rifle, gas mask and water bottle, Danny was toting a heavy sack of Mills bombs.

John was walking several yards ahead, and Danny kept his eyes trained on the back of John's head, his height and his broad shoulders singling him out and making him easy to follow. Every now and then Verey lights lit up the sky making the blackness of the night more intense as the flares faded.

It was late September and Danny was imagining walking through the russet and gold leaves in the People's Park with Darcy by his side, the rosy glow of sunset lighting their path. Lost in his thoughts, he stumbled on, the ground beneath his feet stony and slimy. *Don't fall now*, he told himself, the thought of tumbling into a waterlogged shell hole filled with the detritus of rotting human flesh making his guts heave and his mouth go dry. He quickened his pace, wanting to draw level with John, but just as he did so he lost his footing and would have fallen had an arm not grabbed him from behind.

'You awright, mate?' Tommy Spivey jerked Danny back onto the track. 'You don't want to lose your concentration, otherwise you'll lose your bloody life.'

Danny wasn't sure at that moment that he cared one way or the other. But, only yards later, when Tommy himself tripped and fell, Danny lunged to help him. He held out his rifle, butt end forward. 'Grab hold, Tommy, I'll pull you back.'

Oozing black slime sucked at Tommy's legs. He floundered, his hand grasping then slipping away from Danny's rifle.

Flat on his belly, his pack pressing him down, Danny stretched further, feeling himself slithering into the sticky morass. He let out a scream as the mud threatened to envelop him along with Tommy, who was still kicking his legs and hanging on to the end of the rifle. Danny muttered a prayer as the foul, stinking mud sloshed under his chin. *Goodbye, my darling Darcy.*

Then he felt two strong hands gripping his ankles and yanking him backwards. Up he squelched, a hideous human head bobbing up beside his own as he was dragged clear. Somehow, he was still clasping his rifle as though glued to it, and Tommy was still clinging on the other end. Like subterranean creatures emerging from the bowels of hell, they rolled on the path, gasping and crying.

'You nearly had your chips there,' John said as he knelt at Danny's side, scraping handfuls of mud and filth from his face and uniform.

Danny jerked his head to one side and spewed, his stomach cramping as it emptied. His teeth chattering, he could barely form the words as he said, 'I think I am done for.' Groggily, he got to his feet and stood, shaking uncontrollably.

'You're all right now,' John said, throwing his arm round

Danny's shoulder and holding him close. 'You don't think I'd let owt happen to you, do you?'

Tommy was sitting in a mud-soaked, trembling heap on the ground. He looked up at Danny, his eyes burning with gratitude. 'Thanks pal,' he mumbled.

'You would do it for me. We do it for one another,' Danny said shakily, then gave John a thankful smile.

By dawn they had reached their destination, a warren of muddy trenches on the front line between the towns of Flers and Courcelette – or Flo's Corsets, as some wag had christened it. They dug into position under a sickly yellow sky, the air sulphurous and rank with cordite – and fear. A pale September sun forced its way through the clouds with its meagre heat. Lumps of caked mud fell from Danny's uniform as it dried, making him look like a bird breaking out of its shell.

The guns, which had been silent in the early hours, suddenly roared into life and a barrage of fire from their own lines burst out over no man's land.

The whistle blew. A shout of, 'Come on, lads! This is it,' echoed in the trench. Danny and John, burdened by their packs and equipment, hauled themselves up the ladder and over the top into open land that was lit by explosions, flames and tracer bullets as they scuttled towards the German lines.

'Keep your head down,' John yelled as he surged forward, Danny at his heels.

Machine guns clattered and shells whined, then explosions sent shrapnel flying in all directions. Horses shrieked, men screamed and in front of them the tanks moved at a snail's pace, mowing down stumps of blackened, burned-out trees and anything else that got in their way.

There had been a frisson of excitement when the troops heard that tanks were to be used in battle for the first time, but these lumbering monstrosities were doing little to prevent the carnage that was taking place behind them. Danny dropped to his belly, crawling through the mud like a demented beetle until he came to the lip of a shell hole. He had thought to roll into it for cover but the crater was filled with sluggish water. He cast his eyes round for sight of John and was about to worm his way over to him when a bullet fired from a German pillbox shattered the head of the man next to him, his blood and brains spattering in Danny's face.

His gorge rising, he wiped the warm, fetid mess from his eyes with the back of his grimy hand. When he peered through the smoky haze something more than disgust gripped him. A sheer panic, icy and corrosive, clutched at his innards and inside his head. Something was telling him he needed to stay close to his friend. They had stuck together and watched one another's back so far and that's what he should be doing now.

He saw John making a move, going forward, and began crawling after him. Shrapnel skittered over the patch of scrubland but Danny was oblivious to it as he crawled closer to John. He heard the whining, felt the air shake then the almighty thud as a shell from a German minenwerfer bit into the scrub, tearing the ground in front of him and exploding in a mighty roar. He saw a body flying through the air like a filthy rag and he knew it was John's. Danny followed its trajectory, then he leapt to his feet and ran.

'I'm here. I've got you,' he cried, slithering to his knees by John's body. He slid his hand under John's head, desperate to let him know he wasn't alone. He wanted to cradle him in his arms, tell him that he was loved and had to live for those who loved him.

'Don't lift that man!' The barking voice broke through Danny's nightmare. The stretcher-bearer pushed Danny to one side then ran a practised eye over the casualty. Danny had heard it said that the stretcher-bearers knew more about life and death on the battlefield than anyone else. He slumped back on his hunkers and let them do their work. He realised that he was crying when he felt hot tears trickling into the neck of his tunic.

'Your pal's lost his leg,' the stretcher-bearer growled as his partner wrapped a large, loose dressing round what remained of John's left leg. John groaned and opened his eyes. One of the stretcher-bearers asked Danny for his water bottle. He slipped three small blue morphine tablets onto John's tongue and washed them down his throat before handing back the bottle. Danny's heartbeat, already pounding, quickened its pace. His friend was alive.

'It's me. Danny,' he said, placing his head close to John's. 'I am here. You will be all right.' He felt John's warm breath on his ear as he let out another groan. It gave him hope.

The stretcher-bearers lifted John onto a stretcher. For the moment the guns had ceased save for the crack of snipers' bullets. The battlefield was littered with wounded and dying men amid the debris. As Danny followed the stretcher, he tried to block out the cries of the men at his feet, not daring to look down and meet the pleading eyes. Each step of the way had its ration of bodies, living and dead, and blood bubbled up from the ground under his boots.

At last they reached the field ambulance and loaded John inside. Swaying with exhaustion, Danny looked at the bloody mass of soaked dressing on John's left leg. He grabbed the edge of the ambulance door, ready to heave himself up and inside. He wasn't leaving him now.

'Come back that man!'

Danny heard Sergeant Clapper's bullish voice. He climbed into the back of the ambulance. 'Here, mate you can't go—' The stretcher-bearer got no further.

'I go with him.' Danny turned on him so ferociously that the weary man merely shrugged and slouched away.

Danny stayed with John right to the field station and until he was in the care of a doctor. John, who could leap and tumble better than any man he knew, had lost his leg and Danny wasn't going anywhere until he had seen him in safe hands.

Of course, there was a price to pay; two weeks of digging out the latrines was worth it, but now he was without the shadow of John to shelter him and his war had taken a different turn. John's war was over.

The night that Danny wrote his next letter to Darcy he cried bitter tears that blotched the paper, making his words almost indecipherable.

25

They do say that all good things must come to an end and that pride goes before a fall, and when Darcy arrived home from work at midday on a Saturday in late September 1916 she felt the full brunt of the old adages.

She was feeling rather pleased with herself. Several months after the night Danny had called her up to the stage to sing with him at The Canterbury she had been approached by the manager, who had invited her to give a solo performance. The audience had liked her and this had led to two further engagements; she was making quite a name for herself, and her ladies' choir was also going from strength to strength. She missed Danny dreadfully, her heart yearning for him and her body aching for his touch, but she dared not succumb to the misery his absence caused her. She had to stay positive, as much for Betsy and Angela's sake as for her own.

Autumn leaves, burnished russet and gold, crunched under her feet as she strode up Pellon Lane, and a watery sun shone on her face. She was hoping there would be a letter from Danny, or one from John, when she arrived home. It always brightened the day to know they were safe and well.

The minute she pushed open the door and entered the house she knew that something was wrong. She thought she could smell it, and as the sound of copious weeping reached her ears she knew she had been right. She raced into the parlour.

Betsy was slumped in the chair by the fire, Angela kneeling at her feet with her arms round her mother. They were both sobbing hysterically, the shape of their huddled bodies and their pitiful cries tearing at Darcy's heart and chilling her to the bone. Her first clear thoughts were for Danny and John and her heart lurched painfully against her ribs.

'What is it? What's happened?' Darcy's cry bounced off the walls.

Neither of them answered, and she went over and tried to take Angela in her arms. Angela clung to her mother. Betsy had torn at her hair, the usual neat rolls hanging like tattered curtains, and when she did eventually raise her head, her eyes were so bleak that Darcy thought she was looking into the hobs of hell.

Angela struggled to her feet. 'It's me dad,' she howled, brushing tears from her red-rimmed eyes. 'A soldier came from the barracks an' told us. I knew he wa' from the Dukes by his cap badge. He said he wa' sorry.'

Darcy froze. Told them what? Had John been killed? Suddenly feeling woozy, she flopped down on the couch, her legs giving way under her.

'Is he...?' She couldn't say the word.

'They've sent him back,' Betsy mumbled, seeming to have regained her wits. 'He's in a hospital in London. His injuries are serious but the lad didn't say what. We can get passes for t'train to go an' see him.' All this was delivered in a monotone, flat and grating. She sank back into the chair, raised her gaze to the ceiling and bit down on her bottom lip.

'He's alive, Betsy, he's alive!' The surge of relief that flooded through Darcy was so intense that it made her feel dizzy again. She shook her head to clear it. But would he still be alive by the time they went to see him?

'I'll go up to the barracks and find out what I can and collect the passes,' she said, desperately feeling the need to do something meaningful. She turned to Angela. 'Be a brave girl. Your dad's going to be all right. Make your mam a cup of tea and have one ready for me when I get back.'

Darcy ran out into Pellon Lane, haring through the town to Wellesley Barracks. The sergeant on the desk was sympathetic. He told her that Corporal Carver had sustained severe injuries and been shipped back to England three days ago. He provided her with train passes for two adults and gave her directions to Queen Mary's Hospital.

Darcy glanced at the two passes. 'He has a daughter as well. Can she visit?'

'What age?'

Darcy told him.

'Not allowed, too young,' he replied.

On her way back to the house, she tangled with very mixed emotions: reproaching herself for feeling glad that it was John and not Danny who had been injured, and at the same time thanking God for sparing both of them from death. Then she thought how lost and lonely Danny would be without John by his side. She wept the rest of the way home.

Later, Darcy called at the Hanlons' house to make arrangements for Angela.

'Thanks ever so much, Nora. I knew I could rely on you.' Darcy glanced over at Angela and the two young Hanlons she was playing with. She'd got over her upset at not being allowed to go and see her dad and was quite excited about staying overnight in the noisy, happy house.

'I hope he's not too badly hurt,' Nora said, then closed her eyes and covered her face with her hands. Darcy knew she was thinking of Bob. He had died of his injuries. Nora gave herself a shake. 'She'll be all right with us. The young'uns'll keep her occupied. She'll not have time to miss you.'

Darcy kissed Angela goodnight, hugged Nora and hurried back to prepare Betsy for the next day's journey, half-wishing she could have stayed at the Hanlons and put all this misery behind her for an hour or two.

* * *

'Wake up, Betsy, we must be nearly there.' Darcy gently shook Betsy's arm. It felt lifeless in her hand.

Betsy opened her bleary, red-rimmed eyes. She looked around her, struggling to get her bearings. She seemed to have aged ten years, and Darcy's breath caught in her throat as she wondered how on earth she was going to manage this broken woman as they made their way across London.

Neither of them had ever travelled so far from home, and as the train slowly chugged into the city, they peered through the windows at the huge buildings crowded together with barely a space between them. Already, they felt intimidated. The other passengers in the carriage, an elderly couple and four soldiers in uniform, roused themselves. The couple had slept for much of the journey and the soldiers, after making a few unfavourable remarks about the overcrowded train and then some half-hearted comments about the weather, had sunk into their greatcoats, wearied and morose. They were going back to the front.

Darcy gathered their bags as the train wheezed and groaned into the station. The platform was heaving with civilians and soldiers, the noise deafening as doors slammed, porters shouted, and mighty engines rumbled in and out.

'Keep close to me, Betsy. Hang on to my arm,' Darcy urged, panic rising at the thought of losing her before they'd even left King's Cross station. She began pushing through the crowds, Betsy clinging onto her arm but trailing her feet, shambling behind as if in a trance.

Outside the station, already sweating with fear and frustration, Darcy saw a line of hackney cabs. Following the instructions she had been given by the kindly sergeant at Wellesley Barracks, she showed the cabbie the passes. 'Queen Mary's Hospital,' she gabbled, 'please.'

'That's Roehampton, darlin',' he said. 'Hop in.'

Darcy pushed an unwilling Betsy into the cab then jumped in beside her. The cab trundled slowly through the busy streets. Had circumstances been different, Darcy would dearly have liked to see Buckingham Palace and other landmarks she had only seen in pictures. She gazed out at the River Thames and the bridges. But this wasn't a day for sightseeing, she told herself miserably, and wondered what sights they were going to see when they arrived at the hospital. Her hands felt clammy and she shuddered involuntarily. Betsy, in a stupor, looked neither left nor right. They travelled in silence, each lost in their own thoughts, until they arrived at Queen Mary's Hospital.

'Ooh! It looks like a palace,' Darcy gasped as the cab drew to a halt, the hospital's many windows and turrets making a grand impression.

'Are we there?' Betsy turned to Darcy, her panic rising.

Darcy helped her out of the cab, the poor woman seeming incapable of moving under her own steam. Darcy felt her own legs trembling as they entered by the huge front doors. What were they going to find when they saw John? They stood, lost, in the huge foyer, the smell of disinfectant strong in their nostrils.

'I'm scared,' Betsy whimpered. Darcy squeezed her arm encouragingly. So was she. Hoisting her bag on her shoulder, she gazed round and was wondering what to do next when a voluntary aid worker stepped out of a small office and came towards them, smiling.

'Can I help you?'

Darcy told her why they were there.

She led them into a corridor, calling for the attention of an orderly. 'These people are here to see Corporal John Carver,' she said.

'I'll look on the list for you.' The orderly flipped pages on a clipboard, his eyebrow puckering as he ran his eyes down lists of names. 'Oh, here we are. Corporal John Carver. He's in ward seven.' He set off walking at a brisk pace and they followed, Betsy lagging behind and Darcy almost having to drag her along.

They walked through long corridors, the building vast. 'Do you know Corporal Carver?' Darcy panted, keeping pace with the orderly. 'What sort of injuries does he have?'

The orderly slowed down. He gave her a pitying glance. 'It's early days,' he said uneasily, a tic working on his right cheek.

Darcy's blood turned cold.

'What was that?' Betsy's wail filled the corridor. 'What did he say?'

The orderly opened a door, spoke to a nurse just inside the ward and left them. The nurse beckoned them inside. Darcy felt her heart hammering; now for the moment of truth. The nurse smiled. 'Which one of you is Mrs Carver?'

Betsy was staring blankly into space, so Darcy answered for her. The nurse took Betsy's elbow, speaking softly to her. Darcy gazed the length of the ward. Rows of iron-framed beds were crammed down either side and in the centre was a long table with vases of flowers on it. Men of all descriptions lay in the beds, the sheets covering some of them held up from their bodies by some sort of structure. Others were swathed in bandages and dressings. Most of them lay very still and for the most part silent, only an occasional moan or groan letting her know they were still alive. She wasn't sure if the cloying smell came from the flowers or the wounded men but she began to feel nauseous.

By now, the nurse was physically supporting Betsy and trying to calm her. Darcy intervened, taking a crumpled Betsy into her arms and rocking her gently. She gave the nurse an enquiring look.

'I was just explaining that Corporal Carver has lost his left leg and that the wound is infected,' the nurse said calmly. 'We're clearing the infection but he is still in great pain. He's not always aware of his surroundings or what has happened to him. You might not get a lot of sense out of him at the moment.'

Darcy was stunned. John had lost his leg. Tarquin the Tumbler was no more.

'I'll take you to him.' The nurse set off walking sedately down the ward, her soft shoes making hushed squishy noises on the linoleum. Darcy tried not to look at the men in the beds, but one young lad sitting propped up on his pillows called out, 'Good afternoon, ladies.'

Darcy smiled at him. Only then did she notice that he had no arms. She swallowed hard to prevent herself from crying out. The nurse stopped by a bed with raised sheets. She nodded her head at the figure in the bed and then at Betsy and Darcy. 'He appears to be sleeping. I'll leave you with him for a while,' she said.

There were two chairs at one side of the bed, so Darcy helped a quivering Betsy into one then sat down beside her. Betsy stared at her husband, her eyes bleak. John lay there, his mouth slightly open, his breath sighing steadily as his chest rose and fell. He looked gaunt and pale, deep lines etched around his mouth and puffed, purple bags under his eyes. He shifted slightly and let out a low, agonised groan. The sound brought Betsy back to reality. She leaned forward, placing her trembling hand on his arm and began stroking it gently. His eyelids fluttered.

'John, it's me. Betsy. I'm here, love,' she whispered.

He didn't immediately show any signs that he had heard her, but as she continued brushing the palm of her hand up and down his bare arm, he opened his eyes. He blinked rapidly and his lips moved soundlessly.

'He knows I'm here.' Betsy was suddenly animated. She turned to Darcy, her lips wobbling into a travesty of a smile. 'He's going to be all right.'

Darcy could barely conceal her amazement at the change in Betsy.

John seemed to be dozing again, so they sat on, not speaking, and an orderly brought them cups of tea. Shortly afterwards, the nurse stopped by. 'Time to go,' she said. 'You can come again tomorrow.'

Betsy glared at her. She wasn't leaving her John. The nurse looked anxiously at Darcy as if to say *She's your responsibility. Get her to leave quietly.* Darcy took hold of Betsy's arm, but she shook her off. 'We haven't come all this way for him not to know we're here,' she told the nurse, her voice raised in protest.

John's eyes flew open. 'Betsy,' he slurred. 'Betsy, is that you, love?'

Darcy let go of her, and Betsy placed a hand on John's cheek. 'It is, love. Me an' Darcy are here to see you.'

He struggled to raise his head, the nurse hurrying to assist him. His eyes lit up. 'By, bloody hell! I thought I wa' dreamin.' He placed his hand over Betsy's, still on his cheek. 'It's you, lass,' he croaked. 'You're really here.'

His smile widened. And seeing it, the nurse said, 'Maybe just a little longer.'

'I've lost me leg, haven't I?' He looked from Betsy to Darcy for confirmation.

'You have, love, but we'll manage. We allus have,' Betsy said stoutly.

'We'll all pull together, John, just like we always do.' Darcy, heartened by Betsy's show of spirit, gave him a reassuring smile.

'It's me left, in't it? I can still feel it, an' it's bloody sore.'

'The nurse says they've got the infection under control,' Darcy told him.

'Aye, well I've still got me right one,' he said musingly. 'I can still work me treadle wi' that. I could have lost 'em both.' He sounded stoic, and so much like the old John that Darcy wanted to cry.

'My goodness, you've worked miracles,' the nurse said when she came back.

Betsy kissed John goodbye, promising to return the next day, and Darcy clasped his hands in hers, imbuing all the strength she could muster. John was alive, and like the nurse said, seeing Betsy had done him the power of good.

They spent the night in a small hotel that the sergeant at the barracks had told them about. When they visited John the next day he was in even better spirits. They talked about Angela and Danny, John saying that, whilst he was glad to be back in Blighty, he'd miss being with Danny. 'He'll be all right,' he said to Darcy. 'He's a good soldier, an' a damned good mate.' His eyes moistened. 'I seem to think he wa' wi' me when it happened.'

Darcy shivered. Had the explosion that stole John's leg taken Danny's life? She prayed not. Surely she would have heard by now, and telling herself not to be foolish, she smiled warmly at the man who had rescued her when she was alone in the world.

* * *

Danny's letter was waiting for them when Betsy and Darcy arrived back from London. They wept to learn what had happened, Darcy's heart swelling with pride to know that Danny had stayed with John until they reached the field station and a doctor, and then giggling when she read that he had 'shovelled shit for two weeks' for disobeying orders. She loved him all the more, and at night she prayed that God would return him to her, safe and sound, and that they would all have something to smile about before this war was over.

And miraculously, God did.

In the final weeks of 1916, things seemed to move at a remarkable pace. John had been transferred to Spring Hall, a convalescent home in Halifax only a mile from home. He was discharged three days before Christmas Day. Darcy sang at a Christmas concert at The Canterbury, and the Dunkirk Ladies' Choir gave yet another performance at Heath Villas. Betsy's knitting circle received accolades for making the largest contribution of any of the local circles sending comforts to the troops at the front, and Angela played a leading role in the school's nativity. The only disappointment as far as Darcy was concerned was that Danny wasn't there to enjoy any of it.

'If anybody had told me three months ago that I'd be the happiest woman in the world, I'd never have believed 'em,' Betsy said on the night before New Year's Eve, beaming across at her husband seated opposite her by a roaring fire.

'Aye, things didn't look too rosy back then,' he agreed, 'but look at us now. It hasn't allus been easy, but patience is a virtue an' God's good.'

'That's what Miss Chippendale says,' Angela chimed. 'I waited ages for her to call out my name and give me a part in the play, and afterwards she said I was the best Angel Gabriel she's ever had.'

Her parents smiled proudly at one another. They had invested so much in her future and were reaping the rewards.

Darcy looked up from her book and smiled also. She was equally proud of Angela and looked on her as a little sister. 'When you made the annunciation I thought I was listening to a real angel,' she said, a sharp rap at the door accompanying her words.

'Hey up, Gabriel's come calling again.' John chuckled, and lifting his crutches from either side of the chair he swung lithely upright.

His forthright acceptance of his disability often brought tears to Darcy's eyes. He whom she'd first met when he was leaping and tumbling and amazing the crowd with his agile feats never once complained. And these days none of the others rushed to answer the door for, as master of the house, they knew John felt it was his place to do so.

Betsy glanced at the clock. 'Who can it be at this time? It's near ten.'

'God in heaven,' they heard John cry, 'if it isn't Sergeant Danny Capp.'

Darcy was on her feet in an instant, almost unbalancing John as she pushed him aside to fling herself at her husband. John tottered dangerously, Danny grabbing hold of his shirt with one hand to steady him and embracing Darcy with his free arm. Then Betsy and Angela joined them and they all clung together, laughter mixing with tears of pure joy.

'I see they promoted you then.' John tapped the stripes on Danny's sleeve as they went to sit down. Danny pulled off his tunic and tossed it on a chair.

'Only because there is no one else,' he said modestly.

Darcy looked at his muscles rippling under his shirt, hardly daring to believe he was really there. Her Danny had come home to her, just as beautiful as he had ever been, she thought, gazing at his face and seeing the weariness round his eyes and the creases etched round his mouth. Danny had aged. He was no longer the carefree young boy who had gone to war, he was a man who had seen and done things no man should ever see and do. Every line and crease had been hard earned and she willed away the tears that welled behind her eyes.

'Why didn't you let us know?' She put her arms round him and nuzzled his cheek with her own, the stubble on his chin like tiny darts of invigorating electricity as it prickled her face. For the first time in months she felt utterly alive and whole.

'I had no time. They say you go on the next boat and here I am.' He gave Darcy a smacking kiss. 'I am here for ten days.'

Darcy's euphoria faded. Ten days. Then he would leave her again. She clung all the tighter to him, breathing in his smell and melting under the feel of his arm about her shoulders. When he removed it to hug Angela, she felt a sudden chill.

Then Betsy, Darcy and Angela hurried into the kitchen to make him a meal. 'I bet he's starving,' Angela said, buttering bread for her hero. 'A girl in my class said they have to eat rats 'cos they don't get enough food.'

Betsy hushed her with a tap on the back of her hand with the ladle she was using to stir the pot of soup.

As the women clattered in the kitchen, John stood with Danny in front of the fire, and taking advantage of their absence he said, 'How is it out there?'

Danny grimaced. 'You should know. No better, no worse, no end to it.' He shook his head despairingly.

John sensed that he didn't really want to talk about it, but he had something he needed to say. Trying for a lighter approach, he continued, 'I heard you had some pretty unpleasant shovelling to do after they took me off.' He grinned wryly.

'It was worth it,' Danny said solemnly, his dark eyes warm as he gazed directly into John's.

'Darcy told me what you did,' John said gruffly. 'Thanks, pal.' Then, almost choking on his emotions, he let one of his crutches fall, and placing his arm round Danny's shoulders, he pulled him closer. 'You're t'best mate anybody could have.'

On New Year's Eve, the Carvers and the Cappelinis stood out on the pavement in Pellon Lane with their neighbours, listening to the church bells ring out the old year and chime in the new. As the carillon of bells pealed out their joyful message, every man, woman and child in Pellon Lane hoped that 1917 would bring an end to the war.

Darcy could feel Danny's heart beating against her shoulder blade as she leaned back in his arms, his chin resting on the top of her head. It was bitingly cold, the blue-purple sky a patchwork of brittle stars, but she felt safe and snug. Danny turned Darcy round to face him and kissed her. 'Happy New Year, my love,' he whispered in her ear.

'Happy New Year, the love of my life,' she said, kissing him back then giving him an impish grin. 'Now we have to go first-footing.'

'Not again! You make me do this every year,' Danny laughed as Darcy handed him a lump of coal and led him to the house next door.

'Go on, bring them a bit of good luck,' Darcy cajoled. 'It only works if a dark-haired man is the first to cross the threshold after midnight and wish them a peaceful and prosperous New Year.' She pushed him forward.

Betsy and John had agreed that Angela could stay up late and carry the bucket of coal, so she ran and knocked on a neighbour's door.

'Eeh! He's t'best lookin' man wi' black hair that ever crossed my threstle,' Sally Moore gushed as Danny charmingly performed his duties.

They went to the doors of four more houses, handing their neighbours lumps of coal until Danny laughingly protested.

'I have a much better idea of how to bring in this New Year,' he whispered in Darcy's ear. 'Let's go home to bed and I will show you.'

She went willingly.

* * *

Ten days of living in a dream was ten days too little.

Darcy had sought Joseph Bentley's permission to take a week off work. 'I think we can manage without you, Mrs Cappelini,' he'd said, smiling at his 'little songbird', as he called her. He admired her fortitude. Darcy and her ladies' choir appealed to his philanthropic nature, and it had enhanced the reputation of his mill.

On Danny's last night before his return to Wellesley Barracks, Darcy lay naked in his arms, savouring the taste and touch of him. In a few short hours he would go again, leaving her bereft. Lazily, Danny stroked the smooth skin on her thigh. His eyes were closed but he was seeing a battlefield, stumps of blackened trees in swirling mud and blood, and the fallen men crying out in agony as they drew their last breaths. He shuddered so violently that his body lifted off the mattress.

'What is it, love?' Startled out of the glorious stupor of their lovemaking, Darcy clung to his trembling body until he stopped shaking.

'It is nothing,' he reassured her, rolling on top of her to make love for what he feared might be the very last time.

26

He was gone, and once again Darcy felt as though she had lost part of herself. One moment her world was a shining, golden glass bubble and the next it was shattered into a million pieces. Slowly, she set about putting it together again. She accepted an offer to sing every other Saturday night at The Canterbury. Singing always made her feel closer to Danny.

The small theatre had a new manager, and it was he who had approached Darcy. Herbert Booth was a man of middle years, affable and fatherly, and Darcy liked him instantly. He had worked in musical theatre for many years, and she was fascinated by his stories about the show people he had worked with in better times. So, with this new interest to occupy her, and her continuing friend-ship with Nora, life didn't seem all doom and gloom even if it wasn't what she would have chosen. It wasn't within her powers to have Danny by her side – the kaiser and the king had put paid to that – so she was making the best of what she had. And she wasn't the only one.

'I'm reopening the shop and going back to cobbling,' John

announced one Saturday afternoon in March, when Darcy was just home from the mill.

Betsy looked up, surprised. 'Will you be able to manage?' She tried to ignore his missing lower leg and rarely commented on it, but she'd grown used to having him about the house all day and was reluctant to be apart from him even for a few hours.

'I can't sit on me backside for the rest of me life, and in a week or two I should be gettin' me false leg.' He'd been to St James' Hospital in Leeds to be measured for one and was now waiting impatiently for the final fitting.

'I think that's a great idea,' Darcy said, taking the cup of tea Betsy handed her.

She sipped reflectively. At least John was getting his life back on track.

'But how will you manage to mend shoes an' serve in the shop at the same time?' Betsy said, throwing another spanner in the works.

'Ah, well, that's just it.' John's smile was enigmatic, and Darcy thought he was about to suggest she return as his assistant. She'd hate to disappoint him, but she didn't want to leave her job in the mill. 'I think I have the answer to that,' he continued. 'When I wa' in Spring Bank I met this young lad who'd worked in Schofields in Leeds. He knows all about sellin' shoes, an' he said he wouldn't mind learnin' how to make an' mend 'em. I told him that if I started up again he wa' welcome to join me.' He glanced from Betsy to Darcy for their approval.

Betsy frowned. 'What was he in Spring Bank for?' She was thinking that if he'd lost an arm or a leg he'd not be much use to John.

'Same as me, except that his was his right leg.' He grinned. 'We'd be like a pair of book ends proppin' one another up.' He paused thoughtfully. 'He'll have his prosthetic by now, I should think, so I'm going to get in touch with him an' see what he says.'

* * *

On a cold, frosty morning about two months after Danny had returned to France, Darcy was kneeling over the lavatory bowl being violently sick. She had felt odd from the moment she'd wakened and got dressed, but it wasn't until she went down into the kitchen and smelled the tea brewing on the gas ring that her insides churned and she'd had to dash out to the closet.

She sat back on her heels trying to remember what she had eaten the night before, then, like the fluttering wings of a butterfly, another thought came into her head. Was she...? Could she really be...?

She scrambled to her feet, the sharp smell of the whitewash on the closet's walls making her feel queasy again. She leaned back against the closet door and began counting the weeks. Her heart began to pound. The last time she'd had her monthly show was just before Christmas. She counted again. *I must be pregnant*, she thought, the realisation making her head spin.

She stepped out into the yard, a stiff breeze tugging at her long, blonde hair and whipping her skirt against her legs. She gazed up at the scudding clouds. She was going to have a baby, going to be a mother. And Danny was going to be father. Oh, how she longed for him to be here to see the wonder in his beautiful dark eyes when she told him. She walked back into the house on legs that felt as though they didn't belong to her.

Betsy was in the kitchen frying slivers of streaky bacon, a Sunday morning treat because, like everything else, bacon was rationed. Darcy's stomach churned again and she thought she might have to dash back to the closet. The nausea passed and she stood watching Betsy, questions burning on her tongue.

'I've just been sick,' she said.

Betsy spun round from the cooker, concerned.

'Do you think I could be having a baby?'

Betsy turned out the gas and gave Darcy her full attention. She was smiling broadly. 'I don't see why not. You an' Danny spent enough time in bed on his last leave. When did you last have...?'

Darcy told her.

Betsy chuckled. 'Then by my reckonin' I think you must be.' She threw her arms round Darcy. 'Congratulations, love. I'm thrilled for you.'

Then Betsy popped her head round the kitchen door, laughing as she called into the parlour, 'John, you're going to be a granddad, an' you Angela an auntie.'

They both whooped their delight, and at that moment Darcy felt very loved and very precious.

Later that afternoon, Darcy called on Nora to share her news.

'How did you not know you'd missed your period?' Nora looked askance. 'I'd know if I missed mine.' Her cheeks reddened as she added, 'Me an' Bob did it a couple of times afore he went away an' I wa' on eggshells waiting to see if I'd fallen.' Her face crumpled, tears spilling down her cheeks. 'I could have had his baby,' she sobbed. 'That way I'd have had somethin' of him now.'

Darcy shifted up on the bed in Nora's room and pulled her close, rocking her gently and making soothing platitudes, at the same time thinking that if her Danny didn't come back she at least would have a part of him.

Nora pulled away and wiped her eyes on her cardigan sleeve.

'I'm glad for you, Darcy, I really am,' she said, making a great effort to push aside her grief.

'So am I, but I still can't really believe it.'

'I'm sure your Danny will be over the moon. I read somewhere that Italians love babies, that they're a lot more loving with their children and their old people than the English are.' Nora frowned. 'Do you think that's true?'

'I don't know.' It was Darcy's turn to frown. 'Danny doesn't know he's going to be a father. I'll write to him tonight. I'd like to think that what you read is true. Danny's the most loving person I know.'

* * *

The estaminet was noisy and thick with smoke. Danny sat with his legs stretched out in front of him and a glass of brandy in his hand. He tilted his head and swallowed, the fiery liquid slipping down his throat like nectar from the gods. His battalion had been stood down for four days somewhere near Arras, and the lads were making the most of it.

'There's some cracking lasses through by there.' Taffy Jones nudged Danny with his elbow as he sat down beside him. 'You want to get yourself in there, boyo,' he crowed, pointing to the yard at the rear where a queue of eager soldiers awaited their turn outside the prostitutes' huts. 'I'll guarantee you'll have a good time.' He picked up a glass and drank greedily.

'Not for me,' Danny said dreamily. 'I do not need their good time.'

More than once during his time in France he had been tempted to seek the pleasures of a woman; after all, he was a healthy young man and it had been a long time, but when he'd entered the sleazy huts reeking of cheap perfume and semen he'd reneged on their sexual favours and just sat talking. He enjoyed female company but he did not desire their bodies, not when there was the most perfect, luscious body waiting for him at home. And tonight the thought of taking another woman filled him with revulsion.

He patted his breast pocket where, next to his heart, was the letter telling him he was going to be a father. The euphoric feeling of pure unmitigated joy that had been his from the moment he had read Darcy's words now seemed like a cruel dream sent to taunt him. He drained his glass, tears moistening his eyes as he imagined his beautiful Darcy's body blooming in pregnancy and him not there to witness it. His fingers itched to stroke the mound of her burgeoning belly and her swelling breasts. Lifting the bottle, he replenished his glass. He felt such a deep sense of despair that it made his breath catch in his throat. His dark eyes mirrored all the sadness in the world as he slowly sipped his brandy, praying that he would live to see his child.

* * *

Colin Whittaker arrived in Halifax some six weeks after John had written asking him to come and work in the shoe shop. He was a tall, bony man, his thinness accentuated by the too-large suit that the army had provided him with on his return to civilian life. He walked with a loping gait, his false leg swinging in a little circle before it touched the ground. His sandy hair flopped over his brow and his soft brown eyes spoke of a man who had known great pain and suffering.

'He's not much to look at,' Betsy whispered as she and Darcy went into the kitchen to make tea, leaving Colin in the parlour with John.

'I don't think John's employing him for his looks.' Darcy filled the kettle and put it on the gas. 'He looks all right to me, and John seems to have faith in him.'

Once the tea was brewed and served, Darcy put a pale blue cardigan over her white dress with a sailor-suit collar. The dress was loose at the front and hid her thickening waistline, of which she was immensely proud. She didn't bother with a hat, the May weather being warm and sunny, and her blonde hair hung silkily about her blooming cheeks.

John and Colin were in deep conversation in the parlour, Betsy hovering and listening to what they were talking about.

'I'm meeting Nora,' Darcy announced, 'so I'll see you all later. Bye, Colin, nice to meet you.'

He gave her a grateful smile. *Poor lad*, she thought as she walked from the room, *He's as nervous as a kitten*. She supposed that losing a limb would sap anybody's confidence. Then she thought of John. It seemed to have had the opposite effect on him. These days he was all drive.

Nora was waiting for her on the corner of Pellon Lane and Silver Street. She was looking extremely attractive in a dark green, calf-length dress with a square-necked bloused top, the new shorter length of her skirt accentuating her height. She, too, was hatless, and she'd rolled her long, red hair into a loose chignon, leaving a few soft wispy curls round her face.

'You look nice,' Darcy said warmly. 'That green goes really well with your hair.'

'You don't look so bad yourself,' Nora quipped. 'Nobody 'ud ever guess you were four months pregnant.' When Nora had said she was thrilled about Darcy's pregnancy she had truly meant it and took as much interest in Darcy's condition as she herself did.

'I'll not look like this much longer. Some of my skirts are already a bit tight. I might not be showing much, but in there is a lively little girl or boy. When I was getting meself washed I thought I felt a little jiggle.'

Arm in arm, the two girls strolled into Cheapside and on to Borough Market.

Darcy bought fine lawn cotton to make little nightdresses, and Nora some buns and a quarter of Bassett's Liquorice Allsorts to take home for the young 'uns. As they perused the stalls and then went into the Piece Hall, Darcy reflected on the days she and John had performed there or on the street corners round the market. She thought fondly of the first time she had heard Danny singing 'The Rose of Tralee' outside the Piece Hall and her heart filled with anxiety for him.

On their way back up Pellon Lane – Nora was calling in for a cup of tea with Betsy before returning to the chaos in Silver Street – they came to the shoe shop. The door was ajar.

'Oh, look, John must be showing Colin round the shop.' Darcy had mentioned him to Nora as they'd walked round the market. 'Let's go in.'

Colin was standing behind the counter, and when the girls went in he stepped out from behind it, his false leg swinging a little as he came towards them. He smiled when he recognised Darcy.

'Are you sizing the place up? Seeing what you can make of it,' she said.

He nodded shyly, but his eyes were on Nora. And when Darcy glanced at Nora she saw that her eyes were on him, a gentle smile curving her lips.

'This is my friend, Nora Hanlon. Nora, let me introduce you to Colin Whittaker.' They shook hands for a little too long.

'I'll just pop in and see what John's up to.' Darcy walked through to the workshop where John was tinkering with his sewing machine.

'We're starting up on Monday,' he said when he saw her. 'I'm just oiling the machinery. Colin seems pleased enough, an' he's full of good ideas. He's talkin' of me makin' bespoke boots an' shoes.'

'Bespoke!' Darcy's eyes twinkled. 'Very lah-di-dah.'

She left John to it, and returning to the shop she found Nora and Colin deep in conversation. They broke off, both looking a little bit embarrassed.

'Are we ready for going?' Nora sounded slightly disappointed.

'He's lovely, isn't he?' she said when they were back on the street. 'I could have talked to him all day.'

Darcy chuckled. 'Miss Hanlon! Do I detect more than a glimmer of interest in our Mr Whittaker?'

Nora blushed. 'I don't know.' She sounded bemused. 'I never thought I'd look at another man after losing Bob, but the minute we started talking – no, even before that – I felt drawn to Colin. An' I think he felt the same. We just sort o' clicked.' Nora pulled Darcy to a halt, her expression a mixture of confusion and hungry longing as she said, 'Do you think I'm being daft?'

Darcy felt choked. 'If you think you've found a new friend, I'm glad for you. It's about time you had some love in your life.'

* * *

Darcy sat in her room writing to Danny. In her lap was his reply to her letter telling him he was going to be a father. Of all his letters, this one was her favourite. She knew it by heart but couldn't resist reading it again, every word beautiful, spelling mistakes and all.

My Deerest Darcy, my bellissima wife,

Me and you, mamma and pappa. My hart is big and molto felice (crossed through) verry happy. I not care if bambina or bambino as long is all well. If bambino I hope he look like me. And if bambina she will be bellissima like mamma. Mia cara, my hart is yorrs. You make me molto fiero (crossed through) verry prowd. I will be good husband and pappa I promiss you.

In his own sweet way, Danny went on to tell her how much he loved and missed her. She told him about the baby jiggling, and about Nora and Colin.

Then she poured out her heart in loving words for the rest of her letter – for until this awful war was over words were all they had.

27

'So, I'm being stood up for Colin Whittaker am I?' Darcy laughed mischievously. It was a Friday evening in June and she and Nora were walking home from work.

'I know we said we'd go to see that new film on at the Electric but' – Nora's cheeks had gone quite pink – 'when Colin asked me I didn't like to say no.'

'I'll bet you didn't.' Darcy chortled.

'You don't mind do you?'

'I'm pleased for you, love. I truly am. Anyway, I stood you up last Saturday when I went for tea with Herbert.'

'Aye, you did. What was it like? You haven't said owt about it.'

Darcy pulled a face. 'Like you, I didn't like to refuse.' She shrugged. 'He's such an old-fashioned gentleman. He kept steering me with his hand on my elbow as we walked to the teashop, and when we were sitting down he kept patting my hand, the dithery old goat. Mind you, he tells some wonderful stories about the theatre, and he's been ever so kind giving me regular slots at The Canterbury.'

'Aye, keep well in with Herbert.' Nora gave Darcy a sly nudge and winked.

Darcy grimaced. 'I will. I'm on again tomorrow tonight.'

* * *

Herbert Booth stood in the wings of the small stage in The Canterbury, his heart filled with longing and his eyes filled with lust. Oh, but she was such a beautiful creature, with a voice to match. He tugged at the front of his trousers to ease the fire in his loins.

Darcy was centre stage, bathed in a soft pool of light, her sweet voice soaring to the rafters. She looked like an angel in her white dress made from flimsy muslin and her flowing, pale hair sweeping her shoulders. The dress, caught in under the curve of her swelling breasts, fell loosely to her ankles, hiding the small mound of her belly. As she reached for the high notes at the end of the aria, she felt a trickle of moisture running down her inner thigh. Her voice faltered. Then, making a quick recovery, she brought the song to an end, took her bow and swiftly left the stage.

'Goodnight, Herbert,' she said, brushing past him in her panic to find out what was happening to her. She was oblivious to the effect her fleeting touch had on him as she hurried down the corridor to the dressing room. Grabbing a clean handkerchief from her bag, she rushed to the lavatory. Her heart fluttered painfully as she dabbed between her thighs then peered at the hanky. It was moistened with a watery pink fluid. Darcy's heart missed a beat.

Breaking into a sweat, she dabbed again. Was that blood? Sally in the weaving shed had had to go home when something similar had happened to her – she'd lost her baby. Tears sprang to Darcy's eyes. She had to get home and get a doctor.

Back in the dressing room to get her bag, she sensed someone behind her.

'You sang magnificently tonight, my dear.'

Darcy turned. Herbert blocked the doorway, his florid face wreathed in a sweaty smile. He quivered, almost slavering with pent-up longing. His gaze drifted from her lovely face to her curvaceous figure and he thought of his fat, frowsy wife. He had to have her.

Darcy stared back at him. Why was he looking at her like that?

'I really must dash, Herbert.' She moved to push past him but he caught her wrist.

'You must know how I feel about you, Darcy,' he panted, his pot belly forcing her further into the room and up against a wardrobe. She twisted her arm to release his grip but it only excited him more. He pushed his face into her breast. 'If I can't touch you I'll go out of my mind,' he mumbled, his lips hot and wet on her skin as his hand pressed frantically over her dress and between her legs. 'I have to have you!'

Darcy froze. It was happening again. Abe Earnshaw! Norris Firth! The sickening smell of lust! The frantic hands! Her mind seemed to have stopped working – but feeling a warm wetness oozing between her thighs, she came hurtling back to reality.

'Let me go, you filthy pig! I'm pregnant! I might be losing my baby!'

Her screams brought Herbert up sharp. He saw the terror in his angel's eyes and the smears of blood on her white dress. He reeled, feeling physically sick. What had he been thinking? 'Darcy! Darcy!' he cried, falling to his knees.

But Darcy wasn't there. She had fled.

28

A year had passed. A year in which the war had not come to the hoped-for end. A year that had brought its fair share of sorrows and joys. And on a glorious day in April 1918, as she stood before the altar in St Mary's church in Gibbet Street, she was once again filled with the promise of a brighter tomorrow.

The organ pealed out the 'Wedding March' and Nora and Colin walked down the aisle smiling and nodding at family members and friends, who were all smiling back and offering their congratulations. Nora was radiant in a white lace dress trimmed with green ribbons, and Colin smart in a new grey suit. She matched her step to his, slow and steady, although he'd got used to his prosthetic and no longer swung his false leg quite as much. The smile on his face was one of ecstasy. Darcy walked behind them, pretty as a picture in a blue satin dress, and a circlet of white flowers crowning her pale, silken hair.

A shower of rice met them as they came out into the bright April sunshine. As the wedding guests clustered round the bride and groom, Darcy hurried over to Betsy, John and Angela.

'Has he been good?' she asked anxiously, 'I didn't hear him cry.'

She peered into the pram where Luca gazed up at her with his father's soulful Italian eyes, then he pursed his rosebud mouth and blew a bubble. Darcy reached in and lifted him. He smelled of milk and talcum powder, and she nuzzled her nose into the fold of his neck. At six months old, Luca Thomas Cappelini was the bonniest baby in the world. He had Danny's looks, just as his father had hoped, and he was just as sweet-tempered. He gave a tiny burp as he settled in his adoring mamma's arms.

'He was as good as gold, not a murmur out of him,' Betsy replied.

'But he did jump when the organ crashed out that first hymn,' Angela piped.

'Aye, well, "Now Thank We All Our God" is enough to make anybody jump.' John chuckled. 'Especially when t'organs playin' at one speed an' t'singers are three notes behind it.'

They all laughed.

There had been several fraught weeks after Darcy's ordeal with Herbert, and she had struggled for the sake of her baby not to let it overwhelm her. As she desperately held on to the little life inside her, she hadn't allowed herself to dwell on the fumbling of a frustrated, silly old man.

'The trouble with you, Darcy, is that you don't realise how lovely you are,' Betsy had said. 'I know you don't go out of your way to give men like him any encouragement, but when they look at you they see what they've been missin'.'

Darcy had blinked with surprise at Betsy's philosophical take on the incident, but it had helped put it into perspective, so much so that she'd giggled at Betsy's perspicacity. Betsy was a bit of a dark horse, and Darcy often thought she didn't give her the credit she deserved when it came to reasoning the mysteries of life.

Nora bounced over to them. She was positively glowing.

'Isn't it just perfect? You know, there was a time when I thought

I'd never find happiness again, but look at me now.' She performed a dizzy twirl.

Darcy handed Luca to Betsy then caught Nora in a big hug. When she let her go, Nora cried, 'Just look at him, he's beautiful.' She gave the baby a rapturous smile.

'So is his dad.' The joy Darcy was feeling slipped suddenly away as she thought of Danny. He had yet to meet his son.

In November 1917, only a month after Luca's birth, Danny's regiment had been transferred to Italy; he had gone home, but not in the way that he had imagined. He wasn't crossing the River Arno by way of the Ponte Vecchio, strolling past its intriguing little shops with Darcy on his arm. Instead of showing her the splendours of his native Florence as they had dreamed and planned of doing one day, he and his comrades were holding back the Germans on the River Piave.

Darcy sent photographs and weekly accounts of Luca's progress, but they were small compensation. Now, as she relieved Betsy of her son, Darcy wished with all her might that her husband was here to share this joyful occasion.

Throughout the summer months that followed, she frequently dwelt on all the things Danny was missing, and as Luca's first birthday approached it broke her heart to think that his father hadn't been there to see his first smile or his first tooth, or to attend his christening. Luca had taken his first steps and said his first words and his father had yet to hold him in his arms. With each passing day she wondered how long this war would go on.

The war had been lucrative for Abe Earnshaw and the sawmill. Harry Chadwick had managed to secure a contract with the Ministry of Defence to supply timber to make duckboards for the trenches and pit props to shore up the tunnels. As Abe's profits increased, so did Harry's dislike and distrust of him.

'The men are demanding an increase in wages,' Harry told Abe one morning in May as Abe sloped into the mill.

Abe responded with a sneer and a dismissive wave of his hand. He was about to walk away but Harry blocked his path. 'Not so fast!' he barked.

Startled, Abe shuffled his feet uneasily. 'I'm listening,' he growled.

'Way back in 1909, when you took over, you cut their wages to next to nowt,' Harry continued, 'an' it wa' 1915 afore you brought 'em back up to what they had been, an' that wa' only because we threatened to go on strike.'

'I increased them again in 1916 when we got the contract,' Abe blustered.

'Aye, well, now we're in 1918 an' we want a better cut,' Harry sneered. 'An' if we don't get it, we're withdrawing our labour.'

Abe looked about to explode. 'I'll consider it,' he roared. 'Now get out of my way.'

'Aye, do,' Harry roared back, throwing caution to the wind. 'An' whilst you're thinkin' about it get Miss Darcy back from t'Lake District. She's turned twenty-two, an' by rights she should be in charge here. It's what Thomas wanted.'

Abe's blood ran cold. Damn the man! Was he never going to let it drop?

He scuttled off, muttering under his breath. He'd long since given up hope of finding Darcy or the documents that proved her ownership of the mill. He'd convinced himself that she was ignorant of her father's wishes and therefore had no reason to return to Bradley Brigg. Whenever he was drunk – which he often was – he liked to fantasise that she was dead.

Cursing Harry Chadwick for all he was worth, Abe drove back

to Northcrop House. Polly had gone for the day; the house empty and cold. He stood shivering in his overcoat. Damn it! It might be summer, but he'd light the fire and open the new bottle of brandy, and to hell with them all.

He shambled into the pantry where Polly kept the sticks and paper, then back at the hearth in the parlour he knelt to fill the grate. Shaking loose the pages of a newspaper he began screwing them into balls. A sheet fluttered free, and as he reached for it a picture of a girl caught his eye. His hand froze in mid-air. He peered at the photograph, his heart jumping into his throat.

My God, it was Darcy! He'd recognise that face anywhere. His hands shaking, he scanned the article, an evil smile curving his lips. Now he had her.

Forgetting about the fire, Abe hurried out to the trap and drove to a secluded house on the edge of the town. Cissie Sharp greeted him with a smile on her fleshy, motherly face. Anyone seeing Cissie would have found it hard to believe that this homely looking woman was a procurer of young girls and boys, and that her neat, cosy house was a den of iniquity.

'Abe. You're in nice time. We're just getting started.' She led him through into a comfortable parlour.

Abe couldn't believe his luck. Dr Paddy Flynn and Josiah Pemberton, the local magistrate, were both present. He nodded to them and took his seat lustfully, eyeing the half-dozen or so semi-naked young children who were moving about the room serving drinks and sweetmeats to the gentlemen whose proclivities matched his own. He chose a waif-like girl of about thirteen years of age. She had long blonde hair and striking blue eyes.

Later, his sexual needs satisfied and arrangements made with the doctor and the magistrate, Abe drove home triumphant. It was amazing what money and subtle threats of revelation could achieve. He laughed out loud to the night sky as he recalled the magistrate's ashen face when he'd hinted that the law and the town council would take a dim view of his leisure activities. The poor chap had almost shat himself. He'd blustered, claiming that Abe was as guilty as he was, but common sense had ruled that his reputation would be tarnished, and sullenly he'd acquiesced to Abe's demands. Paddy Flynn had been much easier to persuade. He was a drunk and a gambler, and up to his ears in debt. His eyes had glittered greedily when Abe told him what he was prepared to pay for his services. Now, with the required public officials in the bag, all Abe needed to do was find Darcy. Thanks to the newspaper article, he knew exactly where to look.

'He grows bonnier every day,' Betsy gushed as she came from the kitchen into parlour, drying her hands on her apron. 'Luca, come to Nana Betsy,' she cooed.

Darcy's face glowed with love and pride as she watched Luca pull himself up onto his feet with the aid of the couch. He toddled unsteadily over to Betsy wearing a gummy smile and his plump little arms outstretched. She swung him up, plopping kisses on his rosy cheeks. Luca giggled and smacked his lips.

He was just approaching his first birthday. He was his mamma's pride and joy, her greatest treasure, and for Nana Betsy he filled the yearning hole left by not having given birth to a boy: a son for John and a brother for her darling Angela.

'Can I take him out for a walk in his new pushchair this afternoon?' Angela looked on Luca as the baby brother she had never had and loved showing him off to her friends. 'That's because he's an Italian baby,' she would say when they commented on his big dark eyes, his swarthy complexion and black curly hair. She was now eleven and Darcy trusted her implicitly with Luca.

'Not today, love. I'm taking him with me to Hebden Bridge,' Darcy said, pinning on her hat in front of the mirror over the sideboard. 'I'm going to meet the lady who's asked me to sing at her daughter's wedding, and it'll be a treat for Luca. He's never been on a bus before.' Her hat in place, she fetched the collapsible pushchair from under the stairs. 'You can dress him for me though. He'll need his coat and cap on. I know it's only September, but there's a definite nip in the air.'

'Aye, wrap him up well. We don't want him catching a cold.'

Darcy shuddered at the thought. Nervous Betsy lived in fear and dread of any one of them falling ill.

Angela jumped to do Darcy's bidding. Luca was far more fun than a doll. Dressed in his warm navy cloth coat and navy and white sailor's cap, Luca looked a little dandy.

'I'll be off then,' said Darcy, putting on her own coat then lifting Luca into the chair. Angela wheeled him out to the street.

'I don't know why the woman couldn't come to see you here,' Betsy complained as she followed her to the door. 'It's an awful long way to trail that little lad.' She gave Darcy a winning smile. 'You could always leave him with me.'

'She says she's infirm and can't travel, and now I'm not working in the mill I need to earn something,' Darcy replied as she relieved Angela of the pushchair and set off for the bus stop.

'You take care,' Betsy called out anxiously. 'Don't be sitting next to anybody who's coughing on the bus.'

The journey was a great success, Luca thrilled by the bus's jouncing motion and the countryside flashing past, and Darcy taking great pleasure from pointing out cows, sheep and horses in the meadows, and anything else that might interest Luca. Thankful for the collapsible pushchair, Darcy lifted it off the bus, unfolded it then strapped Luca in.

His new experiences making him sleepy, he lolled in the

pushchair, his head falling to his chest and his eyes closing long before they reached Moss Lane. The house wasn't quite what Darcy had expected, its windows grimy and its tiny garden a patch of mud and weeds. An uneasy feeling made her hesitate. Then she reminded herself that Mrs Derby was infirm. She wheeled the pushchair through the gate. Luca was fast asleep, his chubby fist tucked under his chin and his long, dark lashes fanning his cheeks. Her heart rejoiced at the beauty of him; he was so like Danny.

Rather than disturb him, she decided to leave him outside. She'd make it quick. Find out the details of time and place, what songs to sing, and then leave. It would only take a few minutes. She gave Luca a final, loving smile then knocked on the door. It opened, and Darcy was gripped by a pair of strong arms and dragged inside. She fought to free herself, kicking and screaming and biting at the hand that was clamped over her mouth. After that she felt nothing.

'Bring the car round,' Abe Earnshaw panted, tossing the chloroform-soaked rag to the dusty floor.

Seth Senior looked doubtfully at Darcy, who was lying in a heap on the filthy lino, her clothing dishevelled and her long golden hair straggling free of her chignon. Her hat lay close by, lost in the struggle.

'Go on, you dolt. Don't just stand there gawping,' Abe snarled.

Seth's mate, Ronnie, hovered nervously behind Seth. 'Is she dead?' He sounded as though he might cry.

'Of course she's not dead, you blithering idiot. Get a move on before the chloroform wears off.' Abe gave Seth a hefty shove.

Seth skittered out of the house, cursing under his breath as he hared up the street to where he had left the stolen van. He should never have got involved with Abe Earnshaw.

Ronnie followed him to the door. He peered out. 'There's a

baby out here,' he croaked, dearly wishing he were anywhere else but with the madman inside.

Abe hurried to the door, his face grim when he saw Luca. The child must be hers. They couldn't leave it here for someone to find. It would give the game away. 'Take it up the street. Leave it outside the shops. Somebody will find it but they won't connect it to us.'

Seth arrived back with the van and he and Abe trailed Darcy into it. They picked Ronnie up outside the shops. Untroubled, Luca Thomas Cappelini slept on, unaware that he had been abandoned.

'She shouldn't be this late,' Betsy said, wringing her hands and glancing at the clock for the umpteenth time. 'Luca will be hungry. Where can she be?'

'Well, she's not at Nora's,' John said, having just returned from there, 'and she didn't visit anybody in Burgos Court 'cos I called in there as well.' He thumped his fist into his palm, his face grim. 'Summat must have happened. Maybe she's had an accident.' Unable to stay still, he paced the floor, his false leg thudding. 'That's it. I'm going for the police.'

Reeking of whisky, Dr Paddy Flynn signed the forms with a flourish. Josiah Pemberton did the same and Arnold Beck, the superintendent of the asylum for the insane, witnessed them.

'Well, gentleman, that's the formalities seen to.' Arnold took the document and placed it in his desk drawer.

'I'll be off then,' said Paddy, eager to get to the nearest pub.

Pemberton glared at the doctor, the unspoken message being *keep your mouth shut.*

Abe, looking extremely sanctimonious, addressed the superintendent. 'Such a pity,' he whined. 'She was such a lovely girl' – he paused dramatically – 'but her mind isn't her own. Grief, you know, ever since she lost her parents.' His eyes slid to the superintendent to judge the effect his lies were having. 'She lives in a fantasy world – thinks she's married and has a child. All nonsense of course.' He sighed heavily. 'And she's morally corrupt. She spins dreadful stories about me, when all I've ever done is try to care for her. Sadly, she's now beyond my control. She can be very destructive and violent.' Faking a sob he said, 'I'll leave her with you.' He shuffled out of the office, barely able to conceal the evil smile twitching at the corners of his mouth.

Darcy was huddled in the corner of a bare, narrow room with barred windows in one wall, the vestiges of chloroform still on her lips. Her hair hung in tatters about her dirty face, and her eyes roamed wildly from floor to ceiling, wall to wall. The wooziness was wearing off and she was struggling to understand where she was – and why.

She wiped her face on the hem of her dress then forced herself to take deep, calming breaths. The last thing she could remember was smiling at Luca, asleep in his pushchair. Her heart jolted. Where was he? She scrabbled upright, frantically looking round the small room and saw nothing but bare walls, a bucket in a corner and a padded pallet on the floor. Staggering to the door, she searched for a handle, and not finding one she beat on the panels with her fists.

'Let me out!' she screamed. 'Open this door.' She continued

pounding and screeching until her knuckles bled and her throat was raw. From his observation point outside the room Arnold Beck watched impassively.

'Just as the doctor and Mr Earnshaw described,' he said to the keeper at his side. 'One minute passive and detached and the next a deranged virago. Keep an eye on her. Don't let her injure herself further.'

Unconcerned, the keeper nodded. She'd seen it all before.

Arnold walked back to his office. He hated his job. Dealing with pauper lunatics, demented alcoholics and the manically depressed brought no rewards. And now he had an increasing number of soldiers suffering from shell shock to attend to; yet another burden on an economy that regarded asylum patients as low priority. He was weary of the poor standards of care and treatment and the shortage of nurses due to the war. Darcy Earnshaw was of no particular concern.

Olive Bottomley, the keeper, watched impassively as Darcy threw herself at the door. She'd grow tired eventually; they always did.

Darcy's sudden burst of furious anger and frustration had sent the blood rushing to her brain and her mind cleared. She flopped onto the pallet to think. Olive smirked. Darcy began ordering her thoughts. She'd knocked at the house door – a man she didn't recognise had dragged her inside – she pictured his face – like a weasel's – he'd seemed nervous as he'd trailed her across the floor to where another man...

She leapt up from the pallet as it all came flashing back to her with a clarity that made her tremble. Abe Earnshaw, her Uncle Abe, he had been there. He'd sneered at her and said, 'I've got you now, Darcy.' Then he'd grabbed her in an iron grip and... She shook her head. He must have brought her here. And where was Luca?

Darcy ran to the barred window and, peering through it, she made out the shape of a woman on the other side. She waved then tapped the glass and, raising her voice, she spoke rationally and succinctly. 'Please listen to me. There's been some mistake. My uncle brought me here against my will. You have to let me out. I must go and find my son. He's all alone and he'll be frightened without me.' As she said this, the thought of Luca waking and not finding her with him made tears spill over her cheeks. 'Please,' she sobbed, 'I can explain.'

Olive's stare was implacable. Beck had passed on the detail about the patient thinking she had a son. Darcy, seeing that her pleas had no effect, shrank away from the window and sank down on the pallet, exhausted. She buried her head in her hands, desperately trying to make sense of what was happening.

A tea trolley came rattling down the corridor, pushed by a skinny waif with lank, black hair. Olive stopped her. 'She's calmed down,' she said, 'you can go in an' give her summat.' She unlocked the door. 'Watch her though.'

The girl placed a slice of buttered bread on a small metal tray and poured tea into a tin cup. Balancing the cup on the tray, she entered the room. Darcy looked up, her face flooding with hope. Quickly, the girl slid the tray towards her. 'It's your supper,' she muttered, and just as quickly backed out of the room. The key turned in the lock.

Darcy stared at the meagre offering. Her throat was parched and her belly empty but she'd rather starve to death than let them think she was accepting the situation. She crawled nearer the tray, sorely tempted to drink the hot tea. She licked her dry, cracked lips. Then, burning with outrage, disgust and despair, she flung the tin cup against the wall, and jumping to her feet she trampled the bread and the tin tray underfoot.

'Luca,' she screamed. 'Luca, where are you? Oh God! Danny

please help me!' She tore at her hair, bounced off the walls and rolled on the floor. She kicked the tin bucket from one end of the room to the other time and again, her agonising cries continuing long after the lights in the corridor had dimmed. No one came, God didn't hear her frantic prayers and, thoroughly spent, she fell to the floor and finally into a ragged sleep.

She wakened sometime later and, lying flat on the uncomfortable pallet in the cold, bare room, she opened the darkest chambers of her mind, letting out all the detestable things she had buried there. Out they flew, evil, slimy and black. Darcy felt their agitation in the air as they hurtled through the darkness: Abe's stinking, hairy worm; Norris's clawing hands, the broken bottle and the blood. She screamed and screeched, tearing at her hair and her skin, but no one came to comfort her. Shivering uncontrollably, she slept again.

* * *

The key scraped in the lock and Darcy opened her eyes. They felt gritty and sore. Peering through the blur, she saw that the lights in the corridor were bright. Oh, God, she was still here in this place. She struggled to sit up. Her dress felt damp under her and she realised she must have lost control of her bladder during the night. Her face burned with shame.

The same girl who had brought the tray the evening before crept into the room carrying another tray. She set it down under the window. She saw the puddle. 'You're supposed to pee in the bucket not on the floor,' she said, eyeing Darcy warily as she cleared the mess of trampled bread onto the tray and lifted the battered tin cup.

'It's bread an' dripping an' tea,' she said, nodding over at the other tray. She looked weary and scruffy, her drab grey dress too big on her skinny frame. Her hair was lank with grease and her cheeks blotched with sore, red patches. Even in her own distressed state, Darcy felt pity for her.

'Where am I?' she croaked, her throat so raw that the words stung.

The girl gave her a strange look. 'Storthes Hall,' she replied. Darcy looked bemused. 'You know,' the girl continued, 'the lunatic asylum near Huddersfield.' She walked towards the door carrying the dented tray and cup and the mess of bread. She rapped to be let out.

'I'm not mad,' Darcy said pathetically.

The girl sniffed. 'They all say that in here.' She rapped the door again but no one came. She shrugged. 'That's Olive for you. She must have skived off for a fag.'

'What's your name?' Darcy felt desperately in need of a friend right now.

'Grace Hill.'

'I'm Darcy Cappelini.' She smiled.

'You mean Darcy Earnshaw. That's what it says on the card on the door.'

'No!' Darcy began to gabble. 'I'm married. I have a husband. My baby needs me. Fetch somebody for me to talk to. I shouldn't be here. I'm...'

The key turned in the lock and Olive opened the door.

'None of us should,' Grace replied grimly as she trotted off.

Darcy spent the rest of the morning much as she had the day before, bouts of extreme rage and pleading alternating with exhaustion. When Grace arrived to take away the tray, Darcy was at her lowest ebb.

'Please get someone to come and talk to me so that I can let them know that I'm not insane,' she begged, her eyes dark blue pools of anguish.

'Keep carrying on like you have been doing an' they'll be convinced you are. If you don't want them to think you're a mad woman, don't act like one.'

Grace's pragmatic remark brought Darcy up sharp. She had been acting like a mad woman – with just cause – but she saw the reasoning in Grace's remark. In future, she'd sit calm and collected. Then they'd see the real Darcy Cappelini.

She must have slept through lunchtime, for when she woke she saw the dish of cold stew and a hunk of bread. By now she was so ravenous and thirsty that she gobbled it down. Then she felt sick. With the nausea came tears, and she cried until she was empty. She had to find a way to make them let her go.

When Grace arrived with her tea tray, Darcy eagerly engaged her in conversation, anything to retain her own sanity.

'Are you a maid here?'

Grace gave her a lopsided smile. 'No, I'm like you. I'm an inmate.'

The word 'inmate' grated on Darcy's nerves. 'You don't seem mad,' she said.

'I'm not,' Grace replied firmly, 'but I will be if I stay here much longer.'

'Then why are you here?'

'I had a baby when I wa' thirteen an' me dad had me committed. He said I wa' a stain on the family's reputation,' Grace said flatly.

Darcy gasped. 'What about your baby? Where is it?'

'Don't know, never even saw it.' Grace clamped her lips to stem her tears.

'That's terrible. They can't keep you here for that,' Darcy protested.

'They can if nobody signs you out.' Grace seemed to shrivel with despair.

Olive unlocked the door. 'Finished, have you?' she snapped, addressing Grace and then Darcy. 'You're going to the general ward when you've had your tea.'

* * *

The general ward was a large, cheerless room around which were scattered chairs of all shapes and sizes and a few high and low tables. At this time in the evening the inmates, many of them in a dazed state, lolled in the chairs or sat at the tables listlessly making handicrafts. As Darcy entered, she was struck by the cloying smell of human bodies. She wrinkled her nose and walked over to stand by a window, where she gazed out onto a lawn and distant trees. Dusk had fallen and a sickly yellow light hovered on the horizon. Somewhere out there was her son, all alone. She let silent tears fall.

29

'She has to be somewhere,' Betsy cried, distraught that after two weeks of futile searching John returned with no more news. 'People don't just disappear off the face of the earth without somebody knowing something.'

John sank wearily into the chair. 'It seems they do, love. The police haven't a clue to go on.' He scratched his head, frustrated. 'When I told 'em she might have gone back to Bradley Brigg they sent a chap over there, but he came back with no idea where she might be. I did tell 'em about her dad having owned a sawmill, but the man they spoke to said he hadn't seen her in years.'

'What are we going to tell Danny?' Betsy looked pointedly at the unopened letter on the mantelpiece. 'He'll worry if she doesn't write back.'

'We can hardly write an' tell the poor lad his wife and child have gone missin'.' John grunted. 'He'll have enough troubles to deal with over there.'

'Aye, you're right,' Betsy agreed. 'Although they are sayin' it'll soon be over. Only this morning the coalman wa' tellin' me that our lads had seen the Germans off at Arras, wherever that is.'

'Aye, there's a lot o' talk of victory,' John said grimly, 'but talk's cheap. I'll not believe it till the Germans surrender.'

'Even if the war is soon over an' we've won, there'll be no joy in it for me,' Betsy moaned as she folded a little shirt of Luca's that she had just ironed. 'If we don't find our Darcy an' that little lad, I'll never be happy again.'

* * *

That little lad, Luca Cappelini, was happily chewing on a jam sandwich, watched over by his adoring 'aunts', Violet and Posy Lander.

'He's an absolute joy,' Violet gushed, 'and so biddable now that he's stopped fretting.' She clapped her plump hands, her fat cheeks wobbling with delight.

Violet, the more motherly of the two spinster sisters, stooped to wipe a blob of jam from Luca's chin with a lace-edged hand-kerchief.

'He's certainly brightened up our days,' Posy twittered, her thin, bony fingers flicking wool round her knitting needles: a little bonnet for Luca.

The two elderly sisters had first seen Luca outside the hard-ware store when they were visiting a friend who lived above the shop. They'd cooed over the sleeping child then gone upstairs to take tea and chat. More than an hour later they had descended to find Luca crying pitifully. Filled with outrage at such flagrant neglect, they had gone in search of the child's mother, without success. None of the shopkeepers or their customers knew where the child had come from. A visit to the police station had resulted in the constable on duty telling Violet and Posy that if the mother couldn't be found then an officer would deliver the child to the workhouse.

Horrified, for they had already grown attached to him as they had stilled his tears with the help of an ice cream and jelly babies, the sisters told the constable they would take him to their own home and keep him there until the mother was found. The constable, glad to be relieved of the responsibility, let them go. He could see that the child was in good hands for the time being, and no doubt somebody would claim him soon enough. It didn't seem worthwhile filling out a report. Paperwork got his goat.

Two weeks on, Luca was now established in the comfortable cottage on Sandy Gate. The sisters, after some considerable deliberation, decided to call him Henry.

Luca still cried for his mamma now and then but, like all children of a tender age, as long as he was fed and cuddled and felt safe and warm he soon forgot his sorrows. And Luca had all those things in abundance as Posy and Violet ministered to his every need.

* * *

Each morning and all through the day and for much of the night, Darcy's thoughts dwelt on Luca. Where was he now? She saw his face clearly, and let his entire short life unravel in her mind's eye: from the moment the midwife had placed him in her arms to the last fond smile she had given him as he lay sleeping outside the house in Moss Lane. Her heart warmed as she recalled his smile and his first steps, and the way he held out his plump little arms for her embrace. Then she plunged into the reality that he might be living in squalor at the hands of a cruel warden in a home for abandoned children – or, worse still, not living at all. These thoughts tortured her day and night but she was helpless to prevent them. Her only hope was to survive this terrible ordeal and live to find him, so she struggled through each long day.

If you don't want them to think you're a mad woman, don't act like one. Bearing those words in mind, Darcy hurried across the ward to restrain Gladys, who was rhythmically banging her head on the wall. Gently, she caught the disturbed, frowsy girl in her arms. 'Come on, Gladys, let's me and you go and sit down and you can tell me about your dollies.'

Gladys's head met the panelled wall one more time then, docile as a lamb, she let Darcy lead her to the chairs by the window. 'This one's Susan and this one's Elizabeth,' she said, gesturing to the two grubby rag dolls that she carried with her, everywhere. Darcy knew better than to touch them. These were Gladys's lost babies and nobody was allowed to touch them. To do so would turn feeble, skinny Gladys into a raging lioness protecting her young.

Frances, the keeper on duty, passed by the chairs remarking, 'Good lass, Darcy.' Like all the other keepers on the general ward, she was used to Darcy helping out with the other inmates. Whenever she intervened they raised no objections: she made their job easier. She herself gave them no trouble, and they all questioned the reason for her having been committed.

'She wa' wild enough when she wa' first admitted,' Olive reminded them.

'So would you be if you knew you were sane an' shouldn't be locked up here in the first place,' Frances snorted. 'I've worked here long enough to know the difference between sanity and madness.'

'Arnold Beck seems to think she's delusional,' Olive retorted. 'She wrote some letters on scraps of paper she took from the handicraft box and asked could they be posted – one to 'er 'usband in the army an' another to someb'dy in Halifax.' Olive sniffed disparagingly. 'Beck chucked 'em in t'bin.'

'Did you tell her that?'

'Not my place,' Olive said. 'An' anyway, I didn't want to start her off again.' Bored with the line of conversation, she changed the subject. 'The new doctor starts tomorrow. He's a young lad not long back from France. Dr Steel.'

Frances pulled a face. It was well known amongst the keepers that Olive was Beck's favourite and always knew things before anyone else. 'Well, if he's as useless as Dr Gibb an' Dr Miller, he'll be no use at all,' she said, sourly referring to two of the asylum's resident doctors.

'Oh! Oh! There goes Mary.'

The two keepers jumped up and dashed to where Mary was beating another inmate over the head with a cardboard box. Darcy reached Mary before either Frances or Olive, and between them they calmed her down. Sadly, incidents such as this happened all the time, and when they did the ward became noisier and more restless than usual. Janey the alcoholic began roaring. Sylvia the manic-depressive began wailing like a siren.

Darcy listened to the rising crescendo, sorely tempted to scream and join in the cacophony out of sheer frustration. How much longer would she have to live like this? She was sick of the other inmates' dirty habits, their incontinence and their aggressive outbursts.

Frances led Mary off, no doubt to administer a strong laxative. Dr Gibb firmly believed that profuse diarrhoea calmed his patients – and it did. They were so weakened that they didn't have the energy to be disruptive. Darcy was now familiar with the stink and mess of the aftermath, and her stomach churned. Steeling herself to remain in control, she swallowed the urge to scream and shout. Stupid outbursts served no purpose. She went and sat with Janey. The aged alcoholic liked to sing, and as Darcy sang along with her, she determined that in future she would not allow such incidents to affect her, or to weaken her resolve to find a way out of this terrible place.

By midday the following day, Dr Gavin Steel, with Arnold Beck at his elbow and Dr Gibb trailing behind, had finished his introductory rounds of the asylum and reached the conclusion that he didn't like Gibb, Beck or the treatments the patients received. He was passionate about mental health, having seen so much of it in the trenches where men were driven out of their minds by the continuous bombardment of shot and shell, sleep deprivation and homesickness. He detested the cruelty some officers meted out, calling the men cowards and worse, or executing them for deserting their posts. The mind needed nurturing not punishing, and that's what he hoped to do in his new position.

Now, as he entered the general ward, he made a beeline for Darcy and Janey. Smiling, he joined in the last lines of 'Pack Up Your Troubles in Your Old Kit-Bag and Smile, Smile, Smile'. He enquired after their names.

'Well, Darcy and Janey, I'll come and sing with you again tomorrow,' he said before Dr Gibb urged him on with a none too discreet cough and a nudge.

Darcy liked Dr Steel immediately. Within the next few days on the general ward he ordered that, instead of the brief ten minutes of exercise out in the yard, the inmates should be allowed to walk in the grounds for half an hour each morning. He introduced more meaningful activities and clamped down on the overuse of electric baths – wooden tubs with flat copper electrodes covered with towelling and connected at each end to a battery through which electricity passed.

'This is barbaric,' Darcy had said the first time Frances had asked her to assist in giving Gladys a bath. When she heard that Dr Steel agreed with her she went out of her way to speak to him. Not so much to talk about the treatment of the inmates – that would have been too presumptuous – but to let him see that she was perfectly sane. But Dr Steel had already singled her out, observing her behaviour on the ward, noting how clean and tidily she presented herself: she even managed to make the drab grey dress that all female inmates wore look smart. Then he perused the committal documentation and found no connection with that and her alleged insanity. He was intrigued.

* * *

'And how are you two young ladies this morning?'

Darcy looked round with a smile when she heard Dr Steel's voice. She was walking around the grounds with Gladys on their early morning exercise when he came up behind them. It was a crisp, cold day at the start of November. He had a bright red scarf wound round his neck, and Darcy was reminded of the red shawl she had worn on the day she'd first met Danny in the Piece Hall. It seemed like a lifetime ago. A lump rose in her throat. She swallowed noisily.

'We're fine, doctor, thank you for asking,' Darcy replied, 'although Gladys's feeling the cold.'

The shivering girl was standing with her mouth hanging open, staring vacantly into space.

Gavin cast an eye over the thin, drab grey coats Gladys and Darcy were wearing. 'I'm not surprised. It is bitterly cold. We'd better keep moving or we'll turn into blocks of ice.' He fell into step with them.

'Proper brass monkeys, that's what John called it,' Darcy chirped, her impish smile suddenly fading and her eyes clouding at the memory.

'Who's John?' Gavin seized the chance to learn more about her away from the prying eyes and ears of Dr Gibb and the keepers.

Darcy immediately grasped opportunity to talk about her life before she had been committed to Storthes Hall, and the words spilled out of her. Bit by bit, sometimes with tears and anger and at other times pure, undiluted joy, she told him her story. Gavin listened, horrified by some of the things he heard, and heartbroken by others. She spoke so succinctly, her words alight with truth and sincerity, that not for one moment did he believe it to be a fabrication or the delusional meanderings of someone of unsound mind.

By now, the exercise period was over and the keepers were ushering their charges back indoors. Gavin and Darcy, and poor shivering Gladys, dawdled to the door, he captivated by the beautiful young woman with golden hair and intelligent blue eyes the colour of cornflowers, and she rejoicing at having had the opportunity to explain why she had been committed to the asylum.

'So you see,' she said softly, her face crumpling and tears threatening again as they entered the building, 'all I can hope and pray for is that one day somebody will realise I shouldn't be here and let me go.'

'Come on! Hurry along, Darcy,' Olive bawled, ignoring the fact that Dr Steel was talking to her. She'd already made up her mind, along with some encouragement from Arnold Beck, that this new doctor was interfering with the asylum's regime, and that could only lead to new duties to adapt to, and more work for them.

* * *

Less than a week after Darcy had divulged her story to Dr Steel the kaiser was forced to abdicate. Germany surrendered and peace was declared: the war was over. Then the celebrations began. The streets came alive with bunting and flags and music and drinking. Street parties were organised, people danced the conga, brass bands played at all hours, and cheering could be heard from Land's End to John O' Groats.

But sadly, in many houses throughout the country, the raw emotions of loss, grief and suffering prevented many of the people from rejoicing, none more so than in the Carvers' house in Pellon Lane.

'I've lived for this day,' Betsy moaned, 'an' now it's here I take no pleasure from it. Without Darcy an' our little Luca there's nowt to celebrate.'

'I know it's bad, love, but I can't help feeling glad for our Angela's sake. At least she'll grow up in a country not ruled by bloody Germans.' John was just as miserable as his wife, but he tried to stay positive for the sake of his family. For weeks he had clung to a faint hope that wherever Darcy was she would still be writing to Danny. But when two of Danny's letters were delivered to his address, John had bitten the bullet and written back telling him that Darcy and Luca had suddenly and mysteriously disappeared from their lives. Now, he was more or less resigned to never seeing Darcy and Luca again, and he dreaded the moment he might have to tell Danny face to face.

The end of the war meant nothing to most of the inmates in the asylum – they were too involved with battling their own personal wars – but for Darcy it brought fresh hope. There wasn't a minute in the day that she didn't grieve for her son and her husband, but life was only bearable if she firmly believed that she would see them again one day. So she held on to her hopes and dreams with every breath in her body.

30

'It's good to see you again.' Albert Farrar clapped his hands on Gavin Steel's shoulders and pulled him close.

The old codgers huddled round the blazing fire supping their stout in the taproom at the Black Bull public house raised their eyebrows as the young men embraced.

'Good to see you, and glad that we both made it back to Blighty in one piece,' Gavin said as he returned the hug. Both men had been to hell and back and were thankful to be alive. They had met in a field station near to Vimy Ridge where Albert had sustained a bullet wound and Gavin had been the doctor on duty. Since then, having learned that Albert lived in Brighouse and that Gavin's home was two miles down the road in Rastrick, they had swapped addresses and kept in touch.

They took off their overcoats and scarves and sat by the window that looked out onto Briggate and the solicitor's office where Albert was a junior partner.

Albert called two pints and they talked about their time in France.

'So, how's the new job? Bit of a change working in an asylum after the chaos in France, or is it much the same? Madness whichever way you look at it.' Albert had thought it highly amusing that Gavin had chosen to work in a madhouse.

'I'm enjoying it. The location's pretty decent, good buildings, nice grounds, but some of the staff are a bit dodgy, and the treatments are outmoded. The whole system is in sore need of an entire overhaul.'

'My God! A man with a mission – lucky you. I was dragged into doing law by my father and grandfather. I was never given a choice, and Christ, is it tedious.'

Albert swigged his pint and Gavin called for refills.

'There's nothing tedious about the asylum. In fact, it's positively intriguing.' Gavin's eyes lit up. 'There's this inmate, a girl...' He told him about Darcy.

Albert only half listened, but when Gavin repeated the girl's name, it rang a bell. 'Hold on, what did you say they called her?'

'Darcy Earnshaw – although she insists her surname is now Cappelini. She's originally from Bradley Brigg. Her father had a sawmill there.'

Albert almost choked on his pint. 'Good God!' he declared, the memory of the file in his office, the sleazy uncle and the details of the document suddenly flooding his mind. 'Earnshaw,' he spluttered. 'Sawmill in Bradley Brigg.' He drained his pint with alacrity and slid off his stool. 'Let's go.'

Mystified, Gavin emptied his glass. Albert led the way across the street. As they entered his office, he cried, 'Oh! Have I got something to show you, Dr Steel.'

* * *

Abe Earnshaw strutted through the cutting shed in the sawmill, a smug smile curling his lips. This was all his for certain now that

Darcy was incarcerated in the asylum at Storthes Hall. When he saw Harry Chadwick he quickly altered his expression to one of extreme sadness.

'Ah, there you are, Chadwick.' Abe faked a shuddering sob. 'I've just received the most dreadful news. Miss Darcy... she... she's no longer with us, poor girl. Killed in a traffic accident in the Lake District.' He crumpled his face. 'Those blasted new-fangled motor cars have taken the dear girl from us.'

At first Harry was shocked. Poor, lovely Darcy. But knowing Abe as he did, his sadness quickly turned to scepticism. He found it difficult to believe a word the man said. However, he had to concede there might be some truth in it. He himself had no proof otherwise. He was grieved to think that she would never return and fulfil her father's wishes. Harry had held on to the belief that once Darcy turned twenty-one she would come back and claim her inheritance, but with the passing of another year, he had sadly resigned himself to never seeing her again. 'It looks like we're stuck with that vile, bloody taskmaster, lads,' he said when he gave the workers the devastating news.

Whilst Abe Earnshaw was congratulating himself, Danny Cappelini was lying in a bunk aboard a ferry bringing him back to England. In the last week of October he had sustained a severe shrapnel injury on the Asiago Front and then he been shunted from a front-line field hospital to a casualty clearing station and then a base hospital where they had removed as much of the shrapnel as they could before finally transporting him by lorry to the port at Cherbourg. The long and arduous journey had taken its toll.

The pain in his right shoulder gnawed with every movement of the buffeting sea, but it was nothing when compared to the agonising pain in his heart. In the breast pocket of his torn, blood-stained tunic was John's letter telling him that his beloved Darcy and his son, Luca, the child he had never seen or held, had suddenly left Halifax and hadn't been heard of since. He had suspected something was amiss when weeks had gone by without a letter from Darcy, but the post was erratic at the best of times and he had consoled himself that the fault lay with the delivery system. Now he knew different. She hadn't written at all.

In trying to make sense of it, he arrived at the heartbreaking conclusion that she had tired of waiting for him to return and had met someone else with whom she wanted to share her life. He found it hard to believe, for Darcy was the soul of integrity, but what other explanation could there be? He had no doubt that she had loved him just as deeply as he loved her, but they had been apart for far too long, and the pressures of war did strange things to people's minds. As soon as he was released from hospital he'd go in search of her. If she no longer loved him, he would have to accept that, but she couldn't stop him loving her and their son. He took the battered, fraying photographs from his tunic pocket, gazing with hungry longing at Luca.

* * *

Albert was like a dog with a rabbit. He had unearthed the dusty file he had abandoned when he had enlisted in the army, and he and Gavin perused it avidly, Albert reaching the conclusion that here was a case well worth pursuing: not just some boring transaction of property but a real live human investigation. Albert had got his teeth into the case of Darcy Earnshaw and there was no stopping him. Gavin was delighted.

'I'll meet with her to assess whether she is the Darcy Earnshaw mentioned in the will,' he told Gavin. 'Although from what you've told me, it seems highly likely your patient and my client are one and the same.'

Albert went to the asylum demanding that the superintendent allow him to meet with Darcy. Arnold Beck's shifty manner convinced him that Darcy had been committed illegally, which led to some in-depth questioning. Albert came away reassured that Darcy was indeed the daughter of the late Thomas Earnshaw, timber merchant. Evidence in hand, he wasted no time in contacting the police and the relevant authorities, informing them that a grave injustice had been done, and immediately serious enquiries gathered momentum.

When Albert called at the asylum the next day to tell Darcy that he had set the wheels in motion to gain her release she bombarded him with questions.

'Were the police at Hebden Bridge Police Station able to tell you anything about Luca?' she cried, her voice high with anxiety and expectation.

'Sadly, no,' Albert replied, his disappointment as crushing as Darcy's. 'They had no record of an abandoned child being brought to them on that date.'

Darcy buried her head in her hands, and as she wept Albert held her to his chest.

'But fear not, the police and the authorities are dealing with your case, so they're sure to turn something up before too long,' he said, sounding more hopeful than he felt.

* * *

The Black Maria had arrived in the early morning at Northcrop House. Four burly policemen had paid little attention to Abe Earnshaw's violent protestations of his innocence and he was now awaiting trial in Wakefield Gaol. Seth Senior was in the next cell. Kidnap was a serious offence. Dr Paddy Flynn and the magistrate, Josiah Pemberton, were also under investigation for falsifying evidence leading to the committal of a person into an asylum.

'I can't believe it,' Darcy cried as she threw herself into John's waiting arms. He had come along with Albert and Gavin on the day of her release and they were now in the asylum's entrance hall, Darcy dressed in clothes that Betsy had sent with John. She was ready to return to the life that was rightly hers, and to find her son.

'Oh, my lovely girl,' John exclaimed, swinging her up into his arms. 'You can't imagine how worried we were an' how much we've missed you and little Luca.' He set her down and turned to address Gavin and Albert. 'If I ever get my hands on that bugger, Abe Earnshaw, I'll tear him apart.'

'We'll leave the law to do that, Mr Carver. I like to think that a long, arduous prison sentence is much harder to bear than instant death. He deserves to suffer.' Albert adopted a serious tone, somewhat diminished by the grin on his face.

'Aye, you're right there,' John agreed, 'but still...' He rubbed a powerful hand over his clenched fist, a wicked gleam in his eye.

Darcy had said her goodbyes to Grace and the other inmates, many of them tearful and some deeply envious. Now, as she stepped outside, she turned to give one final look at the grim building, her kind heart aching with misery for those she had left behind. Gazing out over the gardens blanketed with a fine layer of snow and breathing in the fresh, clean smell of chilly air, she rejoiced in her freedom, her heart swelling with a steely determination to find her son.

Her eyes glistened with unshed tears as she hugged Gavin and then Albert. 'I can't thank you enough for believing in me,' she said. 'I thought I'd never be free.' She had thanked them a hundred times before, but now that they were parting company she felt the need to thank them again. The smile she had been wearing ever since they had come to collect her slipped, her elation immediately swamped by the sadness that invaded her mind day and night.

'Now I can start to search for my darling Luca.' Darcy began to weep.

'We'll find him, love,' said John, holding her to his chest. 'If we have to go to the ends of the earth, we'll get him back.'

'Actually, I've been thinking about that,' Albert announced. 'If you tell your story to the newspaper, someone, somewhere, may know what became of him.'

They arranged to go to the offices of the *Halifax Courier* the next day.

Later that same evening, when Darcy sat down to write an urgent letter to Danny, John gave her the letters he had sent to Pellon Lane in her absence. Looking extremely pained, he confessed that he had written to tell Danny that she and Luca were no longer living there and that he had no idea where they had gone.

'I'm sorry, lass,' John said remorsefully. 'But I had to let him know.'

Darcy wept. Poor Danny. He was somewhere in Italy living with the idea that she had given up on him. Scribbling furiously through her tears she filled three pages explaining why she hadn't been able to write to him, and letting him know that she loved him above all else. However, she could not bring herself to tell Danny his son was missing – she wouldn't burden him with that – because she was determined to find her little boy before his father came back from the war.

* * *

Betsy couldn't stop crying. Tears of joy at Darcy's return mingled with copious weeping at losing Luca. 'Somebody must know where he is,' she sobbed. 'A bairn doesn't just disappear in thin air.'

When Darcy and John met with Albert and the newspaper reporter, Peter, a friend of Albert's, they went to the house in Moss Lane. Darcy sobbed as she gazed at the neglected little garden where she had left Luca. Peter took photographs and then they made enquiries at the neighbouring houses and the shops round the corner, but without success. Darcy had given Peter a photograph of Luca, a copy of the one she had sent to Danny. Peter had then taken a photograph of Darcy and gone off to print his story.

In the days that followed, Darcy and the Carvers waited with bated breath for the story to appear not only in the *Halifax Courier* but also in other local editions. 'Spread the news,' Peter had said. 'Everybody buys newspapers.'

Posy Lander pushed Luca's pushchair away from the shops and towards their cosy home on Sandy Gate as her sister, Violet, waddled behind carrying the shopping bags. The two elderly spinsters had revelled in caring for the little boy, and with each passing day they had breathed a sigh of relief that no one had come forward to claim him. In their youth both sisters had dreamed of marrying and giving birth to such a child. Sadly, the opportunity had never arisen and now Luca was the recipient of all their motherly yearnings.

'You put the shopping away, Posy, whilst I give Henry his bread and soup,' Violet said, lifting the little boy from the pushchair and propping him against her ample bosom. He snuggled his face into her fat chins and she crowed with delight. 'Who's his Auntie Violet's best boy?' she cooed, plopping a kiss on the end of his nose. Then, settling him into the corner of a deep armchair, she began preparing his dinner.

Meanwhile, Posy had put the bread in the crock and the butter and bacon in the pantry and was now sitting at the table with the newspaper spread out in front of her. She skimmed the reportage on the Spanish Flu, shuddering as she read the death toll. Then she quickly turned the page.

'Oh, my goodness gracious, Vi,' she squawked. 'Henry's picture is in the paper.'

The spoon in Violet's hand wavered in front of Luca's mouth. She plopped it back into the dish and came upright. Luca let out a frustrated yell.

'Oh, deary, deary me,' Violet moaned, peering over Posy's shoulder. Ignoring Luca's cries, the sisters read the article, their hearts sinking. Then they looked deeply into one another's eyes, their crestfallen faces acknowledging that they had to do what was right. As one, they scooped up their bundle of joy, holding him between them and kissing away his tears.

* * *

The constable who had dealt with the Misses Lander and the abandoned child was also staring at the newspaper article, the heartburn from which he constantly suffered setting fire to his chest. He ran his fingers through his thinning hair and belched noisily but it brought him no relief. He hadn't pursued the case with any vigour and now he was regretting his neglect. Kidnapping and leaving a child unprotected was a serious business. How would this look on his record? He was due to retire at Christmas. He shambled to his feet. He'd better get round to the Landers' house immediately.

* * *

'Mamma! Mamma!' Luca cried when Darcy rushed into the Landers' sitting room. He was playing on the brightly patterned pegged rug amidst a pile of soft toys as Violet and Posy stood, one on either side, wearing anxious expressions.

'We did our best to care for him properly,' Posy twittered.

'He hasn't been unhappy,' Violet assured.

Darcy faltered in her steps, her eyes filling with tears as she gazed at the little boy she had thought she had lost forever. He was dressed in a bright yellow and red striped cardigan and red leggings, handknitted – clothing she would never have chosen – but he looked healthy and happy, clean and well fed.

'I can see that,' she said when she found her voice, the words coming out in a choking gasp of relief. She hurried further into the room and lifted her son, her tears wetting his hair as she cradled him to her chest.

'Mamma,' Luca said. Darcy had never heard a more beautiful sound.

'Yes, Mamma,' she cried, smothering him in kisses.

'We did try to find you.' Violet appeared anxious to reassure Darcy that, in keeping Luca, their intentions had been purely honourable. 'We did notify the police.'

'We couldn't let them put him in the workhouse,' twittered Posy.

Darcy smiled from one sister to the other, her eyes alight with admiration and gratitude. 'I couldn't have wished for him to be found by anyone better. You're a pair of guardian angels and I'll never be able to thank you enough.'

Violet and Posy blushed. 'A little visit now and then will be reward enough,' Violet said. 'We wouldn't want to lose track of the little fellow. He's been a joy.'

'I promise I'll bring him to see you often,' Darcy assured them. 'He's an extremely lucky boy to have "aunts" as wonderful as you.'

The sisters positively glowed.

* * *

'There are some wonderful people in this world,' Darcy said late that same evening, Luca once again in his own cot and Angela and John having retired early after all the excitement of the day. She and Betsy were sitting by the dying fire in the Carvers' kitchen, Darcy still coming to terms with all that had happened in the past few days, and deeply saddened that Danny wasn't with them to share her joy.

'Aye, and there are some bad 'uns.' Betsy grunted, still burning with anger at Abe Earnshaw's cruelty. She wasn't one to easily let his atrocities go.

'That's true,' Darcy agreed, her blue eyes darkening at the memory of how her Uncle Abe had tried to ruin her life, not once but twice. She shook her head to dispel the anguish he had caused, refusing to dwell on the misery. Then, her indomitable spirit recaptured, she added, 'but like Albert says, he and his cronies will receive their just deserts.'

She reached out and grasped Betsy's hand. 'When I think of all the people who have saved me time and again I know I am blessed. First it was John and you, Betsy, and I'll never be able to repay your kindness.' Her voice shaking, she smiled warmly into the gentle face gazing into her own. 'And my beautiful, wonderful Danny never gave up on me, even though I was cruel to him at times,' she added, a sob catching in her throat. 'Then there was Mr Bentley who gave me the chance to do something worthwhile with my singing, and I'll be forever in Gavin and Albert's debt. They pulled out all the stops to secure my release from the asylum.' She paused, her eyes alight, the wonderment of it all bringing a lump to her throat. 'And Luca couldn't have been found by anyone better than Violet and Posy Lander. Yes, I truly am blessed.'

'Aye, when you look at it that way, you are,' Betsy said, 'but a lot of it has to do with the sort of person you are, Darcy. You're a lovely, kind, intelligent girl, an' nobody could say different. John 'ud never have brought you home if you hadn't helped him out like you did that day in the Piece Hall, an' Joseph Bentley saw that in you an' was proud of your ladies' choir. As for Danny, he loves you that much he'd never have given up on you – or you on him. No matter what life's thrown at you, you've allus kept strong.' She squeezed Darcy's hand, smiling fondly at her. 'That's what I love about you. You make me feel strong, an' goodness knows there's been times when I would have gone to pot if it hadn't been for you.'

'Oh, Betsy, you are a love.' Darcy's words came out in a rush of emotion.

Yet again she thought how all too often she had underestimated sweet, simple Betsy who was wise beyond words.

Betsy flushed with pleasure. 'I'm only saying what's true. You'll allus survive, 'cos life's not just about stayin' alive, it's about holdin' on to what matters.'

Darcy was close to tears as she remembered the rampaging and raging she'd done in the asylum. She recalled Grace's wise advice – *if you don't want them to think you're a mad woman, don't act like one.* It had made her hold on to the belief that one day she would be free, and find Luca. 'There were times when I came close to letting go,' she said, her voice wobbling.

'But you didn't, an' that's what counts,' Betsy said pragmatically as she got to her feet. 'I'm going to make us a nice cup of cocoa, then we'd best get off to us beds. John'll think I've got lost.'

Betsy went through to the kitchen and Darcy gazed into the embers of the fire. *Where are you now, Danny?* she asked silently.

Her heart lurched as she thought of one terrible reason for his absence. She shook her head vigorously to dispel the thought. She'd know if he was dead. She'd feel it in her heart.

* * *

The pearly light of a cold December dawn shone faintly through the hospital's window letting the nurse know that the night shift was almost over. On feet that barely made a sound she moved from bed to bed in the ward at St Thomas's checking that her patients were comfortable before she went off duty. She had recently returned to England from a hospital in Étaples and had decided to stay on in London for a while before going back home, even though the war was over.

But for some the war would never be over, she thought, as she adjusted the pillows on the bed of a young lad, no more than eighteen. Not only had he lost his sight, his face was a raw, ravaged mask of hastily stitched flaps of flesh.

'They're transferring you to Queen's Hospital in Sidcup tomorrow morning, so I'll say goodbye now and all the best,' she said softly, as she gave his hand a gentle squeeze.

He mumbled what might have been thanks and closed his sightless eyes. The nurse had heard about the wonderful work the plastic surgeon Major Harold Gillies did there, and she dearly hoped he would do something for this poor boy as she moved on to the next bed.

The soldier appeared to be sleeping, the raging infection from a shrapnel wound to his right shoulder now under control. For three weeks he had lingered between life and death and she had grown fond of the stoic man who never once complained no matter how much he suffered.

Sensing her presence, he opened his eyes and gave her a drowsy smile. She smiled back thinking how handsome he was.

'I'm going off duty for five days, and now that you're well on the road to recovery they might transfer you to a hospital nearer home. I'll say goodbye in case I don't see you again.'

'Home,' he said dreamily, the smile that had welcomed Victoria slowly fading as he added, 'I will go home to find my wife and son.'

Tears welled in his dark eyes and he sounded so hopeless that the nurse, reluctant to cause him further distress by pursuing the conversation, wished him well then said, 'So many lives have been destroyed or families separated by this rotten war. I'm sure you'll soon be reunited.' And giving him an encouraging smile, Victoria Schofield resumed checking on her patients, unaware that the broken man was the husband of the woman her mother had mentioned in one of her letters, whose choir had sung at one of the Bentley's fund-raising events back home in Halifax.

Danny Cappelini watched her go and prayed with all his might that her parting words would prove to be true.

* * *

'I'm taking Luca and going down to see Nora,' Darcy announced the following afternoon as she pulled on her coat.

'An' me an' Angela are going to buy her a new frock for Christmas,' Betsy replied. 'I've already warned her that we're not going to every shop in town tryin' one after another on before she makes up her mind.'

Angela pouted. 'You've got to look round to make sure you get what you want.' Twelve years old and now a pupil at the Girls' Grammar School in Brighouse, Angela was full of her own opinions.

Leaving mother and daughter at loggerheads, Darcy pushed Luca's pushchair down Pellon Lane, the soft, slushy snow churning under its wheels. It felt good to be walking the familiar street and doing the ordinary things that had been denied her during her time in the asylum. She pointed out the holly wreaths on doors and decorated spruce trees in windows of the houses as they passed by. 'Look, Luca. Christmas is nearly here,' she said, 'and Father Christmas will come down the chimney with lots of presents for you.'

'Kissmiss,' Luca echoed, then made a brave attempt at 'presents' which came out sounding like 'peasants'.

His mother sighed. The only present she wanted was the return of her beloved husband. *Where are you, Danny, where are you?* The words drummed inside her head in tandem with the sound of the pushchair's wheels.

When they came level with the shoe shop, Darcy halted. She lifted Luca out of his pram and went inside. She drew in a deep, pleasant breath as the tang of new leather tickled her nose. Colin Whittaker was serving a customer. Giving him a nod and a smile, Darcy went through to the workshop where John was stitching a welt to a sole, his machine clacking and whirring. Luca's eyes grew round and he clapped his hands.

'Busy as usual.' Darcy cast a glance at the loaded shelves.

John raised his head and grinned. 'What do you think?' He grimaced at the shoes waiting to be repaired and the bespoke designs yet to be completed.

Darcy smiled warmly at the man who would always be her hero. Even though he had lost his leg in the war, John Carver was a man to admire. *He held on to everything that was worthwhile,* Darcy thought as she struggled to contain her excited son. John stopped his machine, and getting to his feet he took Luca from Darcy's arms, swinging him high in the air. Luca laughed then squealed, 'Again, Ganda, again,' and John obliged.

Darcy's heart melted at the happiness radiating from the two faces she loved.

Although John was less than twelve years her senior, she looked on him like she had her father and he returned the compliment by loving her and her son as much as he loved his daughter, Angela.

Leaving Luca with John, busy showing him how the machines whirred and clacked, she went through to the shop. The satisfied customer had left and Colin was putting shoes back in boxes. 'I'm off down to see Nora. How's she doing?'

'She's as fit as a fiddle. Another eight weeks and you'll be an auntie,' he replied, his face beaming with pride.

'And you'll be a dad,' Darcy chirped.

Colin's expression became serious. 'I never thought I'd get the chance to be a father,' he said, tapping his false leg. 'I didn't think anyone 'ud ever want me.'

'Well Nora did, from the minute she clapped eyes on you.'

'I know, and I consider myself to be the luckiest man in the world.'

You are, Darcy thought. *You'll be there when your child is born. You'll be there to see him or her grow, whereas my poor Danny...*

'Here, you'd best take this little lad afore he takes over my job,' John said, coming out of the workshop to hand Luca back to Darcy.

Laughing, she stowed Luca back into his pushchair and went on her way.

31

His greatcoat buttoned up to the chin against the chill wind, and the snow on the pavement hampering his weary feet, the soldier trudged along Pellon Lane with his head down and his hands deep in his pockets. After the warmer climate he had known in Italy for the past year and his prolonged stay in one stuffy hospital after another, England seemed much colder than he remembered, but the inclement weather had little to do with the icy chill that surrounded his heart.

He knocked on the Carvers' door. No answer. He knocked again then slumped down onto the step, burying his face inside the upturned collar of his coat. He'd wait. He had all the time in the world. Soon he would know the truth. His heart missed a beat as he thought of his beloved Darcy and his son. How was it that a love that had endured so many hardships had suddenly disappeared leaving him with no answers as to why? John's letter had let him know she no longer lived at this address, but he had to find Darcy and Luca and his search would begin here.

* * *

Darcy stayed much longer than she had intended as she and Nora talked babies, the mother-to-be bubbling with joy, then horrified when, at her insistence to hear all the details, Darcy related the terrifying ordeal of her kidnap and loss of Luca, and then about her time in the asylum.

'Oh, Darcy, I don't know how you managed to survive it all,' Nora cried, wiping tears from her cheeks.

'I knew I had to if I was ever to see Luca again,' Darcy replied, her chin jutting firmly and a steely glint in her eyes. 'Now all I have to do is find out where and what has happened to Danny,' she continued, her tone desolate as she looked at Luca. 'Then we can start to rebuild our lives.'

The two friends parted with hugs and kisses, and Darcy began walking back to Pellon Lane under a darkening sky which threatened more snow. The biting evening air had hardened the slush to ice and the going was slow, the pushchair bumping over frozen ridges and Darcy and Luca's warm breaths clouding in front of them.

She saw the figure huddled on the doorstep before he saw her. Instinctively, she knew who it was and let out a cry of pure joy. She quickened her pace, her heart thudding and a glorious feeling of warmth enveloping her from head to toe. The crouched figure heard her cry.

'Danny! Oh, Danny!'

He raised his head, amazement lighting his face as he scrambled to his feet. Darcy hurtled the pushchair forwards, its front wheels colliding with the toes of Danny's boots as he, overwhelmed with wonder and love, stared down at his son. The little boy, exhilarated by the speed at which he and his mother had just covered the last few yards, laughed up into his father's face.

'Luca!' The name tumbled from Danny's lips. 'Luca. My bambino.'

Darcy fell against Danny's chest, smothering his face in kisses. His heart swelled and his fears that she no longer loved him were vanquished by the intensity of her cries.

'Oh, Danny. My love, my life. You've come back to us.'

He crushed her in his arms, his lips covering hers with a kiss of such intense passion that it left them both reeling. Then, letting go of Darcy and falling to his knees, Danny embraced his son, his tears wetting Luca's cheek and the stubble on his chin making the little boy chuckle. Darcy stooped, and releasing Luca from his reins, she lifted him into Danny's hungry arms. Then, with Luca pressed between them, they kissed cheeks and lips, each clinging to the most precious things in life.

ACKNOWLEDGEMENTS

I would like to extend my deepest gratitude to the following people who help make my books possible. Judith Murdoch, my agent, and Sarah Ritherdon, publishing director at Boldwood, for their continuing faith in me. I am truly grateful for their enthusiasm and encouragement. Many thanks to Candida Bradford and Helen Woodhouse for their superb editing. Their sharp eye for detail sorts out all my errors. Thanks also to the Boldwood marketing team, Clare Fenby, Nia Beynon, Isabelle Flynn and Marcela Torres for publicising my books, and all the production team. Where would we be without them?

Grateful thanks to my family for the support and patience they offer every day as I sit at my computer living vicariously through the lives of the characters I create. I love you all.

ABOUT THE AUTHOR

Chrissie Walsh was born and raised in West Yorkshire and is a retired schoolteacher with a passion for history. She has written several successful sagas documenting feisty women in challenging times.

Sign up to Chrissie Walsh's mailing list here for news, competitions and updates on future books.

Follow Chrissie on social media:

x.com/walshchrissie

facebook.com/100063501278251

ALSO BY CHRISSIE WALSH

The Weaver Street Series

Welcome to Weaver Street

Hard Times on Weaver Street

Weaver Street at War

Standalones

The Midwives' War

The Orphan Songbird

Sixpence Stories

Introducing Sixpence Stories!

Discover page-turning historical novels from your favourite authors, meet new friends and be transported back in time.

Join our book club Facebook group

https://bit.ly/SixpenceGroup

Sign up to our newsletter

https://bit.ly/SixpenceNews

Boldwood

Boldwood Books is an award-winning fiction publishing company seeking out the best stories from around the world.

Find out more at www.boldwoodbooks.com

Join our reader community for brilliant books, competitions and offers!

Follow us
@BoldwoodBooks
@TheBoldBookClub

Sign up to our weekly
deals newsletter

https://bit.ly/BoldwoodBNewsletter

Printed in Great Britain
by Amazon